MICHILIMACKINAC
A TALE OF THE STRAITS

Meet the Author

DAVID A. TURRILL was born and raised in Saginaw, Michigan, where he has lived most of his life, though he has traveled extensively throughout North America, Europe, and Asia. The author has bachelor's and master's degrees in history from Saginaw Valley State University and has been a teacher of literature and history in Michigan secondary schools for thirty years. He served in the United States Air Force as a combat photographer from 1966-1970, including a tour of duty in Vietnam.

Mr. Turrill currently lives in Grand Rapids, Michigan and is the Director of Theatre at Belding High School. He is also the author of *A Bridge to Eden.*

MICHILIMACKINAC
A TALE OF THE STRAITS

DAVID A. TURRILL

Library of Congress Catalog Card Number 89-040415
ISBN: 0-923568-48-4

Fourth printing, revised   2001

Cover art by Bruce Worden

Cartography by Marjorie Nash Klein

 Wilderness Adventure Books
P.O. Box 856
Manchester, MI 48158

Manufactured in the United States of America

Dedication

To MY WIFE, JAN; my daughter, Amy; and my son, David; who give my life its consummate meaning and its greatest joy. To my mother and father, who always gave me books as a child and throughout my life have never failed to believe in me, no matter the particular endeavor . . . and to June Roethke (sister of the famous poet Theodore), who was my teacher and who carefully and firmly developed my love for literature, and who made teaching, in my eyes, a most sacred profession.

Author's Note

THIS IS A WORK OF FICTION. I make no claims on Dame History other than to use the characters and events She has so generously provided.

My primary concern in writing this novel has been to bring the story of Michilimackinac to life and to rescue its ghosts from the penitential fires of obscurity. On occasion, this task has required some 'truth enhancement'—what writers like to call 'poetic license.'

What happens in this book is very close to what really occurred, but to me, the 'sense' of drama is more crucial to understanding than the accurate portrayal of individual lives. The whole, in other words, is superior to its parts.

I have supplied the dialogue and applied some make-up, but "the play's the thing."

"Now to Mitchilimackinack
We soldiers bid adieu,
And leave each squa a child on back
Nay some are left with two.
When you return, my lads take care
Their boys don't take you by the hair,
With a war-whoop that shall rend the air,
And use their scalping knives."

— *COLONEL ARENT SCHUYLER DE PEYSTER*
COMMANDANT, FORT MICHILIMACKINAC
1779

Contents

BOOK ONE: LA FAMILLE DE LANGLADE

1.	Augustin and Domitilde	1
2.	The Birth of Charles Langlade	15
3.	Père Du Jaunay	32
4.	The Education of Charles Langlade	58
5.	Constante Chevalier	84
6.	'Akewaugeketanso'	132
7.	La Damoiselle	157
8.	The Great Council	166
9.	Ishnoki and Lo-tah	178
10.	Lo-tah's Vision	189
11.	Vision Confirmed	197
12.	Quebec	206

BOOK TWO: ALEXANDER HENRY

1.	Montreal	213
2.	Arrival	227
3.	Wawatam's Dream and the Maple Grove	246
4.	The Horse and the Star	276
5.	Confrontations	311
6.	The Beaver Hunt	333

BOOK THREE: ATTACK

1.	Conspiracy	343
2.	Baggitiway	355
3.	The Massacre	365
4.	Discovery	378
5.	Isles du Castor	398
6.	Isle du Michilimackinac	405
7.	Skull Cave	425
8.	Arch Rock	442

Epilogue 456
Glossary of French Terms and Expressions 457
Glossary of Indian Terms 460
List of Historic Persons in Order of Appearance 462
Bibliographical Sources 464

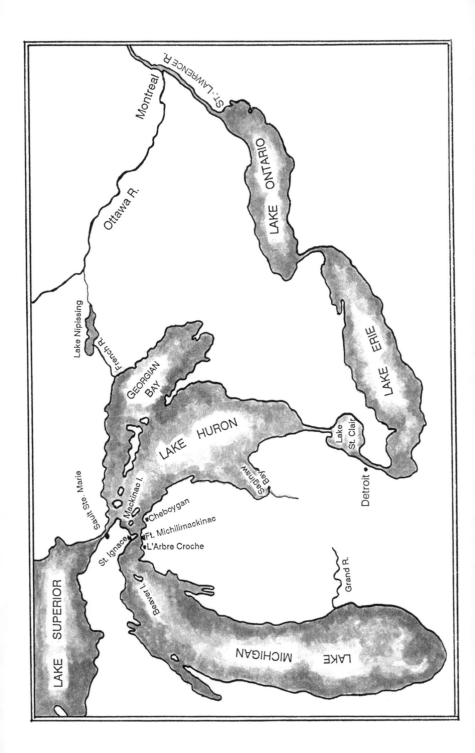

Book One

La Famille De Langlade

Great men die and are forgotten,
Wise men speak; their words of wisdom
Perish in the ears that hear them,
Do not reach the generations
That, as yet unborn, are waiting
In the great, mysterious darkness
Of the speechless days that shall be!

— LONGFELLOW

1

Augustin and Domitilde

Spring had finally come to Michilimackinac. The brilliant warm rays of the sun, hidden for so many months behind winter's dark clouds, began to thaw the frozen strait. The thick ice, looking so incongruent with the budding trees, gradually retreated from the shore and drifted away like the last leaves of autumn tumbling into a swift, bubbling stream.

Losing its grip on the shoreline, the icy remains of winter's corpse floated into the center of the channel which separated the lower and upper peninsulas of Michigan. There, the bobbing little glaciers were drawn into a powerful current, which ushered them into Lake Huron to die a slow death in those cool waters.

The mild winds of the coming summer caressed the beaches, causing the sand to drift up the sloping shore and through the whistling pines which stood sentinel there. The smell of the conifers permeated everything. Meadows blossomed into color and released other marvelous aromas which tried to challenge, without success, the sensory supremacy of the evergreen army.

The black bears, their long sleep ended, lumbered through the forests of birch, maple, oak and cedar, in search of berries and newly hatched insects. Does carefully guided their fawns over fallen timbers and verdant ferns to clover-rich meadows where their offspring grazed for the first time on their still uncertain stilt-legs.

The wind fashioned white-capped waves across the blue water while gulls came out of hiding to wheel and dive in the mild currents. Perch and whitefish and trout leapt among the waves,

1

reveling in the removal of the frozen ceiling which had kept them captive for so many months in their icy, blue-green prison.

The Ottawa and Ojibway had returned to Michilimackinac from their wintering grounds in the south to harvest the sugary syrup which the groves of maple provided. The Indians camped again, as they had for several years, on either side of the French fort, the Ojibway to the east, the Ottawa to the west.

La Fourche, an Ottawa chief, stood by the gnarled, gigantic oak which dominated a little knoll sloping down to the water's edge. The tree was a familiar landmark to anyone paddling through the strait. The French called it *L'Arbre Croche* (the Crooked Tree). The Ottawa liked the sound of it so much that they bestowed the name on their village, located only a few hundred feet away from the oak, just inside the forest's edge.

La Fourche himself had adopted a French *nom de guerre*, his real name being too long and complicated for his European friends to pronounce. The name meant *The Pitchfork*, and though he had never seen one, a soldier at Fort Michilimackinac had told him that it was a three-pronged weapon which could do considerable damage to a human being. It was a fierce name, and suited his temperament.

With a stern expression, La Fourche surveyed the lovely scene before him. His scarred and frowning countenance indicated an inner disquiet which contrasted sharply with the beauty of his surroundings.

The chief had been badly mauled as a boy by *Mag-wah*, the black bear, when he had carelessly fallen asleep in a berry patch. The animal, irritated by this intrusion into his private sweet shop, had raked the length of the boy's face with his sharp claws, from forehead to chin, plucking the lad's left eye neatly from its socket. The intruder had survived only because the bear was more interested in wild blueberries than in vengeance.

The three deep grooves in his face, now white against his dark skin, looked as if a pitchfork had been ripped across his face, giving rise to his name. He was proud of the scars, and used blackberry juice to darken the skin between them, accentuating them even more.

A decorative piece of polished copper, patiently hammered to size, fitted neatly into the empty eye socket, and gave the warrior's face a bizarre, sometimes comic, appearance. His long, black hair hung freely about his shoulders except for one neat braid which bordered the right side of his face and kept hair out of the path of his unilateral vision.

His good eye squinted against the bright sunlight as he surveyed the beach to the east of his camp. It was obvious that he was expecting someone as he stood motionless, the hair on the left side of his head streaming behind him in the mild breeze.

The eye often wandered to the north and east, to Michilimackinac, the Isle of the Great Turtle. The name for the island, and indeed the entire area, including the French fort located only a short distance up the coast, came from an Algonkin phrase, *Mish-in-e-mok-in-ok-ong*, meaning 'dancing turtle spirits.'

The island did resemble a huge turtle, floating in the waters of the strait. It was considered to be the home of the Ojibway guardian spirit, and the Ottawa's primary god. La Fourche could never look at the island without experiencing a sense of wonder, awe, and religious reverence. This too, was reputed to be the birthplace of Hi-a-wa-tha, the Ojibway messiah. It was a very sacred and holy place.

As he stood thus enthralled, La Fourche failed to notice a solitary figure approaching from the east and making his way laboriously through the deep sand toward *L'Arbre Croche*.

The visitor was still a young man in this year of 1728, not yet thirty, but a hint of gray at his temples gave him a look of premature maturity. He was not a handsome man, his features were too coarse, but he could not honestly be called homely either. His black hair was a mass of curls under his red, wool, stocking cap. His full, heavy beard was much the same texture and color.

The most distinguishing characteristic about him was his walk, which was quick and vigorous, yet strangely graceful. It hinted of aristocratic training.

As he moved briskly along the beach, Augustin Langlade thought with great anticipation about his pending visit to his Ottawa friends. He had been to *L'Arbre Croche* before and knew many of the inhabitants well enough to call them by name. It was a favorite place of his, situated on the shore of Lake Michigan (called *Mitchi-Gaumee* by the Ottawa), a few miles distant from his home at Fort Michilimackinac. There he trapped, kept a little garden next to his cabin inside the stockade, and ran a small trading post which catered primarily to the Ojibway and Ottawa who resided in the forests around the fort. At this village he was always welcomed, having gained a reputation among the Ottawa for his honesty in his dealings and generosity with his friends.

Today, Augustin came at the summons of his good friend, La Fourche, the most prominent of the Ottawa chiefs at *L'Arbre Croche*. As he glanced up into the clear, spring sunshine, he saw the rugged warrior standing at the crest of the knoll leading to the village. As he stood by the crooked oak, outlined against the trees behind him, La Fourche looked as if he was in some sort of dreamy trance and seemed to be totally unaware of his guest's approach. It was not until Augustin Langlade called out his name that the Indian turned his attention away from the horizon. Finally becoming aware of the Frenchman's presence, he descended the slope to greet him.

An arranged meeting by an Ottawa usually meant some significant event. The residents of *L'Arbre Croche* were people of few words and not believers in small talk or idle conversation. Thus Augustin approached his friend with a feeling of mild apprehension. Significant news, he had learned through hard experience, was often unpleasant.

La Fourche's scarred face looked stern, giving support to Augustin's suspicions. Only the bright copper, twinkling in its unnatural home, relieved the sour grimace. The lack of head adornment meant mourning, and Augustin steeled himself for unpleasant news as he grasped the forearm of his friend firmly.

The Ottawa spoke first. "You see, my brother, without my voice to tell you. *Pau-guk*, the 'Bringer of Death,' has visited my lodge."

Augustin nodded in acknowledgement, knowing that questions would not be necessary. The chief would explain. To question would be to show a lack of trust, a strong insult.

"Ka-re-gwon-di, my sister's husband, has lost his spirit from his body. He died a warrior's death. A Chick-a-sau band killed him in the Moon of Flowers. He took four *coups* before his death. His name will be honored for many moons, over many fires. He will be remembered."

La Fourche explained that a warrior band of fifteen had been gone for much of the winter, young men mostly, bored with the inactivity of winter. They had gone south into the Ohio Valley in the Freezing Moon (November). In the Moon of Crusted Snow (February), they had been attacked by a group of Chick-a-sau warriors and four of their number had been killed. In a retaliatory battle two months later, Ka-re-gwon-di had perished. They had brought back his still heart to his squaw, Domitilde, and his tomahawk to their infant son, Au-san-aw-go.

This was a great loss to La Fourche, not only because of his close friendship with Ka-re-gwon-di, but now his sister and her child were in *his* care. Though his friend had died bravely, the mouths of his widow and son could not be fed with honor. La Fourche, a bachelor, did not wish to be burdened with another's family.

The Frenchman understood all of this without having to be told. The effects of great familial responsibility had, until recently, laid heavily on him also. Though he was unmarried, the fiscal commitment to his family in Canada had been a tremendous burden. He had been born at the Castle Sarrasin in Basse Guyenne in France. His father, a petty noble of the *haut monde,* had been far better at protecting the family honor than the family estate and had perished in a duel caused by an argument over the addition of a lily to his feudal coat of arms. His jealous neighbor had felt obligated to defend the king's honor, since the lily was the royal insignia of the Bourbons and his pistol put the pretensions of the Sieur de Langlade to rest, along with his body.

This left twenty-one year old Augustin the burden of debt (the castle was heavily mortgaged), and the protection of the family name. Further, his mother and sister depended on him for their survival. He joined the French army (primarily for the officer's *salaire*). Overseas duty paid an additional stipend and so, in 1722, he volunteered for duty at Quebec in New France (Canada).

He quickly discovered that even this money would not suffice to pay for the Castle Sarrasin, so he sold it and moved his mother and sister to a comfortable cottage in Quebec. Preferring practicality to ostentation, away from the prying eyes and vicious tongues of neighbors in Basse Guyenne, they were happier, and closer to him.

Once his tour of duty had ended, he stayed in Canada until the lure of the wilderness of Michilimackinac had seized him. He had been in this area now for two and one half years and faithfully sent money to his mother in Quebec until she had died during the previous winter. His sister had married. The earnings from his trapping and trading presently allowed him some economic freedom for the first time in his life. But he understood the burdens that La Fourche now faced.

"Mon ami," he sympathized, "a warrior like Ka-re-gwon-di is a great loss to your family and your tribe. Your sister is now a *veuve* (widow).

Your nephew is an orphan. You have many things to grieve. I grieve with you."

The Indian nodded his head and signaled Augustin to follow him to his village a few hundred yards away. Once there, he invited Augustin into his lodge, located near the edge of *L'Arbre Croche.*

Inside, the young widow, Domitilde, sat next to the fire, nursing her infant son. At her brother's entrance, she rose quickly, never disturbing the weaning child, to allow the men their privileged place close to the warm embers. La Fourche observed Augustin carefully as he watched the woman settle herself near the birchbark wall. She kept her eyes downcast as was proper.

La Fourche took two pipes from a bag made from a skunk's pelt which dangled by the black and white tail from the sapling frame of the wigwam. He silently filled both pipes with the Indian tobacco, *kinickinick,* lit one for Augustin and then for himself. The two men sat puffing contentedly on the pipes. Conversation was considered *gauche* while smoking, so they sat in silence. Augustin was seated so that he looked directly at Domitilde, probably the exact intention of his host. During the ten minutes in which they smoked their pipes, the men exchanged no conversation at all. The only sounds were the sucking, slurping noises of the hungry child as he attacked his mother's breast. Augustin was taken with the woman's calm and quiet demeanor in the face of such personal tragedy. She was not particularly pretty, but her dark face showed a strength and wisdom far beyond her seventeen years. It was an indelicate and sensuous face with unclassical lines, but honest and strangely feminine. She was clean, and her dark, black hair glistened. Her teeth were straight and white. The slit dress of buckskin she wore showed shapely legs and promised a firm and well-wrought torso.

Throughout the silence, La Fourche kept his one eye riveted on the face of Augustin Langlade and smiled as if reading his mind. When both had put down their pipes, La Fourche spoke sharply to Domitilde. She placed the now sleeping infant on a mound of furs next to her and rose swiftly to his command. She moved forward, out of the dark shadows by the wall and into the sunlight next to the smoldering fire, provided by the smoke hole, her eyes continually studying the ground.

La Fourche growled again, and the girl obediently untied the rawhide pulls at each shoulder. The dress slipped to the ground as she wriggled her shoulders and hips to accommodate its descent. She lifted her eyes then and looked proudly at the Frenchman.

Confronted so suddenly and unexpectedly with her naked beauty, Augustin blushed, causing La Fourche to grin broadly. Langlade's eyes remained safely on her face. Her nose was broad and flat, with flaring nostrils. Her cheeks were full and her red lips were twisted in a wry grin which displayed pride in her body. The smile widened, revealing beautiful teeth. Inevitably, and much to the satisfaction of both La Fourche and his sister, Langlade's eyes moved downward.

Her breasts were normally large and now, gorged with milk, they were disproportionate to her delicate neck and shoulders. Her stomach was flat and her hips were broad, indicating a proclivity for childbearing which had already been substantiated. Her hands were dainty, her legs, shapely.

Augustin finally managed to stammer: "My good friend, have her dress herself, *s'il vous plaît.*"

La Fourche frowned deeply in disappointment. "She does not

please you. I am sorry. She is too old. I should not have insulted a friend. Forgive me."

Domitilde's eyes lowered again, this time in shame. She could tell by her brother's expression and tone of voice that she was not pleasing to the white man. She dressed quickly at La Fourche's irritable command and resumed her place by her sleeping child. The pride she had shown moments before vanished, and her eyes filled with tears.

Augustin, seeing her shame, felt terrible for having hurt the young woman for the sake of his own sense of propriety. He hurried to make amends. *"Non, mon ami,* she is *très belle, agréable.* She is a worthy woman."

La Fourche again smiled. Domitilde showed no emotion, but kept her head bowed, watching her baby. La Fourche was beaming so broadly that he almost forced the copper from his empty eye socket.

"She would make for you a good *noko,* wife, *n'est-ce pas?"*

Augustin did not know how to answer. He had not expected such an offer. He slowly came to the realization that this had been the primary purpose of the summons from La Fourche and he felt deeply honored that La Fourche would want him as a brother-in-law to replace the fallen Ka-re-gwon-di, but at the same time apprehensive about caring for the man's sister and adopting his nephew.

Augustin had not considered marriage with anyone. He had been too busy caring for his own family. Now, only a little while ago, that burden had been lifted. The swelling between his legs had convinced him that the need was there as he had gazed at Domitilde. He was often lonely. He looked again at the squaw and her child. He imagined her feeding the child in the rocker by his stone hearth and her body pressed close to his own on bitterly cold, winter nights. The expectant face of La Fourche awaited an answer.

He heard himself say, as if he were some third person who was merely observing, *"Oui, mon frère, mais oui."*

🦋 🦋 🦋

Fort Saint Philippe de Michilimackinac was built in 1715 by the French as a precaution to protect the strategic straits area against the Iroquois, the British, or both. It was situated close to the water's edge, right on the southern shore of this strait. Its location marked the northernmost tip of the lower peninsula of what is now the state of Michigan.

It was not square in the usual fashion, but more of a pentagon shape with four bastions armed with cannon at the more pronounced corners. The stockade wall was eighteen feet high, built three feet into a trench which was then filled in with dirt to support the structure. The pickets measured twenty-one feet from pointed top to soil-supported bottom and were fashioned from cedar trees.

There were two gates, one facing north, out onto the water, and the other facing south toward the forest. Over each gate, a sentry box was suspended, supported by the stockade wall and additionally strengthened by means of strategically stationed poles cutting at an angle from the sentry box to the ground inside the fort.

A beaten path ran between the gates, trampling the grass that grew wild within the compound. This small, dirt path was called the *Rue Dauphine* by the civilian occupants of the fort. Running across it from both sides was another 'street.' On the west side of the *Rue Dauphine*, the path was called the *Rue du Diable* and on the east side of the main thoroughfare, it was termed the *Rue de la Babillarde*.

In the northeast corner of the fort was the commanding officer's house and in front of it, the parade ground. Also in this area, adjoining each other, were the cabins of the blacksmith, Jean-Baptiste Amiot and the carpenter, Joseph Ainsse. Across the *Rue Dauphine*, the barracks were located, housing about twenty French soldiers.

In the southeast corner, where the *Rue de la Babillarde* and the *Rue Dauphine* intersected, was a house which provided for a single family and was owned by the merchant, René Bourassa.

Across the *Rue Dauphine* and running along the southern side of the *Rue du Diable* was another cabin built with walls of upright logs in the *poteaux en terre* design and chinked and fitted with wattle and daub. The bark-covered roof was high and steeply inclining in the French fashion to let the rain and snow slide off as much as possible.

To this little niche in the southwest corner of the fort, Augustin Langlade brought his bride, Domitilde, and her son, Au-san-aw-go. Once inside, he moved to the small hearth and put fresh wood on the burning coals. They quickly blazed into life, illuminating the room with an orange glow. Domitilde looked at her new surroundings, searching for opportunities to make her mark on this bachelor's cabin. She noticed, in the corner closest to the fire, a rough bed whose frame had been hewn from pine logs and held together with leather thongs. Flat boards lay across the frame, supporting the goosedown mattress which had been brought over from France and had at one time been a part of the lavish furnishings of the Langlade estate.

A crude table stood quaintly in the center of the cabin on awkward legs that belied their origin because of the bark that still encircled them.

The opposite corner from the bed contained a large trunk which concealed blankets and linen. Close by, against the wall, were implements of labor; a broad axe and hoe, as well as a Charleville musket.

Hanging on the walls all over the room were various traps which Augustin used in the pursuit of his livelihood and snowshoes, indispensable for the violent winters of the straits area. A cooking pot and several pans hung on the surface of the fieldstone fireplace. They appeared to have been used little and abused greatly. Domitilde saw much work to be done, but that would come later.

She thought of Ka-re-gwon-di whom she served so often in the last two years. She had become his *noko* at the age of fourteen. He had been as much a father to her as a husband. Now . . . she had to stop thinking of him. His spirit was gone. She had a new husband and she was pleased to think that she would no longer be a burden to her brother, La Fourche.

He was always so kind, in spite of his gruff manner and fearful countenance. He had had to make the decisions for the family since he was twelve, when their father had fallen through the ice on a pond while hunting for beaver, and had never surfaced.

One such difficult decision was to let their mother die in the forest during the Moon of the Crusted Snow when he was but eighteen years old. She had become an intolerable burden because she could no longer use her legs. He left her in the snow without blankets among the rubble of their previous campsite. Domitilde would never forget that stoic look their mother had given them as they walked away, that approving, proud, stare. She had sat in the snow by a tree, awaiting death with a fierce eye and haughty expression, set against the cold wind and freezing sleet.

Domitilde sighed with relief at the glow of the fire and its warmth which so vividly contrasted with her cold thoughts. She had been afraid then. She knew how hard it was for La Fourche to provide for her and her son. Indeed, he had not pursued a wife because of her. Ka-re-gwon-di had come along at last to pay the dowry price.

Her husband had been rough with her, but not cruel by Ottawa standards. He had provided well and she had cooked well (he always had grunted contentedly when he ate). He had relieved her of that burden of guilt which she so often had felt in the wigwam of her brother. She had become tolerably accustomed to Ka-re-gwon-di and his hardness, and the day drifted back to her mind when little Au-san-aw-go had been born. Ka-re-gwon-di had smiled broadly at her and kissed her as she presented him with his son. It was the only kiss she had ever received from him that was tender and devoid of lust. Then he had gone to fight the Chick-a-sau and once again it fell to her brother to take her into his lodge, with the additional burden of a child. Throughout the last long season of cold, no Ottawa male had shown an interest in her. She knew she was not beautiful, but she was physically sound and had proven her ability to bear sons. She had suffered intensely from her dependency because, like her mother, she was fiercely proud. At fifteen, she was experienced in love and knew how to please a man. However, rejection and dependency had fostered in her a wariness and apprehension of her own worth. What she saw as Augustin Langlade's apparent lack of appreciation for her body, her only source of pride, had done nothing to alter that conception.

As she stood by the door, thus absorbed in thought, she failed to notice Augustin's attempts to register her attention. He was signaling her to lay the sleeping Au-san-aw-go in the small basket he had filled with blankets and placed next to the fire, which now warmed the small cabin. Finally, he spoke her name, which broke her reverie and brought her senses quickly back to her. He beckoned her toward the home-fashioned crib once again. She practically flew across the room and laid her baby down gently, mentally cursing herself for her lapse of attention to her new benefactor. She wanted so much to please. To be returned to her brother by this man would be a disgrace she could never live with. She turned and faced Langlade who had been studying her as she bent over, appreciating the shape of her *derrière* and her legs, which showed below the edge of her doeskin dress.

"*Ma femme,*" he said, surprised at the use of the term, "it is time to sleep." He motioned for her to come to the bed. She did not understand. She had never slept on a bed before, nor seen the interior of a white man's dwelling. When she did not move, he frowned (unintentionally), and this disturbed her greatly. It frightened her. In desperation and fear of rejection, she ran to him and threw herself on the floor in front of him, circling her arms about his knees and sobbing in agony, utterly petrified at the possibility of being sent away.

This behavior puzzled the Frenchman. Her obvious fear and terrible misery were a mystery to him. She was perhaps afraid of love-making he thought. Could this be why she had not found another husband sooner? Is this why Ka-re-gwon-di had been so eager to leave her to go on the raid against the Chick-a-sau? "*Mon Dieu,*" he mumbled under his breath.

He reached down and grabbed her arms firmly, bringing her to her feet. "Domitilde, don't be afraid of me, I won't hurt you," he whispered gently.

She looked up into his kind face, tears running slowly across her high cheekbones. He wiped them dry with the back of his hand and kissed her softly on the neck. The expression of fear began to dissipate to one of sweet anticipation. "You want me?" she asked.

This last was said with such a degree of desperate searching that he answered her quickly in Algonkin. "Yes."

A smile appeared on her round, tear-streaked face that, had it been converted to light, would have lit the world. She loosened the sinew ties that held her doeskin tunic at the shoulders and let it slip away. Augustin kissed her cheek and lifted her tenderly into his arms. He carried her slowly across the firelit room and laid her on the bed. He watched her with appreciative eyes as she quickly discarded the small loincloth which she wore beneath her dress and held out enthusiastic arms to him. Her face, once fearful and worried, now carried a smile that was positively lascivious, as he undressed and slowly mounted her.

Moments later, they lay quietly in each other's arms and watched the flickering firelight on the stone hearth. Augustin soon drifted into contented sleep, but the young Indian girl could not. She was deliriously happy. He had been pleased with her. He had enjoyed her, and she, him. He was a gentle and considerate lover.

She propped herself on one elbow and looked deeply into her new husband's face. It was a charitable face, but one that had seen much worry and knew how to be firm. His thick, black hair was turning prematurely gray at the temples. His beard covered a chin that she imagined was square and rigid. The whiskers had tickled her face and she could never understand why white men seemed to take so much pride in their hairiness. Indian men thought their smooth chins and hairless faces to be beautiful. Kissing Langlade, she decided, was rather like kissing an animal pelt, except for the exciting things he did with his tongue, which she had never experienced before.

Though she had been married to Ka-re-gwon-di for almost two years, and had borne him a son, she had never experienced sexual release until this night. Her new husband had somehow cared about that and, she felt, purposely delayed his own pleasure to increase hers. He had been slow, teasing her and himself with long, deliberate, strokes until she had begun to shudder with joy. Then, he had quickened the pace, bringing them together in their rise to mutual fulfillment.

Now, as she rested her head once more on his shoulder and

nestled closer to his warm skin, she watched the moonlight filter through the cabin window and caress the floor. She listened to the gentle breathing of Au-san-aw-go and the heavier respiration of her new husband, and settled contentedly to sleep in the soft down of the French mattress.

Chapter
2

The Birth of
Charles Langlade

MONTHS PASSED, and the happiness that Domitilde had found did not diminish. Not once had Augustin lifted his hand to beat her nor had he shown any inclination to do so. His only sign of displeasure with her was when she fell while carrying firewood and had sprained her wrist. Though she did not allow this to interfere with her work at all, her injury seemed to irritate him immensely. It was not until much later that she came to understand that this was genuine *concern* for her.

She worked hard cooking, cleaning, gathering wood and laboring in the small garden at the side of their cabin. He, in return, provided well for her and seemed to enjoy the presence of little Au-san-aw-go. He was often gone, especially during the cold months when the furs of the woodland creatures he trapped were at their thickest and most luxuriant. By spring, large numbers of hides were dried and piled into a corner of the small cabin for trade with the merchants of Montreal.

He had already been to Montreal twice with a load of furs and had returned after weeks of travel to the fort at Michilimackinac. He had brought back a dress for her and a bonnet which she took great pride in, as well as a new cooking pan and several good cutting knives. She was very pleased and felt somehow undeserving of all the attention.

She had applied herself in his absence to learning French so that she would be able to better communicate with her provider. What little verbal intercourse transpired between them had been the result of his somewhat limited knowledge of the Algonkin tongue.

In this well-intentioned effort, she was assisted by Madame Amiot, the wife of Jean-Baptiste Amiot. He too worked as a fur trapper (as did almost all of the French settlers in the fort), but he also toiled as a part-time blacksmith, repairing muskets, axes, and various tools for the other residents of the fort for a small remuneration. Eight years earlier, he had married Madame Amiot, a Sac Indian woman, and had brought her back to the straits. She was a quick learner and had been instructed by the Bourassa family in both the French tongue and faith. She had been baptized a Christian by a visiting priest (since the little community had no permanent cleric) and given birth to five healthy children, all of whom lived together in the small house in the northeast corner of the fort across from the carpenter, Joseph Ainsse.

The kindness and instruction given to Marie Anne by the Bourassas, Madame Amiot was now determined to impart to Domitilde who, though an Ottawa, reminded her so much of her-self when she had first arrived among the whites.

Marie Anne had made the first visit to Domitilde only days after her arrival at the fort when Augustin was in the forest, hunting rabbit for their evening meal. Domitilde had been sitting outside leaning against the cabin wall, watching the French sol-diers curiously, as they drilled on the parade ground. She enjoyed the small respite from her chores in spite of the nippy October air. She was musing about the precision of the soldiers' movements and the necessity of such apparently inane behavior, when Marie Anne approached her from her left side and startled her momentarily.

After the initial shock, they had chattered away in Algonkin until the piercing wail of one of the Amiot children had forced their separation, with a promise to talk again.

Since that introductory meeting, the two Indian women had become fast friends. Whenever their husbands were gone, they were constantly in each other's company.

On one cold and snowy December day, Domitilde, knowing that Jean-Baptiste and Augustin would be absent for several days, bundled little Au-san-aw-go in a heavy, woolen blanket and trudged steadily through the heavy snow five hundred feet to the Amiot cabin.

She waved at the homely carpenter, Joe Ainsse, as she spotted him working in the little open shelter next to his cabin that he referred to as his *fenêtre d'étalage*, or store front. He was always working, and seemed to be a very lonely young man. He lived a solitary life. He had no woman that Domitilde knew of, and no parents or relatives that anyone else knew about. He seemed to like living alone, though he always had a sort of mournful look about him.

Physically, he was not to be envied. His nose was very big and, in a sense, that was fortunate because without it his huge ears would have seemed vastly out of proportion. His dirty, brown hair was thin and matched the wispy, youthful beard that surrounded his large mouth. His eyes were blue and sharp, but often overlooked because of the nose. He was always friendly, but painfully shy and his face reddened every time he spoke to anyone, but especially women. Today, as he labored diligently on the construction of a table for Amiot, his cheeks scarleted again as Domitilde shouted her greeting. Even so, he smiled amicably and waved back.

She was greeted as usual by the boisterous Amiot children as she approached their dooryard. They were busy caking each other with snow and yelping at the top of their lungs as they chased each other joyously around the cabin. Marie Anne welcomed her at the door by first yelling at her own *enfants terribles* and cooing over Au-san-aw-go who slept peacefully in his blanket despite all the noise and confusion. After the sleeping child had been laid quietly next to the two youngest Amiot children in a sort of bin designed for napping, Marie Anne motioned her new friend to sit next to the hearth and pulled another chair over next to her.

"*Ma soeur*, how happy you look today," she said.

Indeed there was a glow about Domitilde that made her look positively pretty.

"I have reason to feel happy. *Je suis enceinte.* My bleeding has stopped. I will give my husband his *own* son."

Marie Anne, who was herself pregnant again, smiled know-ingly. "You have been busy," she said.

Domitilde laughed outloud and the two women broke into giggling. Au-san-aw-go decided, as he opened his black eyes, that there was very little humor in the situation and began crying loudly. Domitilde lifted him quickly from the crib-bin and walked him back and forth across the room, while Marie Anne stirred the *matelote* (a kind of fish stew) which bubbled in a large kettle over the hot coals.

"How long have you known?" she queried.

Domitilde believed most certainly that their first coupling had resulted in her pregnancy. "I have not bled since I have been here. Augustin has not had to send me away once," she said proudly.

Madame Amiot chuckled. "The French don't send their women away during the bleeding time."

At first Domitilde thought that her confidante was joking, but then realized that what she said had been spoken without any hint of duping or trickery. "You mean that they still sleep with them?"

She made such a revolting face that Marie Anne could not hide her amusement. *"Mais non, ma chère,* but they do not send them away. It is better. A squaw does not have to be shunned for something she cannot stop or control."

Domitilde still looked very unsure of the accuracy or wisdom of that statement, but in the back of her mind, she was relieved that she would not have to spend part of each month out of pregnancy, separated from her husband.

They sat and talked most of the afternoon before the Amiot children stormed into the cabin demanding warmth and food. Domitilde was invited to stay, but she knew that Augustin would not be pleased if she neglected their home. She wished her friend good-bye and, amid cries of *"bonne nuit"* and *"bon soir"* from the young ones, she carried Au-san-aw-go out into the darkness. Joe Ainsse had gone inside because of the cold and falling shadows, but the noises emanating from within the log walls indicated that he was still hard at work.

As she crossed the parade ground, she glanced briefly at the commandant's house, with its back to the water wall of the stockade. Its chimney smoked vociferously and the light streaming from the windows indicated warmth and comfort. She had seen the commandant and his wife, but she did not know their names nor had she ever had occasion to speak with them.

She turned south onto the dirt path called the *Rue Dauphine* toward her own home. She looked through the falling snow at the pine trees towering above the stockade wall, prominent in their blackness against the gray-white sky. She felt, momentarily, like a prisoner. She was not used to the confines of a walled village and though she was very happy, she sensed that she was somehow caged.

She missed La Fourche, who had not been to see her since her departure from *L'Arbre Croche*. She wanted him to be proud that she carried another nephew and that her man was happy. They had played together a great deal as children until her brother began to understand his male role in their culture and he had become suddenly cold for reasons which had been beyond her childish understanding. When he had been brought back to their camp as a teen-ager, horribly mutilated by the bear and close to death, she had cared for him tenderly and nursed him back to health. When their father had died, he had shouldered the responsibility for her and her mother. He had taken care of her ever since, except for her short marriage.

The barking of the Bourassas' dogs startled her and returned her to the present. René and Marie Bourassa lived just opposite the Langlade cabin on the *Rue de Babillarde*. Domitilde had discovered, as her French improved, that her own home rested on the *Rue du Diable*.

The Bourassas had been very kind to her, making her feel welcomed to the little trader/trapping community in the French fort. Madame Bourassa had given her the woolen blanket that Au-san-aw-go was presently bundled in and had spent additional time familiarizing her with cooking utensils and garden tools which were foreign to her.

The Bourassas had no children as yet, but the last glimpse of Marie Bourassa that Domitilde had had, convinced the Indian woman that it wouldn't be that way for long. Fort Michilimackinac would see many babies in the spring.

A chill ran through her and she shivered, not knowing whether it was because of the cold or because of the excitement a new baby generated in her. She had felt her child begin to move inside her and she was convinced that it was a boy. She knew too that he would be a special boy, half-Ottawa, half-French, a good combination.

She had had a dream that first night in the stick-house, before she knew she carried a child. She had seen a huge turtle floating in the water. A great warrior stood on its shell. His left side was entirely white, beginning with the hair and traveling down his entire left side. Even his left eye was white. His right side was red, including the right eye and the hair on the right side of his head. Likewise, the loincloth he wore was half-white/half-red. In his hands he held the reins that traveled through the nostrils of the great turtle and as he jerked at them with one hand or the other, the turtle would respond by obediently moving in the direction it was bidden. The warrior enjoyed himself greatly, and the sun shone on him as he propelled across the water like a king.

The next morning, Domitilde's first inside the fort, Jean-Baptiste Amiot brought a gift to Augustin to congratulate him on his new bride. The door to the Langlade cottage had long been supported by leather hinges which had worn thin. The door had to be lifted to bring it shut and would soon become a problem with cold weather approaching.

Amiot had surprised them with a pair of iron hinges to replace the damaged leather ones. What had shocked and pleased Domitilde was that the hinges had been wrought in the shape of turtles. She thought of her dream and understood.

Now, as she approached her doorway to escape the snowy, December night, she saw the hinges which held the door firmly, felt the child move in her womb, and smiled.

🐢 🐢 🐢

AUGUSTIN LANGLADE WAKENED SLOWLY. He had been sleeping soundly, but the heat in the cabin was suffocating and he was perspiring profusely. In the last week, he had not had to build a fire in the hearth, a rare circumstance in the area of the straits. It had been a terribly hot July and he had spent the previous evening sitting late outside the cabin, talking quietly with René Bourassa who had become a new father in May. He had named his son Ignace after the sainted Loyola. It had been the recommendation of Jean Cuchoise, a French *coureur de bois* (unlicensed fur trapper) who lived with his Chippewa wife in her village about half a league from the fort. Cuchoise had a brother who was a Jesuit priest and a great admirer (as most good Catholics were) of Ignatius Loyola. So Bourassa accepted the idea.

That evening outside the cabin, they had discussed names for the expected Langlade child, and swatted at mosquitoes. Domitilde slept fitfully inside the cabin. She had been very uncomfortable in the last two weeks and Au-san-aw-go, timing his development properly, was keeping her busy all the time. Her delivery was very near, and Augustin had alerted Marie Bourassa to assist in the birthing.

Augustin and René sat up late, reluctant to go inside because of the intoxicating, light breeze which found its way across the lake and through the water gate to make breathing easier and the rum taste better. Bourassa had even treated Augustin to a perfect gentleman's brandy, kept by for special use. Their state of intoxication soon matched that provided by the breeze, and as dawn rose over the stockade and between the pines, the two roisterers finally bid each other *adieu* and went to bed.

Augustin did not remember now, that ending to their pleasant discourse and as he rose painfully from his bed and set his feet upon the plank floor, he noticed that Domitilde was not in the cabin. Au-san-aw-go too, was absent. Langlade went deliberately to the wash basin by the door and splashed the tepid water in his face and ran it through his dark hair. He heard outside, the clammering hammer of Amiot at his forge, the squeals of children at play, and the barking of dogs. He pulled on his breeches and staggered out the door, wincing as the bright sunlight struck him.

Judging by the intense heat and the activity around him, he guessed that it was mid-afternoon. He looked at the Bourassa house to his right. Madame Bourassa sat in front, underneath the extended roof in the shade, rocking little Ignace. Augustin thought of Domitilde. It was unlike her to leave him alone without telling him where she was going. His head throbbed.

In a few moments, fighting off the stabbing pains in his head, Augustin Langlade cut across the *Rue Dauphine* and then across the parade ground in front of the commandant's house, heading for the sound of the hammer and Amiot's cabin. As he passed the residence of Joe Ainsse, he saw the carpenter at work repairing the doubletree on the front of a regimental wagon. The young man glanced up and said softly; *"Bon jour,* Monsieur Langlade. *Comment allez vous?"* The sweat poured down his homely face and drenched his calico shirt. *"Très bien,"* the trapper answered automatically, his pallid face and drawn features revealing the truth. *"Et vous?"*

"Je vais très bien aussi," Ainsse rejoined shyly and bent his head as much to avoid further conversation as to continue his work.

Langlade hurried past Ainsse and cut between the carpenter's cabin and Amiot's, almost tripping over the Amiot children as they came racing around the corner.

As Augustin had suspected, Amiot was at work at his makeshift forge. It had been constructed under a small enclosure which stood between the back of his cabin and the wall of the fort.

Amiot was a small man, but very powerfully built. He had his shirt off and his huge chest and arm muscles bulged as he brought down the heavy hammer time and time again to shape the piece of hot iron against his anvil. His thick wrists and hands were covered with dark spots that looked like large moles. They were scars from accidental burnings that had occurred many times in his work as a smithy.

When his hammer stopped, he studied the shaped metal in his clamps, grunted his approval, and thrust it into the water bucket where it steamed and bubbled until it cooled.

As he looked up briefly from his work, he saw the gaunt Langlade standing before him. *"Bon jour, mon ami.* You look terrible. Has your *femme* delivered yet?" He smiled as if he expected a positive response.

"I haven't been able to find her," he sighed. "When I woke this morning, she was gone from the cabin."

At that moment, Marie Anne came around the corner of the house. In her arms, she held little Au-san-aw-go. Langlade looked at Amiot. "Then she is here. Why hasn't she come home? *Par la sambleu!*" Concern converted to anger in Langlade as a dark frown spread across his countenance.

At that moment, the Amiot children again came screaming into the yard. It was Amiot's turn to be angry now. "*Arrêtez!*" he shouted loudly in his full bass voice. His offspring stopped immediately. Marie Anne said softly; "*Va-t'en,* be off now. You bother your papa."

When the dark-haired and half-naked little brood had disappeared again, Marie Anne said: "Domitilde is not here. She is birthing."

"What?" Augustin almost shouted. "You mean she is having my child? Where is she? Why is she not in bed?" He became extremely excited and agitated.

Jean-Baptiste explained: "It is the Indian way, Augustin. They go off to the woods to have their babes. Don't like their men to see them in pain or a bloody mess. It's a good custom as far as I'm concerned. I've never seen any of mine born, and much the happier for it I suspect."

"Where did she go?" Augustin pleaded.

"She came here early this morning," the blacksmith said. "The pains had come before the sun and she knew the time had come. So she left Au-san-aw-go with us and went out of the fort. She'll be back, *mon ami,* probably very soon."

"How could you let her go?" Augustin roared accusingly. "There is no *sage-femme* (mid-wife). She will suffer, perhaps die, without assistance. How could you let her go?" The poor husband was totally distraught and the dull ache in his head turned to soaring pain. "I must find her," he mumbled and headed for the fort gate by the lakeshore.

Amiot yelled after him. "She will be hurt and embarrassed if you see her. Leave her alone!"

Langlade shrugged off the warning and hurried his pace.

🦋 🦋 🦋

H E HASTENED ALONG THE BEACH, following the small moccasin prints in the damp sand that he knew to be Domitilde's. He had gone perhaps three hundred yards from the fort in a westerly direction, when the footprints abruptly left the beach and moved into a grove of cedar trees. Twenty-five feet in from where the line of trees began, he spotted her. She was squatting in the sandy soil, and judging from the dark color of the ground beneath her, he could see that her water had broken and the child was on its way into the world.

He thought momentarily about announcing his presence, but remembered Amiot's warning and instead concealed himself behind a bush, comforted with the knowledge that he would be of no help to her and it was too late now to move her anywhere else.

She held a garter snake in her left hand, the one she had kept in a box in the cabin for the last several weeks. When Augustin had asked her why she wanted to keep it, she had only smiled. Now she picked up a sharp piece of broken shell in her right hand, and as the snake writhed crazily in her grip, she severed the head from the rest of the squirming body, then let the bright drops of red blood fall into another half-shell which was partially filled with water. She mixed the strange concoction and lifted it to her lips, swallowing it in one,long gulp. She then discarded the struggling, headless reptile and concentrated on the task at hand.

Augustin was at once fascinated and repelled. He noticed that she was wearing her doeskin dress. It was the first time she had worn Ottawa clothing since he had brought her the outfits from Montreal. She pulled her dress up above her waist and began grunting hard and breathing heavily. Blood dripped to the ground as the force of the child's head began to tear her flesh. She gripped her knees tightly as if to coerce her legs into position for the birth. She grimaced from the pain, but continued to push hard, sweating profusely. A horsefly landed on her exposed buttock and bit into the soft skin. Seagulls whirled and cried in the blue sky above her. The wind off the water blew steadily through the cedar trees. None of these things seemed to distract her in the least, so totally was she concentrating on the baby, whose head now appeared, gray and bloody between her legs.

She gasped for breath as she continued to push with all her strength. The blood began to fall in a steady stream now to the ground beneath her. Flies concentrated in large numbers around it.

She muttered something in the intensity of her pain, but Langlade could not quite make it out. He thought he heard the word *michi*, but it made no sense to him. He was too awed by the struggle of his wife with her body to give it much thought. He wanted so desperately to help her, but understood that there was nothing he could do except to add mental anguish to the physical distress she was already confronting so courageously.

After a moment which lasted a thousand years, the shoulders of the infant struggled through the fleshy door of its prison and it fell rudely into the air, plopping dully into the bloody sand below. Domitilde, gasping for air and obviously greatly relieved, fell backward onto the sand, listening happily to the child cry helplessly, but somehow aggressively, between her shaking legs. As she lay there on her back, staring at the jet-blue sky, she suddenly yelled, startling her concealed husband.

He would have run to her immediately had he not recognized at once that the cry was one of ecstasy and triumph, a shout of achievement and fulfillment, a warrior's whoop of victory. Her eyes tightly closed, her mouth drawn up in an ecstatic smile, she seemed to be in some sort of religious trance as the neglected infant continued to wail. Langlade heard her repeat, *"Me-daw-min, Me-daw-min,"* over and over again.

He knew that among the Ottawa, *Me-daw-min* was a spirit, the Ruler of the West Wind. After what seemed like a very long time, perhaps lengthened for Langlade by the anxious cries of his new son, Domitilde shook off her reverie and sat up, wincing from the stomach muscles which now rippled in spasms, making her nauseous.

She ignored the sensation and pulled her doeskin dress above her head and flipped it aside. She sat down, fully naked, in the sand. She reached for her screaming child, lifted him from the ground, and guided his mouth to her breast. The sudden silence was broken only by the west wind in the cedars, and the cries of the gulls. The child (a son, as she had known it would be) sucked greedily and sloppily at her nipple as she stood on her knees and grunted again, forcing the milky afterbirth to plop heavily onto the sand. Her long, black hair clung to her sweaty face and shoulders as she turned her attention to her new child. His hands were large and pounded against her collarbone and sternum as he drank contentedly. His feet were constantly in motion. He had the dark complexion and high cheekbones of his mother's people. His nose was Gallic, almost Romanesque. When he had had his fill, he closed his eyes and Domitilde sang a song to *We-eng*, the Bringer of Sleep, as the baby rested contentedly in her arms.

She lifted the child's torso to her face after he seemed relaxed and composed from his ordeal, mystifying her secret observer. Her jaws began moving in a chewing movement and Augustin realized that she was severing the umbilical cord with her teeth. The child slept peacefully through the entire procedure. Then she laid their son gently in the sun-warmed sand, stood up painfully and walked awkwardly to the beach, bypassing her husband by only a few feet. She waded into the water and lowered her torn and still bleeding groin into the cold lake.

Moments were sufficient for cleaning and coagulating the wound. She returned to the birthing place, wrapped her damaged torso in white rags, and pulled on her dress. She carefully buried the afterbirth and blood in the loose sand and limped back to the beach to wash the child, passing close again to the spot where her watchful spouse had been. She was unaware of his absence. She had never known he was there.

🐚 🐚 🐚

WITHIN TWENTY-FOUR HOURS, the news of the birth of the Langlade child reached the village of *L'Arbre Croche* and La Fourche set out immediately to visit his sister and new nephew. He started for the fort, taking the quickest route along the beach, accompanied by Wawatam, a boy of eleven summers whom he had taken into his care. The boy's mother had perished delivering him into the world. His father, the warrior Gubichi, had died of an *oqui*, a devil who made him cough up his own blood. He had suffered bitterly through the long winter and his soul was finally released by *Gitchi Manitou* in the Moon of Flowers.

Knowing that *Pau-guk*, the Spirit of Death, with his skeletal body and burning-coal eyes would soon be upon him, Gubichi had summoned La Fourche, the 'man-who-lives-alone,' to his wigwam, and had drawn from him a promise to care for his son. La Fourche had given his word, while the squaws bled Gubichi and the *shaman* tried to suck the evil spirit from his body through hollow swan wing bones applied to his chest. Still he continued to cough his bloody sputum into a hollowed gourd.

Wawatam had shown remarkable courage at his father's passing and had displayed admirable respect and proper reverence for his benefactor. La Fourche liked the boy, though he believed him to be too sensitive and gentle of spirit to ever be a great warrior. Perhaps he would be a wise *shaman* someday? Time would tell.

The lad had to almost run to keep up with La Fourche's long strides as they moved swiftly along the waterline. The sky was blue and cloudless. Though the sun sparkled brightly off the water, the temperature was cool.

Wawatam had become used to La Fourche's scarred face and fierce expressions, but walking with him at hip level, he was still fascinated with the geometric designs tattooed on his new father's thighs, and the large, steel knife attached to his hip by the same rawhide string that held his breechclout. Wawatam looked down at the bright cloth that now covered his own loins, a gift from La Fourche. He no longer ran around naked as the 'little' children did. La Fourche already had taught him to hunt, and he looked forward to the day when he could take his place in the warrior's circle.

Wawatam had never seen a white man's village before and he was awed by the stockade as they passed through the watergate. La Fourche knew the sentry well, a young soldier named François Cardin. As the two adults spoke pleasantly to one another in the French tongue, Wawatam's curious eye scrutinized the log buildings inside and he wondered how the whites would break camp. They must have great strength to move such dwellings when the game grew scarce. Though the Ottawa rarely moved more than twice a year, it was still a major undertaking, and this would be well-nigh impossible for his own people.

The boy suddenly realized that he was left standing alone, as he spotted La Fourche heading down the *Rue Dauphine* toward the Langlade cabin. He caught up with him just as he reached the cabin door and then he almost ran into his patron. La Fourche had stopped dead in his tracks and was staring incredulously at the turtle hinges that Amiot had made for the Langlades. He went a step closer and ran his rough hand over the surface of one of the hinges very tentatively as if he expected to receive some sort of shock from it. Wawatam could see that he was profoundly solemnized and appeared to display a sort of obeisance to the iron objects.

La Fourche was startled by the unexpected opening of the door. Domitilde stood in the portal, obviously delighted to see her brother. "I have come to see my nephew," he said, abruptly and with no apparent emotion.

She bowed low before him and signaled him to enter. As he stepped forward, he lightly and purposely touched her arm. It was a gesture that would remain imprinted in her memory for the rest of her life. It said, 'I am proud of you' and 'I have missed you.'

Inside, Langlade was kneeling by the fire, scraping the rust from his traps. On La Fourche's entrance, Augustin rose, bowed politely, and signaled the Ottawa to sit down.

"You honor me," he said solemnly. La Fourche sat down and remained silent for several moments. Wawatam stood behind him, reveling in the respect shown his new father. Finally, La Fourche began to speak in his low voice and broken French. "Domitilde, my sister, has borne you a son. She has done well."

Augustin nodded his head as he glanced at his wife who still stood by the door, flushed with pride. "You were a good friend to let me have her. She serves me well and is obedient." Augustin knew these two things were terribly important attributes for Ottawa women to possess and that his brother-in-law would be happy to hear that she was behaving as she should.

La Fourche's mutilated face broke into a scarred smile and even the socket of his eye seemed to twitch into a grin. His powerful shoulders were erect in pride. He grunted his contentment.

Langlade's curiosity finally got the better of him. "Who is the boy?" he queried.

The Indian then spoke for perhaps a quarter of an hour, explaining the circumstances under which young Wawatam had come to be his ward. Augustin was about to ask another question when La Fourche said bluntly: "I have come to see my sister's son. Will you show him to me?"

Augustin nodded at Domitilde. She went to the cradle by the window and lifted the dark infant into her arms. She crossed to her brother, unwrapped the child from his blanket, and proudly displayed him. The boy wriggled and fussed, but did not cry. La Fourche grinned broadly at the sturdy little naked body and bright, black eyes.

Augustin took the child from his wife. "It is time my son is baptized," he said. "Domitilde, fetch some water."

Her heart began to beat violently as she sensed that her husband was about to perform some masculine ritual. From experience with her own people, she knew that any ceremony involving males was likely to be painful and include some kind of self-mutilation. She feared for her son's safety. She watched apprehensively as Augustin took the water, scooped some from the bowl with the hollow of his palm, and poured it over the black hair of his son's head. "I baptize you in the name of our Lord Jesus Christ," he said. "Since no priest is here to do it, I take this responsibility upon myself. May He give you eternal life! I name you Charles Michel Monet de Moras, Sieur de Langlade. The Blessed Virgin confirm it."

He poured water once again on the child, not realizing in his ignorance of theology that only an ordained priest of the church could perform the rite to the satisfaction and approval of God. He rose and held up Charles for all to see. Domitilde was greatly relieved that this ceremony had not involved any test of courage; her baby was too young.

Dispelling her peace of mind, La Fourche stepped forward, drawing his large, hunting knife. Domitilde did not understand what he intended. Whatever it was, it was not anything she had ever seen as tradition among her own people. He had not behaved in such a manner at the birth of his other nephew, Au-san-aw-go, who now slept peacefully on the Langlade's down mattress. She fought back the maternal impulse to interfere, and swallowed hard.

La Fourche raised the knife, now liberated from its sheath. He placed its point against his chest and pulled it firmly across his breast, leaving a thin line of blood dripping behind it. He then calmly replaced his knife in its sheath and stood staring at little Charles, almost as if mesmerized. He seemed to be studying the child, searching his countenance for something. Wawatam shuffled his feet, and looked impatient. Augustin held tightly to his son, wondering at the maniacal grin on La Fourche's hideous face and concerned over his self-inflicted wound.

The chief lifted his hands to his chest, smearing them with the blood that had already begun to coagulate. He took a step toward the father and son. Augustin wanted to retreat, but something told him to remain where he was. La Fourche placed his hands on the child's head, rubbing the blood into his hair and across his face and neck. Little Charles looked at him defiantly, uncrying and too young to be afraid. They were to discover later that there was very little in the world which would make Charles fearful, even when he understood the meaning of it.

The Ottawa finally spoke: "You are blood of my blood. You will be my song of life. The blood of the Ottawa will be filled in your body and you will not die by your enemies. You will live long upon the earth and be a great warrior. The sign of *Michi-mak-i-nac* is upon you."

With this pronouncement, he turned and left the cabin, Wawatam hustling after him. Augustin looked at Domitilde. "What does it mean?" he asked.

She shrugged in genuine confusion. He could see that she did not understand it either.

Years later he would comprehend more, but never fully know. He somehow sensed that this son he held in his arms was not really his, name it what he will. He would recall looking down at his bloodied child on this baptismal morning and remember the peculiar shape of La Fourche's handprint on the child's forehead. It resembled a turtle.

Chapter
3

Père Du Jaunay

IN 1735, SIX YEARS AFTER THE BIRTH of Charles Langlade, Pierre Du Jaunay arrived at Michilimackinac and the occupants of the fort were very pleased to know that the Church had finally sent them their own parish priest. Du Jaunay was a 'black robe,' a Jesuit, who had spent the last ten of his thirty-one years working among the Huron, Ottawa and Ojibway Indians of the straits area. He had labored for several years among the Huron in the western part of the Upper Peninsula before reestablishing Père Marquette's mission at St. Ignace just across the strait from the fort. That having failed, the last six months of his missionary activity had found him among the Ottawa at *L'Arbre Croche*.

La Fourche and his people were willing listeners, particularly when Du Jaunay had given them new, shiny crucifixes to wear around their necks. Still, these Indians too had been reticent and when the bishop of Montreal ordered him to accept the settled parish at Fort Michilimackinac, the good Father was almost relieved. Though he hated to admit failure, he was certain that God wanted him to serve the little French community and he was still close enough to the Ottawa tribe at *L'Arbre Croche* and the Chippewa village east of the fort to gain some converts among the Indians yet.

Père Du Jaunay had reported to the French commandant, Pierre-Joseph Celoron de Blainville, who had replaced Jean-Baptiste René, Legardeur de Repentigny the previous year. The commandant was very cordial and receptive, and arranged a small *soirée* for the priest in his living quarters so that he could meet his parishioners. The reception was very formal and quiet with cider being served and small French pastries prepared by Madame de Blainville. All residents of the fort were invited and Augustin and Domitilde were among the first to arrive with seven-year-old Au-san-aw-go and six-year-old Charles. Augustin's hair had grayed even more and his beard was salt and pepper, although he looked very happy with his Domitilde and the two boys.

René and Marie Bourassa were there also with Ignace, and Marie was again very obviously pregnant. A beautiful young woman of twenty attended with them. René had brought her back from Montreal on one of his rare visits to see his brother who was a cloth merchant there. He was surprised to find that this brother had taken in the young lady, then fifteen, the daughter of a friend who was recently deceased and had left her an orphan. His *frère* was beside himself because he had promised his friend to care for the child, but his own brood numbered eight and he was having great difficulty in providing for so many. René had arranged to take the girl to his home on the frontier, if the girl would agree to servitude until she should be properly married. The young lady, named Constante Chevalier, had readily acquiesced. She had taken an instant liking to René and later, to Marie. She had been an excellent servant and boon companion to them both. The Bourassas had almost come to regard her as their daughter. She was vivacious and witty and quite beautiful, with lovely, blond hair and sparkling, intelligent, blue eyes. She always seemed happy, despite her difficult early years and, though not a student, she was bright, and loved quick conversation. She was immensely popular with the men of the fort, and was intensely desired and pursued to the point that René and Marie worried. She seemed to revel in these innocent flirtations, her favorite pastime. Yet she performed her domestic tasks well and was an excellent governess to little Ignace, who adored her. René wondered how Marie had ever gotten through her first pregnancy without Constante to help.

Also in attendance at the reception was Joseph Ainsse, the carpenter. He, like all the other males, was enraptured with Constante. He had made a small cedar jewelry box for her and left it anonymously at the doorstep of the Bourassa house in January of that same year. He had delivered it in the middle of the night during a terrible snowstorm, believing with certainty that no one would notice the clandestine benefactor. Yet the soldier, François Cardin, had been on sentry duty and had spotted the dark figure by the Bourassa cabin. He had not recognized Joseph in the shadows and snow, even though he had approached to within twenty feet of the hapless, gawky phantom and had shouted loudly to frighten the culprit. Having the desired effect, poor Joseph just about leapt from his skin and, slipping in the wet snow and ice, had fallen spread-eagled on his back, right in the doorway of his belovèd's home. A rush of light suddenly flooded the poor man as Monsieur Bourassa and Constante peered through the door opening. He mumbled that the box was for her. Rising, flushed, and wishing himself dead, he humbly apologized for his *gaucherie* and for disturbing their household. At that moment, François came running the last twenty feet from his sentry post, and becoming instantly cognizant of the situation, he gallantly remained silent as Joseph Ainsse retreated to his own cabin.

As the carpenter sat now at the reception for the priest, and watched Constante enter with the Bourassas on this May evening, the wretched recollection of that night flooded his mind and he remembered the amused expression on Constante's face as she looked at him, sprawled out in the snow. But imbedded much deeper in his distressed memory was the wanton look she had directed at the handsome soldier, who had smiled back in zealous agreement before Madame Bourassa ushered her away from the door.

Joseph sat quietly, by himself as usual, as he watched her cross the room. He had avoided her nervously throughout those winter months since his humiliation, and these first weeks of early spring. Now she walked directly to him and sat next to him on the bench close to the wall.

"*Bon soir,* Monsieur Ainsse," she chirped. "It is a wonderful night when so many people are together at once, *n'est-ce pas?*"

Joseph turned scarlet and shuffled his big feet. "*Oui,*" he mumbled. He stared steadily at his hands which gripped his knees, as if letting go would permit his entire bone structure to collapse and convert him to a mass of jelly.

"I beg your forgiveness," he stuttered.

"What?" she said, her eyes engulfing the busy scene before her.

"Please, forgive me."

"Why? For what?"

"Because I need to know you don't despise me."

"For what?" She suddenly gave him her attention. "Why would I despise you? You are so sweet and kind, and I adore the little jewelry box. Why should I not be fond of you?"

"Perhaps," he said wryly, "because of the manner in which it was given."

She could see that the memory of that night caused him great consternation and embarrassment. Out of pity for the poor man, she put her hand on his cheek and forced him to look at her. *"Mon cher,"* she said. "That was a lovely experience that I will long remember. *Merci,* I will not forget your kindness."

She kissed him lightly on the cheek, then bounced away to socialize with the others, pleased with what she felt was a return of kindness. The Bourassas followed behind her.

His heart pounded rapidly in his chest and the continual ache of combined loneliness and longing left him for the first time in years. He felt positively handsome, and smiled.

Typically, Constante Chevalier was instantly surrounded by other fascinated males. Among them were Commandant de Blainville, several French soldiers in their best dress uniforms (including François Cardin), and the rough but personable *coureurs de bois,* Jean Cuchoise and Jean-Baptiste Cadotte.

Cuchoise and Cadotte were usually absent from the fort, preferring to spend their time in the Ojibway camp which was in the forest east of the fort. When they heard of the arrival of the priest, however, they had hurried to meet him. They were formalistically religious men. Their spirits were rarely touched by the raw emotions which motivated men like Du Jaunay, but they enjoyed immensely the trappings and rituals of the Church. Very little emotion or intellect filtered through their coarse, inelegant

and rude exteriors to touch the heart. Yet they both wore crucifixes about their necks, believing them to bestow God's protection. They faithfully attended confession and Mass (when a
priest was available), then went about their daily lives of drinking and debauchery with their Ojibway women, feeling perfectly
free from conscience, knowing they had paid their debt to the
Church which guarded their souls.

They looked out of the place with the other guests because of
their Indian leggings (the *ceinture flechée),* and their buckskin
shirts and moccasins. They were unshaven and unbathed for
many months, and they presented quite a contrast to the commandant who stood near them in a crisp, blue uniform, shiny
black boots, with shaved face and powdered wig. Yet they were
good souls who had done many favors for the denizens of the
French community and showed little regard for money or power.
Their opiate was freedom, which they imbibed in unrestrictively
and guarded jealously.

Constante Chevalier was fascinated by them and their stories,
but she reserved special looks for the soldier, Cardin, who stood
directly across from her and stared right through her as she
laughed and was charmed by the adventures of the *coureurs de
bois.* There was little doubt that he was captivated by her charm,
but he moved slowly away when he saw Joseph Ainsse come
forward.

Ainsse, however, was intercepted by the blacksmith, Amiot,
who talked rapidly to him in excited tones as Joseph strained to
hear the conversation between Constante and de Blainville.

At this point, the priest raised his voice to invite everyone to
sit down on the wooden benches that were ordinarily used for
military meetings and were facing a makeshift podium that
served the commandant and his wife as a dining table. Joseph
Ainsse saw his opportunity, and quickly sat on one side of Constante as the Bourassas were seated on the other. Père Du Jaunay took his place behind the table. Cuchoise and Cadotte removed their beaver hats and stood, heads down, in the back of
the room.

Père Du Jaunay was a small man who, at age thirty-one, was
balding rapidly. He was very thin from continual fasts, and al-

though not a complete ascetic, a good measure of the physical deprivation he had enforced upon himself showed in the lank frame and slender face. His blue eyes sparkled and were an enigmatic contrast to the stark and gaunt cheekbones. Constante Chevalier, though not very religious, was fascinated by him almost as much as the men in the room had been impressed with her.

He wore a long, black robe, common to his order, stretching from the clerical collar to his feet. The robe was fastened with many buttons down the front and the entire gown was accented by a large and extraordinarily heavy-looking silver crucifix. His voice was gentle but firm, and easily carried across the room.

"Mes amis," he began, "I am delighted to be with you in this place. The Lord, through the Primate of Montreal, has determined that I should serve you here. I thank you for your most gracious welcome and the hospitality shown me by Commandant de Blainville. Monsieur Amiot has arranged for me to stay temporarily with his household until permanent quarters can be arranged. The king's memorial has determined that Monsieur Amiot shall be bonded to my service for the remainder of my stay here, and he will be compensated by the Crown."

Amiot smiled proudly while Marie Anne fussed with the children who became somewhat excited at the mention of their family name.

"I understand," the priest continued, "that we have a very talented *charpentier* among us." Joseph Ainsse bowed his head and squirmed in his seat, trying to escape notice. Constante patted him on the knee. "This is good, for soon a church must be constructed for the use of this parish and its people." There were general exclamations of approval and even some light applause by the Bourassas. "In the interim, Holy Mass will be performed outside on the parade ground each Sunday and Holy Day at sunrise. In inclement weather, the Eucharist will be celebrated under a temporary shelter. Confession is available at any time and we trust that you will all come and take advantage of the penance offered. Feel free to visit me at any time to request the assistance of Mother Church in any sacrament. You will be expected to tithe to the Church and the Holy Father in Rome will

be well pleased with you." Having concluded the informational
part of the meeting, he gave them his blessing. *"Vade in pace.
Omnia ad Dei gloriam* (Go in peace. All things for the glory of
God). He made the sign of Christ's cross over his audience whose
heads hung in sacred humility. The evening ended with the
chanting of the *Te Deum.* Forty-five minutes later, the room was
empty and the commandant and his wife had gone to bed.

🦋 🦋 🦋

ONLY MOMENTS AFTER LEAVING the reception with the Bourassas,
Constante had noticed Joseph Ainsse standing by the water gate
of the fort. He had apparently been waiting to talk to her, or so
she assumed. The night air was cool and refreshing after the
closed and smoky atmosphere of the commandant's quarters. She
made an excuse to the Bourassas to enjoy the air for a few moments and René, in a hurry to get the pregnant Marie to her bed
and rest, capitulated.

Once they had left, Constante moved directly to Joseph who
had been watching her closely. He took several steps toward her,
not out of boldness, but a desire to escape the prying eyes and
curious ears of the sentry at the gate.

As she approached, he whispered a barely audible, *"Bon soir."*

"Oui, it is a beautiful evening Joseph. It has been a wonderful
night. So many people, so much to do, how different from the
winter months! The air smells so good. The pines and the water
give off such a marvelous scent. I love the sounds of the birds
and insects, and the laughter of friends and the sunshine! I am so
happy I could burst!"

She had not noticed that the homely man had walked away
from her and seated himself on a stack of firewood which was
used to heat the soldiers' barracks some thirty feet distant. She
had been so engrossed in her own joyous mood that she had
quite forgotten whom she had been addressing. She could see
him clearly by the glow of the bright moon and, escaping her
reverie, approached him again. "What's the matter Joseph? Are
you all right?" Her expression of genuine concern moved him.
She sat down next to him and placed a hand on his slumped

shoulder.

"What is it?" she sympathized.

The words suddenly poured forth from him in a torrent. "Constante, I am so unhappy and alone. I have always been alone it seems. It's very difficult for me. I'm ugly and clumsy. I don't know how to talk. You . . . you're so beautiful, so happy and comfortable among people. You seem to fear no one. I . . . I want to be your . . . friend. I like you very much. You're in my thoughts, even my dreams . . . all the time. You're *more* than a friend. But, you see, I'm too ugly. I have no hope."

Constante was somewhat taken aback by this sudden emotional outburst, but she seemed to understand his suffering. She had never been coquettish, and her concern for him was genuine, but she didn't know how to reply without hurting him or verifying what he had said. "You are *not* ugly," she said. "I find you . . . charming. You are not handsome, but neither are you repulsive. Most people fit into that order somewhere. You are kind and thoughtful and you make beautiful things with your hands. The way you are is enough."

He was not convinced. Living had taught him differently. "Enough for what, Mademoiselle? Enough for you?" He did not wait for an answer, perhaps because he felt he knew what it would be. "I *do* try to be kind, but it has not gotten me a wife nor has it gained any friends for me. The looking glass tells me the truth. It doesn't care what I think. Kindness doesn't give me hope. My craft doesn't give me hope. My image mocks me. I hope only in you, Constante."

He suddenly grasped her small hands in his rough, huge ones, enveloping them and squeezing them as if they were the channels to life itself. For the first time in his experience, he looked boldly into the face of another human being and the fierceness of his eyes and appealing expression of ardor, momentarily overwhelmed Constante. His eyes she thought, reminded her of her dead father's eyes, blue and brilliant and piercing when aroused to strong emotion. Tears of fear and confusion welled in her own eyes, as she pulled her hands roughly from his and broke the discomfiting contact.

Joseph looked down again, believing that he had been vindicated in his assessment of human love and motivation. He smiled bitterly, as a man might smile as he put a gun to his head.

"*Maintenant. Est-ce que vous comprenez?*" (Now. Do you understand?) he said. "Do not feel badly or pity me. I have felt that too. It's all right. I had no hope before, I have none now. I have only embarrassed myself . . . again. It will be the last time." This last was spoken with such a deadly finality, that Constante shivered with fear.

He stood up resolutely, and took a step forward then stopped, his back turned toward her. She noticed his shoulders stiffen in resolve. She sensed that he was through with any further attempts to open himself to another human being. He would deny himself, to avoid destruction of self. The commitment hardened in his strong, broad back as he muttered, "Please forgive me for any discomfort I may have caused you, Mademoiselle. *Au revoir.*"

She stood, watching him walk away, dreading what might happen to that delicate psyche and her contribution to its destruction. Impulsively, she shouted his name and rushed to him. He turned warily and the moonlight on his face made him look ethereal, almost ghostly. He said nothing.

She slowed her pace and stopped inches from him. She looked up into his face which seemed steely and hard, no longer subject to shyness, or any emotion. It was a face that said only; 'I expect nothing. Dismiss me and let's be done with it.'

'How did this happen?' she thought. 'I wanted to show I care. He seemed so lost and harmless.' She looked past his contorted features, at those burning blue eyes. . . . She felt his arms around her waist. She put her hands on his red cheeks, pulled his face to hers, and kissed him for a long moment. She finally broke away and began to walk toward the Bourassa cabin.

"*Merci, ma chère Constante,*" he mumbled. "I will take hope, even out of pity."

She halted and turned, facing him angrily. "I did not kiss you out of pity or to give you hope. I did it because . . . because I wanted to." Her tone was harsh, almost bitter, mixed with confusion.

"Forgive me, Mademoiselle," he managed to stammer. "May I

see you again?"

"If you wish," she said abruptly, knowing there was no other answer.

She saw his large mouth open in awed excitement and joy as she again turned to home. Her thoughts flashed to the image of her dying father and she remembered how he had kept her close to his side with words of filial duty and obligation. When he died, she mourned, and yet she felt unencumbered. She had known such a great sense of relief and freedom . . . until now. She was sympathetic tonight to a renewal of that burden. Those terrible eyes . . . that destructive frown. . . .

She was chained again and she sensed it. Yet she contented herself to believe that when the time came, she could be freed by a few kind words.

François Louis Cardin's eyes followed her into the Bourassa cabin as they had watched her from the barracks window ever since she shouted Joseph's name, drawing Cardin's attention. He sighed deeply and went back among the snoring sounds of his comrades. He lay back down on his cot and stared at the ceiling, deep in thought, until the first light of dawn erased the darkness from the room.

🐾 🐾 🐾

PÈRE DU JAUNAY WAS KEPT VERY BUSY in the next few months. He heard confession often and said Mass frequently. He labored diligently among the French soldiers who were often negligent in their devotion to Mother Church and the mystery of the Eucharist. He spent much time instructing Domitilde and her two sons in the Roman Catholic faith and he found in the Indian woman an apt and eager pupil. The boys, one full-blooded Ottawa and the other a French half-breed, were bright enough, but too restless and impatient to learn without discipline. Besides, the priest found that for every bit of progress he made in their religious instruction, their uncle, a deformed Ottawa chieftain called 'the Pitchfork,' seemed to undo those accomplishments with bloody tales of giants and cannibals and forest spirits. They spent large amounts of time with this uncle on hunting trips and other excursions, and their father, though French, seemed to heartily approve of this association. The mother, being a good Indian wife as well as a student of Catholicism, always deferred to her husband's judgment and authority and so the boys continued to be seen in the company of their savage uncle and to be deeply influenced by him. Strangely, the half-breed (Du Jaunay believed him to be named Charles) was more Indian than his full-blooded brother (whose more difficult Ottawa name the priest could never remember.) Little Charles was darker than his half-brother, with straight black hair that hung to his shoulders in Indian fashion. His dark eyes were fierce and strangely cold sitting behind his high cheekbones, like animal eyes staring from dark caves on some fleshy precipice. He was a quiet, withdrawn and serious boy, not at all like the other Langlade child who laughed and romped and generally seemed to be full of the pleasure of living.

Oddly enough, little Charles was fond of wearing French clothing and he appeared disgusted with his older brother who ran about naked or only with a loincloth to gird him and protect his minimal modesty. While Au-san-aw-go could not sit still for his instruction from the Jesuit and had to be scolded often, Charles sat quietly, staring at Du Jaunay until he felt almost uncomfortable. Yet, when questioned about his catechetical absorption, he was always able to recite in his prematurely adult voice, the lessons taught him, and he never failed to comply with instructions. While Charles was the better student, Père Du Jaunay thought he liked the other boy better. He acted more like a boy than the inquisitional, dark little judge who tested his composure and silently devoured his thoughts.

In the early part of August, only weeks after his arrival, he was called upon to carry out the rite of baptism. It was Domitilde's desire to be consecrated into the Christian faith and she earnestly desired the same for Au-san-aw-go. Though in Domitilde's mind, Augustin's baptism of his own son had been sufficient (now that she understood its significance), it was the good Father's wish that Charles should be baptized properly, knowing that the mystical powers of the priesthood wrought true sacramental grace and not the imitative action of a simple, unordained trapper, as devout as he might be.

So on a hot, August morning, several members of the French community of the fort gathered at the Langlade cabin to see the triple baptism. The Bourassas were there with little Ignace, Marie Bourassa looking large and uncomfortable, a *femme grosse* indeed. Constante Chevalier was with them too. She stood near Joseph Ainsse who unabashedly had placed his arm about her waist smiling proudly and possessively. Constante appeared happy enough and comfortable with his closeness, but somehow she had changed and was not as full of the *joie de vivre* as she had once been. René Bourassa attributed the change in attitude to maturity and made well-known his approval of the industrious and honest carpenter. Marie knew it was something else.

François Louis Cardin knew also. He was in attendance, wearing a ruffled linen *jabot* and tight breeches with his royal blue uniform coat. Though he was perspiring profusely in the heat, he cut a handsome figure. His classical features and thick, wavy hair tied neatly in the back with a ribbon, gave him an air of nobility. His chin was dimpled and when he smiled, the indentation would momentarily disappear. Vulcan and Adonis in one place. The comparison did not escape the blonde Venus they both desired.

Amiot and Marie Anne were there with their many children. Cuchoise and Cadotte would most certainly have attended had they known, but they were away at the Ojibway village.

The Ottawa relatives of the Langlades had not been notified. Most likely they would not have seen much use in attending, since Father Du Jaunay's magic had not made much of an impression on them when he worked among them. To the Indians, his claim that he had transformed some bread and wine into flesh and blood was not substantiated by the physical evidence, and so they saw him as somewhat of a charlatan, albeit a kind and caring one. After La Fourche had shared his opinion of the priest with his French brother-in-law, Augustin decided that it would be better that the chief not attend.

The pious Jesuit saw the sacraments as miracles of God's power and he smiled broadly now as he sprinkled the holy water on Domitilde and Au-san-aw-go, who was given the new Christian name of Jean-Paul Langlade. When the serious little Charles stepped forward, the priest hesitated momentarily, unaware of the reasoning behind his recalcitrance. After he had poured the water on the child's black hair, he ended the ceremony as he had the previous two baptisms with the traditional; *"In nomine Patris, et Filii, et Spiritus Sancti"* (In the name of the Father, the Son, and the Holy Spirit).

Amiot, whom Du Jaunay had grown close to while living with his family, had been given the honor of assisting the priest at Mass and at special sacramental ceremonies such as this. Today, he held the chalice containing the holy water blessed by the cleric. As Du Jaunay completed the baptism of Charles, Amiot turned to put the water back on the makeshift altar when the chalice slipped from his hands and fell with a splashy thud onto the ground. There was a hushed 'ah-h-h' which came spontaneously from the small congregation as they gasped at the desecration. Père Du Jaunay knelt and touched the damp earth at the feet of young Charles, who had not moved. He looked slowly up and noted that the eyes of the young boy were riveted on his. Their mutual staring was suddenly interrupted by the groaning of Madame Bourassa who, strained by her pregnancy, the heat, and this terrible accident, had swooned and fallen to the ground. Father Du Jaunay rushed to assist the poor woman and her distressed husband. She was carried to her cabin across the *Rue Dauphine* where, within the hour, she was delivered of a six pound baby girl who was promptly named Charlotte by her proud papa. As the new child cried for the first time, Charles and Jean-Paul Langlade came out of their cabin on the *Rue du Diable* and noticed that the moisture in the soil where the chalice had fallen had completely evaporated.

ALTHOUGH LA FOURCHE did not attend the official baptisms of his sister and nephews, and was unaware of the birth of the little Bourassa *enfant,* news did arrive at *L'Arbre Croche* of another significant birth only weeks later as the air began to turn cool off the lake and the 'Season of Colored Leaves' continued.

The squaw of the Ojibway chief, Minavavana, had given birth to a son. La Fourche was on excellent terms with the Ojibway, although the fort was a dividing landmark between their respective hunting grounds and they both honored an unspoken agreement not to trespass unless invited. Minavavana, known as the *Grand Saulteur* (Great Chippewa)[1], had invited many Indian leaders to his camp for a feast on the occasion of the birth of his son, who was given the name Wenniway. La Fourche was accompanied on his short journey to the Chippewa village by his adopted son, Wawatam, who was now seventeen and regarded as a full-fledged warrior in the Ottawa camp. He had become a very big man, standing over six feet tall and powerfully built. The chest underneath his quill-decorated buckskin shirt was broad and promised great strength. His black hair was pulled together at the top of his skull and wrapped with rawhide lacing so that it jutted straight up toward the sky. The rest of his hair, made shiny with bear grease, fell below his shoulders. A single eagle feather had been forced into the rawhide ties in his top-knot. He wore the *ceinture flechée* over his legs and a breechclout to cover his loins. Garters worn over the leggings just below each knee were decorated with brightly-colored porcupine quills delicately interwoven in geometric patterns. His moccasins too were embellished with quills. His ear lobes had been split with a knife and, once healed, swansdown had been thrust into the slits and copper rings attached to the bottom of the lobes. He carried a *mocock,* or birchbark box containing gifts for the new father and mother and their son.

Wawatam's face was handsome by Ottawa standards. He had a long, aquiline nose and large, brown eyes. His chin was completely hairless and he was much admired among the women of the camp. As yet, he seemed to take no notice of them and despite his powerful build, he was very gentle, an attribute that

---

[1] Other Indians called these people Ojibway, which means 'pucker-up,' a reference to their moccasins, which puckered at the ankles. They called themselves the Anishnabeg. 'Chippewa' is a mispronunciation of Ojibway. The French sometimes called them *saulteurs* because they first encountered these people fishing in the shallow rapids, or *'sault.'*

made him even more desirable to Ottawa maidens.

The scarred and one-eyed La Fourche, looking fifteen years older than his twenty-seven winters, presented an interesting contrast to his son as the two men walked side by side through the forest, following a pathway that had been in use for years, long before the fort was built. The sylvan setting they traversed was beautiful, dotted with black and white spruce; striped, red, and sugar maple; slippery elm and yellow birch, jack pine and white pine. The forest floor was littered with purple spiderwort and green ferns, pink arbutus and thickets of hawthorn wherever the sun managed to peek through the arboresque ceiling. Elderberries grew wild along a little brook which roughly paralleled the path. Though the two travelers did not comment on the particular excellence of their world, they understood its value and knew its worth. They did not have to write odes to it or attempt to reproduce it on canvas. Their praise was in being *in* it, living as part of it.

They knew that such beauty could suddenly turn to their destruction. La Fourche thought of the day many years ago when he lay contentedly full, in a blueberry patch, idly watching the clouds form their nebulous shapes. His stained mouth was opened in a lazy smile when the mountainous shape of *Mag-wah,* the bear, had risen over him, blocking the sky and obliterating half his vision of the world in a single swipe of his paw. On that day, he had become the 'boy with the scarred face,' later refined by his French friends to La Fourche—The Pitchfork. That day, nature had made its mark on him. He was not bitter. He had learned a lesson that would enable him to survive. He knew the value of the experience. He never got caught in idyllic reverie again. The poet's soul was exchanged for the warrior's wisdom, to harden him for additional painful experience. Nature was beautiful, but She was also exacting, austere, unsympathetic, insensitive and unyielding. Life must be lived Her way, or not at all.

None of this was said by the two men, or even consciously thought about, as they approached the Chippewa camp in silence. Their Indian brethren had known of their approach for several minutes and the squaws and their naked children came running to see the 'Scarred One' and his adopted son.

Scars represented difficult triumphs and were regarded with awe by most Indian men in general and the Chippewa in particular. They were viewed as signs of courage and many a young man, unlucky enough not to have them, scarred himself in hope of recognition and worth. Almost everyone knew that La Fourche's mutilated face had been caused by *Mag-wah,* an animal held in great veneration by the Chippewa for his strength and courage. To have lived through an attack by *Mag-wah,* particularly unarmed and as a child, elicited tremendous respect from these people.

Their camp, about two miles from the fort, was haphazardly constructed. The center of it was dominated by a huge community fire. Wigwams with sapling frames, covered with birchbark, dotted the clearing. From the most central of these emerged the young Chippewa chief, Minavavana. Like La Fourche, only in his twenties, he was already greatly respected by his people for his prowess as a warrior and his wisdom in council. Perhaps the only man more esteemed by this company was the forty-year-old *shaman,* Ishnoki, who was revered for his power to heal and his magic. The one held the respect of a soldier, the other the regard of a priest.

In spite of the chilly air, the 'Great Chippewa' was dressed only in loincloth and moccasins. He was powerfully built too, like Wawatam, but much shorter in stature. His head was shaved on both sides, leaving only a single row of thick, black, hair, combed erect, stretching from his forehead to the nape of his neck. Most noticeable however, was the massive tattoo of a turtle on his naked torso, reaching from his navel to his neck. The reptile was designed so that its shell faced the observer, and was positioned to appear as if it were crawling up his body toward his head.

Few among the Ojibway could wear the sign of the *Michimak-i-nac,* the Great Turtle. Yet Ishnoki, the *shaman,* had seen in a vision that this must be for Minavavana. Though the chief was yet to prove himself to his people in many ways, Ishnoki was known to have the ear of, and be the mouthpiece for, *Gitchi Man-i-tou,* the 'Great Spirit' and 'Maker of All Things.' No one doubted his wisdom.

Minavavana stepped forward to offer his hand in friendship to the two Ottawa. His voice rang in a sharp, guttural bass; "Welcome my brother and his son. You are well? I am honored that you have come to my village on this day."

La Fourche gripped his arm tightly and held it firm. The Ojibway chief never failed to be awed by the massive ruin of this man's face. He noted that a new lesion stretched across his chest just below his collarbone.

La Fourche spoke through scarred lips: "My dear brother, my son and I find great pleasure in your invitation, and honor in your wish to share your happiness with us. I know what you feel. I felt this way also on the birth of *my* son." He placed his arm on Wawatam's shoulder and grinned happily. (Though all present knew that Wawatam was adopted long after birth, so total was La Fourche's acceptance of the young man that he had obliterated any memory other than that of purely genetic fatherhood. To La Fourche, Wawatam was his natural son, and the strength of his love abolished memory, as well as the logical fact that he would have had to become a parent at the age of ten in order to be Wawatam's natural father.)

At a signal from La Fourche, Wawatam unshouldered the pack he had been carrying and revealed the gifts they had brought for the family. Minavavana watched with stoic patience as Wawatam laid the pack on the ground and placed each gift at the feet of the *Grand Saulteur*. Included were a piece of iron pyrite for the new mother to light the lodge fire; porcupine quills dyed with bloodroot, wild plum bark and blueberry juice for the infant's first moccasins; some beautiful *migis* (cowrie shells) for the father; and for the whole family, fresh fawn's tongue, a great delicacy and rare treat. The expression on the Chippewa's face showed clearly his obvious gratitude and pleasure at the gifts.

Minavavana spoke with solemnity, masking his excitement over the gifts. "La Fourche and his son are men of strength and courage. Your presence here, on this day, shows your wisdom and the greatness of the Ottawa people. Come, see the reason for our celebration."

He turned to his wigwam, raised the deerhide cover over the entrance, and beckoned La Forche and Wawatam to enter. The presents were left on the ground where they had been placed to be admired by others of the Ojibway band. The possibility of theft did not occur to them and the gifts were later delivered to Minavavana's wigwam intact. Only the fawn's tongue was removed from the ground by the new child's maternal grandmother, to keep it from the dogs.

Upon entering the smoky domicile, La Fourche immediately spotted the mother, sitting against the wall, feeding the infant. She rose painfully, babe still attached to her breast, and smiled shyly. She had never seen La Fourche before, and his fierce appearance intimidated her. Once on her feet however, she stood silently, awaiting instructions from her husband. Minavavana signaled her to remain still and the two Ottawa approached to get a better look at the baby.

The child was handsome and physically perfect, with sturdy little fat arms and legs. He bore a luxurious crop of black, silky, hair.

"He will be called Wenniway, 'Untroubled One,' because he does not cry," the proud father announced grandly.

"It is a good name," La Fourche mumbled, and Wawatam nodded his assent.

🏵 🏵 🏵

In the feast that took place later that night, there was much to eat and good company. La Fourche, normally not a man of huge appetite, stuffed himself with venison, *masquinonge* (muskellunge), *mez-he-say* (turkey) and handfuls of a type of wild rice the French called *avoine folle* (crazy oats). Wawatam too enjoyed the meal immensely. The pair sat around the communal fire in the center of the village after eating, and smoked *kinickinick* with other guests who had traveled several days' journey to be in attendance.

Thus relaxed and warmed by the huge fire, they exchanged tales of the *Puk-wudj-in-i-nees*, fairies of the land who lived in and around them and played tricks on mortals, and of the cannibal giants, the *Wen-di-goes*.

The most fearful story however, came from Wing-ge-zee-

awn-day-gog (Eagle Crow), who was the chief of a small band of
Ojibway called the *Mas-ke-gon* who came from an area south of
Michi-mack-i-nac on the shores of the lake called Huron. This
young chief told of the fearsome *Red-Gee-bis,* sorcerers who lived
in caves and consorted with *oquis,* or devils. He related the story
of a young man who went to the island of *Michi-mack-i-nac* and
found a cave which he entered to escape the rainy, foul night. As
he lit his fire, sorcerers oozed from the stone walls of the cave,
and their green eyes, penetrating and feline, drove him mad so
that he drew his knife and slit his own throat. Such action could
only be motivated by the *Michi Man-i-tou,* the 'Spirit of Evil,' he
said.

Wawatam was fascinated by these stories and showed a keen
interest in them. Any reference to the 'Isle of the Great Turtle'
always aroused his curiosity. He had heard many stories about
the Great Turtle, the guardian spirit of the Chippewa and Ottawa, and had gone to the island several times with the 'other
man' (his real genetic father) when just a small boy. Though in
daylight it could be seen clearly from the fort that took its name,
the Isle du Michilimackinac was never visited by the white men.
Even Cuchoise and Cadotte, who lived among the Chippewa and
had been seen this very day by Wawatam, paying their respects
to the *Grand Saulteur,* had never ventured onto its shores. Cuchoise had told him some months ago that it was a heathen den
of evil and good Christians avoided this 'place of devils.'

Though Wawatam did not fully understand the meaning of
Christianity and even less of the church, he proudly wore the
crucifix Père Du Jaunay had given him. He understood that
somehow the little 'man-with-nails-through-his-hands' had the
power to drive away evil. Evil he understood (having lived all his
life among his fellow creatures), and would use any such talis-
man to keep it away.

He knew that the Great Turtle guarded his people (much like
La Fourche had protected him) and that this spirit lived on the
island (or rather, *was* the island), floating firmly in that one spot
to watch over his own. He was distracted from his thoughts by
the tired voice of La Fourche: "My son, we must leave," he said,
getting to his feet. "I will inform our host."

He walked in the direction of Minavavana's wigwam. Wawatam realized then that only he and Eagle Crow were still by the fire. The Mas-ke-gon spoke to the younger Ottawa: "Your father is a good man. May he live long upon the earth and have many grandsons."

After a thoughtful pause, Wawatam rejoined: "I will be dutiful in trying to provide them."

Eagle Crow smiled broadly. "That is one of life's sweet duties," he quipped. The spreading grin on the face of the young Ottawa pleased him. "My *noko* will be delivered of a child soon. You will visit my village then too?" Wawatam, honored, shook his head affirmatively.

Unknown to Eagle Crow, his squaw had already given birth to his own son at their village only minutes earlier. The boy would come to be called Matchekewis, and grow to be a close companion of little Wenniway, who slept peacefully, while his father bid *adieu* to La Fourche.

🐢 🐢 🐢

CONSTANTE CHEVALIER had kept very busy throughout the summer, tending to six-year old Ignace and the delicate little infant, Charlotte, as well as cleaning, cooking, and doing other household duties which had been assigned her by Madame Bourassa. Joseph Ainsse had become her constant companion. When he was not occupied in his carpenter shop, he was eternally near her, drawing water for her, carrying wood, or even plucking fowl and shucking corn. She had grown fond of him too, and had begun to depend on him for so many things that she had slowly come to the realization that she could probably not get along without him. Certainly she knew he could not live without her, and the probability of her ever telling him to leave became more and more remote. She rationalized that he was a good man, kind and hard-working, who would never see her suffer. She found him to be gentle and devoted. But when she dreamed passionate dreams, it was François Cardin who held her. It was he she coupled with in her secret bed. Even when she kissed Joseph, her eyes closed to reveal the handsome soldier's face. She sensed that she loved François and perhaps that he loved her, yet she had never talked with him, nor heard his confession of passion. Only his eyes had said it at chance meetings with hers. Constante had seen him only once since the baptisms of the Langlades a month earlier, but again, he had pierced her through with his strong, unflinching stare and made her flesh quiver with excitement—even lust. However, occasional momentary eye contact was not enough to triumph over the persistent Joe Ainsse, whose daily assaults on her emotions and conscience wore away romantic idealism.

Joseph did not demand. He waited to be ordered. But both of them knew that he was the master of this relationship, wielding guilt, pity and obligation like weapons, to beat devotion into her and destroy her heart's defenses.

When she was in the company of her carpenter, she felt like a little child. Several times she had tried to tell him how she felt (though as time passed, she began to become unsure of what she had intended to say). He would listen to her so intently, smiling so warmly and trustingly, that she could not bring herself to hurt him by sending him away. Eventually, she gave up, and forgot her commitment to her own heart.

Her years of poverty and her servitude contributed to her lapse of memory. Although she knew herself fortunate to be cared for so assiduously and with such parental devotion by the Bourassas, she remembered, nonetheless, that her position was that of bound servitude, and servants had no right to dream of perfection, but should content themselves with the more pragmatic matters of survival and comfort. Love was a luxury she could ill-afford.

Joseph's business thrived. He received orders daily for wagon repairs, furniture, crates, chests, caskets and all manner of things which required his considerable skills. He was prompt, his prices reasonable, and soon the little open-air, roofed shelter had become an enclosed shop. The cabin, which had served as a work place in the winter months, became a home. Monsieur Bourassa could not say enough about the man's thrift and industry, commenting that he would one day be rich, while winking the conspirator's eye at Constante.

Only days after La Fourche's visit to the Chippewa camp, Joseph came to the cabin to request of Monsieur Bourassa, as guardian of Constante, permission to pursue her as his spouse. René was delighted and shook the carpenter's hand enthusiastically. Moments later, as Constante entered the room, and in the presence of the Bourassa family, he begged her to be his wife. She had both anticipated and feared this moment and each time the thought had occurred to her, she had quickly put the discomforting idea from her distraught mind. Now there was no escape. She knew a negative response would destroy Joseph and deeply disappoint her benefactor who stood waiting expectantly. She also understood that a positive answer would give her security and a cessation of her emotional torment and indecision.

The image of François Cardin momentarily drifted before her mind like some ghostly premonition of haunting days and years of regret. She appeared briefly to be dazed or drugged, and Madame Bourassa looked concerned for her, when she suddenly broke from her mesmerization and resolutely looked each of the occupants of the room in the face, as if to find somewhere, on some countenance, the answer to her dilemma. Joseph was not a simpleton and he could not ignore the terrible struggle that so plainly manifested itself in her expressions. Finally and abruptly, she accepted, and his eyes welled with the tears of a man who had just escaped the grave.

In the days that followed, the coming nuptials were publicly announced and plans were made. Joseph was seen each day, whistling merrily as he went about the business of building an addition to his cabin which would become a private bedroom, separate from the rest of the house (no small luxury at Michilimackinac) and adding real glass to the windows, which he had ordered from Montreal.

Constante was honored by Madame Bourassa by the latter's offer to allow her former servant to wear the wedding gown she had worn when taking her vows to René in that same city. It was a beautiful dress of white lace and satin, and Marie was touched by the tears which trickled down Constante's cheeks as she tried it on. It had to be taken in at the waist, but otherwise it was a perfect fit. Madame Bourassa was never sure if the tears were those of a humble girl's overwhelming gratitude, or those of sorrow at something lost.

Marie Anne Amiot and Domitilde Langlade had promised to provide the bulk of the food for the wedding feast and Père Du Jaunay had been engaged by Joseph to say the nuptial mass. Invitations were delivered to almost all the occupants of the fort by young Ignace Bourassa and everyone, it seemed, was busy in preparation. The women especially anticipated the coming event with great excitement and all appeared to look forward to the break in their routine with complete accord—with the exception of François Cardin.

The beautiful girl's betrothal to the homely carpenter had struck him as wrong. It was not so much the physical disparity between them that bothered him, but he was sure that she did not love her intended. (The only other person to even remotely suspect such a possibility was Marie Bourassa, but she too, had been captivated by Joseph's excessive, obsessive and energetic determination.)

François thought he had seen in her blue eyes where her real love lay. Though they had never spoken, he sensed her tender passion for him instinctively. However, doubt reared its head at times in his assesment of the situation and he could not be absolutely certain that what he felt was reality. He determined that the only way to be unequivocally sure was to speak to Constante. He had avoided approaching her prior to this time because he had genuinely believed that she loved *him,* and the apparent infatuation with Joe Ainsse would fade away and her true feelings would be revealed. But now. . . . He must speak with her before he lost her permanently. This was no jealous ruse. This was not playful flirting. The game had gotten out of hand and he must know what she felt for him, if anything, and hear it from her lips.

An opportunity presented itself several days later when he was leaving the fort to walk along the beach in off-duty idleness. Constante was standing alone on the strand. Her feet were only inches from the waterline. She was staring out across the lake. Her long blond hair drifted in the gentle breeze beneath her white mob cap. She wore a boned stomacher about her waist which tied in front and a plain skirt which fell to her shins. As she turned to see who the intruder was, he swallowed hard, knowing that he *must* say something now. The stomacher, he noted, emphasized her hips, by reducing her waist, and forced her firm bosom to jut upward, almost overflowing the low-cut peasant's blouse. Her skin was a creamy-rose hue, complementing and accentuating the beauty of her blue eyes and soft yellow tresses. Her red mouth was open in astonishment at his approach. She had obviously believed that he was someone else when she heard him behind her. She held his eyes captive for a moment, then forced herself to look away again, toward the lake.

"*Bon jour, Mademoiselle,*" he said, bowing with exaggerated gallantry. He kept walking until he stood by her side.

"*Voyez!*" she said, scanning the horizon and pointing. "There is the island the Indians call the 'Great Turtle.' Domitilde Langlade told me about it. It does look like a turtle's head and shell floating there in the water, don't you think?"

Cardin had seen it many times. His eyes were not on it, but on her, and she knew it. "*Mais oui.* It does. The Indians have called it that for many years. Is this the first you have heard of it or seen it?"

"I never bothered to look," she lied nervously. She could feel his gaze, and it excited her. He sensed this and stood in front of her, forcing her to face him.

"I have heard, Mademoiselle Chevalier, that you are to be congratulated."

At this her coy expression became serious, almost pained. "What do you mean, Monsieur?"

"I mean that you are to be married soon. How very happy you must be. Monsieur Ainsse is a *bon homme*. He will provide well for you." As he spoke, Cardin searched her countenance, studying every expression, watching every reaction, hoping for some verification of his belief. Her face was stone.

"Joseph *is* a good man as you say, and he loves me." Her chin rested almost on her bosom after she spoke as if to look at him further would cause the *façade* to crumble.

François knew that he was risking great embarrassment and was guilty of a terrible effrontery, but he was driven to know her heart. He placed a finger under her chin and lifted her face so that she was forced to look at him. The lack of resistance on her part, and the tears forming in her haunting eyes, emboldened him to ask: "Do you love him?"

Her lower lip quivered violently as she struggled with her emotions. At the point of surrender, she realized that the walls that Joseph had worn away in the past weeks were being reconstructed in moments by this strange man who pulled at her heart and made her throat constrict until she found it difficult to catch her breath.

"Why should I not love him?" she said angrily, tearing herself away from Cardin and walking in the opposite direction down the beach. She turned back to him, smiling and collecting her emotions, wiping away tears. "He loves me!" she almost shouted. "He wants me and would die for me *and is not afraid to tell me so.* He would never desert me or leave me alone. Yes," her voice shook, almost sobbing, "yes I *do* love him."

Overcome by her emotions, she whirled and ran. She jumped up the little knoll and was racing along the stockade wall, when Cardin overtook her, grabbed her by the arm, and turning her toward him, kissed her passionately. Her arms resisted him at first, but the hands which tried to push him away soon slid around his neck, her tear-stained face moving salaciously against his, twisting and turning, as if to devour him in her passion.

He was overcome by her fervent intensity, lost in the sweetness of her mouth and the salt taste of her tears. "You love *me,*" he said huskily. "I knew you loved me. *Je t'adore,* Constante." He kissed her wildly, again and again. She reveled in his attentions. Here was happiness. Here was the life of dreams.

But the dream was abruptly broken by the image of her father's face, drifting sadly and mournfully into her mind's eye. His blue eyes burned into hers, angry and betrayed. She immediately became stiff and unyielding in Cardin's embrace. He drew his lips from hers and looked at her, puzzled. She appeared to be lost in a sort of trance as she stared straight ahead and seemed to be unaware of his presence, whereas moments ago they had been pressed together in such oneness that they had almost been a single entity. Now, they were apart—worlds distant.

The apparition of Constante's father continued to hold her vision in sway. She felt desiccated and winnowed, like the chaff from grain. Gradually her father's countenance faded, and was replaced by the kind, smiling face of Joseph Ainsse. His homely, good-natured smile could only accuse.

She suddenly became animated, broke the young soldier's hold on her arms, and dashed toward the entrance to the fort, her beautiful golden hair flowing behind her. She heard Cardin yelling: "Wait, Constante! Please wait, my love," but she did not stop.

A few days later, Joseph Ainsse and Constante Chevalier were united in marriage by Père Du Jaunay and took up residence in the carpenter's cabin across the parade ground from the soldier's barracks.

4

The Education of Charles Langlade

AUGUSTIN LANGLADE had become concerned about his sons. They were growing up rapidly, and although they were very intelligent and had been taught to read and write, they knew little of their French heritage. La Fourche had taught them well about the customs and religion of the Ottawa. They spent a great deal of their time with him and their cousin, Wawatam. Yet they knew little of Augustin's people. He was frequently gone, and so it was natural for the boys to be with their uncle.

Augustin did not object. He was very fond of La Fourche and trusted him implicitly to watch over them. As much as he loved Domitilde, and as hard as she had tried to become a God-fearing, Christian, French wife, she was still a product of her own Ottawa upbringing and she, like Marie Anne Amiot, paid little attention to her children and let them run wild in the Indian fashion, never disciplining them. She saw to it that they ate and were safely inside the cabin at night. Other than that, she rarely paid any attention to them, though she adored them both. She was still only twenty-five herself, and spent the more monotonous moments of Augustin's absence with her special friend, Marie Amiot, although those visits were becoming less and less frequent. Jean-Baptiste Amiot seldom left the fort anymore now that he was in the full-time employ of the parish priest and Marie, as Domitilde understood, must be with her husband. She had, over the course of the years, come to know her close neighbor, Marie Bourassa, very well and also spent time with Madame

Ainsse, although *her* husband was always in attendance and left them no time to talk privately as they would have liked to do.

She saw her brother, La Fourche, more and more, since the boys spent most of their free moments in the Ottawa village, and the conscientious uncle would always pick them up in the morning and escort them back to the fort at night.

Augustin knew that La Fourche was especially fond of little Charles. The chief felt that there was something very unique about the boy and spent many hours with him, working with him and telling him stories about the Great Turtle while Au-san-aw-go (now Jean-Paul) played merrily with the other children of the camp, unaware of any favoritism. Indeed, young Jean-Paul felt that he held a special place in his uncle's heart because he was not made to be the student and he could spend time with his cousin, Wawatam, learning to hunt and fish.

All of this Augustin understood and accepted. Unlike the English, who regarded the Indians as savages, the French saw through the barbaric exterior and recognized the simplicity and beauty in the Indian lifestyle. Nevertheless, Augustin was concerned that perhaps his children (especially Charles) were not receiving enough instruction about the French side of their heritage. So he engaged the priest to teach his sons French history and geography, to add to their weekly religious catechism.

Charles, always serious, was a model student whose voracious appetite for knowledge wore out the good Father. As in the Indian camp, Jean-Paul eventually was allowed to run free, unable to bend his mind or body to academic discipline. Charles was told of the conquests of Pepin and Charlemagne, great heroes of the papal cause. He listened to the exploits of Hugh Capet and Louis, the 'Spider King,' Charles the Bold and the great Sainte Jeanne D'Arc. He listened as Du Jaunay described the wrestling match on the 'Field of the Cloth of Gold' between Henry VIII of England who gave away his religion and his soul for a woman, and the French monarch, Francis II, who defended Holy Mother Church. He told of Henry of Navarre, the traitor in league with the damned souls called *Huguenots,* who returned to God and was rewarded with the Crown of France. He told of 'Le Grand Monarche,' Louis XIV, his brilliant advisor, Cardinal

Mazarin, and how they struggled with the unholy English in their quest for empire in the New World.

He showed the willing boy maps of Europe and talked of the Hundred Years' War and attempts on the part of the British to steal Normandy, Aquitaine and Anjou. He rolled out charts of North America, pointing out the English colonies along the coast and the French settlements in Canada and along the Mississippi. He told of Champlain and La Salle, Marquette and Joliet, Brulé and Sieur de la Mothe Cadillac.

Young Charles listened to all of this with utter fascination and began to comprehend something of the global significance of his country and people. In these weeks of instruction, a fierce loyalty to France began to disclose itself and a fidelity to the king and Church which would serve France well in his adult years.

All of these exciting lessons, however, did not overcome his fierce Indian nature, which was so much a part of his daily life. The Ottawa were with him each day, teaching, instructing, molding his adolescent psyche to their way. The king and pope, living across the sea, depended on a lowly priest to do their work. Still, the lessons took, and Charles understood that he was a part of France and a child of God. These were lessons he never forgot. Most importantly, as far as Augustin was concerned, he learned to hate the *Anglais* and would use the lessons of both cultures to try to destroy them.

🦋 🦋 🦋

EARLY ONE SEPTEMBER DAY IN 1739, La Fourche visited the Langlade cabin at Fort Michilimackinac. The sky was extremely overcast and dark clouds rolling in the heavens spewed torrential rains on the straits. Huge waves pounded the shore so viciously that the spume splattered against the stockade.

The Ottawa chief arrived soaked and chilled, and Domitilde fussed over him until an angry glance from his good eye convinced her that she should stop. La Fourche had removed the precious copper from his eye socket and his face had a strange, wrinkled look, like a mouth without teeth.

Domitilde and Augustin assumed that their brother had come

to take the boys for the day back to *L'Arbre Croche* and Jean-Paul had already jumped from his bed in joyous anticipation. Little Charles however, sensed that something else, uniquely significant, was afoot, and waited to hear more.

Augustin offered La Fourche a chair by the fire when he saw that the Indian wanted to speak to him and sat down opposite. Domitilde stood a short distance away.

"My brother," La Fourche began, "I have come to tell you of a proposed raid against the Chick-a-sau by my people. I have waited long, and the time has come. Already fifty warriors have drawn the wampum and we will leave soon."

Domitilde remembered when La Fourche had built a bark lodge before and had hung a belt of purple wampum painted with vermilion inside. Fifteen warriors had entered, smoked *kinickinick,* and pulled the wampum belt through their left hands, symbolizing their enlistment in the raid. Ka-re-gwon-di had been one of them.

"The Chick-a-sau," continued La Fourche, "have shown themselves to be enemies to the 'Out-ou-ais.' They are filled with greed, and hate the earth. It is their association with the *Anglais* which has corrupted them. They are no longer people, but Saugunash." (Algonkin for 'English.')

Augustin listened intently with a concerned frown. Domitilde instinctively sat beside little Charles on the bed and put her arm around him. He submitted to this quietly, but his dark eyes blazed with excitement.

"I have come to see you my brother," La Fourche said, "to ask for your son, Au-san-aw-go to accompany us and taste the warrior's blood."

Augustin seemed pleased, but at the same time surprised and cautious. He knew the boy would be well protected and had to learn of the world and its demands eventually. Yet he had his reservations. "Jean-Paul is only eleven years old," he said. "A warrior's age is more than this. Why do you wish him to go?"

La Fourche answered Augustin calmly, knowing the father's concern. "The-other-man-who-gave-him-life" (a reference to Jean-Paul's genetic father, Ka-re-gwon-di) "came to me in a dream. He told me to take the boy along, and vengeance on the

Chick-a-sau would be successful. A man cannot go against his dreams, and *Me-daw-min,* the Sky Spirit, weeps at my delay. So I come. You know I will watch over him. He is of my blood. No harm will befall him."

Of this, Augustin was convinced. He glanced at little Jean-Paul whose expectant face was bursting with anticipation. Then he looked at Domitilde who was now clutching Charles to her breast. He could see the anxiety in her face, but he would see it there if the boy were twenty-five. In the *pays sauvage,* the back country, one must grow up in a hurry, or perish.

"You may accompany your uncle, Jean-Paul," he said flatly.

"*Allons! Allons!*" Au-san-aw-go yelped, jumping up and down ecstatically. La Fourche turned toward him and silenced him with a glance. He was not acting with a warrior's dignity and, realizing it, he calmed himself.

"I want to go *aussi,*" came a small voice from the other side of the room. Charles had risen and was approaching his father and uncle after wresting himself from Domitilde's arms.

Augustin looked at his son, so small and dark, dressed in his French clothing, even suffering the ruffled *jabot* around his neck. He was such a contrast to Jean-Paul who always preferred loin-cloth and Ottawa leggings.

"You have no reason to go, Charles," Augustin told his son. "The Chick-a-sau have done nothing to you. No payment need be met there."

But Charles was adamant. "The Ottawa are my people too. I will avenge my mother's husband, my brother's *père.*" His dark eyes flashed fiercely and his black, shoulder-length hair glistened in the lamplight. "I am protected by the Great Turtle. La Fourche, my uncle, has told me of the symbols and visions regarding my birth."

Domitilde thought of her strange dream of the half-white, half-red man, riding the back of the turtle. Though she was a Christian now, that dream seemed to stay with her and she was not unaware of its significance. She looked puzzled at her little boy who spoke like a warrior.

La Fourche beamed proudly. He had intentionally ignored Charles, hoping that the boy would step forward on his own. To have held back would have destroyed the chief's assessment of Charles' significance. He had passed the test. He looked at Augustin and shrugged his shoulders as if to say, 'the decision is yours.' Yet Augustin knew it was not.

"You may go," he said abruptly, without looking at Domitilde.

Charles, whose little fists had been clenched, ready for more of an argument, suddenly relaxed. He said: *"Merci, mon père,"* and calmly returned to his anxious mother.

The following day, the sky was blue and brilliant. Though seasonably cool, it was still warm enough to travel without overgarments. The raiding party left at dawn, heading south along the eastern shoreline in a flotilla of ten canoes.

La Fourche led the party accompanied by his 'son,' Wawatam, who had been given charge of the boys. Au-san-aw-go crouched on his knees near the front of the birchbark vessel, trying to look sophisticated and fearsome, Ka-re-gwon-di's tomahawk held securely in hand. Charles knelt near the rear, dark eyes surveying the wooded shoreline suspiciously. His gaze shifted occasionally to the broad back of Wawatam in front of him as he labored with the paddle. Then he would glance behind him to see the other ten canoes, containing forty-eight warriors, gliding smoothly through the calm waters.

The island of the Great Turtle was on their left and then quickly behind them. They moved deliberately past the island east of it which was called 'Bois Blanc' (White Woods) because of its many birch trees, and then abruptly moved south, leaving the straits of Mackinac to their rear, diminishing in the distance as the bright sun began to disperse the lake mist.

The soft light of morning gave way to the hot rays of the afternoon sun, which eventually surrendered to the red gloaming of dusk. They camped along the shore that night. Day after day they pushed forward, seldom resting, eating only at dawn and dark. As the chilly evening of the fifth day descended upon them, the little armada pulled into the shoreline just north of the Bay of Saguenaum, unseen, and headed down the *Rivière Ste. Claire.* By dark, they reached Fort Ponchartrain at a place the French called *D'étroit* (meaning 'of the strait').

Antoine Sieur de la Mothe Cadillac had established this

stockade some thirty years earlier to, like Michilimackinac, protect a strategic passage from one large lake to another. This fort was very active and the population around it was primarily Indian; Ottawa, Potawatomi and Ojibway, although a few French settlers had established 'ribbon farms' along the *Rivière D'étroit* and along the *Rivière Rouge* nearby.

Here they camped for a full day and Wawatam and La Fourche proudly displayed their young progeny to the French soldiers in the fort and to the Indian leaders of various bands camped around it. Little Charles was particularly impressed with a very young Ottawa chief whose bearing was monarchial and whose enormous wisdom surpassed the experience of his twenty years. He was called Pon-ti-ac by his people. He told La Fourche that the young French-Ottawa (Charles) was destined for great things. The two Ottawa chiefs talked long into the night by a fire, while Jean-Paul slept in Pon-ti-ac's lodge. But Charles lay awake, attending to their every word. At one point, they disagreed sharply and their voices were raised in anger. Though Charles could not hear all that transpired outside the wigwam, he was able to discern that Pon-ti-ac, for some reason, was opposed to the intended raid on the Chick-a-sau, muttering something about all Indians being brothers (except the Iroquois), and they should behave as such. In spite of the disagreement, their conversation ended amicably enough and Charles was asleep before La Fourche entered Pon-ti-ac's lodge for the night.

The following day found them entering another great lake. On the southern and eastern shores lived the people the Iroquois called the *Erieehronons* (People of the Panther). The French titled it *Lac du Chat* (Lake of the Cat). Here they disembarked and hid their canoes, abandoning them for the remainder of their journey and continued their southern march on foot.

IN THE WEEKS THAT FOLLOWED, the Ottawa crossed the river called *O-hi-o* by the Iroquois, and passed into the lands of the Cherokee and Shawnee. They were careful to skirt this territory since they had little or no contact with these tribes and did not know how they would react to any intruders, especially a band traveling without women and therefore obviously belligerent.

Once they had bypassed the Shawnee, they had merely to circumvent a large Cherokee village called *Tenasie,* and then move west until they were within striking distance of the Chick-a-sau.

One cloudy morning, advance scouts informed the main body that the Chick-a-sau camp was about half a league distant, and the village was still asleep. Even the dogs had not suspected their presence because they had approached downwind.

La Fourche called a quick halt to their march and the column of fifty Ottawa all fell silent and broke into cover among the trees. On his instruction, they prepared for war, painting themselves in elaborate colors and readying their weapons. Wawatam was told to remain concealed in the woods and watch over the boys while La Fourche led the attack.

The invaders moved silently forward and, upon reaching the Chick-a-sau camp, the Ottawa chief saw that what the scouts had reported was true. Fires from the previous night smoldered, and it appeared as if the Chick-a-sau, concealed by their wigwams, were still sleeping soundly. The camp was guarded only by two sentries, one at the opposite end of the village, and one just a few feet away, sitting by a dying fire, with his back to them, swatting flies.

Wawatam, standing with Charles and Jean-Paul, was opposite the clearing from his father. He watched with great interest as La Fourche stepped noiselessly from the copse where he had hidden and approached the closest sentry. The Chick-a-sau, preoccupied with flies, never knew what hit him. La Fourche grabbed him from behind and slapped his large left hand over the mouth of his victim while, at the same time, jerking his head back so that he almost lost consciousness. It would have been better for him if he had. Swiftly, and with silent precision, La Fourche drew his deadly knife across the unfortunate man's throat, the blood spurting from his torn jugular, his windpipe hissing as it was exposed to the open air. The only other sound was a dull thud as his body slumped to the ground.

The Ottawa's concentration on his victim was broken by a

yelp, and he glanced up to see the other sentry racing toward him and shouting the alarm to his sleeping comrades. La Fourche signaled his warriors forward and they leapt from the forest, raising a frightening din that was bound to alarm the Chick-a-sau.

From a wigwam in the center of the camp, the *Tishomingo* (war chief) came running. He was entirely naked since he had been roused from slumber and he had had only enough time to grab his warclub. When he realized that his camp had been thoroughly infiltrated with the charging Ottawa, he looked for their chief. He found him bending over the dead sentry, relieving him of his hair. The *Tishomingo* recognized him by the special paint and tattoos.

He came at La Fourche from his blind side with such speed and velocity that he drove him to the ground, knocking the wind from him, before the Ottawa even saw him. La Fourche, gasping for air, threw aside the bloody scalp that had been torn away from the sentry as he was struck, and instinctively reached for his knife. No sooner had he drawn it from its sheath, than he was struck a crushing blow on the arm, from the *Tishomingo's* warclub. The blade tumbled harmlessly to the ground.

The Chick-a-sau chief raised his club again, this time to deliver a death blow to the head. La Fourche, his arm broken near the elbow and weaponless, could not move and awaited his fate calmly.

At this point, young Charles, who had been watching from a safe distance with Jean-Paul and Wawatam, burst from the cover of the trees and dashed across the Chick-a-sau camp amid the shouts of warriors and the wailing of women and children.

As he drew closer to his helpless uncle, he grabbed a still-smoldering log from the central fire of the camp and, without hesitation, jabbed the red-hot timber into the *Tishomingo's* bare back as he had raised his club to kill La Fourche. Yelping in pain, the Chick-a-sau turned and struck the boy a telling stroke across his face, breaking two of his teeth and rendering him unconscious. Wawatam and Jean-Paul, in pursuit of Charles, now came upon the scene, distracting the Chick-a-sau warrior again from his murderous intent.

La Fourche, taking advantage of the momentary reprieve, picked up the knife with his good arm and plunged it into the back of the astonished chief, burying it to the hilt in his well-muscled flesh. He dropped to his knees, the club falling uselessly to the ground, as La Fourche pulled the blade free and drove it into the *Tishomingo*'s neck.

Ripping his knife free, the Ottawa chief surveyed the camp as Wawatam and Au-san-aw-go tended to the stricken Charles. The raid was an obvious success. The Ottawa had managed to catch the Chick-a-sau by surprise sufficiently well enough to destroy most of the warriors who were in camp. The remainder had fled into the forest, leaving the women and children at the mercy of their captors.

Some of the more attractive women and healthier young ones were rounded up to return to Michilimackinac as slaves of their Ottawa conquerors. The rest were left to mourn their dead.

Charles eventually regained consciousness, looking unsure of his surroundings and bleary-eyed. The left side of his face was swelling badly and turning a purplish-red. Blood oozed from the corner of his mouth, and as he spit in the dirt to rid himself of the taste, a tooth came with the spittle. La Fourche's face revealed his concern, but he said nothing as Wawatam helped Charles to his feet. The boy staggered momentarily, but then seemed to gain his equilibrium and dusted off his clothes.

A steely glance from La Fourche indicated to Wawatam his father's displeasure in failing to protect the two young brothers. Charles, looking through only one eye (the other was swollen shut), looked down at the corpse that lay sprawled at his feet and then up at his uncle. La Fourche grinned broadly.

Within minutes, the wigwams of the Chick-a-sau had been set on fire, prisoners chosen, scalps taken and booty packed for the return trip. Once preparations for their journey had been completed, the Ottawa gathered around La Fourche who still stood by the body of his fallen foe. He spoke so all members of the assemblage could hear: "My brothers," he began, "we have come far to seek our vengeance. We have destroyed the murderers of our kinsmen, and now their spirits may rest. We have acted in honor, and honor is our victory." He handed the scalp of the Chick-a-sau war chief to Au-san-aw-go, who received it with great satisfaction. "Ka-re-gwon-di," he shouted. "Your death is avenged and your enemy's scalp will hang from the belt of your son!"

At this, there were general shouts of acclamation and joy. The Ottawa took a familial pride in their conquest and this vindication of tribal honor was a great moment for them. The general whooping and hollering settled down after a few moments, and La Fourche spoke again: "We must leave now. The murderers will be back soon with their brother-devils. Yet, there is one thing more to be done."

He knelt above the corpse of the *Tishomingo,* rolling it over on its back with his uninjured arm. He then removed the bloody knife from its sheath and plunged it into the chest, using a sawing motion to open the torso from collarbone to groin. He then stood up, handing the knife to Wawatam and signaling him to continue.

Wawatam's warm smile indicated his understanding of the gesture. To be allowed to participate in such a ritual was a great distinction for one who had not fought in the battle, and was a manifestation of his father's forgiveness. He knelt and thrust his arm into the red maw left by the knife. Wawatam forced his hand through the still-warm flesh and under the sternum until he had a firm grip on the warrior's heart. He pulled at it forcefully, finally having to sever most of the major arteries attached to it before he could free it from its scarlet chamber.

Once liberated, he held it high in the air for all to see, generating more yelling and cries of victory. His father beckoned him to cut the heart into several pieces which he did, then offered it to La Fourche. But the one-eyed chief shook his head and pointed to Charles. Wawatam obediently proffered the offering to his cousin, who did not recoil from it, but took a small piece of the raw, red meat and throwing his wounded head back to accommodate its descent, he dropped it into his mouth and swallowed it whole.

Amid exclamations of approval, La Fourche followed suit, then Wawatam and Au-san-aw-go. This done, the Ottawa chief spoke again: "This day we have not only killed our enemy, but we have taken his heart. His courage is now ours. He has nothing left. His women and children are ours. His spirit will walk in cowardice and he will be the last of his line. So die the enemies of the Out-u-ais!"

More yelling and cheering followed as the other warriors lined up to take a piece of the corpse. They cut away whatever portion of his anatomy they felt would benefit them, then the mutilated corpse was pitched into a fire, denied a proper funeral. Such was the hate of the Ottawa for the Chick-a-sau, such was the sweetness of their revenge. Eleven-year-old Au-san-aw-go and ten-year-old Charles never forgot that day.

🦃 🦃 🦃

THE WAR PARTY HAD BEEN GONE from Michilimackinac for several weeks, and as the weather grew colder and the distant shoreline turned golden red, dotted with evergreen, Domitilde became more and more worried and fretful. She did not reveal her true feelings to Augustin, but he knew her state of mind. She ate little and slept even less. She spent much of her time patching the boys' clothes or standing by the shore, looking out at the lake and the Great Turtle, floating serenely in the strait. Augustin understood her fear and apprehension, because he felt a good deal of disquietude too and had experienced some misgivings about his decision to let the boys go. Yet he was determined not to allow Domitilde to see his perturbation and he belittled her for hers, calling her 'an old hen.'

Finally the day came when, toward evening, the French soldier on sentry duty called out to announce the approach of canoes. Augustin and Domitilde ran down to the beach, joined by Joseph and Constante, the Amiots, the Bourassas, and most of the French garrison who were eager to hear news of the raid or news of any kind from outside their little world.

As the small craft were landed, Domitilde could see the silhouettes from a distance of both of the boys and they looked well. (Jean-Paul was jumping from the canoe with his usual youthful vigor.) She resisted a strong maternal urge to run to them. La Fourche stepped from his canoe and Domitilde could see that something had happened to him. His arm was splinted with tree branches and wound tightly in cloth.

Jean-Paul came running to his parents. Exuberant and boastful, he recounted the story of their great victory over the Chick-a-sau which would be told around the council fires for many winters to come.

"Look, mama," he shouted happily, and pulled the *Tishomingo's* scalp from his belt. Domitilde winced at the sight of it, though she was used to such grisly trophies. Her first husband had had his own collection of hairpieces, as did her brother, but she had never quite become accustomed to their presence and the thought of them repelled her. But she hid her feelings from her son and tried to look enthused.

As La Fourche approached, Augustin spoke: "My brother," he said. "I am so happy to see you are returned safely. You have kept your promise to see to the protection of my sons. I hope all has gone well for you." He noticed the injured arm, but knew enough of Indian etiquette and La Fourche's standards of honor, to make no reference to it.

The Ottawa chief gave no explanation for it, but spoke of other things. "We have avenged our brothers," he said. "The Chick-a-sau have been destroyed. Their women mourn, some of their women and children are now slaves of the Out-u-ais, their wigwams will be cold and without food in the season of snow. Their chief is dead, killed by me with the aid of your son. He saved my life. He will be a great warrior."

Augustin, assuming that his brother-in-law was referring to Au-san-aw-go, looked at him proudly. He was showing his prize to the Amiot children who giggled and fussed over it.

Charles now stepped away from the canoes and approached his parents. Somber and serious as always, he greeted his parents with a nod of his head. As he did so, Domitilde saw that the one side of his face was a deep purple color and badly swollen. His one eye was completely shut and, in some odd way, reminded her of her brother. She took a step toward him, but Augustin gripped her arm and restrained her.

"It was Charles who helped to kill the *Tishomingo*," La Fourche said flatly. "The scalp was given to Au-san-aw-go because it belonged to his father's killer, and now frees his father's spirit from the earth."

Augustin stared at his son and found it difficult to believe that the boy had sprung from his loins. Though he was very proud of Charles, his lack of emotion worried him. He was so much like La Fourche that Augustin sometimes thought that the child must be his in some mysterious spiritual way. Now, with his damaged face, he even resembled his uncle physically.

"Charles," Augustin said softly, "go with your mother and let her treat your injuries. You have done well to save your uncle, for he means much to us and to his people."

The boy left obediently with Domitilde, but very reluctantly. As they approached the water gate to the fort, Charles stopped momentarily to look at the delicate little Bourassa girl standing next to the stockade wall with Ignace, her brother, and their parents. She was now four years old, and was dressed in a frilly little blue dress and hoop skirt. Her golden hair was done up in a mass of beautiful curls. Her appearance was totally incongruous with the scene which surrounded her. She looked so frail and vulnerable among all these dark and savage men. Yet when Charles, with his damaged, violet, face and fierce expression, stopped to look at her, she was not intimidated or frightened by his serious frown. Domitilde noted, as she ushered him away, that for the first time in her memory, she had seen a faint smile on her son's sober countenance.

🕸 🕸 🕸

As AUGUSTIN AND LA FOURCHE followed Domitilde into the fort, the chief could see that changes had taken place since his departure weeks ago. Pierre-Joseph Celoron de Blainville had ordered that a separate house be constructed for the priest and it was now under construction on the western side of the fort, beyond the *Rue Dauphine* and the soldier's barracks. Furthermore, the commandant had declared that a blacksmith's shop should be attached to it with a decent forge and proper walls to facilitate Amiot's work in harsh weather.

Joseph Ainsse had been placed in charge of the building

project and was given the assistance of several soldiers of the garrison, including François Cardin. By the time of La Fourche's return, they had completed the skeletons of the two structures and Joseph had assured de Blainville that both dwellings would be ready for occupancy before the first snow.

As usual, he attacked his work like a demon, laboring from first light to dusk to make good his promise. He often took his meals while working, brought to him in a tidy basket by Constante. For the first time in his life he felt secure and alive, reveling in the envy others displayed when looking at his beautiful wife with appreciative eyes. He was not jealous, because he believed that his wife was absolutely loyal. She showed him unflagging devotion and worked hard to be a proper companion. He was immensely proud of her.

She was often seen around the work site, delivering water to her thirsty husband and his crew. At first, she kept her eyes lowered when Cardin dipped his cup in the water bucket, too embarrassed by their encounter on the beach and the knowledge of his true emotions to look him in the face. But as the days wore on, she inevitably confronted him and he held her eyes to his with his earnest gaze.

She began to bring water four times daily instead of twice, and Joseph bragged to Cardin about her wifely concern.

Though they did not speak, Cardin could see a prisoner behind her noble *façade.* The hard-working, sober, and thrifty Madame Ainsse was a far cry from the beautiful, vivacious woman he had met at the reception for the priest. Her delicate hands had developed calluses, her hair had lost its curl and her step, its bounce. Her actions were slow and methodical, not quick and spontaneous as they once had been. When she spoke, it was with the cautious speech of one who holds a terrible secret and must guard her words or reveal her feelings inadvertently, leaving her carefully constructed world in a shambles.

All this and more was sensed by Cardin. But whenever he reached out his hand to touch her as she poured the water, or attempted to whisper to her, she shot away in utter terror. Cardin was convinced that she still loved him, despite her actions, but would never tell him.

What he did not know, nor could he understand, was that she loved Joseph also. But it was filial love, not a love that comes with acceptance and easy surrender, and Constante, for all her effort, still did not accept Joseph as her own. With the exception of their intimate moments, which were infrequent at best, she loved him as she had loved her father. She knew that she was his, like a master owns his slave, but *he* was not *hers*. In both senses, she was a secondary figure, loved and isolated, a lonely idol tired of being worshipped, a statue waiting to come to life, wanting to possess as well as to be possessed.

She knew instinctively that François loved her and was *her* slave and she, his, in effect eliminating *any* slavery and democratizing devotion into love. But another, darker emotion, kept Constante enslaved. She had been raised to worship the god 'Guilt,' assisted by his henchmen, 'Duty' and 'Sympathy.' This terrible trinity had wrought a tremendous impression on Constante, to the point that they commanded her decisions and controlled her actions. Still, Cardin knew that her imprisoned heart would manifest itself on occasion, and it drew her to the building site more and more often.

As Joseph and Constante came back from the beach after welcoming the Ottawa home from their raid, Joseph decided to work until dark and asked Cardin and the other soldiers assigned to the task to join him. Constante walked back toward their lonely cabin, as Joseph climbed up the ladder to complete work on the roof of the priest's new house. Cardin joined him while the others worked as sawyers down below in the sawpit, fashioning boards. Cardin watched Constante as her sweet, solitary figure drifted away. He jumped when Joseph spoke to him.

"She is a beautiful woman, *non?*" he said, having observed Cardin's attendance on Constante's movements.

"What?" Cardin's face flushed, as if Joseph had read his mind. "Oh. *Oui.*"

"She is not only beautiful outside," Ainsse said, turning to his work, "but she is beautiful in the heart. I do not know what would happen to me if I ever lost her. I must confess, *mon ami,* that I have been very lonely most of my life, but no longer. I have not your looks, Monsieur, but I have her, and she loves me.

It is something to marvel at, *n'est-ce pas?* I work and live for her, and she loves and comforts me. May God give every man such happiness."

Cardin listened to the homely carpenter and felt a sort of resentful comraderie with him. 'Such life-giving love,' he thought, 'God does not grant to everyone, my fortunate friend, though they too may require it like water and air.''

As Joseph returned to his work, somewhat embarrassed by his emotional outburst, Cardin's gaze shifted to the Langlade cabin where Augustin and La Fourche stood by the entrance, engaged in what appeared to be a rather animated discussion. He did not know that La Fourche was informing his brother-in-law that because of the lateness of the season, the Ottawa, for the first time in many years, were not going to camp along the *Rivière Grande* in the south, but winter where they were, close to the fort at *L'Arbre Croche*. Cardin saw the Indian point to the dark clouds gathering in the north with his uninjured arm, and remembered that the Ojibway had left for their southern wintering grounds weeks earlier.

'The snow will come very early this year,' he mused, and bent to his work.

🥀 🥀 🥀

Winter did arrive early, and with a vengeance. That February of 1743, Wawatam came to the snowbound fort in search of his cousins. It had snowed steadily for almost a week, and the stuff had drifted off the icy lake almost to the summit of the stockade wall. Except for the evergreens, the trees stood black and skeletal against the grey sky. The shoreline, no longer distinguishable from the lake, received the brunt of a bitter and frigid wind, and as Wawatam slipped inside the gate and passed the bored and chilled sentry, he was grateful to evade its bleak and biting wrath. He was welcomed with great enthusiasm by his young cousins and Domitilde, who could not conceal her delight at this opportunity to escape boredom. Augustin had been away for most of the day each day, checking his traps in spite of the inclement conditions, and with her work done and the boys outside all morning among the Amiot children, she was beside herself with the inactivity. Though Marie Anne came to visit as much as she could, the continued growth of her family (she was again pregnant), and the fact that Amiot's new position with the priest kept him at home most of the time, and perhaps her own subconscious resentment of Marie's fertility in the face of her own obvious barrenness, led to a severe curtailing of their usual mutually pleasurable companionship.

Domitilde was understandably joyful then at the sight of her nephew and fussed over him excessively when he entered the cabin. She noted that his boyish good looks were maturing and that his personality had become more like that of the majority of Ottawa men, serious and condescending. In the few short months since she had seen him last, he had taken a *noko,* and it was apparent that his marital status had changed him significantly in his attitude toward women.

Perhaps the presence of the young boy he had brought with him had something to do with his new posture. The lad was about nine years old, small for his age, and very thin. He did not look healthy. Though dark-complexioned like the rest of his race, he appeared to be almost pale, his gaunt face delicate and hollow. But for his personality and robust, intelligent eyes, Domitilde would have thought him quite ill. His buckskins hung from him in drape-like fashion and he appeared very small next to Wawatam.

Charles observed this stranger with great curiosity, but it was Jean-Paul who, characteristically, blurted out the question everyone wanted to ask. "Who is *he,* cousin?"

La Fourche would have been extremely angry with such effrontery, but Wawatam, more patient by nature and young enough to understand the impatience of youth, simply smiled. "His name is Okinochumaki," he said indulgently. "He is the brother of my *noko,* my new squaw."

At this pronouncement, Domitilde became extremely inquisitive. This was the first she had heard of Wawatam's marriage and she was very eager to know all about it. Yet she understood that it was not proper for a woman to interrogate a man about anything, so she sat silently until Wawatam, in his laconic fashion, decided to relate the story of his connubial adventure.

It appeared, from the narrative which followed, that he had married the fifteen-year-old granddaughter of a *shaman* of the *Wabeno* class of medicine men of the Chippewa tribe encamped near the fort in summer, now gone south for the winter. Her grandfather's name was Ishnoki and he was reputed to be among the wisest of all the Chippewa *shaman*. The *Wabeno* class were highly respected among the Ottawa and they were well-known for their worship of the rattlesnake spirit, *Kinabig Man-i-tou,* whom they referred to as their 'grandfather.'

Wawatam had met the girl, named Ti-bikki, when he had gone with La Fourche to the Chippewa camp on the occasion of the birth of Wenniway, Minavavana's son. She had been only twelve years old then, but Wawatam had seen in a vision (a circumstance he was often subject to) that he would some day take her for his wife.

Before leaving on the campaign against the Chick-a-sau, unbeknown to La Fourche or anyone else, he offered a rich supply of tobacco and wampum to Ishnoki for his granddaughter. (The *shaman* was her guardian since she had been orphaned shortly after her birth.) The wampum, little beads fashioned from clam shells and strung together, were almost entirely purple. Much work was needed to produce one tiny, purple bead, since the largest part of the shell was white or pink in color. A good-sized shell might produce, after tremendous labor, two small purple beads. Wawatam had offered Ishnoki a band of purple wampum six inches across and four *feet* long. The rarity of the color and the tremendous work required to carve the beads, made it a veritable treasure. Wawatam had spent, on and off, six years of laborious searching and endless drudgery to produce this single band.

Nevertheless, Ishnoki was not quick to reply, and it was not until just before their departure on the Chick-a-sau raid that the *shaman,* after much consultation with *Kinabig Man-i-tou,* had agreed to the union. The Chippewa, after all, believed that a husband should reside with his wife's people and the Ottawa maintained the opposite point of view.

In the end, Ishnoki had released his granddaughter to live

among the Ottawa, converted by his respect for Wawatam's vision, the advice of the 'Rattlesnake Spirit,' and the purple wampum. But more than anything else, he admired Wawatam's tremendous curiosity and interest in his snake cult, and promised to instruct his new 'son-in-law' in its finer idiosyncrasies upon his return from the latest of his 'medicine quests' (a journey to obtain certain herbs, barks, mosses, and small animals used to effect his miraculous cures), and the winter camp.

As Wawatam told his story, he said very little about the young girl who had become his wife, but Domitilde had gleaned enough from his sparse description to understand that she was quite attractive and obedient, and already pregnant. Her name, which translated into something like child-woman, indicated that she was quite small and Domitilde tried to imagine her sleeping with the large man who stood before her. If her brother, Okinochumaki, was any indication of family genetics, she was small and child-like indeed and Domitilde thought that Wawatam must smother her when he laid upon her. The happiness with which she received the news of the impending birth was clouded by her own distress at having produced no more offspring for Augustin, though he had made no reference to the barren years since the birth of Charles and still seemed happy to join her in the down bed. She was relieved when Wawatam continued his discourse, explaining that his young brother-in-law had stayed behind when the rest of the Chippewa band moved south because Ishnoki had dreamt that he, too, must live among the Ottawa and become one of them, joining Wawatam and Ti-bikki in their lodge. Wawatam had readily agreed to this presumptuous proposal because he, too, put great credence in visions and because he was genuinely fond of the boy.

The winter had not been good to the Ottawa, Wawatam continued. Game was scarce and they had been reduced to eating *Wahkoonun*, a black-looking, leathery, lichen which, when boiled, became a starchy lump, resembling an egg in its consistency. It had a bitter taste and was consumed only in winter when more palatable fare was not always available. Most of the Ottawa had subsisted on this meagre diet for the last few weeks and even this unsavory plant was fast disappearing.

In concern over his wife's condition and the wasting frame of Okinochumaki, Wawatam explained to the assemblage that he had left *L'Arbre Croche* in search of game and was determined to kill *Mag-wah*, the bear. He would be happy, he told Domitilde, if his young cousins would be allowed to join in this adventure.

It must be understood that the Ottawa regarded *Mag-wah* with great reverence. His size and strength were legendary and tribal members rarely hunted him unless they were, as in the present situation, desperate for food or, as was also the case with Wawatam, seeking out the spirit of *Mag-wah* to advise and direct.

Until this pronouncement, Charles had remained typically silent and sedate, but the possibility of accompanying Wawatam on this special adventure, after the cold boredom of long winter months, was too much for even him to retain his composure. "Oh, may we, Mama?" he chirped.

Domitilde believed that it was the first time since Charles had been born that he had actually betrayed his boyishness. She had almost come to regard him as an adult, and often depended upon him for consultation on some domestic matter or other when the oft-absent Augustin was not around. Now she saw him as the little boy he was, as Jean-Paul too chimed in and clamored for permission to go.

Domitilde, as usual, was very reticent. She had seen on her brother's face the track of the 'bear-god' and she knew well that Ottawa arrows and knives had little affect on him. The same weapon that would drive through the head of a rabbit would bounce harmlessly off the thick skull of *Mag-Wah*. Outside of man himself, the bear was the most difficult animal on earth to destroy, and she knew it.

She began to respond, when she caught Okinochumaki's eyes. His young face, gaunt and pale, needed filling. For her to offer food to Wawatam and his charge would be fruitless, she knew. No Ottawa would ever be reduced to begging. Though the Langlade's larder was well-provisioned, Wawatam would never accept food from them. A weapon, trinkets, or practically anything else would be acceptable as gifts, but victuals were a man's *responsibility*.

In addition, she recognized that her instinctive *non* would be regarded as offensive to Wawatam, signifying her distrust of his ability and his word.

She thought it puzzling that Wawatam or any other Ottawa should be so affronted by a mother's concern for her children. Yet Domitilde was all too familiar with his reasoning. She understood that Wawatam would lay down his life in the protection of her sons, but she also realized that this should be satisfaction enough, and the noble gesture would give Wawatam's memory great honor, whether her sons perished or not. It was this male obsession with honor and the corresponding recklessness with which they lived that disturbed her. Yet she knew, as always, that there was no escape from honor, and she could not risk insulting both her brother's adopted son and her own boys. Most importantly, she was sure that Augustin would have given permission had he been there. Reluctantly she assented, and Charles returned to his sober and dignified manner, perhaps somewhat embarrassed by his momentary lapse into childhood, while Au-san-aw-go hastily fetched his good luck charm, the scalp of the *Tishomingo.*

🦫 🦫 🦫

WITHIN THE HOUR, the three boys and their adult guide were deep in the forest behind Fort Michilimackinac. The Langlade brothers and Okinochumaki had carried on a lively conversation ever since their departure, and were quickly becoming fast friends as they tramped happily through the snow on the heels of the silent Wawatam. Though Charles said little, it was obvious to Okinochumaki that he was enjoying their company and regarded them as his comrades-in-arms. Jean-Paul, on the other hand, chattered incessantly and could not be silenced until a signal from Wawatam made it clear that they were approaching their quarry. They had arrived at a small clearing in the center of which stood a majestic northern red oak, its circumference at the base several times the width of a large man's shoulders. There were no tracks in the newly fallen snow, but claw marks at the base of the tree, indicated to the boys by a gesture from Wawatam, promised that *Mag-wah* was nearby.

Though the boys searched the surrounding brush with wary eyes, they could see no other evidence of the creature they sought and they relaxed somewhat. Charles assumed that their real prey was a good distance away and was thus puzzled as Wawatam approached the massive oak with such caution. While the three boys watched, their protector dropped to his knees in front of the tree and began to dig in the snow. This labor was interrupted occasionally by placing his head in the hole he had formed, apparently listening for some sound, then resuming his task until he saw fit to halt and eavesdrop again. This pattern of behavior continued until Wawatam was almost standing on his head, and only his leggings, topped by his beaded moccasins, showed outside of the hole which could now be more accurately described as a tunnel.

Confused and puzzled by this aberrant behavior, the boys moved closer to the tree in an attempt to find some reasonable explanation for such ungainly deportment. Gradually, Wawatam's shifting torso appeared to the grey light of day as he wormed his way backward, escaping the subterranean shaft. As his face appeared, he found the boys only a few short feet away and beckoned them to come closer. Charles was the first to step forward, curiosity consuming him. Wawatam motioned for him to place his head, and only his head, into the entrance of the opening. As he did so, Charles could immediately detect the heavy breathing of some beast as it echoed up the snowy tunnel to his ear.

Smiling broadly with comprehension, he moved out of the way to let Jean-Paul and Okinochumaki have a listen. Once all had had a chance to hear, Wawatam moved them a safe distance from the tree and explained: "*Mag-wah* has found himself a home for the winter-sleep. He has dug in among the roots and rests peacefully in the empty tree."

"We should kill him while he sleeps in his den," Jean-Paul volunteered.

"No, cousin," Wawatam warned, "he can defend himself too easily there. We would be torn to pieces trying to get through the small tunnel. To strike at his weakness, we must get him into the open." He looked around briefly and then ordered the boys to gather dead, brown, pine branches and green cedar leaves, and deposit them in the hole he had fashioned, which they promptly did.

Then, ordering the boys to back away, he used a small piece of pyrite to ignite the tinder whose viridity caused it to smoke lustily. Wawatam packed the opening of the hole with damp snow, leaving only a tiny orifice which he blew into several times before closing the tunnel entirely and retreating.

At first, the only sound the Indians could hear was their own breath, frosting immediately upon the frigid air. Gradually, they began to discern a sort of rumbling growl, interspersed with a hacking cough. The ground, it seemed to the boys, began to tremble beneath their feet and branches from the dead oak fell as it, too, was shaken from its rooty base. Suddenly, the snow surrounding the foot of the tree erupted into the air like some icy volcano and the black and snarling visage of *Mag-wah* appeared.

Wawatam stepped forward quickly, arming his bow. He knew that the bear must be dispatched immediately while it was still in its stuporous, torpid state. Its eyes were glassy but viperous as it struggled to remove its torso from the den and stagger to its haunches.

Wawatam took dead aim at the creature, but was slightly off the mark. Having aimed for its neck, he struck the enraged animal in its shoulder. The boar halted momentarily, staring dumbly at the feathered shaft embedded in his flesh almost as a man might observe a mosquito on his arm, annoying but inconsequential.

This pause allowed Wawatam an additional moment to unsheath another arrow and no sooner had he fingered it to his bow, than the beast charged, lumbering forward in ignoble rage.

Jean-Paul unconsciously stepped backward, behind Wawatam. Charles stood stoically at his cousin's side. Okinochumaki, on the other side of Wawatam, actually stepped ahead a pace or two, fascinated by the frothing bear. Charles looked up at his cousin who seemed to show no trace of fear, but had centered his entire concentration on his charging enemy. His one eye was closed, narrowing his vision down the shaft and into the bear's neck. The swansdown in his split earlobes moved lazily in the breeze, but apart from that, he stood as motionless as a statue.

Wawatam waited for what seemed an eternity, but Charles knew he could not release the arrow until *Mag-wah* stood up. In its current running position on all fours and head on, no vulnerable spot was open. To release the arrow now would mean only a small wound, or the dart would simply bounce off the black behemoth's thick skull. If the bear did not raise itself up on its haunches, one, or all of them, would die. The boar was within several yards and closing fast, when a blast of thunder came from the trees to the right of the clearing. At the sound, all three boys jumped and Wawatam, startled by the sound, let loose his bowstring. The arrow sailed harmlessly over *Mag-wah's* head, but the animal, much to the amazement of the hunters, lay prostrate and gasping for breath only a few steps away. The bear was not dead, but dying, and they could tell from the gurgling sound and the spouting, red fountain in the side of his neck, that some missile had found its mark.

All four heads turned in the direction of the explosion and across the clearing they spotted a lone figure stepping from the protection of the forest, the barrel of his smoking 'Charleville' preceding him.

"Mon père!" Jean-Paul cried, and went running to greet Augustin, tripping and falling in the deep snow several times before reaching him and hugging him fiercely around the waist. The Frenchman's one shoulder was weighted down with traps, while the other was covered with beaver skins, held together by a rawhide thong threaded through small holes punctured in their flat tails. Augustin later commented that the shot was nothing short of miraculous because he had really had no room or time to shoulder his musket and had literally 'shot from the hip.'

He and Jean-Paul joined the other three who had managed to collect themselves and were congregated around the now lifeless body of *Mag-wah*. Charles greeted his father politely as always, but with little emotion, though in truth he had been greatly relieved at his father's sudden appearance and intervention.

Wawatam expressed what they all felt when he said: "Good Uncle, you have saved us. My life is yours now. Wish anything of me and I will do what I can to fulfill it. Honor me now, and join us in the taking of the meat."

They worked at dressing the bear for over two hours. The fat on the boar was six inches deep in several places and was put aside for candle making and other purposes. While Wawatam cut huge slabs of meat, Augustin fashioned a *travois* sled out of pine boughs which could bear the weight of their burden and, pulled by the boys, would move fairly easily over the frozen surface. The hide was given to Augustin who would lay it on the floor of his cabin by the hearth. It would serve as a constant reminder to the boys of their adventure.

The leviathan's head was taken back to *L'Arbre Croche,* painted red, and placed on a pole in the center of the village where *Mag-wah* could see his body being put to such good use. His spirit would not haunt them. To further appease him, Wawatam blew the smoke of peace into his dead nostrils and gave prayers of thanks to him each day as he watched Okinochumaki gain weight and grow strong and saw the expanding girth of Tibikki as his own child developed.

Charles, lying still that night in his bed, as Jean-Paul slept beside him, thought about that day. He had learned respect for *Mag-wah*'s power. He had felt fear again, but had been exhilarated by it and not cowed. Though he had been impressed by the courage of the Ottawa as exemplified by Wawatam, he had acquired first-hand knowledge of the power of the white man's mind, which could invent such a formidable weapon as the musket. He had seen the 'Charleville' around the cabin, but he had never understood its deadly strength until *Mag-wah* fell to the earth in a bloody lump.

He had also found a new respect for his father, whose dress he preferred, but had imitated La Fourche in every other aspect of his life. Augustin had saved his life with his quickness of mind and accurate eye. He began to comprehend the value of his double heritage more fully and that, in itself, would prove valuable to his primitive instruction.

Chapter

5

Constante Chevalier

Winter eventually faded as the snow drifted into oblivion to reveal a verdant, green landscape dotted with blossoming flowers. The Chippewa, returned from the south, tapped the maple trees, draining the sweetness from them like the bees in nearby meadows gathering their own nectar.

Like the little pollen-bearers, the residents of Fort Michilimackinac were busy in their wooden hive, building and planting, cleaning and repairing. Joseph Ainsse was one of the most active of these workers. He had been contracted by Père Du Jaunay to begin construction of the church which would be attached to the rectory on one side, with Amiot's blacksmith's shop already affixed to the other.

As the warm weather approached, Ainsse had been closeted with the good Father on many evenings, laying plans for the church. The priest was often at the carpenter's cabin, and he took an instant liking to Madame Ainsse who, though he had seen her before and been formally introduced, had never had the pleasure of her company or conversation. She was such a bright and personable young lady who, the priest came to believe, was starved not for attention (which she really had an abundance of), but rather for witty and intellectual company. Her husband, though well-meaning and obviously deeply in love with her was, nonetheless, a rather dull companion whose simple requirements were enough work, enough food, and enough Constante. (The latter category he seemed unable to fulfill.)

At dinner, the priest and Madame Ainsse would carry on lively conversations about theology (his interest), music and fashion (hers), and politics (theirs), while Joseph nodded at the table and eventually excused himself to nap by the fire.

One particularly fine evening, Du Jaunay and the carpenter had completed their usual discussion about the building of the church after a fine dinner of *poisson blanc* (whitefish), and *gallette au beurre* (butter and milkbread), when Joseph announced that he had something important to say. He smiled proudly, as if he had discovered something that might be of interest to them both and make him less a conversational boor.

He addressed himself primarily to the priest. "As you know, Father, having performed our wedding mass," he began, "Constante and I are very much in love." He looked sheepishly at Constante, reddening somewhat on either side of his prominent nose and reaching across the table to grasp her hand. "It has always been my wish to have children, and now it appears that God has granted my request."

The priest beamed happily and was quick to offer his congratulations to the prospective parents. Constante's pretty face seemed genuinely pleased, though she appeared to be puzzled at Joseph's announcing the event as if she had no knowledge of it. She cast her eyes downward when the priest glanced at her. She believed that a child would increase her passion, deepen her love for Joseph, change her somehow. She hoped it would make her happy and content. Whatever the reason, she wanted the child desperately and looked forward to its birth. She knew that Père Du Jaunay could read her mind.

"When will it arrive?" the priest asked. This most natural of questions under the circumstances was directed to the future mother. She opened her mouth to reply, but Joseph quickly interjected: "In the fall, before the snow comes, I hope. We will have the church completed by then, Father, and he can be christened there. It is exciting to think that my son will be the first child to be baptized in it, *n'est-ce pas?*"

The priest smiled kindly and winked at Constante. She liked this Jesuit so much. He seemed to understand her completely and it helped her to bear her burdens when she knew someone as bright and lively as herself could discern her thoughts and feelings without explanation. She knew that she could talk to Joseph for hours, and he would listen patiently, that adoring smile carved into his face, but comprehending nothing of the real intent of her conversation.

Père Du Jaunay gave her another paternal grin and then turned his attention to the animated carpenter.

"How do you know the child will be a boy?" he asked.

At this, Joseph's face grew serious and thoughtful. "I don't know Father," he muttered. "I suppose, I assumed . . . well, I don't know. I guess I just feel it will be a son."

"You would not be disappointed though if it were a girl?" the priest said, laughing.

Joseph did not answer, but seemed to be mulling the question over very carefully in his mind. Finally he said; "*Oui*, yes, Father, I think I would."

Constante raised her head and looked at her husband with some degree of surprise. Joseph was ordinarily very predictable. She was not used to surprises from him. She did not like this one at all.

When Joseph saw the expression on her face, and the mild astonishment on the priest's countenance, he decided he had better try to explain himself. "I do not mean I would not love the child," he hastened. "I only meant that I have always wanted a son, someone to carry my name; someone who can help me in my labor as I grow old; someone to give an inheritance to, and train and mold."

"Can't those things be given and accomplished with a girl?" Constante looked at him with accusing contempt.

Joseph could see that he had offended his wife and this horrified him. He was quick to try to make amends. "My dearest Constante," he said. "Please don't be angry with me. I never meant to upset you."

The priest expected to see tears from Constante, but they never came. Her eyes flashed with anger. Père Du Jaunay began to think that perhaps she really didn't care which sex the child might be, but rather her consternation seemed to stem from a now-thwarted ambition to engage in some lively argument with her timid spouse. His apologetic tone however, left little hope of any such achievement. He hung his head miserably, looking very much like a beaten and obedient dog.

Constante knew very well why her husband was so enraptured with the idea of a son. He had been, like herself, an orphan, only at a much earlier age. His uncle, who thought him a dull and stupid boy, had apprenticed him to a carpenter in Quebec, where he had learned his trade. At the age of sixteen, he had accompanied an expedition of six soldiers and several carpenters from Quebec to Fort Michilimackinac. The carpenters had been commissioned to build chairs, tables, stocks, and other necessities for the commandant as well as even some luxury items (like a billiard table), which could not be accomplished with unskilled labor.

The commandant had been so impressed with his ability that he asked the young apprentice to stay, and Joseph, hating his existence in Quebec, and being appreciated and wanted for the first time in his short life, wrote a brief note to his uncle explaining that the commandant had paid up the monetary obligation on his apprenticeship and he was determined to stay. Joseph never received a reply.

A son, Constante knew, meant security and family, genealogy and status, stability and pride to her insecure and emotionally starved husband. A daughter would be loved she knew, but a son would be worshipped and lavished with all of the attention that was now hers alone. She welcomed the thought of sharing that pedestal with someone else, but her heart cried out for the companionship of a daughter.

Though Joseph's statement had angered her, the priest was correct in guessing that his immediate obeisance when she showed the least displeasure, irritated her more. She wanted very much for him to just once tell her that she was wrong and argue with her. She often felt like a child whose parent, unable to cope with any childish noise or distraction, gave the perpetrator a piece of candy to quiet her, rather than bothering to reason with such an immature mind.

The condescending smile on his face exasperated her even more. Père Du Jaunay, a sensitive and observant man, could not help but see what their relationship was, and he saw tragedy in it.

"Please forgive me dear one," Joseph said softly. "I did not mean to offend you. Of course I will be overjoyed at the birth of our child, no matter what its sex. It can't help but be perfect, since it was conceived and nurtured in you."

Constante's desire to fight subsided as the fire in her eyes slowly died. Père Du Jaunay could see that the anger had not dissipated in a healthy manner like a fire burning itself out in bright blazes, but rather had died as an act of will, smothered by another's action. Constante simply said: "It's all right my sweet. I know what you meant."

Thus reassured, Joseph slipped away to the fire and was snoring loudly within minutes. Somehow, the conversation between the humble priest and the curious girl turned to world affairs. Constante was the type of person who longed to know more about the wide world outside of her wilderness home. Under different circumstances, she would have been perfectly at home in a big, metropolitan city, the witty hostess of many *soirées*. Life had given her a different environment, but her curiosity of bigger things was unquenchable and she longed to know about the people and events which shaped the world. "But why do you, a man of God, detest the *Anglais* so much Father?" she said. "Doesn't God love all his creatures?"

"God loves His Church and those who defend it," the priest retaliated. "The *Anglais* have been excommunicated and declared anathema by the Holy Father in Rome."

"Forgive me Father, but everything seems to come back to the Church. Theology is your love, not mine. Aren't there other reasons for the animosity between the French and English? Why? Why must there be blood shed between our peoples?"

At this, the priest paused to sip his tea and smile lovingly at his inquisitor. Such wonderful curiosity, he thought. "People must sometimes be willing to die for what they believe in my child. Look at the examples of the martyrs. Why, our Lord Himself . . . " The look in her eyes told him he was again regressing so he paused, thought a moment, and after another sip of tea continued: "Several years ago, Marie Thérèse acceded to the

Hapsburg throne of Austria. She is not the rightful heiress to this great dynasty and therefore our most gracious majesty, Louis XV, supported the true sovereign in his quest to ruin the plans of the pretender Marie, and all seemed well. Yet, as is to be expected in all cases involving the French nation, George II of England and his scheming minister Walpole (who only last year died and now suffers in perdition), took the side of this insufferable woman in order to strengthen France's enemies. This scheming has resulted in skirmishes between our peoples in both Europe and here. I expect that competition for land unoccupied between us in *L'Amérique,* along with continued bickering over the Austrian succession, will again lead to war between us in the very near future."

Constante was fascinated by all of this. "Why does our king care who rules in Austria?" she asked.

"There is so much to know and lowly priests are not always privileged to know it, but I believe that His Majesty would like to see the Germans grow stronger and the Austrians weaker so that the Hapsburgs will not threaten the power of France."

"If that is so," Constante persisted, "will not His Majesty come to fear the growing power of the Prussians and someday need to help the Hapsburgs to contain Frederick?"

"Ah, Constante," he sighed, "you rattle my poor brain with all your questions. I have no more answers for tonight." He rose, painfully stiff from the hours of sitting in the wooden chair. As he opened the door to leave, he noted that the sun was gone and darkness enveloped the little cabin.

"Forgive me, Father, for having kept you so long," she said, oddly pleased that he had addressed her by her first name. "I do so enjoy talking with you."

"*Merci,* my daughter, for the dinner and your delightful company. Don't worry too much on the world, but think more of your home and your husband." He nodded at Joseph, slumped in the chair by the dying fire. Constante sighed.

"I sense, my child, a discontented spirit," he said. "Your mind is so active and bright and inquisitive, and you ask many questions to satisfy your intellect, but you say nothing of the matters of the heart. I will not pry, but I am concerned. If you ever wish to unburden yourself, I am always at your disposal." He put a gentle hand on each of her arms. She suddenly threw those limbs around his waist and hugged him. Her cheek, pressed against the black buttons of his robe, became moistened with tears. He put his hand to her head and patted it softly. "Tears are good," he whispered. "They dampen the fire of the heart's rebellion. They help to produce harmony in the soul."

Constante stood up straight and looked into the benevolent face of the kindly priest. "I know Father," she choked. "But I have never been able to understand the difference between peace and death. They seem to me to be so much alike."

Père Du Jaunay looked at her sympathetically. "Death is not peace dear one," he said. "Death is torment and everlasting agony. Life is victory and peace."

"And where does one find life, Father?"

"In Jesus Christ my child," he said with absolute certainty. He took her hand in his and patted it lovingly. "Find Him, and you find peace. Nothing or no one else can do that for you."

When the priest said *Him*, against her conscious will, the face of François Cardin appeared in her mind. "I know you're right, Father," she said with a surety that amazed him. "But sometimes what one wants and what one *must do* are different. Yet I believe *he* will come to me."

"Most assuredly He will. God bless you child." The priest took his leave, and later that evening in the privacy of his bed, he prayed that Madame Ainsse would be delivered from her troubled state and find the peace she so desired. While he did so, the subject of his prayer sat by the hearth in the darkness of her own cabin, listening to the snores of her homely spouse, slumped only inches away in his rocker, and she too prayed for deliverance, but she knew that her saviour could not hear her, because *he* was only flesh and blood.

🦋 🦋 🦋

THE SUMMER PASSED SLOWLY. Constante rarely visited the construction site where her husband labored with the soldiers who had been chosen, because of their experience in building the priest's rectory and the blacksmith's shop, to assist in the construction of the new church. When Joseph inquired as to her reticence to do so, she complained of morning sickness. He, of course, begged her forgiveness for being so thoughtless and demanded (if she would be so inclined) that she rest as much as possible. He smiled and placed his broad, callused hand on her growing mid-section and commented that she must be careful of *him* so that *he* was born healthy.

In truth, Constante had not experienced a moment's pain or discomfort in her pregnancy thus far, but had promised herself that she would avoid contact with Cardin as much as possible and push him from her thoughts. She was relatively successful with the first resolution, but failed miserably in the second.

She passed the hot, humid days of July, sequestered in the sweltering cottage, glad to be relieved of the company of her too-agreeable husband, and pining for the man she was sure had put *her* from his thoughts. She left the cabin only in the cool darkness, while her exhausted spouse slept peacefully. It seemed that all he did was work and sleep. He appeared to be fatigued most of the time, a condition which was not at all natural to him. He was up before light and labored until dusk, and such was his piety and devotion to Père Du Jaunay, that his other work suffered because of it. Though he never discussed it, Constante was convinced that he saw the building of the church as a kind of holy mission, one which would be the ultimate 'Good Work.' The priest, as much as he desired the completion of his church, cautioned Joseph against excess, and compared the two of them to Michaelangelo and Julius II, a jest that was lost on the simple carpenter.

Constante was genuinely concerned for him. She saw his obsession as foolish. To her mind, in his attempt to escape his sins, he had created his own terrestrial purgatory.

His appetite too, had waned as hers increased, and she found herself eating the remains of his meal as well as consuming all of her own. He lost weight and complained of dizzy spells to Cardin, but said nothing to Constante.

She sat outside in the shadow of the stockade wall this evening, on a small bench attached to the exterior of the cabin wall. The sky was a brilliant red and gray as the last rays of the sun painted the horizon. Joseph had quit early, come home an hour ago, and fallen asleep without eating. Constante thought it best not to disturb him, so she ate her own dinner in silence and then wandered outside.

As she rested there, she could see the steeple skeleton rising above the soldier's barracks in the foreground. A monument to what? Light twinkled from the windows of the soldier's lodging and boisterous laughter and cheering came from within as some of the men pursued a lively game of darts and others gambled with dice. She enjoyed the masculine sounds, so alive and cheerful.

At that moment, Cardin came through the barrack's door, his shirt off, water dripping from his black hair, toweling his face. As he lowered the towel, he looked toward the Ainsse cabin as he habitually did each time he passed through that portal. Seeing Constante there surprised him. She was never outside. As their eyes met, a lump formed in her throat and her eyes became moist with tears, but she could not pull herself away, mesmerized by his gaze. He froze where he was, and stood so still that he resembled an animal, caught in a hunter's sight, its only escape its camouflage, the slightest movement, destruction.

Their vision thus linked, they remained in this attitude for several moments until a righteous kick from Joseph's heir-apparent reminded its mother of her loyalty. Constante arose quickly and retreated inside, François' eyes following her every step. Once sheltered, she pulled aside the corner of a curtain and looked through the window. Cardin stood in the same spot, looking in the same direction. She almost believed that he could still see her, concealed though she was, except that he then lowered his head and looked away. As he turned to go back inside, his toe stubbed against a stone which he picked up in his hand, studied for a moment, and then pitched in one angry motion over the stockade wall. He stood immobile then, attempting to compose himself, but his shoulders slumped and the towel in his left hand went to his face.

Constante saw his misery and frustration and her heart ached for him, but his actions brought a kind of selfish joy too, for she was convinced that he still cared for her. The child in her womb gave her another kick as she watched Cardin re-enter the barracks and she went to attend to her restlessly sleeping husband.

🦋 🦋 🦋

CONSTANTE'S TIME CAME LATE IN SEPTEMBER. Since August, Joseph had been feeling stronger and more energetic each day and, but for a slight cough, had pretty well returned to normal. The work on the church had continued without interruption and was almost complete. The exterior was entirely finished and the bell, a parting gift of Commandant Pierre-Joseph Celoron de Blainville who was being reassigned soon, was even established in its belfry. Only the planks needed to be placed across the floor joists and the pews installed upon them to complete the interior.

As Joseph's health improved, he spent less time sleeping and thus became more of a nuisance to Constante who determined to end her self-imposed isolation by visiting. She began to spend a great deal of time with the Bourassas. She adored the little girl, Charlotte, and was disappointed to learn that her parents would soon send her away to Montreal to get a 'proper education' and to be instructed in the niceties of Gallic society. They were concerned about her maturing into a 'barbarian' as Marie phrased it, and were determined to place her into an environment more befitting her sex and status.

The Bourassas enjoyed Constante's visits almost as much as she did and noted that she seemed to be in a better humor as each day passed. She confided to Marie that their company was of great comfort to her and her conversations with the woman who she almost regarded as a mother, centered around the subject of childbirth and its consequent trials. Constante had a normal, healthy, fear of pain, and although it was not an obsession with her, she quizzed Marie almost daily on the intensity and range of it in connection with childbirth.

Marie attempted to make light of it, but Constante knew it was not something to be taken lightly, and thus she went to Domitilde to ask her opinion, one which she accurately supposed would not spare her feelings, but be brutally honest.

Domitilde remembered that day on the beach almost fourteen years earlier and a similar, more difficult one in the forest near *L'Arbre Croche* the year before and, she told Constante very frankly, that 'it would hurt her more than anything in her life.' When Madame Langlade saw the frightened look on the young woman's face, she attempted to soothe her, but not with falsehoods.

Birth, she had explained, had much in common with death. The person experiencing it felt little of it and remembered nothing. It was always those around the person who suffered. In both cases, it was the mother who hurt the most. But mothers, she said, if they were lucky, would not outlive their children. Birth, however, was unavoidable. She said that, in a sense, getting ready to deliver your first child was somewhat like dying. You knew it was going to happen, you knew it would be painful, you knew a fresh life would come of it and that the suffering was temporary. That, she quipped, was the difference between men and women. Women knew something of death and thus respected it and avoided it more. Men plunged in with little regard for its power. Men, as a result, often died violently, women peacefully, because they had had more practice with it. But, she said in a more serious vein, birth, like death, had its great rewards and was only a momentary trial which passed quickly.

Constante left the Indian woman feeling somewhat more nervous than when she had come, but more realistically informed and she fortified her courage with the knowledge that although the experience would be hard, she had talked to two women who had lived through it very nicely and seemed to be none the worse for wear. In addition, both had promised to be in attendance at the great event and help her through it.

It was not long before Joseph came running to their respective doors one especially hot autumn evening to enlist their promised assistance. When they arrived at the Ainsse cabin, Constante was lying on the bed, crying and perspiring profusely. Their smiles vanished when they saw the great pool of blood on the mattress and, with closer examination, no indication of the infant having made any progress down the birth canal.

Their expressions frightened Constante who had heard them

arrive and stopped crying in momentary relief. Now her heart began to beat rapidly and her eyes betrayed her fear with a wild, cornered look. "What is it?" she gasped between hard breaths.

Marie looked questioningly at Domitilde who was rolling up her sleeves. The Indian woman was blunt. "The child is not moving and must be helped. You must push hard."

Joseph was beside himself. "What can I do?" he moaned.

Marie left the bedside of the frantic wife and, approaching the worried husband whispered, "Get the priest!"

🦋 🦋 🦋

PÈRE DU JAUNAY AND JOSEPH sat on the little bench outside the cabin and waited in the darkness impatiently for what seemed like many hours, but actually was less than two. Standing nearby was René Bourassa who had joined them less than an hour ago, leaving Ignace to watch over little Charlotte. Augustin Langlade had arrived, back from a day's hunting and also huddled with the worried men.

They sat and stood alternately, glancing at each other with concerned and solemn expressions, but no one spoke. They seemed unable to get comfortable. The only sound was Joseph's mumbling and the clicking of his rosary beads as he counted off his prayers.

In the twilight, two shadows approached and as they drew nearer, it was obvious to all that it was the Amiots. Marie Anne hustled wordlessly inside while Jean-Baptiste joined the husbands.

"How is she?" he said.

"We don't know," René Bourassa answered.

The agonizing sounds brought several soldiers from the barracks, François Cardin first among them. When he saw the source of the torturous noise, he ran across to the cabin and arrived simultaneously with its conclusion. Seconds later, Domitilde and Marie Anne Amiot came from the house. The two Indian women looked profoundly sad and tired. Domitilde's hands and forearms glistened with blood. Joseph came to her, awaiting some explanation.

"I'm sorry Monsieur Ainsse, but your child is dead," she said. "She was dead in the womb and we have done nothing but bring her out. Take heart, your *femme* is young and there will be others."

Cardin waited for Joseph to inquire after the welfare of his wife, but when he did not, and simply stood there, head down and shoulders slumping, the soldier said: "And Madame Ainsse? She is well?"

Père Du Jaunay looked at the handsome young man, wondering about his especial concern in the matter.

"Madame Ainsse has lost much blood, but I believe she will be fine," Domitilde responded. She then requested that the priest enter as Constante had asked for him. Joseph too, went inside. Cardin, feeling conspicuous, turned to his barracks, while René Bourassa, Amiot, and Augustin Langlade waited to escort their wives home. They came out directly, and the couples left silently.

Inside, Constante lay exhausted. Her skin, normally rosy, was pale-white and her hands were cold and clammy from her blood loss. Tears ran down her face as she watched Joseph hunch over the little wooden crate in which their daughter lay. Domitilde's words returned to her: "Birth, like death, is painful, but fresh life comes of both." She saw no life here, for all her pain, and her heart was embittered.

Père Du Jaunay stood by her bedside, smiling kindly at her, but even that sweet face could not intrude upon the terrible hate that was beginning to fester in her breast.

"I am so sorry my child," the priest said.

"It's all right Father, don't be sad," she returned sarcastically through her tears. "I have become accustomed to suffering."

He told her to be silent and rest, but she continued. "What answer do you have for me now? How will I find peace out of this? Can the church bring my sweet child back to life? Shall I push the corpse back into my womb and start over? What solution have you, good priest? I want to know!"

At this she fell to sobbing hysterically as Joseph came to the bed. "Constante," he pleaded, "do not talk to a man of the Church in such a manner. It is sacrilege!"

She whirled violently. "Don't talk to *me* of sacrilege husband." She almost spit the words at him. *"That* is sacrilege," she shouted, pointing at the little box with its grisly contents. "You scrape and genuflect and grovel to your precious priest and his church. What has it done for you? Behold! God's gratitude for the church you have built Him," and again she pointed at the box.

"Constante, my sweet wife . . . " Joseph mumbled in miserable confusion.

"There is another sacrilege," she laughed bitterly.

Père Du Jaunay bent over her and wiped the sweat from her brow, but at his touch, she turned her face to the wall to draw away from it. "Go away," she muttered.

The Jesuit moved away from the bed and signaled Joseph to pick up the box and leave the room with him. Once he had closed the drape separating the bedroom from the rest of the cabin, Joseph stood helplessly holding the box and staring at the small, still form it contained.

The priest went to him, taking the box from him. "Joseph," he said. The carpenter did not seem to hear him and kept staring at the floor as if he still held his dead child. "Joseph!" The stricken man raised his tear-filled eyes. "The Lord has taken your daughter to Heaven. Do not grieve. She sleeps in her Saviour's arms. I have baptized her. I will take her body away and discuss with you later the last rites. For now, pull yourself together and tend to your wife."

"Father, I am so sorry for her cruel words, she . . . "

Père Du Jaunay raised his hand to silence him. "Nothing needs to be said. She was not herself and her words are those of a grief too difficult to bear right now. I understand. Go to her and comfort her. She needs your strength now."

Joseph nodded and obediently returned to the bed where Constante lay, as the priest took his leave, the box in hand. Constante lay still as a corpse, pale and worn, her golden hair matted and disordered. She stared straight up at the ceiling, her eyes free of tears, her face set in grim determination. As Joseph approached the bed, he took her hand, which she did not resist, and he brushed her damp hair from her forehead.

He kissed her hand and knelt by the bed, hiding his face in

the blankets. Her eyes remained riveted on the ceiling as he spoke. "Do not be bitter, Constante. Do not talk to the Father so. He cares about you and loves you." As he spoke, no change appeared in her expression. She was like stone. Even her hand was cold and hard and it frightened Joseph. "Constante, these things happen. We are young. We will have more children. I too grieve for our daughter, but . . . "

"But what?" she suddenly lashed out. She pulled away her hand and glared at him bitterly. "But what, Joseph? At least she was not a boy? What a great tragedy that would have been. But this was only a girl. This was only Marie Coussante *Ainsse*. She would lose her father's name eventually anyway, eh? So let's be done with her now. So, bastard, you have gotten your way. Be happy. You will not have to suffer a daughter's presence in your house!"

Joseph backed away from the bed, his mouth yawning in an expression of horror. He stared at Constante as if she were possessed by some demon and indeed, the thought had occurred to him.

"Constante, how can you say this to me? Do you believe I willed our child's death? Can you really think me capable . . . " He stopped in mid-sentence, his voice choking with emotion. "I love you, Constante. I would do nothing to hurt you, you know that. Your love has made me . . . "

"Get out!" she screamed. She threw her pillow at him, striking him squarely on his nose. "Get out and stay away from me. Your presence sickens me. I've had enough of guilt and duty. I don't love you. I never have loved you."

His face twisted in pain. His heart beat violently and his supplicating voice changed to a direct and passionless tone which almost matched hers in its bitterness. "Then why did you consent to our marriage?" He asked coldly.

Constante knew she had overstepped her bounds and was entering forbidden territory, but she could not turn back. Sorrow and resentment pushed her relentlessly on. "It was pity," she mumbled softly.

"What?" He thought he had heard her, but he wanted to be certain.

"Pity," she repeated clearly. "I married you out of pity, Joseph."

"I see," he said. "It has always been my greatest fault to listen to my heart instead of what my better instincts tell me. Good-bye, Constante." He turned, pushed aside the drape over the bedroom entrance, and was gone. She called after him twice before she heard the door to the cabin close, and she knew he had left. She collapsed back onto the bed and, after crying bitterly, fell into an exhausted and fitful sleep.

🦋 🦋 🦋

PÈRE DU JAUNAY found Joseph the following morning, lying in his own vomit in front of the church he had worked so hard to construct. He was very drunk and semi-conscious. He babbled and sobbed while the priest helped him into the rectory, gave him tea, and assisted him into his own bed where, within moments, the tortured husband was sleeping soundly.

The Jesuit then prayed briefly after lighting a candle which rested at the base of a small statue of the Blessed Virgin in a niche in the wall. Thus fortified, he went out the door, crossed the parade ground, and entered the Ainsse cabin.

He knocked on the frame of the doorway to the bedroom and, receiving no reply, he pulled aside the drape and stepped in. Constante lay in her bed, a confusion of arms and legs intertwined with sweat-soaked sheets. He felt her feverish brow and as he did so, she opened bleary eyes which looked confused and disoriented. When she realized who he was, she spoke through parched lips. "Forgive me, Father. I was cruel and . . . "

"Sh-h-h," he whispered. "I know. Rest now and we'll talk later." He went out to the other room, found a wooden bucket in a corner, and went outside to draw water. At the well, he encountered Charles and Jean-Paul Langlade who had come on a similar errand for Domitilde.

"Ça va?" the priest asked.

"Très bien," Jean-Paul returned happily. Charles characteristically said nothing, but nodded in acknowledgement.

"Boys," the cleric continued, "I have a request of you."

Charles and Jean-Paul looked at each other, the latter shrugging his shoulders to indicate his ignorance of the proposed petition to his brother. "Madame Ainsse is quite ill and her husband cannot attend her because . . ." (here he paused momentarily, trying to be tactful, yet avoid equivocation) "because her husband is sick also. She wants care which would better be supplied by one of her own sex. Would you ask your mama to come?"

Jean-Paul assured him that he would, and the two teen-agers wandered off in the direction of their own home while the priest drew a bucketful of water and returned to Constante. Using a rag which had once been part of a pair of breeches, he moistened it, placed it on her forehead, then fetched her a cup of water. She had been without sustenance since before her ordeal yesterday, and she drank greedily.

When she had finished and was better able to speak, she said weakly, "Father, where is Joseph?"

"He is with me and he is all right," he answered gently.

"I hurt him very badly, Father. I, I told him . . . I told . . ." Her voice drifted off and her eyes closed.

The Jesuit tried to arrange her bedding to make her more comfortable, disentangling her legs and arms with the sheets. She moaned painfully in her sleep. He decided to disturb her no further and retreated to the adjacent room.

Moments later, Domitilde arrived and promised the priest that she would remain with Constante until he, or someone else, should return to care for Constante. Reassured, Père Du Jaunay returned to his own quarters.

By mid-afternoon, the unusual heat wave began to dissipate and more seasonal temperatures prevailed as dark storm clouds rolled across the lake from the north. The cooling air seemed to revive the unhappy Joseph, who could now add the trauma of physical pain to his emotional torment, as his head pounded unmercifully.

He rose from Père Du Jaunay's humble bed and staggered across the room he himself had designed and built. The priest was at prayer before the statue of the Virgin in the little alcove off the main room. Hearing Joseph's movement, he hastened to end his petitions and greeted the carpenter with a hardy *salut.*

Joseph slumped into a chair, put his face to his coarse hands, and began to sob bitterly. Père Du Jaunay thought to himself that there was no sadder sight than that of a big man, so often a symbol of strength, reduced to tears.

"Joseph, Joseph," he said softly. "What is it, my friend? Can you tell me?"

"She does not love me," he blubbered. "She never has. I have been played for a fool again. I can't suffer it, Father. I won't survive it."

"Nonsense," the priest corrected sharply. "She spoke badly to me too. She was suffering immensely from the death of her child. She did not know what she was saying. You know so little of her, Joseph, if you will excuse my boldness. She doesn't mean what she says. Her grief confounded her and she struck at the nearest targets, myself and you. She has already expressed her regret to me about what she said in anger, and has asked of you."

Joseph raised his head slowly, his face daring to look hopeful. "She has asked for me?" he said.

"She asked *of* you," the priest said, "which shows her concern for you and her devotion. You cannot accept everything people say, my son, when they are under such duress."

"What should I do, Father? Should I go to her?" He had such a miserable expression of confusion on his homely, tear-streaked face that the priest felt deeply for him in his innocent suffering. The good Father thought of a dog he had had when he was a small child in France. It was an ugly, loving little beast which was constantly getting into mischief. When it troubled a nervous ewe into a miscarriage with its incessant nipping and barking, Du Jaunay's father had beaten the poor animal mercilessly. The priest remembered the event forever after. The eyes of the pup kept coming to his thoughts and presented themselves in occasional dreams. The eyes always looked so hurt and misused, as if to say: 'I feel the pain of life to its fullest. I know somehow that I deserve it, but I don't understand it, and will never know *why* I deserve it.' Père Du Jaunay, looking at Joseph, wondered why that particular moment of his past should come to him now. He shrugged it off as Joseph spoke again.

"Father?"

"What? Oh, I'm sorry, Joseph. I was thinking. Perhaps you should wait until evening and allow your poor wife some time to rest and consider her situation. In the meantime, I will get you something to eat and we will discuss the rites of the church for your child."

The afternoon passed slowly for Joseph. The unpleasant details of his daughter's funeral, the pounding rain on the roof, the storm in his head and the anxiety in his heart, all slowed the passage of time to a crawl.

The tempest eventually abated in the evening, and Père Du Jaunay finally suggested that they go to see Constante. The coolness of the rain-purified air helped to clear his aching head, but Joseph's heart remained cloudy as they entered his cabin.

Domitilde sat faithfully by the hearth, enjoying the warmth of the fire. She related to them, upon the priest's inquiry, that Constante had slept much of the day, taken some nourishment in the form of a special herbal broth, and appeared to be much improved both physically and emotionally, though she was still dozing most of the time. The Jesuit encouraged Joseph to go to his wife and accepted a chair next to Domitilde to await his return.

Joseph entered their bedroom cautiously, as if his very appearance might occasion the flight of some missile more fatal than a pillow. His apprehension however, was unwarranted. Constante bestowed a sympathetic look and seemed very calm. He shuffled forward sheepishly, like a small child, or a chastised pet, the desire for forgiveness apparent in every motion and expression. She held out one thin, pale hand to him and he took it gratefully, covering it with tearful kisses as he knelt beside her. "Forgive me, my darling," he sobbed. He was not sure why he needed forgiveness. One might assume that true repentance requires some knowledge of one's sin. Such was not the case with the poor carpenter. He only knew that his precious Constante had been angry with him and this was transgression enough to demand contrition.

Constante sighed mournfully and looked pityingly on the pathetic figure of her husband. "It is I who require forgiveness, Joseph," she moaned. "I spoke to you in anger . . . out of bitterness . . . because of the loss. . . ." She began to weep. She wept for her lost child, for her husband, for her own cruelty and guilt, and for another, perhaps even deeper loss. She cried and cried, and Joseph wept with her.

She finally composed herself and asked Joseph for a hand-kerchief to dry her face and eyes. He quickly returned with it, having doctored his own moist features. He stood and watched her as she collected tears and her scattered emotions.

Presently, he knelt again by her bedside. He surrounded her prostrate form with his arms, and rested his head gently on her breast. His face was turned away from hers. She put a hand on his thick, curly hair and caressed it in a maternal, comforting fashion.

Joseph sighed, and in that sigh was the release of a legion of demons which had possessed him since the night before. Though he knew it, he needed confirmation from his exorcist. "You love me, then?" he said meekly, his head still turned away.

"Yes," Constante answered without hesitation or emotion.

"You will not go away?"

"No."

All other questions went unasked. Joseph did not need to, or want to, know anymore. There was no subsurface probing, no reading between the lines, no request for explanation of previous words spoken. Love was confirmed, nothing else was wanting. They remained in their strange embrace for several minutes, not speaking or wishing to, then Joseph stood up, bent to his wife, kissed her tenderly on her cheek, and exited.

Upon entrance to the adjoining room, Père Du Jaunay looked up hopefully and could see from the placid smile on the carpenter's face that all was well with him. He turned to Domitilde, dismissing her with sincere gratitude and, patting Joseph on the shoulder as he passed, entered the chamber of his dear friend. He, too, was greeted with tears, but this time the pleas for forgiveness came from her.

"Father, I ask your pardon," she pleaded. "You are my good friend and I would not injure or insult you for the world. But I am so hurt, so completely torn apart. I beg your forgiveness."

"And I give it freely, dear child," he said, taking her hand.

"Oh Father, you are so good. You can be so wise, but I know you can't explain this to me. The hurt of this will never go away. How can I face each day with such a burden?"

"God can give . . ."

"Please Father," she interrupted. "Do not talk to me of God. I don't want to hear of spirits I cannot see. Give me a closer comfort, one I can touch or feel."

"My dear daughter," the priest whispered. "You want your child back, and I cannot give her to you. The only physical solace I have is the hand that you hold so tightly now. It will always be there for you. You're right about explanations. I have none for what has happened to you. My only source of comfort is that which comes from God. Though you object to it, you will come to learn that only He can put your heart at ease and your mind at rest. Won't you pray with me to that purpose?"

She shook her head from side to side and she could see that her answer pained the gentle cleric. "Father, your God must be good somehow if *you* have found Him worth serving. He is alive for you because you want it so. You are honest and loving, so you must attribute your noble qualities to something outside yourself, because your humility does not allow you personal credit for such lofty emotions. But me, Father, my feelings would insult the great God you so adore. They are base, selfish, and ignoble. So I find it best to credit them solely to myself and not injure another being, spiritual or otherwise, with their burdensome weight."

"Constante," he rejoined, "that weight will ease with time and that burden would be lighter if it were shared."

"Thank you, dear priest, for your forgiveness. Don't abandon your mission to show me God. Don't let my apostasy confound you. But I beg you not to look too deeply into my soul today. You won't like what you find." The terrible look on her face scared him. "I'm worn out Father," she mumbled, closing those demonic eyes.

"Very well, child," he said, preparing to leave. "We will talk again."

"Don't desert me, Father," she called after him. "I should be lost without you."

"I won't," he reassured her. *"In cruce spero."*

"What does it mean?" she asked.

Père Du Jaunay smiled at her young, care-worn face. "I hope in the cross," he said. As he left the room, Constante answered him without his hearing. "I hope in someone to relieve me of my cross," she muttered.

The single word, 'François' passed her lips, before she crossed over into the land of dreams.

🦋 🦋 🦋

THE FUNERAL SERVICE for Marie Coussante Ainsse kept Michili-mackinac in a solemn mood for weeks afterward. The child was laid to rest under the floor of the new church which bore the ap-pellation of 'Sainte Anne de Michilimackinac.' Joseph struggled through this church ceremony which was to have been the bap-tism of his son, but instead was the last rites of his daughter, as Père Du Jaunay committed her soul to God and her remains to the dusty earth. Joseph had requested that she be buried there before they sealed off the last part of the floor, instead of the lit-tle fort cemetery where, traditionally, the dead were interred. The church had been his greatest achievement as a carpenter. It would now serve as her monument.

Constante did not attend. She was neither physically nor emotionally able. Domitilde had made a fur lining for the little coffin which Joseph had built for his daughter. A dress, formerly belonging to Charlotte Bourassa, now long outgrown, was do-nated by Marie to clothe the unfortunate infant.

These two families, as well as the Amiots, Louis de la Corne, (the new commandant), Jean Cuchoise and his Chippewa wife, Jean-Baptiste Cadotte and, in the back, François Cardin, at-tended the solemn ceremony.

Cardin was noticed only by the priest since he had slipped in at the last moment and everyone except Du Jaunay was facing in the opposite direction. Throughout the mournful ritual with its incense and melancholic liturgy, François stood in the rear of the church, shuffling his feet and looking uncomfortable. Perhaps his discomfort could be attributed to his civilian clothing, which he was not in the habit of wearing. The departure of Pierre-Joseph Celoron de Blainville as commandant had also marked the termination of Cardin's enlistment and though he was encouraged to extend his service to the Crown, he declined and opted for civilian life.

He intended to join most of the rest of the French community in trapping and had spent most of his meagre savings in the acquisition of the instruments of that trade. Augustin Langlade, aware that the country was too rich in furs to worry about competition, had been most helpful to him in selecting his equipment and tutoring him in the finer points of the profession.

Langlade liked the young man, as did Domitilde and the boys. He was industrious, honest and personable, yet blessed with a modest confidence which indicated some leadership qualities. Augustin and his two teen-aged sons had volunteered, then insisted that they be allowed to help him in the construction of his home. A site was chosen along the *Rue du Diable* close to the Langlade's, and the laying of the foundation was to take place the afternoon of the funeral in hopes that labor would diminish the stigma of that mournful event.

Seeing that Constante was not there, Cardin slipped out of the church before the actual interment and walked back to the barracks, where he would be allowed to reside until the completion of his own residence. He could determine no movement or activity as he glanced at the Ainsse cabin. He wondered about Constante's absence from her daughter's funeral and he worried about her incessantly, but he could not bring himself to inquire after her. He felt instinctively that his sudden appearance outside the Ainsse cabin yesterday had raised some eyebrows and he did not want to contribute to any further suffering for Constante by being the source of unfounded rumors.

Though he had never acted toward Constante in any way except honorably since her marriage, his secret thoughts riddled him with guilt and he sensed somehow, that everyone could read his mind and heart. His absorption with her had become an obsession and he was convinced that he must do everything possible not to display that to anyone, in order not to harm her.

Yet he had run to her when he had heard her screams, and

he was sure he had seen a knowing expression on the face of the priest. He stared at her door every time he happened to glance in that direction, as he was doing now, and was certain that every occupant of the fort watched him through cracks in their walls or from behind closed curtains. Moments ago, he knew, the priest had seen him in the church and, he felt, glared at him accusingly, realizing that his one aim must be to destroy the happy marriage of the faithful carpenter.

Consciously, François Cardin had no such intent. But he had not told anyone that de Blainville, now departed, had offered him a full commission and a magnificent bonus if he would remain in the service of the King and accompany him to his new assignment as his adjutant. Such an honor and promotion was virtually unheard of in the French military for a man of humble birth like Cardin. It was, in short, the opportunity of a lifetime.

However, the young man had declined, and opted for civilian life because, he insisted to the commandant (and himself) that he had always wanted to try the fur business and such a profession was becoming increasingly lucrative.

He failed to admit to himself, that to leave Michilimackinac was to admit that Constante would never be a part of his life. To face such a prospect was to face self-destruction. This he could not do. He stared briefly at the little house again, and thought he detected a slight movement of the window curtain. When no further motion manifested itself, he retreated into the barracks to spend the remainder of the time in idle dreams, waiting for the assistance of the Langlades.

🐝 🐝 🐝

By THE END OF OCTOBER, François' cabin was virtually completed and he left the barracks to take up residence there. He, Augustin and Charles had worked diligently, chopping trees, digging trenches for the logs (since the house was to be built in the *poteaux en terre*[1] fashion) and collecting appropriate pieces of bark to be molded into shingles for the roof.

---

[1]Posts in the earth.

Joseph Ainsse volunteered to assist him, but Cardin declined, begging that he not neglect his duty to the priest to complete the wooden pews necessary to conducting mass in the new church, and explaining that he already had more help than was needed.

François was impressed with the energy and diligence of Charles who was eager to learn and seemed to be delighted to have some meaningful labor to employ him in his idle hours. Though he was very sober and quiet for his age, François thought, he did the work of a man and never complained.

Jean-Paul, on the other hand, found any and every excuse to escape the regimentation of purposeful labor and often left to hunt with Okinochumaki or wandered away to *L'Arbre Croche*, reappearing only at dusk, the day's work completed and he, safe from contamination for another day.

When Cardin would inquire into his absence, Augustin simply shrugged and smiled pleasantly as if to say; 'It is his nature, *mon ami,* what can I do?' Charles never seemed to resent his brother's indolence or even regard it as such, apparently because he thought himself the fortunate one not to have been born with a frivolous nature.

Whatever their separate personalities, François grew very close to the Langlades as they worked side by side through the decreasing daylight of the October sun. Domitilde often provided their meals, and always greeted Cardin cheerfully and seemed very fond of him.

On the day the last bark shingle was nailed home and a fire was built in the new hearth, Cardin invited them all to be his guests for a picnic lunch and, though the cabin was sparsely furnished, he had enough chairs (with the addition of two thick logs), for them all to be seated for a dinner of venison around the square table he had made himself.

Upon the completion of their repast, he presented each of the family with a gift. For Augustin, he had two bottles of premium rum from the West Indies which he had purchased from the new commandant.

To Domitilde, he gave a beautiful pillow with her name embroidered in gold thread in large letters across the surface of it. (Though he had paid for the materials, Marie Bourassa had done the work.) It was the first time Domitilde had ever seen her name in print and it made her cry, recalling her mother, who had chosen it for her.

Charles received an adze and a well-forged hammer (both from Amiot's skilled hand) which seemed to please him very much, though he said nothing besides a polite *merci* in his typically economical way. Jean-Paul was presented with a small pair of dice which he received with gratitude and an expression of his pride in what he believed to have been an integral role in the construction of the noble edifice.

A good time was had by all, and when François closed the door on their exclamations of *bonne nuit* and *merci,* he decided that he was very grateful for their companionship and simple amity. The silence of the cabin seemed somehow oppressive after such gaiety and to distract himself from it, and the inevitable image of Constante's face, he set about putting things in order.

The following morning found him outside early. As he looked about him, he noticed a small group of people standing by the water gate of the fort. From this distance at the opposite end, he could not make out who they all were, but he recognized the hardy guffawing that he heard as belonging to Augustin Langlade. Espying Jean-Paul and Charles standing in their own dooryard, he called them over to determine if they might know the reason for the gathering.

Jean-Paul, in his gregarious manner, happily volunteered what he knew while Charles, looking somewhat depressed and out of sorts, said nothing, but only shook his head in concurrence.

It seemed that Charlotte Bourassa was about to leave for Montreal to attend a fashionable school for young ladies or, as Jean-Paul put it, a 'fancy manners place.' She was to be attended on her voyage by Monsieur Cadotte, Monsieur Ainsse, and two soldiers.

Cardin wanted to ask why Joseph would be going when his wife was suffering emotionally and slowly recuperating from terrible physical trauma, but Jean-Paul began to answer before he could ask.

The carpenter had asked the Langlades and Bourassas to look

in on Constante in his absence since he felt compelled to travel to Montreal to purchase several tools necessary to his expanding trade. Little Charlotte was to live in Montreal with René's brother for several years as she completed her education. The rest would return in a month, barring any difficulties, and be settled into their normal routines before the first winter storm.

François thanked the boys and returned to his cabin. He took out a bottle of rum, cheaper than that he had given to Augustin, and sat by his table. He took the entire day to find the bottom of the bottle and by then his head was swimming, awash with the form of Constante.

🐦 🐦 🐦

HE FELL ASLEEP at five o'clock in the late afternoon and awoke again at midnight. Seeing how late it was, and knowing from his stiff neck that he had drifted away while sitting at the table, he arose, undressed, and lay down on his makeshift bed, a straw-stuffed mattress, which occupied one corner of the room.

He was awakened again in the middle of the night by a sound which he heard first in his sleep and, upon gaining his senses, was not convinced that he had really heard at all. Detecting no further noise for several moments, he lay back on his bed intending to resume his rest, when he heard the sound again.

It was, he thought, a kind of gentle tapping at the door, since it was so soft and hesitant that it could not really be defined as knocking. He supposed that it could be the scratching of a dog or raccoon, but for the reality of a very discernible rhythm. Determined to solve the mystery, he pulled on his breeches and shirt and approached the door warily before opening it slightly.

What he saw could not have shocked him more if it had been the Angel of Death planted in his doorway. This *was* an angel, but of another kind. Constante stood there, nervously glancing in every direction to see if anyone had noticed her on her clandestine journey across the few hundred feet from her cabin to his.

When the door opened, she started and then, with an embarrassed smile and more anxious looking about, asked to be admitted.

François, feeling stupid for having made her wait outside in such obvious discomfort, begged her to enter and when she did so, he closed the door behind her. They stood in the semi-darkness, seeing each other only by moonlight and the glowing embers of the dying fire. Finally, he moved to light a lamp and invited her to sit down, addressing her as Madame Ainsse, which seemed, somehow, to irritate her. Cognizant of her desire for privacy as evidenced by her nervous actions, he closed the simple curtain which covered the only window in his cabin.

He sat down across the square table from her and the two of them said nothing, perhaps finding it unbelievable to be so close after so many months of separation, their thoughts constantly obsessed with each other, but never communicating.

François spoke first; "I'm so happy to see you," was all he was able to say. It seemed such an absurdly polite and inane statement to make, but his confused brain could find nothing else.

At least it prompted her. "Monsieur Cardin," she said officiously, "I have come here in the middle of the night when my husband has left me alone for the first time since our wedding, to see you and . . ." here she hesitated, "to tell you how I feel and explain myself to the benefit of my marriage and our futures." As she spoke, she could see that he was already reading her mind and knew her heart. "I know you have demonstrated a certain, ah, affection for me and I must be honest and tell you that that affection is mutual. But Monsieur Cardin, this must end. Nothing can ever happen between us or . . . or the consequences would be very dreadful indeed. I have made my decision to marry my good husband and I will not betray him!"

François could see her agitation and her fear. He knew how difficult this speech was for her to make, but also understood that this would probably be his last chance to ever speak to her privately and bare his soul. He did not intend to let her cloud that opportunity with words he knew she did not believe.

"Constante," he said abruptly. "Without touching you or making any attempt to disarm you emotionally or physically, I am going to sit here as calmly as I can and speak my mind truthfully, regardless of the consequences. I tell you frankly that I love you, and that is the *honest* word—not 'affection.' It is a passionate, possessive, greedy and all-consuming love which denial, separation and probably not even your rejection can affect or remove. My desire is to hold you, kiss you, and make love to you. My wish is to care for you, remain with you now and through my old age and, if possible, through eternity itself. I have no intention of being driven away. I can be very patient. My intent is not to hurt Joseph, but I *know* you love me."

She opened her mouth as if to speak, but he would not allow it. "Yes, yes, I know you love him too, but not like you love me. You dream of me as I dream of you and there is simply no hope for it. Deny it to me if you wish, deny it to yourself if you dare, but that won't change it or end it. It will always be there as long as we are alive, and you know it."

She looked at him helplessly, tears welling in her eyes. "Monsieur Cardin, you *must not* say these things. You must leave me alone and let me have some peace."

His heart cried to hold her and comfort her, but he forced himself to talk and remained seated. "You know I have not touched you or attempted to visit you. I did not step forward to challenge your marriage, though it was a terrible burden to bear. Since that time, have you experienced peace? What are you asking of me that I have not already done? Do you wish me dead? I would die for you Constante, but not to make you more comfortable in your choice. I don't agree with your choice and I'll not accept it, but I will leave you alone as I have, if you can find happiness in that."

She wept openly now, unable to speak, overcome by emotion and confusion. Out of pity for her and himself, he violated his promise and reached across the table to grasp her hand. His touch seemed to calm her.

"Dear Constante," he said. "I beg you to understand me. It pains me to see you in such misery. You have had the burden of losing your child. I do not know how that feels and I am so sorry for it. No words can erase such grief. I . . . I only wish the child had been mine, so I could share your sorrow and mourn with you."

She raised her head then and looked into his young and ardent face. Her other hand covered his and she attempted a small smile. Finally, she spoke: "Then what are we to do, my love?" These words caused his heart to race in joyful affirmation of the certainty of her feelings. "If I leave Joseph," she said, "he will die. He tries so hard to please me and provide for me. I cannot, I will not, destroy him. Then do I live in constant agony? Do I mourn you forever as I mourn my little girl? Do I break my own heart? Deny my own life? And what of you, my sweet love? What becomes of you?"

François kept his eyes locked on hers throughout this monologue. The cherished sound of her voice thrilled him. The falling tears seemed to enhance her beauty. He suspected that if she lay dying of the plague, that her beauty would overcome it and he would kiss her and gladly share destruction with her. Yet she demanded an answer. She had to have a solution, and he *must* provide it. He was her hope.

"If I were a godly man, I would release you to your husband," he said, "and voluntarily go away, knowing firmly that right is right and wrong is wrong, and having done right, I would live with a peaceful conscience, awaiting my eternal reward. If I were a noble man, I would lie to you and tell you I didn't care for you and leave you with a broken heart, but render you some peace with my absence, some opportunity to forget. If I were a rogue, I should work for your seduction, fulfilling my own needs and damn the consequences. If I were evil, I would murder Joseph to free you from your bond. If I were brilliant, I would think of some other option which would give happiness to all. But I am none of these. So, precious Constante, I cannot help you, or Joseph, as I cannot help myself."

She released his hand and stood as if to go. He rose also, saying nothing, his fear of her leaving causing him to experience a sickening wave of nausea. Once at the door, her hand on the rough knob, she forced herself to turn and look at him. He stood, leaning against the table for support, his attention riveted on her. His forehead was furrowed, his expression resolute, but desperate. His hand shook and he looked like a man who was fighting some physical infirmity. He stood solidly erect only by sheer force of will. This act of discipline was for her. He would smile for her. He would let her go . . . for her.

She thought of the days ahead. She thought of Joseph and her dead child. She thought of endless days without François and the awful vision was now too close to substance to bear. She finally took her hand away from the latch and faced him. She strode resolutely across the room, the chasm, the universe, that separated them, and into his arms.

The wonderful relief of her body close to his caused him to release his pent up frustration in tears. And while they kissed and kissed, their tears intermingled as he, in snatches of breath mumbled; "No. Dear one, no, no. You cannot, no." Yet he devoured her with his mouth, caressed her with his hands, and reveled in the sheer joy of emotion honestly released and received.

After a moment, Constante pulled away, leaving them both breathless. Cardin feared she would run again, but she took his hand, and with a peculiar expression of resolve and abandon, she led him to the straw bed.

They lay in each other's arms at first, doing nothing except to hold one another and enjoy the delicious warmth their closeness generated. Several times, they both tried to speak, but realized there was no point to it. They kissed, they touched, they luxuriated in the blithesome beauty of their tender regard. At length, Constante rose from the bed, put out the light, removed her clothing and, sighing in contentment and momentary security, snuggled close to François. He followed suit, and for a few moments, they left the world behind and joined their bodies to match their souls. They found escape and release from care, if but for a few moments, in their mutual ecstasy.

🕊 🕊 🕊

CONSTANTE SLIPPED AWAY BEFORE DAWN, unnoticed. Their parting was silent, as they kissed tenderly. There were no promises of reunion, no plans for the future, only a small contentment in momentary fulfillment.

As Constante closed her door on the pink-grey sky of dawn, she removed her *fichu* and sat down by the table in the center of the room. It was so quiet that the silence almost frightened her.

She got up from her chair, pulled open the curtain, and looked about to see if there was any sign of activity. She was petrified that someone may have seen her, and as the sounds of others rising to go about their daily work increased, so did her paranoia.

She did not sleep at all that day. Too many thoughts raced through her fevered brain and tortured heart to allow her any such relief. She would lie down several times on her bed to try, but the sweetness of her recollection of the night before would always be shattered by the accusing and nightmarish face of her husband.

She imagined a myriad variety of unpleasant situations. She saw the sentry pointing at her in pious testimony as Père Du Jaunay interrogated him and Joseph hung his head in the gallery while her wigged and black-robed father sat in judgment. She saw François being lynched by an angry mob of their friends and neighbors, his carcass dangling pitifully from the church spire, his legs flailing in the unsupportive air. She saw herself and François making love wildly on his straw bed while the Bourassas stood watching, shaking their heads in mournful condemnation.

These and many other terrible images flashed into her tired and worried brain throughout that difficult day. But the most hideous anxiety centered around the awful apprehension that she had touched François or spoken to him in intimacy for the last time. This belief was insufferable and distressed her so that she plummeted into the depths of despair. Yet she knew that it had to be that way. No other option was available.

In the days that followed, she became a veritable recluse. She was rarely seen outside her cabin, and then only to draw water from the communal well or empty the chamber pot. Domitilde had come several times, as she promised Joseph, to inquire of her, as had Marie Bourassa, but they left with the impression of being politely tolerated as unwelcome intruders.

She sat day after lonely day, dying each night to repeat her assignation with François, but not daring to. She thought that perhaps she could write him a note and slip it under his door unnoticed. She even wrote it and sealed it, but her courage failed her and she ended by tossing it into the fire.

After ten days of this agony, she awoke to another unhappy

day. The sky was grey and overcast, and dead, dry leaves rustled across the deserted parade ground. The weather fitted her mood. She went first to the smoldering fire, to replenish it and stoke it, before placing the iron pot over it to warm water for her tea.

As she sat at the table to await the boiling, bubbling sounds which signaled its readiness, she noticed a white object on the floor by the cabin door. When she approached it, she recognized it as a folded piece of paper with her name scrawled across its surface.

Her heart leapt to her throat, as much in dread as in anticipation. She brought it back to the table, sat down, and opened it. It was, as she had hoped and feared, a note from François. It read:

My Love,

It is impossible for me. I can't continue to be without you. I must see you again. I must know that you are well. I must know if you suffer as I do. I will come tomorrow night. If you will not receive me, notify me by this same means tonight and I will go away and be done with it. If I receive nothing, I will come.

Ever your devoted one,

F. Cardin

Constante was both thrilled and paralyzed with fear at the thought of seeing her lover again. No reply would bring him, a note would mean she would never see him again. He was forcing her to communicate with him and make a decision.

What torture she endured! She wrote several messages, none of which seemed to express her emotions, none of which would ever satisfy her thoughts. She found it impossible to say goodbye.

Late that evening, she simply scribbled the word *non* on a piece of paper, determined to deliver it. But she feared that François (or others) might still be awake and she did not trust herself with another confrontation. She decided to wait several hours until she was convinced in her own mind that everyone would be asleep. Having made her decision, she lay her head upon the table where she had been writing, and closed her eyes to await the post-midnight darkness.

When she opened them again, she looked down at the sunlight on the floor, then closed them against the unaccustomed brightness. Slowly, the memory of the night before trickled back into her consciousness and she sat bolt upright with a start.

She glanced quickly at her hand and saw the note, still clutched there as if in defiance of her will. She was in a panic now and stood up, pacing swiftly to and fro in the small room. 'He will come now', she thought. 'Why did I sleep?'

"Your God is having fun with me," she said aloud to the church steeple as she looked out her window. The sound of laughter made her look to her right, and she saw the Amiot children playing next door. She seized upon the idea of having one of them deliver the message in her hand for a small remuneration. In the end, however, whether out of fear of discovery, desire, or apprehension, she burned the note with the rest of the attempted communications, changed into her best dress, fussed with her hair, and awaited her lover.

🦋 🦋 🦋

IN THE TWO WEEKS THAT FOLLOWED, Constante and François saw each other every night. He would normally arrive at her cabin at some time after midnight, and return to his own before dawn. As the November nights grew longer, this afforded them usually five hours of love-making, gentle conversation, and simple pleasures. Little of the future was ever spoken of, but as each night flew by, they knew that Joseph would be returning soon and that they would have to end their happiness—or his.

They began to speak on this most difficult subject one night about a week before Joseph was due to return. François, fearing the loss of Constante, finally broached the topic while they lay together in the Ainsse bedroom on a cold, November evening.

He explained to her how much he loved her and attempted to tell her what she meant to him, but these were wasted words, since she already knew what he was feeling.

He suggested that they go away together that moment. They should pack their belongings and escape in the middle of the night, fleeing to someplace where they might start a new life together. He told her that she was the only hope for his happiness, and he, hers.

Throughout his discourse, Constante lay silently in his warm embrace in the soft bed, tears running down her cheeks, realizing the impossibility of it all. The god 'Guilt' would not allow it. At each statement, she snuggled closer to him, but said nothing.

When he stopped talking, he held her even tighter, awaiting the answer that would affect both their lives permanently and, he believed, irrevocably.

She eventually said a simple 'no,' tersely and with finality. She kissed him long and deeply, with desperate passion. Then she got up and dressed and he followed. When both were in the main room, she told him that they must not see one another again. Their affair must end now, permanently. Joseph would be home any day and she had to start over now to clear her head. She had to erase the passion of her heart. François fell to his knees, threw his arms around her small waist, and begged her in agonized sobs not to destroy them. He buried his face in her skirt, his pride in her heart, but she steeled herself against him, pushing him away and turning her back.

He pulled himself together, trying to salvage his dignity, knowing that she would not hear him any further. He stood up and took his cloak, tying it roughly around his neck, wiping the moisture from his face. He went to the door, turned, and said to her back: *"Tout est perdu hors l'honneur."*[2] When the door closed behind him, she sat by the table, her expression void of tears and vacant. She had crossed from agony to emptiness.

Three long days later, Joseph returned from Montreal. He was so overjoyed to be home, that he did not notice the cold misery of his spouse. He was excited to tell her about his visit with Bourassa's brother, about how fond he had grown of Jean-Baptiste Cadotte on the trip, and how much he admired the little

---

[2]All is lost save honor.

girl, Charlotte, who, now delivered safely to her uncle's house, was attending the 'fancy manners place.'

He pulled out his new tools and proudly displayed them to Constante, explaining the function of each in careful detail, oblivious of her deadness. He also brought forth a beautiful, pale blue nightgown made of *mousseline de soie* (a thin, silk fabric resembling chiffon), which he begged her to model.

She obediently dressed, and he was so captivated by her sad beauty that he suggested that they should retire early. In the darkness of their room, in the bed where she had lost her child and her lover, while Joseph thrust at her in ectasy, Constante bore his weight patiently, her eyes staring vacantly at the ceiling.

🦋 🦋 🦋

THE WINTER MONTHS began early and ended late, making the season seem longer than usual. François Cardin kept himself occupied with his traps, learning his trade. He had intended to leave Fort Michilimackinac after his last liaison with Constante, but he hoped against hope that something would happen that would bring them back together.

He did not see her at all except at a distance, and then perhaps twice. She did not attend Mass or any other community function, though he often saw Joe Ainsse in attendance. He spent many nights at the Langlades, including one memorable evening when the Ottawa chief with the terribly scarred face was a guest and entertained them all with tribal history. He was also fascinated by the chief's adopted son with the split ear lobes who chattered incessantly about some religious cult into which he was being initiated that had something to do with rattlesnakes. As they sat around the Langlades' hearth, the expression on his face varied little from that of the boys who were obviously fascinated by their cousin's enthusiastic diatribe.

But for the most part, François dreamed of Constante at night, and thought about her through each day. In the quiet of the snowy forest, he would often sit on a rock or stump, staring off into the grey sky, wishing silently to himself or praying diligently to God, for some relief from the burden that oppressed him. At night, in his solitary bed, he wept unconsciously and cried out her name in his fitful sleep.

Constante did not cry or smile or display any type of emotion. Emotions were for the living. She wandered through her sense-less and insensitive existence from day to day, dutifully fulfilling her wifely obligations, speaking but rarely, and then only in response to some question from Joseph.

She cooked his meals, washed and darned his clothes, allowed him the use of her body. Her emotions were numbed, and had she not moved and reacted on occasion, one would have thought her catatonic. She did not allow herself to think of François or her dead child, or any thought beyond the immediate task at hand.

All of this, of course, did not completely escape the attention of her husband. But he was happy in his work, well-fed, and proud of his beautiful spouse who willingly, if unenthusiastically, gave herself to him whenever he felt the need or inclination.

In this kind of life there was security and peace, and he was not about to muddle it up by pressing for words of explanation that were not necessary. His standing in the community was impeccable, his hard work and piety admired, his wife and growing wealth envied. Little else remained for him to desire except . . . .

One January night, as he lay upon her in the course of love-making, Constante uttered a little cry of pain and when he inquired into the cause (for he was always gentle), she explained flatly that she believed herself to be pregnant and, accordingly, her breasts were tender and his weight on them was cause for discomfort. He got up immediately, begging her forgiveness and expressed his unbounded joy and gratitude, laughing and giggling like a small child. Without expression or any change in demeanor, she rolled over, laid her face on the pillow, and got up on her knees, presenting herself to him in animal fashion. She simply said: "Continue." He looked at her, kneeling prostrate in servitude, and frowned in confusion, but he would not ask.

The next morning, Joseph told everyone he saw of the marvelous news of the conception and many came to offer their good wishes and congratulations. Domitilde Langlade was one of the first and though Constante was polite, the Indian woman could see that this poor, fair woman was deeply distressed and found no joy in her condition. She tried to glean from the suffering thing some justification for her distress, but accomplished nothing.

Madame Bourassa also availed herself of the opportunity one day to offer her felicitations, but was rebuffed by the hard, insentient woman who had once been the gay, vivacious girl who worked in her house. Even the subject of Charlotte did not arouse her from her self-induced torpor and Marie Bourassa told René that evening that Madame Ainsse seemed very 'unnatural' and that she feared for her sanity.

The only person who seemed to be able to carry on a semblance of a normal conversation with her was Père Du Jaunay. Yet much to his chagrin, her interest centered around his person and not his God. She told him frankly that his pleasant humor and loving words eased her pain, but she would not share that pain or enter into his confidence, any more than she would enter his church.

Even her immediate neighbors, the Amiots, saw her seldom. Yet Marie Amiot noticed that she did smile once, while watching the children (now numbering eight) as she happened to see them playing in the snow on one of her infrequent sojourns into the world outside her cabin walls.

Spring grudgingly arrived in mid-May. There had been a violent blizzard in April, dumping more than two feet of snow on top of the previous month's accumulation, making travel outside of the fort dangerous. The first week of May saw another two inches, and it wasn't until the middle of the month that the forest streams began to flow rapidly along their widening courses, fed by the melting snows. A week of bright sunshine and increasing temperatures witnessed the breaking up of the ice on the strait. The honking of wild geese flying north heralded the death of winter.

By the end of May, flowers abounded and rich green leaves and grass appeared in the forests and meadows around Michilimackinac. The Chippewa had returned from the south and constructed a new village just east of the fort.

The shouts of men, barking of dogs, and drilling of soldiers on the parade ground were a welcome contrast to the whistling wind moaning across the barren winter commons.

Constante wandered outside her cabin on one of these late May mornings. She had served Joseph his breakfast and, as usual, he had gone to work in his little enclosed shop, a few yards away. He had been coughing incessantly since the weather turned warm, attributing it to a spring cold. As she left the cabin, she heard him hacking away while he labored, but paid little attention, since she felt she had done more than her duty in regard to him. She strolled away in the opposite direction, leaving the fort through the water gate.

She was getting very big with her child, who was now entering upon its seventh month since conception. She moved slowly and deliberately. She walked along the beach, heading east, resting every few minutes. The pine and cedar trees blocked any view inland until she came to a gap in the trees, half a league from the fort, which opened onto a flower-sprayed meadow of yellow, red, lilac, and orange. She hesitated, then turned toward the meadow, drawn by the color and fragrance. She sat down on a rock by a small brook and pulled a single flower from the soft earth. She seemed mesmerized by its bright hue and she even smiled in a small, unconscious way. She remained for the better part of an hour, breathing in the refreshing air and mixed scents of nature's perfumes.

She finally sighed and stood up, dropping several petals from her receding lap and straightening her dress. As she glanced to her right, she saw a solitary figure standing perhaps thirty feet away at the southern edge of the meadow where the forest began. It didn't take her long to recognize him, and once she had, she turned away and strode quickly toward the beach.

François ran across the meadow after her, shouting for her to stop. She did not, but hurried along, puffing from the inactivity of winter and the additional weight she now bore. Her eyes were wide in fear. She stumbled and slipped to the ground on one knee. While she was attempting to raise herself, he caught up to her and assisted her to her feet.

He turned her to him and held her shoulders. She looked, wild-eyed, into his handsome face that she had tried so hard to erase from her mind. "No-o-o-o, no, no *no!*" she screamed. She began flailing at his chest crazily and yelling at the top of her lungs, but he held her firmly. Eight months of emotional restraint burst as the dam broke its delicate barriers and her feelings flooded forth.

He silenced her with his mouth and the arms that had struck at him in blind desperation now groped for him in reckless, itching, greed. "Oh my love! François, my love! Oh God, God, God!" she mumbled between insatiable, ardent kisses.

He tried to talk to her, but she would not listen, continuing to smother him with her passionate mania. As they embraced, he felt the child in her womb kicking against his stomach, an absurd little movement in an explosion of gyrations. She seemed to feel nothing but him. All the world and universe rested in the sensation of his lips and hands.

When he pulled away to try to talk to her, he found her busily pulling at the buttons of her shirt. "No, Constante. Not here," he said, looking anxiously around him. But she ignored him, pulling the loose-fitting garb over her head and shedding her undergarments on the grass. "No, Constante, we can't . . ." his voice trailed off.

"Why?" she asked boldly. "I did not come to you François, now or last winter. I have fought to keep you from my thoughts each minute, but I almost lost my sanity by doing so. People can only deny themselves to a point. I carry *your* child. I love you, but the powers of heaven or hell who direct my fate have seen fit to keep us apart. We should be lying together in *our* bed, in *our* house, but we can't. So I will couple with you in adulterous lust in a meadow. But I *will* have you and spit in the face of fate for a few moments."

He wiped the tears from her cheek with the back of his hand. "I didn't follow you to make you miserable. I am here because I *have* to be," he said. He smiled at her gently and held her close. "You carry *our* child? My poor Constante. How could you be so cursed as to love me? How could I ever take advantage of you? I didn't follow you to satisfy my . . . own desires. I . . . I . . . don't know. I was . . . compelled."

She stared at him, calmed in his embrace, her blue eyes and

scarlet mouth so pronounced against her fair skin. "François, you don't understand me. I have done what I have done because I am compelled. I do what I do now because I *choose*. I want to feel again. I want to be loved and held and whispered to, for *me*. Do this, and I can bear life for awhile longer."

As the two lovers grasped a moment of happiness, the Chippewa warrior, Tcianung (Big Star), passed by the meadow. His wife, Natomah, had recently given birth to a daughter whose name would be Lo-tah. Although he knew that the coming of a girl-child was not as great a cause for celebration as the birth of a son, he was very proud of the dainty infant and intended to host a feast in her honor, inviting all of his relatives, including his older brother, the war chief, Minavavana. Thus it was that he had spent the early morning hunting game and now carried home his trophies which included two rabbits, several squirrels, a porcupine, three partridge and a turkey.

Assisting him with this respectable catch was his nephew, Wenniway who, even at the age of twelve, showed considerable prowess as a hunter.

Tcianung had not looked at the meadow as they passed silently on the edge of the forest, still hoping to add to his catch and scrutinizing the forest ahead of him. His young companion however, grasped the back of his uncle's loincloth and when the older man turned to see what was the matter, the boy pointed toward the meadow.

At first, Tcianung thought that he had seen two deer rutting and he raised his bow in hopes of adding two sides of venison to his feast. But gradually a smile broke upon his face as he realized they were human. They were standing by a birch tree which the female gripped with her hands. The male stood behind her, his hands on her shoulders, the muscles of his buttocks contracting and expanding as he lunged against her. The woman grabbed the tree tightly at each thrust, throwing her blond hair back and arching her neck, exposing her face to the secret observers, as she shivered in passion. Judging from her swollen belly, Tcianung guessed that what they were so assiduously attending to was not for purposes of procreation. Their clothes lay scattered a few yards away, in the tender spring grass, by a brook.

Tcianung winked at Wenniway whose childish mouth stood open in awe. The uncle kidded his nephew about his surprised expression later that day when they arrived in the Chippewa camp, but Wenniway explained that it was not the act itself which had surprised him, for he had been raised in a culture where privacy was a useless commodity and he had observed his own mother and father engaging in such pleasure many times.

What amazed him, he told his grinning uncle, was that the woman they had seen, he knew to be the wife of the carpenter at the French stick-house, and the man who was with her, well, he was not the carpenter.

🦋 🦋 🦋

IN JULY, on a sweltering day which was so humid that one inhaled the air in chunks, Constante Chevalier Ainsse began her labor. Joseph, as before, ran to fetch Mesdames Amiot, Langlade, and Bourassa. Père Du Jaunay again stood outside with René, Augustin and Jean-Baptiste, to keep Joseph company while he paced and prayed. The poor carpenter was petrified at the thought of what Constante would be like if she lost her second child. She would become a madwoman, and this time there would be no reconciliation.

He had continued his coughing for the last two months and now was regurgitating little globules of blood with each spasm. Père Du Jaunay was extremely concerned for him, but Joseph shrugged it off. He told the priest that he felt well (aside from his apprehension concerning the birth of his child), but he seemed extremely short of breath and wheezed continually between bouts of coughing.

The new commandant, Jacques Legardeur de Saint-Pierre, had recently taken command of the garrison, replacing La Corne who had gone home to France to fight in the war against the *Anglais* which was then raging in Europe. His substitute brought news that the French invasion of Nova Scotia had not gone well, and because of the demands of the military, the doctor who had been promised to the residents of the fort for so many years would not be forthcoming.

So Joseph's affliction had gone untreated and undiagnosed for well over a month, and continued to get worse as Père Du Jaunay had observed. His apprehension regarding the carpenter's health was momentarily interrupted by the fierce, yet helpless cries of an infant. Joseph's large ears seemed to prick up, canine-like, at the sound and his grin almost reached from one to the other.

Madame Langlade emerged from the cabin shortly after and announced to the anxious assemblage that Constante had given birth to a healthy son and that the mother was weak, but all right and in good spirits. This proclamation brought cheers from the little group. Père Du Jaunay whispered, "praise God," as Joseph rushed by him to see his new son.

The child was baptized Joseph Louis Ainsse, though he looked nothing like the beaming father. He had the delicate features of his mother, and his body, though sturdy, was more compact than the lanky frame of Joseph.

Constante attended the baptism and seemed to have become more like her former self, although she was nowhere near the happy, frivolous, child she had once been. She continued to meet François occasionally in the meadow throughout the summer, sometimes carrying along little Joseph Louis so that his real father might have some pleasure with his son.

She always returned from these clandestine rendezvous feeling exhilarated and refreshed, although the dark reality of sleeping with two men often made her feel whorish and cheap. Yet her only happiness was her moments with François, and Joseph was so tired and ill that it was not often a problem.

Even Constante began to worry about his incessant coughing fits which now kept him awake most of the day and night and forced him to try to sleep in a chair for fear that he might choke in his own phlegm if he reclined.

The baby was very good about all of this disturbance and actually coordinated its schedule, rather accommodatingly, to Constante who often held the child to her breast while she prepared some suggested 'home remedy' or other for Joseph—none of which was effective.

Joseph continued to maintain his carpenter shop, though the

joy he had found in his work faded considerably as the struggle with his illness became a major battle.

One night, he was especially ill, and although Constante tried to comfort him, he pushed her away, surprisingly not apologizing for his behavior. He almost acted coldly toward her, but she attributed his conduct to his sickness. That day, she had seen him talking outside the cabin to some Indian, a Chippewa she believed by his appearance. It was unusual to see members of this tribe within the walls of the fort, though the Ottawa were a common sight.

When she asked him why the Indian had come to see him, he told her, rather sharply, that the Indian wanted him to make a wooden spear shaft and would pay in furs. When she pursued the topic, he shouted at her to forget about it and leave him alone. For the rest of that day, he seemed to view her with scorn, and refused any kindness at her hands.

As his condition worsened however, his mysterious attitude softened, especially in October as Indian summer came upon the straits and he had to give up working and became confined to his bed. Constante tried every remedy presented to her by concerned neighbors (with the exception of the priest's suggestion to pray). No one seemed to be able to help Joseph.

By the time the first snow flew, the coughing had abated somewhat, and he sat up at the table for the first time in weeks to share tea with her. He even suggested that perhaps returning to his work might be beneficial, but Constante would not hear of it. At such times, when he was calm and lucid, she would notice how he stared at her, as if he were trying to read her thoughts. His own expressions varied from deep frowns to pleasant smiles, but she never quite understood what was going on in his mind, and he would not say.

In April, the coughing was so much worse that he found it almost impossible to breathe. In addition, his chest suffered a continual burning sensation and a knotty lump, somewhat discolored, appeared at the lower part of his neck, just above his collarbone. He became feverish and occasionally delirium followed. Twice in that terrible month, Constante called for Père Du Jaunay, convinced by her husband's choking that he would not survive the night. Yet each time he seemed to rally and the symtoms would become milder for awhile, except for the tumor on his neck, which grew constantly larger.

By May, the tumor had reached elephantine proportions and was pressing against Joseph's besieged larynx, further complicating the already difficult respiratory process.

During all of this critical time, no one could have been a more devoted wife than Constante. She was nurse, cook, comforter. She had not been alone with François at all for the last few months, the freezing weather preventing any personal contact. They had communicated with each other by means of notes passed under doorways and occasional glances from a distance. Once, they had touched hands briefly while drawing water from the well, but François knew that this was not the time to press his ardor and he contented himself with patience and the sure knowledge of her love. As the warm weather approached again, Joseph no longer seemed to be able to find the strength to make any kind of retaliation against the enemy which assaulted him. On the fourteenth day of May, Constante and François met again in the lovely meadow. She had left her husband in the capable hands of the priest, and their infant son was securely housed with Domitilde Langlade. Both the good Father and the Ottawa woman had readily agreed to assist in freeing Constante from her nursing duties to both spouse and child to allow her some small time to walk and wander by herself. But by previous arrangement, she knew François would be meeting her and she walked with eager deliberation eastward, away from the fort.

She returned, later that sunny afternoon, feeling whole and healed again. François always stayed behind in the forest, hunting for game and not returning until the purple dusk settled, to avoid suspicion.

As she approached the water gate, young Jean-Paul Langlade came running toward her. In excited, and somewhat slurred speech, he managed to communicate to her that her husband had taken a bad turn and was at the brink of death. The priest had sent him to find her.

She rushed to her home breathlessly to find Du Jaunay kneeling next to the bed, his rosary in hand. The stricken carpenter lay there, the purple tumor making an ugly contrast with his pale skin. When she entered, the Jesuit shook his head sadly, and patted Constante on the shoulder as he left them to their privacy. Joseph gripped her wrist hard as she approached their bed. His eyes captured hers with his reproachful stare. He opened his mouth as if to speak, shut it again, then spoke slowly, working hard to produce each sound. What emanated from that tortured throat would remain with Constante always.

"I know. You . . ." he coughed viciously and winced at the pain which rotted him. With herculean effort, he continued: "You and Cardin. I know. I . . . know, and . . . I forgive."

She stared at his emaciated face, horrified. He squeezed her wrist, smiled in the peculiar ugly, yet beautiful way of his, and released his last agonizing breath from his body, seeming to melt into the mattress in the process.

When Père Du Jaunay reentered the room, he found Constante in a swoon, sprawled on the wooden floor, the dead carpenter still holding tightly to her wrist as if to drag her with him to the other side.

🦋 🦋 🦋

THIS FUNERAL CONSTANTE DID ATTEND. Père Du Jaunay did his very best to console her, but it was obvious that this second tragedy had driven her completely away from God or any connection with the church, and almost away from him as a friend. She came to Ste. Anne's for Joseph, and Marie Coussante who lay beneath her feet. She wept bitterly for them both.

This inconsolable grief surprised many of Joseph's friends who, though they were very fond of Constante, had never believed that she cared very much for him. If they had known her heart, they would have understood that if the circumstances of his last moments had been different, if he had carried his knowledge of her disloyalty to the grave with him, she could have mourned him briefly, waited a decorous, respectable period of time, then shed her black widow's weeds and married François, living joyfully thereafter with her great love and their son.

But, like her father, he had laid a burden of guilt on her with those few, brief, terrible words, which would scar her permanently and continue to haunt her conscience, building an indestructible wall between her and fulfillment. Joseph had known enough of her from the beginning to capture her vacant soul if not her love. Now he would continue to hold her, by preventing her from ever enjoying any kind of life with his rival. He left behind a false devotion as well as a false heir, but they were better than nothingness and he had not questioned, only controlled.

So Constante mourned for herself as much as for him. She could not bring herself to hate Joseph (another victory), but neither could she bring herself to marry François.

The funeral was long and difficult. Cardin attended, but made no attempt to communicate with Constante. He secretly and guiltily rejoiced over Joseph's demise, for he expected that now freedom would be theirs and elusive fulfillment could be accomplished. He would be patient now, for hope was not distant, but sat grinning upon his shoulder.

Constante did not look at him at all during the proceedings, but he rationally assumed that this was for the benefit of public appearance and that soon, perhaps by winter's approach, they could be snuggled together in his cabin, a joyful family of three with, perhaps, more members to follow. Secrecy could be eliminated and they could display their affection openly and securely.

As they committed the body of Joseph Ainsse to the little cemetery plot annexed to the church, and Père Du Jaunay read the last rites and prayed for his soul, Constante stood stoically by, tears cascading, holding her infant son stiffly.

When Joseph had been interred, she received the sympathies of their neighbors, and warm embraces from the Bourassas. She rejected many offers of company that afternoon, including the priest's, stating quietly that she wished to be left alone to grieve in her own way and she promised to end her seclusion soon.

The day passed slowly for Constante. It was warm and the sun shone brilliantly, perhaps to mock her mood. She spent the remainder of that afternoon and evening, rocking her baby, feeding him, talking to him, cooing in his ear and kissing his chubby cheeks.

While he napped, she went out to Joseph's workshop, found

a sturdy box, and brought it back inside, packing it with linens. As the sun set on the opposite side of the straits, she lit a lamp, sat at the table, and composed a short message on a piece of paper. This she fastened to the little box. She emptied the cedar case that Joseph kept under his bed and found fifty *livres*, which she also placed in the box. Then she sat by the fire to wait. She did not sleep.

At three o'clock, she took Joseph Louis from his crib and placed him in the box, covering him with the linens. She blew out the flickering lamp, threw her *fichu* about her shoulders, lifted the little box with its beloved passenger, and stepped outside into the darkness.

As she crossed the parade ground, she looked down lovingly at her child who, in spite of the disturbance, slept peacefully. She walked deliberately to François' cabin and set the box down carefully in front of his door. It was only then that she recognized that it was the same box that Joseph had used to remove the corpse of Marie Coussante from their home.

She leaned over the box, to look again at that sweet, living infant face, illumined by the soft moonlight, and sobbed aloud. Frightened by her own sounds, and fearful of discovery, she kissed her son on his forehead in desperation, put her hand over her mouth to muffle any more unwanted noise, and rushed tearfully away. She did not look back at the little box. She did not pause to look at the Bourassa cabin where she had been so happy. She did not look at her own home as she ran sobbing through the gate toward the beach, past the empty sentry box. As light dawned, she moved quickly along the shore until she found the opening to the meadow. There she flung herself to the ground sobbing, and retched violently. In a few moments, she struggled to her feet, moaning in despair, and plunged into the dark and unknown forest beyond.

Chapter

6

'Akewaugeketanso'

About a month after Constante Chevalier Ainsse disappeared from Fort Michilimackinac, that is in the summer of 1745, the British captured the French island fortress of Louisbourg. This citadel, considered by many to be impregnable, guarded the entrance to the mighty Saint Lawrence, and therefore the direct path to the two major settlements in New France, Quebec and Montreal. When it fell, the central object of French strategy became its recapture.

In the following year, a French fleet undertaking this mission was decimated by storms and disease and failed to even get close enough to see the intended target.

In 1747, another French fleet with that same objective was badly defeated on the open sea by the vastly superior naval forces of the island nation which so bitterly opposed them.

A realistic admission by the French government of the inferiority of their navy initiated a change in strategy which manifested itself in a series of raids along the Canadian–New England–New York border in 1748. Although these skirmishes did not accomplish a great deal in themselves, the assistance that the British gained from the Iroquois Confederacy convinced French officials that Indian alliances were invaluable and that the friendship of the tribes of the northwest must be courted.

Though the peace of Aix-la-Chapelle, signed in October of 1748, officially ended hostilities between the colonial powers in North America, there was little doubt that belligerence still remained and both sides set about acquiring as many allies as possible in preparation for a major conflagration that would settle the problem of colonial suzerainty in the Americas permanently.

With this end in mind, the French colonial government in Quebec sent François Duplessis-Faber to Michilimackinac to replace Jacques Legardeur de Saint-Pierre who, although he had done an estimable job as commandant, was not as familiar with Indian dialects and cultures as his replacement, who had gained much valuable experience in this regard by living among the Indians in his youth, his mother being half-Potawatomi.

Upon his arrival at his new assignment, Duplessis-Faber immediately asked to speak with any French families who had Indian relatives or connections. He was disappointed after his interview with the Amiots to discover that Marie Amiot no longer had any contact with her relatives and had not for fifteen years. Her husband, Jean-Baptiste, was also a disappointment since he worked for the priest and was more interested in his smithy work than in politics or warfare.

When the commandant met the Langlades, however, he was overjoyed. The father, middle-aged and graying, was a trapper and did not wish to leave his business to become involved in a struggle which he knew little about. But he had two grown sons, and they impressed him.

The oldest wore only Indian garb and though he carried the Christian name of Jean-Paul, it was clear from his shaved head, pierced ears and general demeanor, and the ease with which he spoke the Algonkin tongue that he was more Ottawa than French. He was twenty-two or three and, best of all, he possessed a truly genuine and admirable hatred of the *Anglais.*

His younger brother was more of a puzzle. Though clothed in formal French attire, including a stiff and formal black cravat over a white lace *jabot,* he did not look at all French. He was five feet nine inches tall, squarely built and heavy, but not corpulent. His black, shiny hair hung loosely about his shoulders and he owned the high cheekbones and black eyes which characterized his mother's people. His high forehead bespoke intelligence and his nose was prominent if for no other reason than it was the only Gallic feature he possessed. He was a year younger than his brother and, much to Duplessis-Faber's delight, shared his enmity toward the English. Though a sober young man in contrast to his personable brother, the commandant could tell that great passion lay just below the surface of that stern *façade* and he genuinely liked the man.

Charles Langlade, though he would not display it, was also fond of the young and warlike commandant who craved action and adventure as he did and disliked diplomacy. It was apparent that they would become fast friends, and Charles invited him to the Langlade house to discuss what he had in mind over dinner.

On a fine summer evening in 1750, Commandant Duplessis-Faber crossed the parade ground where he had personally been drilling his garrison of twenty-six men for the last three days and approached the cabin of his host. As he came into the dooryard, he noticed a man sitting in front of the cottage next to the Langlades'. The man played with a little boy of five or six, whose remarkable resemblance to him led Duplessis-Faber to believe that he was the child's father.

The Langlades later informed him that the man's first name was the same as the commandant's own and that the boy had been adopted by their neighbor when the child's 'real' father died and his mother mysteriously deserted him.

The man seemed to love the little boy a great deal and his kindness to the child, coupled with a certain aura of tragic sadness, impressed the commandant as he greeted the man with a polite *bon soir* and knocked on the cabin door of the Langlades, noting the peculiar turtle-shaped hinges.

He was greeted by Domitilde very graciously. She was quite plain, he observed, and growing plump in her middle-age, but her warm smile made her seem much more attractive than she actually was. She had prepared a sumptuous repast, and while they ate heartily, Duplessis-Faber shared his intentions. He addressed himself primarily to Charles though if someone had asked him why, he would not have been able to tell them.

"The Fox people, in the land of the Illinois," he began between mouthfuls of roasted whitefish, "have levied a toll on passage through the Fox River which, as you probably know, is necessary for travel through that country. The *Anglais* have encouraged them in this as French settlers have been competing with them for the land."

"The Fox, aghh," Charles interjected, drawing two fingers across his face in a sign of disgust and imitating a spitting action. "They, like the Chick-a-sau and Sauk, are barbarians."

Jean-Paul imitated the gesture, while Augustin smiled good-naturedly at his sons.

"My intent," continued their guest, "is to take a force down to the Illinois country and break the blockade and end the toll. But I will need the help of many of your people who love the French king."

Charles answered calmly: "I can find many warriors to fight the Fox. When do you wish to go?"

Duplessis-Faber said: "As soon as it can be organized, a week from now, perhaps?"

"Three days, no more," Jean-Paul said. "We will be ready in three days."

"Au-san-aw-go, my brother," Charles interrupted. "We will need the week."

"Why? I will talk to La Fourche tomorrow and he can have his warriors ready in three days or less."

"You are my older brother and friend," Charles rejoined, "and I would not undertake such an opportunity without you."

Jean-Paul beamed at the compliment.

"How, then," continued Charles, "can the Ottawa leave on such a journey without consulting and inviting their older brother?"

At this, the French officer looked confused as Jean-Paul nodded his head in acknowledgement of his brother's wisdom.

Augustin explained. "The Chippewa, Ottawa and Potawatomi are allied in the Council of Three Fires." (The commandant knew this from his Potawatomi childhood, but said nothing.) "All are related, but the Chippewa were created first, then the Ottawa and the Potawatomi last. Thus the Chippewa are regarded as the elder brother, the Ottawa the middle, and the Potawatomi the younger. Charles is saying that his Chippewa brothers, in deference to their age, must be informed of the expedition and invited to attend. To not do so would be a strong insult, since it does not involve a tribal problem, but one which affects the welfare of all who support the French and detest the *Anglais.*"

"I see," the soldier said, feigning ignorance. "I'm not aware of all of the customs of the Ottawa. You have a week then. This will be enough?"

Jean-Paul nodded his head in affirmation.

Silence reigned briefly. Domitilde, still unused to the idea of her sons making decisions for themselves, rose from the table and fetched their young guest some brandy. Augustin had developed a taste for it since his gift from Cardin, and kept a regular stock on hand.

As she poured, the commandant revived their conversation in order to satisfy his curiosity. "One question more, *s'il vous plaît.* Monsieur Langlade," this he addressed to Charles, "you called your brother Au-san-aw-go, the Squirrel. This is his name *aussi?*"

Charles favored the commandant with one of his rare smiles. "I know, *mon ami,* it is a child's name and my brother is a warrior. But he cannot part with it. It is used only in affection by our family now, and by our Ottawa friends. He is generally referred to by his Christian name among all other people."

Jean-Paul grinned foolishly.

Duplessis-Faber's question showed some grasp of the Algonkin tongue and impressed Charles further. Few soldiers knew any Indian dialect and though he had been raised among the Potawatomi, their language was slightly different. The Langlades were to discover that this bright and energetic man knew several Indian dialects.

Conversation lasted longer than the brandy, and when Duplessis-Faber finally took leave of his hosts, it was close to midnight. As he left their cabin, he expected to see no one, due to the lateness of the hour. But he noticed their neighbor again, and he observed how solitary the man looked, sitting in a chair outside the window of his cabin, illuminated by lamplight from within. He was smoking his clay pipe and staring at the sky as if he expected the starry heavens to open up and reveal some dark secret.

🦫 🦫 🦫

As ANTICIPATED, Charles and Jean-Paul had little trouble convincing their Ottawa brethren to join in their enterprise. La Fourche, now regarded as an *Ogema* (respected leader), was able to convince most of his warriors to go and thirty-seven drew the wampum through their hands. This accomplished, the brothers turned their attention to the Chippewa, and made a visit to their camp.

Minavavana, now thirty-eight years old, greeted them as they approached and invited them to sit in council around the community fire. He welcomed them warmly and listened assiduously to their proposal, after smoking *kinickinick* and inviting them to share in some rum which he called 'English milk.'

Jean-Paul, as always, was fascinated with the tattoo of *Michimak-i-nac* on his torso and marveled that the animal actually seemed to move across his barrel chest when Minavavana exhaled and inhaled.

After listening to the full account of the proposed venture, the Chippewa chief pondered for a moment, then spoke: "My young brothers," he began. "I am pleased that you have come to us to offer your hand in friendship and to consult the elders of our Council of Three Fires before you act. You show great wisdom for your youth." He paused momentarily, rubbing the bald sides of his skull to wipe away the perspiration that had formed there. "I personally would be honored to fight the Fox slaves and their *Saugunash* masters. I will consult the other warriors of my clan and answer for them in the passage of three suns."

Both Jean-Paul and Charles were about to interject that they really didn't have a great deal of time for decision-making, when they were distracted by the roguish laughter of two youths, perhaps fifteen or sixteen years of age, who had crossed the village commons and were approaching a small, bark-covered wigwam which seemed, by intent, to be separated from the rest of the camp. The Langlades understood from Minavavana's cheerful greeting that the one athletic-looking youth with braided hair was his son, Wenniway. The other, it was explained shortly, was an Anishnabeg youth from a more southern village. His name was Matchekewis, the son of Eagle Crow.

As they drew near to the isolated hovel, Charles noticed a

white woman in dirty rags, suckling an Indian baby in the mud outside the wigwam entrance. Even in her filthy condition, Charles and Jean-Paul recognized the beautiful widow of Joseph Ainsse, now absent from the fort for over five years. She had simply disappeared one night, leaving her child with their neighbor, François Cardin. As much as they had assisted him in searching for her, her trail had ended in the forest just beyond the meadow, and they had heard nothing about her since.

As Wenniway and Matchekewis approached her, she put her head down close to the child at her breast, her dirty blonde hair hiding her frightened face from view. Wenniway stood next to her and uttered something which, to Charles and Jean-Paul, was unintelligible. She reacted by shaking her head from side to side. At this gesture, the other Chippewa youth became upset. Matchekewis grabbed her long hair and yanked her head back violently, forcing her to look at Wenniway who stood before her. He grabbed his groin in his right hand and signaled with his left for the miserable woman to enter the wigwam. Again, she shook her head no. This time, Wenniway raised his fist, striking her violently across the mouth, knocking her down. Her child began to cry over the disturbance, and tears ran from her eyes, matching the little red streams of blood flowing from her nose and mouth. Matchekewis added a kick in the back of her ribs for good measure.

Charles glanced over at Minavavana who seemed to enjoy the proceedings, watching his son with paternal pride, winking at Charles as he noticed him looking his way. Jean-Paul looked angry, but wisely said nothing.

The woman finally relented, placing the wailing child in the bough of a pine tree nearby and lacing him to it so he would not fall. She glanced through her rapidly swelling eye in the direction of the Langlades and froze, appalled, when she recognized Jean-Paul and Charles. Another kick from her tormentors brought her back to her situation and she hurried into the wigwam, the two Indian boys pinching her buttocks as she stooped to enter, and laughing hysterically.

Minavavana smiled happily as if the noises of whooping and grunting inside the hovel, and the screaming of the woman and the neglected child were the most pleasant of sounds.

When Charles inquired into the woman's presence in their camp, the chief simply replied that she was a 'whore,' and of no consequence.

After explaining the need for haste in the recruitment of his people, and sharing with the Grand Saulteur the essential plan of attack, the Langlades were about to leave when they spotted Jean-Baptiste Cadotte and Jean Cuchoise, who lived permanently among the Chippewa and had taken Chippewa squaws, coming toward them. As they greeted one another. Wenniway and Matchekewis emerged from the wigwam, grinning and adjusting their loincloths. Matchekewis called back into the entrance, making some reference in his guttural Algonkin to her expertise, and threw a piece of meat, taken from a pouch at his side, into the doorway of the wigwam. A dirty, delicate hand reached out to pull it inside, and no further appearance was made by the pathetic creature until long after the Langlades had left, despite the cries of her child.

🏵 🏵 🏵

On their short journey back to the fort, Jean-Paul and Charles discussed what they had learned from Cadotte concerning the presence of Constante Ainsse in the Chippewa camp.

The warrior, Tcianung, had found her in the forest near their camp, laying unconscious and half-starved, over five years ago. She had obviously been without shelter or sustenance for several days and was in a very weakened condition. Natomah, Tcianung's wife, had nursed her back to health, and Cadotte, hearing of her presence in the camp, and having acquired the friendship of her deceased husband on their journey together to Montreal, came to see her and return her to the fort.

She begged him not to and pleaded that she would take her own life if forced to return. She told him emphatically that no one was to know of her whereabouts. Cadotte told the Langlades that this had puzzled him a great deal until, upon an incidental conversation with Tcianung, it was discovered, from his description of her liaison in the meadow with Cardin, that she was an adulteress and her own shame over her scandalous behavior had probably motivated her disappearance and desire for anonymity.

Cadotte said he had tried to explain to her that the Chippewa had little use for unfaithful wives, and that in their culture, the guilty party would have had her nose cut off to mark her permanently and alert other potential suitors to her infidelity. Further, he explained that these women were often reduced to prostitution for survival and were referred to as 'anyone's woman.' Since she was not a member of their tribe, the former punishment was unlikely, but the latter was a real possibility since no self-respecting warrior would take her into his lodge once he knew of her past, and she would not be able to survive on her own.

This seemed to frighten her a great deal, and she almost left, but she was still weak from her ordeal and really had nowhere else to go. What terrified her to distraction, was the unexpected appearance of François Cardin in the camp, asking questions concerning her location. Cadotte had lied at her request and not revealed her whereabouts, but it had been very difficult to watch Cardin's face fall, walking away, slump-shouldered, as if he held the weight of the world on his back, his disappointment bitter and hard.

After François' initial visit and subsequent return the following week, still with the same object, Constante had decided to stay in the camp, regardless of the consequences. She had found some small pleasure in the companionship of Natomah and the care of her five year old daughter, Lo-tah, until Tcianung, in a moment of drunken lust, had raped Constante. Natomah, returning early from picking wild blueberries, had found her husband in the midst of his debauchery, and had struck him with the birchbark vessel she carried, scattering berries all over. He rose quickly, striking her back and knocking her to the dirt, shouting in rather pious terms that the woman was an adulteress and meant nothing.

This seemed to assuage Natomah's anger with her husband to a considerable extent, but she let it be known that she would no longer suffer the 'whore' to abide under her roof. Tcianung had grabbed the half-naked and hysterical Constante and thrown her bodily from his wigwam, apparently appeasing his wife's wrath in the process and restoring matrimonial harmony.

Cadotte had believed, he said, that the experience would send her rushing back to her own people and damn their opinions of her, but she stayed, sleeping underneath trees and accepting scraps of food from unattached Chippewa males, who now sought her out. It no longer made any difference to her. Death was death.

Cadotte explained that he had built a small shelter for her and she had remained there until the band had broken camp and moved south in the fall of that first year. She had gone with them. Cadotte assumed that she had remained in the wintering grounds and he had not seen or heard from her for several months until she had returned with the tribe in the spring, carrying with her the infant.

When Jean-Paul inquired as to who the father was, Cadotte said that it could be just about anyone, but she called the child Sans-Père.[1]

Cadotte revealed that he had talked to her only a few days ago and she had confided to him that her only wish was to end her life, but that she was too cowardly to do so, and perhaps someone might do her that wonderful favor soon.

Thus, he said, the Langlades had seen her in her present miserable existence and he was convinced that she was in utter terror of discovery. Would they keep her secret?

Charles quickly agreed, but Jean-Paul was reticent. Could she not be rescued from her situation? They all knew by now the extent of Cardin's devotion. Would he not be willing, in spite of her obstinacy, to rescue her and deliver her from her private hell?

Cadotte's belief was that no man would want her now, and to expose her to their neighbor would only cause them both grief and upset their child. It was better, he thought, if all concerned believed her to be dead and maintained the status quo. Cadotte promised to look after her as much as his time and suspicious wife would allow.

This seeming the most sensible course of action, Cadotte thanked them and bid them *adieu*.

---

[1]Meaning 'without a father.'

As they returned home that evening, they saw Cardin teaching Joseph Louis Ainsse how to whittle a cedar branch with François' skinning knife. The child sat on the man's lap, obviously fascinated, as the small whistle took shape.

Charles walked inside immediately, but Jean-Paul, sensitive to the contrast between this domestic scene and the suffering of the child's mother, paused. The boy giggled and seemed delighted as Cardin put the finished product to his lips and made the branch sing. It seemed ludicrous that the missing member of this family was only half a league away.

No one but Jean-Paul knew of the true devotion and love of Cardin for the unfortunate woman he had seen earlier in the day. He, unlike the rest of his family, had heard François' description of the whole sordid business one night when both had consumed too much brandy. He knew how Cardin had searched for her—still searched for her, though less frequently as time passed and hope withered. Jean-Paul knew what a good father he was to the boy and how he had paid no attention, in spite of his handsome features and many opportunities, to any other woman.

Jean-Paul opened the door to his parent's cabin. It squeaked on the turtle hinges that were beginning to show evidence of rust. That night, unable to sleep, he looked out the window and saw Cardin sitting in his chair outside, staring vacantly at the wide universe above.

Something that Cardin had repeated on several occasions during their personal talks suddenly came to mind. "I would forgive her anything," he had told Jean-Paul, "if only she would come back to me."

🦋 🦋 🦋

Two DAYS BEFORE the French and their allies were to leave Fort Michilimackinac for the Illinois country, the Bourassas welcomed their lovely daughter home from Montreal.

In the six years of her absence, she had matured from a child of nine into a young woman of fifteen. She had arrived toward evening in a forty-five foot long *canot du maître* which had been smoothly guided through the wilderness by several trustworthy *voyageurs,* hired for that purpose by her uncle and paid for by her father. Ignace, her brother, had been gone for two weeks, determined to meet his sister en route, and he had hooked up with the small party somewhere near Georgian Bay.

She had become a lady beyond the Bourassas' greatest expectations. Her sophistication and poise, as well as her knowledge, forced them to believe that the investment and separation had been worth it.

She stepped daintily from the canoe in a fancy lace dress of pink and white with a matching parasol to keep the fierce sun off her fair skin. Domitilde worked hard to keep from laughing at the outlandish outfit, with its hoop skirt bulging, so obviously incongruent with the frontier environment of Michilimackinac. She later confided as much to her husband and was surprised and taken aback when Charles, who had overheard, snapped at her, accusing her of jealousy and indicating that her remarks were motivated by envy.

Domitilde was obviously hurt by the remark and Augustin shouted at Charles angrily for the first time in his life. Their brooding son, not comprehending himself the reason for his outburst, begged his mother's forgiveness and even put his arms around her and smiled. But he looked at his father with dark anger.

The morning after her arrival, Charles decided to make a visit to the Bourassa cabin. He told Domitilde, now in much improved spirits, that he had been negligent of his neighbors for some time and should correct his unsocial behavior. Besides, he said, he wanted to invite Ignace to join them in their campaign against the Fox.

When Domitilde hinted that perhaps his sudden concern for the Bourassas' feelings might in some way have something to do with the arrival of their very beautiful daughter, he scoffed and frowned, pulling the door shut sharply behind him.

After his departure, Jean-Paul and Augustin, both smirking, said they believed that there might be some truth in what she said. After some raucous laughter, Jean-Paul announced that he was leaving to do some recruiting of his own with their other neighbor, the one without the pretty daughter. Domitilde stated that she would be happy to watch his son if François should decide to go.

Charles was received with much enthusiasm by René and Marie, while Ignace flung his arm around the shoulder of the friend he had known since childhood. "Welcome, good Charles," Ignace chirped happily. "You have come no doubt to see my sister, her majesty Charlotte, Empress of the Americas." He bowed solemnly with great exaggeration toward the subject of this jest who stood by the hearth, her flushing cheeks contrasting with the light blue dress she wore.

"I should have stayed in Montreal where gentlemen do not embarrass ladies with sarcastic banter," she retorted.

Charles watched her stride across the room toward him, as if her face and arms were protruding from some fluffy cloud, so elegantly and softly did she move.

She held out her hand to him and much to her surprise, he took it and kissed it gently, his long, black hair covering his face and part of her arm as he did so. *"Enchanté, Mademoiselle,"* he smiled, straightening. "We are so pleased to have you back among us."

Charlotte turned to her brother. "You should take lessons," she said, "from Charles."

Charlotte loved his cavalier attitude which, in itself, was indicative of a romantic spirit. She thought he was well-formed, and she regarded with pleasure his sturdy frame. Yet the physical attribute she admired most was his eyes. He was not shy about his appreciation of her beauty and the way he stared boldly at her face and figure excited her. Even as a child, she had known there was something particularly attractive about him, but she couldn't quite pin it down. He was a strange combination of courtly gentleman and erotic savage and though he *looked* barbaric in some respects, he was the perfect aristocrat. This duality fitted her very well for although she appeared the perfect picture of refined femininity, she could be very savage in her own way.

He had always thought of her as beautiful from the time he had first smiled at her as a child when returning from the raid on the Chick-a-sau. In the past few years, she had become refined and genteel, but he knew that there was a basic toughness about her that would suit her to frontier life, contrary to Domitilde's prediction.

As they stood speechless, drinking in each other's closeness and devouring each other with their eyes, the additional occupants of the room became somewhat uncomfortable and René Bourassa cleared his throat, bringing them temporarily down to earth. "My dear young friend," René began. "We are so happy to have you here. Do not credit the bickering of my children. They are entirely devoted to one another and . . . perhaps to you." He winked at Charlotte, who gave her father an embarrassed scowl. "My Charlotte has become quite a young lady now. She will one day equal her *mère* in beauty and grace." He placed his arm around Marie and kissed the top of her head, a habit which had developed because of the differences in their height.

"The Bourassa household is blessed to contain two such beauties," Charles said gallantly.

Madame Bourassa scolded him for being so foolish, but she was obviously pleased with the flattery. Her daughter also was not unaffected by his charm.

"Please, be so kind as to sit down and relieve me of the burden of my brother's empty jests," Charlotte said. Although she invited Charles to speak and tell her about all that had transpired with him in her absence, she did most of the talking. She described the beauty of Montreal and the gaiety and sophistication of that noble city, but she seemed more at home, she said, among the forests and waters of the straits. Though she had been educated to city life, she only felt comfortable in the wilderness, and since her parents had spent a good deal of money on her education, she intended to put it to good use by introducing others in this area of the world to 'proper society.'

Charles appeared to listen intently and nodded his head solemnly at every salient point, but he really heard very little. He watched the way her blonde curls bounced when she displayed a special enthusiasm for some subject. He adored the way she wetted her lips with her tongue when she ventured on to some thesis, the length of which she knew would require special lubrication to complete. He enjoyed immensely the sing-song continuity of her voice as she blithely skipped from one topic to the next. In short, he loved everything about her.

Eventually, her obsession with the city which had been her home for the past six years waned, and she looked to relinquish the floor to someone else. Ignace took the opportunity to ask Charles if there were some special reason, other than to be bored by his sister's narrative, why he had come.

It took the young half-breed a few moments to tear his eyes away from Charlotte and focus his attention on the subject at hand; but once accomplished, he related the inevitability of the French-English conflict and suggested that Ignace might want to join in their raid on the Fox.

Ignace seemed very enthused about the prospect and quickly assented. Charlotte's mood suddenly changed and she became very quiet. Though she said nothing, her very silence indicated that her gaiety had deserted her. She was obviously worried about the safety of her brother and their guest.

When Charles took his leave of them, the atmosphere in the Bourassa cabin had changed from joy to apprehension and he felt badly that he had, with the exception of Ignace, been the cause of their dampened spirits. Charlotte had made him promise to guarantee their safe return, a commitment he was not sure he could keep.

As he returned to his own cabin to prepare for the journey, he saw Jean-Paul next door, engaged in animated converation with François Cardin. When he asked his brother later that afternoon if François intended to go along, Jean-Paul said he did not think so. Moments later, François knocked at their cabin door, asked Domitilde to watch his child (a request which had been granted so often that Joseph Louis looked upon the Langlades as family and addressed Domitilde as *ma tante*[2]) and left the fort at a hurried pace, apparently on some urgent errand.

---

[2]My aunt.

FRANÇOIS RUSHED ALONG toward the Chippewa camp like a man possessed. He tore his clothing and his skin on thorny hickory bushes, but thrust them aside, feeling no pain. He ran headlong through the forest, oblivious of the noise he made and the fierce burning of his lungs caused by the long sprint from the stockade, along the beach, and through the meadow which had once been the scene of great happiness for him. Now Hope had returned, and pushed him insanely forward.

When Jean-Paul had told him of Constante's presence, he had not been kind. Without mentioning her name, he had described the woman in the camp and her condition, leaving out no detail. He had wanted to be bluntly straightforward, and his honesty was brutal. But when he said the name 'Constante,' the rest of the story seemed to evaporate in François' memory and he had rushed away as soon as he could sensibly provide for their son. For some reason he was not sure of, he went to the priest first and told him everything. The good Father listened patiently to François' description of their infidelity, her tortured conscience and eventual flight from the fort, as well as the brief history of her life with the Chippewa and her present circumstances. He did not appear to be shocked or surprised, but an expression of such complete and tender sympathy dominated his smooth and understanding countenance, that Cardin sensed that he had known much of what he had told him already, or had suspected as much. He simply said; "You must go to her now. I will follow shortly."

François' frantic passage through the morass of thicket and foliage came to a sudden halt as a Chippewa warrior stepped from a green copse and stood resolutely in his path. The Indian was called Maingaus (Small Wolf) and he was often chosen for this kind of sentry duty because of his lupine ferocity and sense of the intruder. He was only one of several sentries who surrounded the camp.

Cardin stopped abruptly and signaled impatiently that he wanted to pass. He had been to the camp before, and rarely been delayed. Maingaus did not know him, however, and since the stranger could not explain his reasons for desiring passage because of the language barrier, the Chippewa had no intention of allowing him to continue. The sentry did not understand the desperation of the man before him, but he did comprehend a belligerent action when he saw one as Cardin drew his knife from his belt, obviously intending to fight his way through.

Cardin was suddenly surrounded on all sides by four other fierce-looking Ojibway and he began to realize that his thoughtless abandon could cost him dearly.

Fortunately, at this point, the *coureur de bois,* Jean-Baptiste Cadotte, emerged from the arboresque wall behind Maingaus and, acting as interpreter, was able to persuade his Ojibway brothers that Cardin was not a threat and they should allow him to continue. After the Indians had melted back into the sylvan woods, Cardin explained his purpose and Cadotte, reluctantly, but realizing that her secret had been revealed, agreed to lead him to Constante.

The sun was rapidly disappearing from the sky over the straits when Cardin stooped to enter the wigwam where Cadotte had brought him and then departed.

He barely recognized the filthy creature who lay in the dirt next to the dying fire as the radiant beauty who had dominated his thoughts and dreams for so many years. She was sleeping fitfully, snags of greasy hair hanging in a face that was bruised and swollen. She wore the remnants of a grimy deerhide dress. Her bare shoulders and thin legs, still shapely and feminine, were soiled and her bare feet were caked with mud. The hut was empty except for the fire and a small child who lay snuggled in a bed of leaves and pine branches a few feet away.

François stared at her for a moment, shocked by her uncleanliness and emaciation. She had lost a great deal of weight, and as he drew close to her to push the hair from her eyes, the odor made him withdraw slightly.

She turned from her side onto her back and in doing so, she mumbled his name. He moved closer to her then and with his face above hers he whispered: "Yes, my sweet, I am here."

She opened her eyes slowly and smiled at him, holding out her arms dreamily. She believed, in fact, that she was dreaming, but when he touched her hand, she withdrew it quickly and her eyes popped open, almost starting from their sockets. With dawning horror, she realized that he *was* here, looking at her, an expression of barely concealed disgust on his boyish face.

She scrambled backwards on her knees across the dirt floor until the wall of the wigwam prevented further flight. Her back was against the bark surface. She faced him in terror, shivering with fear. This confrontation was too horrendous to bear and she had to think of some way to escape the unbearable humiliation of his presence.

"Constante," he pleaded. "I love you. Come away now. Be done with this."

She laughed bitterly. "I am a *gourgandine,* my sweet—a whore. If you have the payment, I will be happy to serve you."

She could see this wounded him deeply and knew she had found a weapon with which to drive him off. He stepped toward her.

"I am happy in what I do," she sneered. "The Ojibway have ways to make a woman happy. Would you like me to tell you what they are?"

His eyes clouded with tears, but he did not retreat. He stared at her in disbelief, but she did not detect any loss of conviction. He stepped toward her again and this time she rose in a rage. "I hate you," she sobbed. "Get away from me. Leave me alone!" The venomous glance she threw at him made him halt.

"Do you want to know about our child?" he asked softly. This broke the hard veneer and she began to weep bitterly. But as he came to her and grasped her arms, she broke away and slapped him hard across his face. "Can't you hear me?" she shouted angrily. "I hate you! Get away from me!"

"Constante, I love . . ." he began, but she cut him short by spitting into his face. He stood looking sorrowfully into her cold eyes, the spittle dripping from his cheek. Seeing no regret or bending of her determination, he released her, turned away, and left.

Her eyes followed him out the opening to her hovel, then went to the little child who whined briefly before returning to sleep. She watched the infant for a few moments, but did not pick him up or succor him in any way.

With tears of sorrow and anguish floating down her bruised

and tortured face, she set her mind to a task she had been contemplating for several months, determination and final decisiveness evident in every motion.

She went outside, searching the area behind her isolated wigwam until she found a piece of a thick log. She dragged it back inside, the weight of it causing her to breathe heavily in exertion.

She pulled it into the center of the dwelling and hastily untied the rawhide cord around her waist. She stood on the log and threw one end of the cord at the ceiling, about two feet above her outstretched hand, making several attempts before it looped over the sturdy sapling that held the roof in place. She tied off the loop and wound the rest of the cord around her neck until it was taut. Her tear-stained, dirty, bruised and swollen face was rigid in grief. "François," she whispered. Then, without a moment's hesitation, she jumped from the log and swung into the air.

At precisely that moment, Père Du Jaunay pushed his shoulders through the entrance. As she choked, he grabbed her legs and forced her body upward, relieving the constricting garrot around her throat. "My God, Constante, my poor child," he mumbled under labored breath. Her arms hung limply at her sides and she did not struggle at all. The priest was helpless to do anything but hold her up, praying that she was still breathing.

Fortunately, François had not gone far and his overwhelming devotion had enabled him to cast aside his doubts and return to Constante. As he approached the wigwam, the sounds of the struggle inside reached him and he hurried forward.

The sight he beheld as he entered almost caused him to vomit as he watched in horror the poor priest trying to hold aloft the filthy, thin, wretched creature he loved so dearly, and keep her breath from draining from her forever.

It took sharp words from the struggling Jesuit to bring him to his senses and, drawing his skinning knife, he stepped up on the log and cut the cord from Constante's neck.

🐚 🐚 🐚

WHEN SHE REGAINED CONSCIOUSNESS, Constante was immediately aware of the warm sensation of lying in a clean bed and
the delicious odor of some sort of broth. She was completely disoriented and for a moment believed herself to be back in Montreal and the shadowy figure beside her bed to be her father.

But as her vision cleared, and the shadow clarified into the
benevolent face of Père Du Jaunay, the hellish vision of herself
stepping from the log and the life choking from her came wing-
ing into her mind like some demonic spirit, and she fainted.

Several hours later, unwanted consciousness returned to
torment her again and she wept bitterly as she saw the priest still
standing vigil, like some sentinel at the gates of hell.

After she had cried until it seemed that every drop of fluid
had been drained from her body, the priest, in perfect silence
and composure, forced her to take some sustenance in the form
of the broth she had smelled earlier.

She took it, reluctantly at first, but the wonder of such a
beautifully prepared and aromatic concoction after years of
scraps of tallowy meat, often rancid, was too much to resist and
she consumed it hungrily.

When the last drops were gone from the bowl, she looked up
at the priest guiltily, as if she had just committed some terrible
offense by taking pleasure in a meal. She waited quietly for him
to speak, fully expecting words of rebuke spoken in vituperative
reproof. But those words did not come. His thoughts instead
were spoken with commiseration and compassion.

"My dear child," he began, "how happy I am to see you again.
I have missed our conversations. Your absence has left quite a
void in my life and your return fills it again." He put his hand on
her forehead and rubbed it gently.

She tried to speak, but her throat was very sore and the abra-
sions on her neck burned slightly from salty perspiration. Tears
of anguish and shame mixed with gratitude were wiped away
softly by the priest's indulgent touch. After a few moments, she
took some water and attempted to talk again. The words came
slowly, but with perfect clarity. "François?"

"He is here, waiting. He will not come until you ask for him,"
the priest assured her.

She seemed relieved by this, but also very frightened. She knew she was in the rectory now, inside the fort. How could she face him? How could she face her son? What would Marie Bourassa and Domitilde think of her?

Père Du Jaunay could see what was going through her mind by the wild-eyed expression on her emaciated face. He said: "Let he who is without sin, cast the first stone."

"What?" she asked.

"The words of our Master, Constante—in reference to an adulteress. The Lord took her in His loving arms and forgave her and sent away her accusers with those soft words. He forgives you and me, too. You are His child, His creation. He died for you. Are you not worthy then to live?"

"I have crucified Him again Father. There is no escape from my guilt," she said, almost inaudibly.

"Constante," the benevolent priest asserted, "there is no guilt with Jesus Christ. The guilt you possess in your heart is placed there by *you*. Replace it with your Saviour and He will drive the guilt away and you can begin your ascent to atonement and happiness, free of that kind of misery."

She looked at him long and hard, then pleaded: "Help me, Father!"

He grasped her hands and held them between his own as he began to pray fervently. She closed her eyes, trying to reach for the God she had never known, but needed so badly.

In the months that followed, a gradual healing took place in Constante which was physical, emotional and spiritual. Her first meeting with François was difficult, but he knew what had happened to her and he was very willing to let it go and make it a part of the past, burying her guilt with his own.

Her son, Joseph Louis Ainsse, had no words of recrimination for his mother. He was only happy to learn that he *had* one and his youthful embrace, accompanied with the words *ma mère,* did much to accelerate the healing process.

It had been Père Du Jaunay's suggestion that her other child, Sans-Père, should remain among the Chippewa with Constante's past. The boy would be happier there, he convinced her, and make her adjustment to life in the little French community less burdensome. It was arranged through the good offices of Jean-Baptiste Cadotte, that he should be raised by Wawiekiumig and his squaw, Au-saw-way, who were childless. Though she was reticent to part with him, the child whose father had raped her was unquestionably tied to the horror of her life with the Chippewa, and she had been prepared to abandon him when she attempted suicide, knowing that no child among the Ojibway was ever left uncared for. Her concerns about his welfare thus assuaged, she acquiesced, providing the Chippewa agreed to never inform him of his real mother or her degradation. This was accepted by Minavavana and his people and Constante became a 'non-person' to them. When next they saw her, she was treated as a stranger, as if her experience with them had never occurred. She often wished that she could erase her memory that easily, but every time she saw a Chippewa about the fort (which was not often), the terrible affliction of those miserable years swept through her, and caused her to isolate herself for days before being coaxed by the priest back into the society of her fellow creatures.

François was her constant rock throughout the difficult adjustment period. It was he who nursed her back to health, who kissed her gently, who comforted her and reassured her of his undying love. He forced her to face the Langlades and Bourassas, both of whom accepted her with forgiveness and treated her with kindness and respect. Young Charlotte gave her one of her beautiful dresses to wear and the two women became close friends.

Time worked its healing slowly but with certainty. Constante's emaciated frame began to fill out, the scrapes and bruises began to fade and Charlotte made it her special project to attend to Constante's hair, molding it in the latest Montreal *coiffure*. In short, she began to look herself and, to an extent, be herself, as much as her scarred psyche would allow.

Much of her psychological and spiritual restoration was the result of Père Du Jaunay's effort. He was gentle and yet persistent in his evangelical attempts to bring this lost sheep back to the fold. His stories of the Good Shepherd and the Prodigal Son had a profound influence on her. Yet she enjoyed the story of

Mary Magdalene more than any of the others and marveled at this woman's devotion to the Lord Christ. In time, Constante came to identify with her and, moved by the sanctifying Spirit, began to attend Sainte Anne's, the scene of such sorrow, now overcome by faith.

Two months after her return, on July 6, 1751, Constante and François were married in Sainte Anne's by Père Du Jaunay and witnessed by friends. On that day, the ghosts of Monsieur Chevalier and Joseph Ainsse were finally laid to rest.

❧ ❧ ❧

THE CAMPAIGN AGAINST THE FOX in the Illinois country resulted in a spectacular triumph for the French from Michilimackinac and their Indian allies.

They had broken the Fox toll of the river and opened it up for free passage to the French explorers and settlers who were moving in increasing numbers into the area. This victory had been accomplished in a pitched battle which had taken place near the river's edge only a hundred yards or so from the main Fox encampment. Though François Duplessis-Faber had been the titular leader of the attacking force, the Chippewa had followed Minavavana into battle and the Ottawa, La Fourche.

Charles and Au-san-aw-go were with a small group which included Ignace Bourassa, Okinochumaki, and several other Ottawa, led by their scarred chieftain. They were assigned to attack the enemy's flank, while the main force of French regulars and Chippewa attempted a frontal assault.

In the first endeavor, the attackers were thrown back by the Fox and their Sauk allies, leaving La Fourche's group temporarily isolated. As the Fox prepared for another attack to their front, they began to realize that the small group annoying the side of their body of warriors was in a precarious position and turned their full attention there, forcing La Fourche to retreat.

The French and Ottawa withdrew to a naturally defensible position near a bend in the river which was strewn with fallen trees, eroded by the constant movement of the water against the shoreline. Here they took their stand, using the trees to protect themselves from the onslaught of the angry Fox, hoping that the main body of French and Chippewa would regroup and mount their second offensive soon.

At present, Charles knew, their Charlevilles would keep the Fox at a distance, but when the powder and shot were gone, they would have to engage in hand-to-hand combat and numbers would eventually destroy them. Several young Ottawa warriors, attempting to display their courage, jumped from their protected positions and actually charged the Fox. They were quickly dispatched; the head of one of them, a friend of Okinochumaki, was severed and, after being relieved of its scalplock, thrown in among the fallen timbers, landing with a dull thud near La Fourche.

Charles, concealed behind a large log and seeing what had transpired, sprang from his cover and grabbed the lead Fox warrior who was spearheading the offensive against them. Ignace and Au-san-aw-go watched from nearby as he bashed the head of his enemy against the log which had shielded him, and then dragged his unconscious foe over the timber as arrows whizzed around him.

Moments later, the closest Fox infiltrator was struck in the chest by the severed head of his compatriot and he shouted in fear and anger at the Frenchman who, having hurled the disgusting missile, now calmly held his musket sight steady and put a hole between the eyes of his startled enemy.

Thus fortified by the courageous defiance of, and disdain for, the superior attacking force by his nephew, La Fourche led his group forward just as Duplessis-Faber and Minavavana resumed their frontal assault, throwing the bewildered Fox into confusion and flight.

Ignace had been so inspired by Charles' tranquil bravery, that he leapt from the protection nature had provided and rushed forward at the enemy, firing off his Charleville as they retreated. Unaccustomed to Indian warfare, Ignace was unaware that often older warriors, who had little time left for warfare, would refuse to retreat and remain behind, selling life dearly and leaving behind an oral monument which would endure around family and clan fires for many generations.

Just such an individual appeared from the surrounding brush as Ignace halted to reload his musket. Charles spotted him approaching the young Frenchman stealthily from his blind side. Cognizant of the danger to his friend, and the promise he had made to Charlotte, he ran forward, shouting his warning, with Au-san-aw-go and Okinochumaki on his heels.

Ignace whirled in time to dodge the hatchet which had been intended to become united with his head and to see Charles leap on the back of the old Fox warrior and stab him repeatedly about the neck and shoulders until he collapsed in a torrent of blood.

Ignace winked at Charles who smiled briefly, then the two of them rejoined their group in the routing of the Fox.

After the battle, scalps were taken, the great logs blocking passage on the river were dispersed, the Fox village was burned, slaves were taken and booty packed for the return journey.

As they assembled on the banks of the river to embark in their canoes, La Fourche recounted the battle, honoring the names of those who had fallen and lauding the military prowess of their French and Chippewa brethren.

He then addressed Charles, calling him forward, and looking proudly into his solemn eyes. His grizzled visage beaming with pride, he placed his big hands on his nephew's stocky shoulders and proclaimed to his people: "Behold, the warrior Akewaugeketanso!" The cheers of the French and Indian army resounded throughout the forest.

Chapter
7

La Damoiselle

Upon THEIR RETURN to Michilimackinac, the Chippewa and Ottawa were greeted at the beaches near their respective villages as heroes, while the French returned to the fort to be enveloped in the arms of their loved ones.

Charlotte Bourassa was waiting outside the water gate, looking anxious, her arm entwined around her mother's waist and holding René's hand. She was delighted to see that her brother was alive and well and equally grateful to discover that Charles was among the survivors. As Père Du Jaunay helped to unload the dead and wounded, the Langlades came through the gate, greeting their sons joyfully. Domitilde, in the absence of her brother, unabashedly showered them with kisses and hugs until Charles, who could tolerate no more, impatiently told his mother to stop. She did, at least as far as concerned Charles, but she continued it with Jean-Paul who seemed to relish the attention.

It was not long before all the tribes of the area and the community in the fort had heard of the heroics of Charles Langlade. Ignace was terribly enthusiastic in his description of his friend's preservation of his life, and the Bourassas' gratitude was reflected in an invitation to dinner, several days after their return. Augustin butchered one of the domesticated pigs kept in the sty behind the cabin, and Marie prepared a delicious *languier* (pig's tongue), especially for the honored guest.

Throughout dinner, Ignace described how Charles had severed the head of the lead warrior and tossed it defiantly at the charging Fox (leaving no detail to the imagination), until Madame Bourassa turned quite pale and asked to be excused.

Such graphic illustration did not appear to disturb Charlotte, as dainty as she looked, but rather excited her. As she seized an opportunity to watch him, Charles continued to consume the tongue throughout the story and she wondered to herself how anyone so awfully savage could be the picture of decorum and taste. In chameleon fashion, his colors seemed to adapt him to his environment.

As they enjoyed tea and the men a pipe from René Bourassa's *andoville,* Ignace again recounted the story of his rescue by the refined, richly-clothed young man who now sat opposite him. "You should have seen it, Charlotte," he mused, "to see your idiot brother reloading his musket, contented to let some murdering Fox dispense with him while he blindly fiddled with his piece."

"I'm sure I should be glad not to have been subjected to such a sorry scene," she said.

Ignace laughed. "If not for Charles, some old Fox would be using my hair for his judicial wig."

Charlotte wrinkled her nose at the joke and smiled seductively at Charles. "Monsieur Langlade," she said, "you are far too humble. You say nothing."

"Au contraire, Mademoiselle," he said, puffing contentedly on a pipe. "Your brother exaggerates my poor abilities with such a flair, that for me to interrupt and correct him to a more truthful expression of what occurred would be to my disadvantage. Better to be silent and let him leave you with some good impression."

"Nonsense," Ignace protested while Charlotte and René laughed at Charles' wit.

"Nevertheless," Charlotte continued, fingering her pretty blonde curls, "we are forever indebted to you for preserving my brother. He is simple at times" (with this she winked at Ignace), "but we love him dearly. I'm glad you are a man of your word and kept your promise."

"I hope," Charles replied, "that this opportunity to partake of the pleasure of your companionship is not restricted to a sense of debt, and that I may be allowed to see you again soon."

Charlotte's cheeks flushed and she flashed her pretty blue eyes at her father. Taking the hint, René said: "Our household is open to you at all times, Charles, though you'd best be careful or Charlotte will have the warrior dancing the 'quadrille' or the 'minuet'."

Charles looked puzzled.

"They are dances," Charlotte explained, scowling at her father, "and the *only* person who seems to have any desire to learn them around here is Constante. Thank God for her society or I should waste away for lack of proper companionship."

"Are you referring to Madame Ainsse?" Charles queried.

"Madame Cardin," Marie corrected as she reentered the room looking somewhat rosier than when she had left it.

"I don't understand," Charles responded.

"Constante was brought back from the Ojibway village. She was terribly ill and was nursed to health by Cardin, our neighbor. They became very fond of each other and his devotion to her son made them a natural couple. They were married only recently and we have become the best of friends." Charlotte was very enthusiastic in the description of her new companion. "She is so intelligent and thoughtful and very like a sister to me," Charlotte continued.

Charles remembered the scene he had witnessed at his meeting with Minavavana and he was happy for the unfortunate woman's escape. But he wondered if Charlotte knew the real background of her friend. He said nothing.

"They are so happy together. François is a good man and she will be a faithful wife to him."

Charles smiled pleasantly. "A good wife is hard to find," he said finally. "I hope to do well someday in that regard."

"Perhaps you will," Charlotte teased. "Until that day, however, you may have to tolerate my company."

🦂 🦂 🦂

CONSTANTE CHEVALIER AINSSE CARDIN awoke one morning a week after her wedding and stretched her limbs luxuriantly. She turned on her side to look at her dozing husband and pinched herself to be certain that she was not dreaming. Having reassured herself, she kissed François lightly on the forehead and got out of the bed that he had built for her to replace the straw-stuffed mattress upon which they had first made love.

She pulled aside the little privacy shield consisting of blankets suspended from ropes which sealed off one corner of Cardin's cabin and formed a bedroom of sorts.

She went first to the hearth and stared down at her son who slept soundly in a hammock attached to the thick, shiny logs which supported the roof. This makeshift bed was designed to be taken out of the way during the day and lowered almost to the floor at night to take full advantage of the warmth from the nearby fireplace.

Constante smiled as she watched the innocent face of her son, so sweet in its repose. He looked remarkably like François. She saw so little of herself there except, perhaps, for the fuller mouth and cheeks. He was a darling boy, she thought, never angry, rarely depressed. He always seemed to get along with others and he had a keen mind for languages. He was constantly bothering Jean-Paul to teach him Algonkin, and he took every opportunity to practice. He loved to accompany François on his trap checks and though he had never been told that this wonderful man was his real father, he treated him as such. They had decided to leave him the name he had been baptized with in Joseph's honor. To Constante, it seemed somehow like a little victory, for both her and her deceased husband. He had gotten what he wanted most out of life; now she could pursue her own happiness and that happiness centered around François and this child.

She went, on occasion, to Joseph's grave outside the church and planted flowers there. She even talked to him sometimes and tried to explain what he would never have been able to comprehend in life.

This morning, she smiled at his nominal heir and sat in the chair by the table in the center of the room. She began to pray, as had become her matins habit. The priest had been right. Peace *was* found in this deep and silent communion with God. Nothing else gave her quite as much satisfaction, or eased her guilt as completely. While talking with God, she somehow felt as if she were conversing with Magdalene or Peter, Thomas or the criminal on the cross. It was as if her once miserable spirit found union with these other Fallen, and their spirits, now pure and mingling with hers, white-washed her soul and she could feel clean again.

Having eased her guilt, she went to the wash basin and cleaned her face and hands. She fussed with her hair, put on a dress, and was ready then to fix a meal for her husband and son.

Following a pleasant breakfast in which much lively conversation took place and loving glances passed between her and François while little Joseph babbled on about nothing, she hiked across the fort commons to the church to make her daily confession and volunteer in some small capacity, to assist Père Du Jaunay. When he protested, she insisted that she felt a tremendous need to serve the Master somehow and this, she told him, appeased her and, she was convinced, pleased God. He put her to work cleaning, and smiled to himself.

She spent her afternoons visiting the Bourassas and Charlotte (who practically idolized Constante's piety and devotion), and made herself useful to others by tending to the sick, babysitting, or any other myriad number of chores. She was even able to face Charles, who bowed politely to her and said nothing of his encounter with her in the Chippewa village.

Evenings were reserved for her family, and she and François often sat on the beach talking quietly, working the past away in words, and watching the red sun sink below the horizon while Joseph built fortresses made of sand.

🐝 🐝 🐝

As CHARLES AND JEAN-PAUL GREW OLDER, they spent less and less time at the Langlade cabin. Charles, of course, spent the vast majority of his time with Charlotte, and those moments passed quickly.

It was not long before they were stealing innocent kisses from one another and it became apparent to both Domitilde and Marie Bourassa that their children were devoted to each other and would eventually marry.

Yet in those hours away from his beautiful friend, in his own solitude, Charles found little peace. He was restless and anxious and the only thing that seemed to interest him much was news about the military and political situation in New France received from the various traders and *voyageurs* who visited Michilimackinac. Trapping and fishing bored him and he longed to be in the center of the conflict which he was certain would begin soon. He spent much of his day closeted with Duplessis-Faber, pumping him for information, and his nights were frequently passed at *L'Arbre Croche,* conversing with his uncle.

Jean-Paul lived almost exclusively in the Ottawa village now. He too had become attracted to a woman, an Ottawa maiden of sixteen years named Nodinens (Little Wind). He spent many hours watching her and finally, without ever having spoken with her, asked for her hand by offering her father three knives, four wool blankets, a new hatchet, and several casks of English rum, taken from the Fox.

The happy parent had agreed to the match with the provisions that Jean-Paul live among the Ottawa at *L'Arbre Croche* (a task too easy to refuse), and that he publicly receive his *ododem* (totem mark).

The Ottawa believed that *Nanabozho* had created the earth, and formed man from the dead bodies of the first animals. Each clan then had their own totem, or animal insignia, indicating from which creature their family had sprung. Ka-re-gwon-di, Jean-Paul's genetic father, had belonged to the *Me-shay-wag,* or elk clan and, therefore, Jean-Paul was initiated into its mysteries and given his tattoo, the antlers of an elk, inked into the skin on his right shoulder.

By the conclusion of the summer, he was married to Nodinens and had his own lodge in the village of *L'Arbre Croche.* He did visit Domitilde and Augustin regularly, but his life with them —and Charles—had come to an end. The little boy who had always been more Indian than French, slowly lost any semblance of his French upbringing as he grew to manhood.

One day, Charles was at the village, visiting his uncle and brother, when their mutual cousin, Wawatam, joined them. His squaw, Tibikki, had given him a son, now almost two winters, and she was pregnant again. Wawatam, carefully instructed by the Chippewa *shaman* Ishnoki, had become a practicing member of the rattlesnake cult, and the necklace he wore was decorated with the fangs of that viper.

He had grown wise and mature far beyond his years, and La Fourche had become very proud of his adopted son. He had the mystic's far-away look and avoided conflict whenever possible as disturbing to the spirit. He was not a warrior, but a priest, and highly respected as such, both among his own people and the Chippewa elders.

As Wawatam settled himself next to his relatives outside La Fourche's bachelor wigwam, he was greeted with enthusiasm. "My wise cousin," said Charles. "I am so pleased to see you again. It has been many days since I have had the pleasure of your company."

Wawatam lowered his head solemnly in recognition. "I thank my friend and brother for his kind words," he rejoined in his deep voice, "but my heart is heavy for the bad news I bring. Spirits of evil walk the land all around us." He swept his hand in an arc as if to indicate the universe. "Here there is peace," he said, "but the Ottawa must arm themselves to prepare to drive away *Pau-guk,* the Evil One, and his demons."

Charles waited for him to continue, but he simply sat, legs folded, eyes staring, trance-like, over Jean-Paul's antlered shoulder. La Fourche, though very pleased with his heir's prophetic ability, often became impatient with his figurative language and dreamy attitude, which demanded forbearance on the part of the listener. Finally, he could wait no longer. "The French," he said, "have built a line of stick houses (forts) along the southern mountain river (the Allegheny). La Damoiselle, the great war chief of the Piankeshaws, has led several raids against these strongholds in the service of the *Anglais.* He and his people have become infected with the English milk which makes men crazy." He circled one finger around his ear to illustrate, his copper eye catching the bright autumn sun. "My son has seen a vision in which the *Anglais* and their worthless allies break down all the stick houses and drive our French brothers away."

"What must we do?" Jean-Paul asked, thinking of Augustin and Domitilde.

"We fight!" Charles answered.

🐚 🐚 🐚

HE WAS RELUCTANT to leave Charlotte, and though her sweet, concerned face haunted his mind, Charles was glad to be moving again, applying himself to some purpose.

Jean-Paul bade farewell to his wife as did many other Ottawa. The French regulars in the fort had been ordered to stay put in the event of any British surprises from Canada and the Chippewa had declined to get involved, since it was so near the time for removal to their southern wintering grounds. So the Ottawa left in a small force of about thirty-five, counting Langlade, Cadotte, Ignace Bourassa, and a few other French volunteers.

François had tried to convince Constante to allow him to go, but she would not hear of it. She had learned from others that the chances of success were as small as the expedition's numbers and she refused to risk her new-found happiness for any cause on earth. Charlotte had cried bitter tears after Charles and Ignace left her in the comforting embrace of Constante and the Bourassas, convinced that she would see neither of them again.

As it turned out, her fears were unfounded. They returned once again to the straits with more slaves and more glory heaped upon their heads. This time, Au-san-aw-go had been the hero, rallying their small force to defeat the Piankeshaws who were twice their number. He had eight scalps to his credit and a nasty wound in his leg where an enemy arrow had penetrated just above the knee joint. But he walked proudly erect among the people of his new home, and La Fourche bragged continually about his nephew's courage.

Charlotte had run to Charles when she saw that he was alive and well, and only inquired about her brother after checking him over carefully. Ignace kidded her about it for months afterward.

La Damoiselle had been captured alive and returned to the straits with his captors. He stood stoically by while Charles and Jean-Paul greeted their parents and Domitilde attended to the latter's wound. Duplessis-Faber offered his congratulations, appearing chagrined at having to miss all the action.

That night, the prisoner-chief was staked to the ground in the center of *L'Arbre Croche* and handed over to the women while the men relived the battle around a communal fire.

Tibikki and Nodinens joined in the torture of La Damoiselle and placed bets to see if they could raise a scream or look of fear from this noted warrior. An old Ottawa squaw with a canine face and mottled complexion who was called, appropriately, Kitsamo (Spotted Bitch) and whose son had been killed on the raid against the Piankeshaws, instructed the younger women in the intricacies of causing pain.

They jabbed sharp, dry thistles under his toenails and fingernails until they bled, then set them on fire so that his cuticles were charred. They placed hot coals on his nipples and groin, plucked out his eyelashes, broke his teeth with rocks, burned his hair, jammed pointed sticks into his ears and eyes, and generally did everything in their power to reduce him to a mass of quivering jelly. But the Piankeshaw chieftain was equal to the task. Not only did he not cry out, but he laughed defiantly each time they applied some new technique and his courage so impressed the Ottawa that eventually the men drew around his mutilated body to observe and they encouraged him with words like, "stay strong," and "well done."

Just before dawn, after over five hours of agonizing torment, and now unrecognizable as a human being, La Damoiselle's valiant heart finally stopped, and the women moved away to other work, frustrated at their failure, while La Fourche arranged a cannibalistic breakfast of the corpse in honor of their victory and their enemy's fortitude.

Jean-Paul expressed his appreciation of La Damoiselle's courage during their grisly meal to Wawatam. His cousin simply replied that he should consume as much of the Piankeshaw's valor as possible, for they would need such bravery in the months to come.

Chapter

8

The Great Council

WAWATAM'S VISION of a time of sorrow and foreboding manifested itself in 1753 when Commandant Duplessis-Faber, whom all in the fort esteemed as a strong and noble man, and who was revered by the Indians for his gift-giving and genuine friendship, died in an unfortunate accident.

He had tripped over a chair in his quarters (apparently moving about in the dark, as he was found dressed in bedclothes and no lamps were burning), and struck his head on the fieldstone hearth. He had been a bachelor and lived alone. When his adjutant found him in the morning, the top of his head had been burnt and blackened because of its proximity to the fire and he was pronounced dead immediately afterward by Père Du Jaunay.

Charles mourned him especially, and was disgusted with such an ignoble end to a noble man. He was buried with full military honors and a beautiful eulogy was delivered by the priest, but Charles struggled with it nonetheless, fearing it to be a portent of things to come. His great comfort was Charlotte's loving companionship.

The new commandant, Louis Lienard de Beaujeu, was actually an old one, for two reasons. First, he was almost seventy years of age, and secondly, he had been Fort Michilimackinac's first commandant, and had supervised its construction back in 1715.

Charles believed that perhaps his age would make him a man of peace, at great cost to French integrity and territorial claims,

166

but he was pleasantly surprised to learn that the exact opposite was true.

When Beaujeu asked Charles to visit him in his quarters, he was very much aware of the storm that was gathering, without any visions to assist him and he told the young man so when informed of Wawatam's clairvoyance. The French government, he insisted, would need the military aid of every Indian tribe in the Northwest and, in pursuit of the object, he suggested that an invitation be sent to all of the tribes within reasonable traveling distance of the straits to attend a general council and discuss their positions relative to their fealty to France. He asked Charles to make the necessary arrangements, promising to have many gifts for his red brethren to bolster their patriotism.

Charles happily agreed, delighted to be engaged once more in some adventure which would alleviate the mundane affairs of day-to-day existence.

Runners from *L'Arbre Croche* were sent in every direction; some were absent for weeks in their attempt to communicate the message to distant tribes.

The response was more than Charles and Beaujeu could have reasonably expected. In July, tribal leaders began gathering around the fort, establishing temporary villages. Chiefs of many different nations and bands were constantly in and out of the fort for much of the summer, conversing individually with Beaujeu. Charles acted as interpreter for the commandant and was fascinated by the various leaders who represented the Huron, Sac, Miami, Winnebago, Minominee, and Potawatomi. Sixteen different tribes had sent spokesmen, from people as close as the Ottawa of *L'Arbre Croche,* to the Sioux of far away Wisconsin.

Even enemies of those who lived nearest Michilimackinac, such as the Fox, were in attendance as well as delegates from many different bands of Ojibway and Ottawa.

Minavavana, as well as his eighteen-year-old son, Wenniway, and the *shaman,* Ishnoki, represented the Chippewa village where Constante had suffered her purgatorial sentence.

The *L'Arbre Croche* Ottawa sent La Fourche and his adopted son, Wawatam, as well as Okinochumaki and Jean-Paul Langlade, although the latter were considered too young yet to speak or vote.

The great Chippewa chief called Le Grand Sable was there from the village along the Bay of *Saugenaum* in the south. Charles was fascinated with the physical power of this man who, it was said, had grabbed in his right hand, the fist of some unfortunate who had decided to strike him, and slowly applied pressure until every bone in the aggressor's hand had been disjointed or broken. Charles believed it possible, looking in awe at his muscular frame which stretched over six feet and weighed in excess of two hundred and fifty pounds. The chief was bald, except for the hair in the center of his head which was as erect as porcupine quills from his forehead to the nape of his neck, held in place with glistening bear grease. His most prominent feature however, was the tattoo of a snake, slithering down his forehead between his eyes, to the end of his nose.

He and Minavavana seemed to have been previously acquainted and Charles guessed they might even be related, but would not be so crass as to inquire into something as personal as family affiliation.

Young Matchekewis, Wenniway's friend of the same age who had so abused Constante as a teen-ager, represented the Ojibway group from *Che-boy-gan,* about twenty miles southeast of the straits. He had distinguished himself at a very early age for his courage in battle and at every competitive recreation. He was not noted at all for his wisdom or judgment and he was unnecessarily cruel, vices which his bravery oftened concealed. He looked confused and wild-eyed and though he spoke little, his actions were so erratic and his habits so reckless that there were those among his people who called him 'whirlwind.'[1]

Even his good friend Wenniway, Minavavana's son, feared him. Because stability and consistency were so lacking in his nature, the closest of companions could never predict his reactions. Once, his anger had gotten so uncontrollable (the object of his rage being his toe, which he had stubbed against a root) that he cut off the offending appendage, explaining to Wenniway that it would never cause him pain again and it had been given a lesson

---

[1]A common Ojibway expression synonymous with 'insane.'

in submission.

Another time, he tortured a dog to death with fire because it had awakened him. The irate owner had gone home from his encounter with the wild young man, the not-so-proud possessor of a new scar which Matchekewis' knife had engraved across his chest.

Generally speaking, most of his own tribesmen avoided him or, failing that, took pains to keep him calm. Eagle Crow, his father, was dead, and rumor had it that Matchekewis had been the cause, but this was unsubstantiated. He lived with his mother whom he ruled like a tyrant and she was always relieved when he went north to visit Wenniway's village.

Yet when it came time to do battle, he was always the first to plunge into the fray, fighting with such abandon and reckless courage that on more than one occasion he had led his people to victory. Thus, at this very young age, he had become a war chief, and though he could contribute little wisdom to any council, he was nevertheless entitled to attend and did so with swaggering pride in his own importance.

He and Wenniway were habitually together at the council. Minavavana's son was always recognized as being the smaller of the two young men, as well as the one who had two braids on either side of his square face, one painted yellow, the other red. He wore an otter hat which resembled, in form, a Moorish turban. He was very proud of this headdress, a gift from Matchekewis, and he was never without it though it made his appearance almost comic.

Minavavana, a wise and cautious leader, was also a very indulgent father. He saw only the best in Wenniway and once his son had attained the age of eighteen, took him everywhere. He had insisted that the young man be allowed to attend the Great Council too, and have the right to speak, regardless of his lack of stature as a chief or *shaman*. Langlade had convinced Beaujeu to relent, arguing that the Grand Saulteur was needed at the council. Several of the great chiefs assembled at Michilimackinac resented Wenniway's presence and were irritated by the juvenile conduct of the young man and his friend, who were too fond of rum and full of self-esteem, swaggering among the temporary encampments, spewing *braggadocio* and offending their guests.

At the opposite end of the spectrum of leadership was the Ottawa war leader, Pon-ti-ac, who had come to Michilimackinac all the way from Fort Ponchartrain at *D'étroit,* the strait connecting the lower lake with Lake Huron.

Though still only about thirty, he was always in the company of the elder chiefs and *shaman* who marveled at his wisdom. They were especially impressed with his ability to speak so many Indian dialects and his noble bearing inspired awe. He carried himself with such grace and poise, that when he entered a council or a conversation, others paused to wait for him to speak. The French immediately wanted to know who he was. At this stage in his life, descriptions of him were often legends, based in fact. Before his death, the facts would become legendary.

He was very tall and quite lean, but in a smooth, athletic way —not gawky. He wore his hair in the shaved/topknot fashion, the black pony tail looking just that, as it rose straight up from the back of his bald head and then curved downward, caressing his neck and shoulders.

His face was lean, but not gaunt, and the sobriety of his expression, often mistaken for brooding in lesser men, simply indicated a peaceful and confident seriousness and maturity.

His body was unadorned except for a plain breechclout and a necklace made of copper, deer bones, and a pendant carved from the top of a human skull. His ears and nose, unlike many of the other Indian leaders, were unpierced and he had no tattoos.

Charles remembered visiting Pon-ti-ac's village and sleeping in his lodge with Au-san-aw-go when they took part in the Chick-a-sau campaign as boys. Also fresh in his memory were the sharp words exchanged between La Fourche and Pon-ti-ac over what he later recognized as the latter's philosophy of a universal Indian brotherhood.

Charles wondered how there could be any credence to his theory. There were so many different clans and customs, such varied cultures among the Indians, that Langlade held out very little hope for it. When he was finally, formally introduced to the chieftain, Charles asked him about it.

He was surprised that Pon-ti-ac remembered him, and even

more astonished by his reply. The taller man indicated that one must look, in these days, beyond one's own family, clan or tribe for survival. The conflict brewing now was only a prelude to the coming war (or wars) which would have as its central theme the extinction of the red man from the face of the earth.

He told Charles that he had walked among the many settlements of the *Anglais* and they were more numerous than snowflakes or grains of sand. The French, he said, were alone among the white race in treating Indians with equality, respecting their rituals and customs and recognizing their intellect. Yet the *Anglais* would someday destroy the French if they weren't cautious, and this would divide the tribes into petty, quarreling factions, who in their division and indecisiveness would be trampled and annihilated.

Thus each red man needed the other in the anticipated struggle for dominion and the French must prevail in the conflict or all would be lost. The native peoples of this land, therefore, must not bicker among themselves, but rather assist the French to drive out their common enemy. "The *Anglais* must die," he said to Charles. "The *Anglais* must perish."

🐚 🐚 🐚

THE GREAT COUNCIL took place in the open spaces between the fort and the forest which bordered its eastern perimeter. Le Grand Sable was chosen to preside with Pon-ti-ac and Minavavana sitting on his right and left respectively. Charles was present, acting as adjutant and interpreter for Commandant Beaujeu.

The half-breed spoke first, as was pre-arranged, representing the French government and thus the Intendant, the Governor of New France, and ultimately the king. "My brethren," he began, "we, the children of the French king, are honored to have so many distinguished emissaries accept our invitation to *parler*. The commandant of Michilimackinac bids you welcome and offers you gifts of friendship."

Immediately, French soldiers began to circulate among the assembled dignitaries, passing out knives, hatchets, tobacco, blankets, mirrors, jewelry and other presents. Charles could tell from the grunts and smiles that his audience was pleased. It was a good start. After the soldiers had finished and things quieted down again, he continued: "As you can see, the French king loves his red children too, and wishes to protect them from any harm. My relative, Wawatam, a *shaman,* a member of the *cicigwe* priesthood, is possessed of the *Jessakid.*[2] He had a vision of the destruction of the French and their red brothers by the murderous *Anglais.*"

Upon hearing this, some of the Sac and Fox representatives began to whisper among themselves.

"The *Anglais* have no respect for the rest of humanity. They do not share their labor, wealth or food with others, but put up fences and claim the abundant land for their own, exacting tolls from others who would use it." He glanced quickly in the direction of the Fox leaders, one of whom rose and stomped away in fury. "They do not understand the relationship of civilized people with all the spirits of the non-human world. They burn and kill without regard to the souls of their victims or consequences to the realm of the *manitous.* They are barbarians."

With the exception of the Sac and Fox bands, the other tribal chiefs nodded in assent. "Therefore your French father asks his children to commit themselves to the protection of our common homeland. Who will pledge himself to this worthy struggle?"

Minavavana rose very slowly, an indication of his desire to address the assemblage. Charles, recognizing this, said: "We are honored by the older brother of the Three Fires, the Grand Saulteur, and would hear him."

"The Anishnabeg too, hate the *Saganosh.* My people will join in any effort against them. *Cawin nishishin Saganosh.*"[3] As Minavavana enjoyed the cheers of the surrounding crowd and scratched the shell of the turtle on his belly, Wenniway suddenly sprang up without invitation and shouted: "Our people would follow *us* anywhere. Death to the *Saganosh!*"

A sudden silence fell over the council and its audience at the

---

[2]The power to summon spirits at will.
[3]The English are no good.

youth's audacious outburst. The chieftains scowled at Wenniway and this, combined with the ominous silence, served to keep him quiet for the remainder of the council. Minavavana, looking awkward, seated himself next to his upstart son, apparently having said what he felt was necessary, and too embarrassed to continue anyway.

La Fourche broke the tension of the moment and stood to speak for the Ottawa of *L'Arbre Croche*. "My people," he said, "have always lived in peace, except when provoked by the actions of others." He glanced at the remaining Fox representatives. "No provocation is greater than to steal one's home or destroy wantonly what belongs to all. The *Anglais* care nothing for others and do not respect even themselves. The great Piankeshaw chief, La Damoiselle, also called 'Old Britain,' who kept an English flag over his lodge, died bravely fighting for their cause at our hands. His white allies have joked about his death, saying that he was one Indian who would not stand in their way. I commit myself to our French friends," he winked at his nephew with his good eye, "and all who will follow me."

There was a general applause, followed by hushed silence as Pon-ti-ac rose to address his comrades. "My friends, my people have lived in the shadow of the French stick-house of *D'étroit* for many seasons. These whites have always treated us with friendship, lived among us, and taken our women as their own, thus becoming our brothers in blood. The *Anglais,* however, shun us as savages, and see only themselves as worthy of life. We must resist them, or be reduced to slavery. I will be no man's slave. I will fight!"

Whooping and shouting and jumping up and down took place behind the circle of the council where young warriors and women looked on, ecstatically demonstrating their absolute concurrence with Pon-ti-ac's words. One by one the various delegates stood to voice their assent. Charles and Beaujeu were greatly encouraged because this indicated that the tribes of the northwest were predominantly allied with the French and would offset the British pact with the Iroquois Confederacy.

Only the Fox refused to enter into the verbal treaty, stating their belief that the English were no different than the French and hinting that perhaps all whites should be regarded as enemies. At this statement, even the Sac deserted them.

The younger member of the Council of Three Fires, the Potawatomi, were the last to speak. Their *Wakama,* a fierce-looking brave with bowed legs named Mshike, refuted the Fox. "The *Ktchimokoman*[4] intrude every day into *Kitchi-Gumee,* claiming this land of our fathers and the sacred ground of the *Mshi-Mackina,* for themselves. The white brothers (the French) live among us in peace and make no claims. If the Fox cannot see the difference, they are poorly named and should be called 'slug,' a title more suited to their intelligence."

This statement provoked such intense anger that one Fox warrior rushed at Mshike, determined to defend the honor and name of his people. But as he closed on the Potawatomi, drawing his knife in earnest intent, a strong arm yanked him backwards and he was struck across the face with a mule-kick blow which sent him sprawling into the dust unconscious.

As Le Grand Sable stood over his victim, Charles broke the silence again. "Perhaps if the Fox do not wish to join us, they should withdraw," he said, "before blood is shed among us. We are in council and you have violated a long-standing belief among all our peoples, including your own, that one may say what he wishes in council without fear of retribution."

The Fox leaders, acting on Charles' suggestion and motivated by their minority status, helped their stunned fellow to his feet and began to leave. But one of them could not resist a parting malignity. "You speak thus" (he directed his virulence at Charles), "because you are not true Ottawa. You are infected with white blood—it flows *red* in our veins."

Jean-Paul then began to rise, but Wawatam held him back and told him to be quiet. Charles pulled a knife from his boot, and La Fourche feared that the Fox insult was forcing his nephew to lose his own sense of decorum. Yet Charles did not attack. Instead, he drew the blade across the top of his hand, until the scarlet blood flowed freely. "You see," he said, "that my blood is red, but it makes no difference. My loyalty is with my

---

[4]Long-knives, the Potawatomi word for 'English.'

people whom I love. A man's honor does not depend upon the color of his blood, but the conviction and courage of the heart through which it passes."

A tremendous cheer arose then from the other members of the council, as the encircling crowd shouted *Akewaugeketanso* and the Fox sneaked away in disgrace.

🦋 🦋 🦋

ON AUGUST 12, 1753, Charlotte Bourassa and Charles Langlade were united in marriage by Père Du Jaunay.[5] They had grown closer and closer over the spring and summer of that year, walking along the beach at sunset, picking berries along forest trails, and sitting silently in front of the Bourassa cabin at night, listening to owls and crickets and holding hands like two love-struck schoolchildren.

Matrimony had been on Charles' mind frequently. Their neighbors, Charlotte's good friends the Cardins, seemed so happy and content. The couples spent quite a bit of time together and Charles was amazed at their devotion to one another. They spoke openly of the trials of their romance and Constante had been singularly honest with Charlotte concerning the degradation she had suffered. Charlotte had not been shocked, but rather sympathetic to her friend's distress.

When Charles seemed a bit suspicious about Constante and her motives, saying it was the first time he had ever heard of prudery leading to prostitution, he was scolded roundly by Charlotte who called him 'beastly' and 'insensitive.' Indeed, he began to feel ashamed of himself when he came to know the gentle and pious woman better and there was no question that her husband loved her to distraction and trusted her implicitly. The overcoming of such seemingly insurmountable obstacles in pursuit of their love made him realize the beauty of such faith and solid devotion. It made him desirous of that kind of happiness for himself.

---

[5]This very wedding is reenacted several times each day in a light ceremony in the reconstructed church at Fort Michilimackinac.

He thought of Jean-Paul who also seemed to be contented with his new wife, Nodinens. His brother had confided to Charles that there was no greater pleasure to be had than to make love to a woman and though he was in many ways a man of great passion, Charles was yet naïve in the ways of love. Though he played the *gallant,* he never stopped to consider the end result of his performance or believed that his flirtations would lead to such a serious situation. He both feared and desired that conclusion to their relationship.

He was unsure of marrying a French woman of such taste and sophistication. He seriously doubted if it were possible to keep Charlotte happy in a log cabin, facing extended absences from her husband, battling the everyday trials and boredom of the frontier. This was a lifestyle better suited to an Ottawa woman and that was certainly a possibility, since many maidens of *L'Arbre Croche* had looked at him slyly and sensuously when he visited. Yet he knew somehow, instinctively, that Charlotte had an innate toughness about her which was concealed beneath the surface of frills and lace.

In spite of his inner confidence, before he could ask her to live with him, he wanted her to meet his Ottawa relatives and get an opinion of her from La Fourche, who had only seen her as a child and not noticed her since her return from Montreal.

So after the Great Council had ended, he asked her to go to *L'Arbre Croche.* She was hesitant at first because they had been arguing over a Pani (Pawnee) slave-woman who had been given to Charles as a gift by one of the Sioux chiefs who had attended the Council, in appreciation of Charles' leadership and wisdom. What caused Charlotte's anger was not so much the gift itself, but the youth and beauty of same, living under the identical roof with the man she considered her own. The Pani woman (for so she was called), seemed to show no interest in Charles, nor he in her, but jealousy sprouted nonetheless and a good deal of tension existed between the two romantics for a number of days.

In spite of his icy reception at the Bourassa house, Charles did convince Charlotte to go with him to *L'Arbre Croche.* She remembered how frightened she had been of the horrible face of Charles' uncle as a child, and she was curious to see if such fear was only a childhood reflection or if the Ottawa chief really was so fearsome. It would give her an opportunity also to meet Jean-Paul's child bride and, of course, separate her beloved for a day from the Pani woman.

So one fine morning, around the beginning of August, they roamed along the beach toward *L'Arbre Croche,* Charlotte dressed in a fine, lacy gown, bare at the shoulders, and carrying a parasol to protect her fair skin from the modest summer sun.

Charles believed that the old bachelor would laugh at him for courting a delicate female who appeared to be such a *dilettante* and he secretly wished that Charlotte had worn something less pretentious. Yet the old warrior was completely charmed by her.

She was fascinated by his scars and she asked about them, giving him a chance to tell an old story to someone who had not heard it. She commented on his bravery, on the beauty of his character, on the attractiveness and cleverness of his coin-eye. She asked him to explain the tattoos on his legs. She marveled at the scalps on his lodgepole. She demanded something to sit on besides the dirt floor, but ate the muskrat that he served with vigor. She wanted to hear his stories. She asked about the bear's skull in the center of the camp and questioned why such an oustanding man should remain unmarried. In short, she delighted him and showed Charles what a skilled diplomat he had fallen in love with.

Jean-Paul, Wawatam, Okinochumaki and everyone else she conversed with that day were equally charmed. Tibikki and Nodinens both wanted to know how they could get a parasol, and she promised to find one for each of them. When she left *L'Arbre Croche,* she left behind many new friends.

Two weeks later, Charles married her. Before winter set in, they had their own cabin, with the Pani woman as their servant and a good companion to Charlotte.

Chapter
9

Ishnoki and Lo-tah

THE SUMMER FOLLOWING the Great Council and Charles' marriage, Tcianung awoke at dawn in the Chippewa camp, as was his habit, and looked over at Natomah, his *noko*. She continued to sleep peacefully on her mat, as he rose and rekindled the dying fire in the center of their wigwam. He noticed that their daughter, Lo-tah, was already gone, probably walking in the forest or bothering old Ishnoki.

Normally he would have taken advantage of her absence and the consequent privacy to awaken his wife by lying next to her and arousing himself until she would have to service him. But she had lost their third child only days earlier (the second had died two years earlier), and he thought it better not to disturb her.

As he ate a breakfast of corn and smoked fish, he looked proudly, for the thousandth time, at the feathered spear leaning against the lodge wall near the entrance. It was a very special lance, for its blade had been made by the blacksmith, Amiot, and the shaft had been carved from oak by the carpenter, Ainsse.

He was unhappy that such a skilled craftsman had died, though he had been dead now many years. They had done much business together and Tcianung had hoped that the homely man could make him a fancy war club, but that would never happen now.

He remembered the expression on the poor cuckold's face when he had told him of his wife's infidelity with Cardin in the meadow. He wondered what the unfortunate man would have thought had he known that Tcianung himself had enjoyed her, that she had become a whore in the Anishnabeg camp, and that she was now the wife of her former lover. He grinned at the irony of it and knew that the carpenter was better off dead.

He stepped outside into the shadows of the forest camp, still mostly quiet. He could hear the loons on the lake and see the mist dispelling on its surface through the sentinel pines. He loved the call of the loon. It held a special fascination for him because he belonged to the loon clan. It was the largest of the five clans of the Ojibway and, he believed with familial pride, the best.

His enjoyment of the loon's cry was interrupted by loud snoring which came from somewhere nearby. After investigation, he discovered the source. Lying among some ferns near the camp's perimeter and obviously in an inebriated condition was his brother's son, Wenniway. He must have gotten some more of the 'milk' from his vicious friend Matchekewis, who seemed to have an unlimited supply. Tcianung wrinkled his nose in disgust. His opinion of his nephew was similar to that of most of the village, and that was not good. But Minavavana seemed blind to the young man's faults and would hear no criticism of him.

Tcianung walked away, and headed through the pines to the lake to drink and bathe and perhaps hear the loons again. If Lo-tah was not at home when he returned, he thought, Natomah would have him out looking for her—again.

🐚 🐚 🐚

AS HER FATHER HAD SUSPECTED, Lo-tah was with Ishnoki. Every opportunity she had to spend with the old man was taken, and this morning was no exception. She was fascinated by his collection of snakes, by his stories about anything and everything, and by his peculiar fascination for her.

No other female, adult or otherwise, had the privilege to speak with him intimately. In point of fact, he spent little time with anyone except the most important warriors— and her. He was not convinced himself why he was so taken with the little ten-year-old, but he knew that somehow she was blessed by the *manitous* and that she would someday reach such a complete union with them that she would perhaps herself achieve divinity. Every sign he knew, every portent imaginable in his animistic faith, led him to this conclusion.

Her birth had been heralded in so many ways, that one could not avoid the reality of her uniqueness. On the morning of the day she was born to Tcianung and Natomah, a huge *masquinonge* (muskellunge) the size of a man, had washed ashore, along with the body of a large loon. Later in the day, the decomposed corpse of a crane had been discovered in the shrubbery behind her father's wigwam and a purple marten had landed on the roof of that same dwelling. Then, toward evening, just minutes before her arrival in the world, the Anishnabeg had heard the roar of the great *mag-wah* and though many hunters had searched the surrounding forest, the bear was not seen, nor any trace of it found. The next sound to be heard in the village was the cry of the infant, Lo-tah.

The great fish, the loon, the marten, the crane, and the bear all represented the five clans of the Anishnabeg. That night, a shooting star fell across the wilderness sky and Ishnoki knew with certainty, that this child was special.

As he sat and talked to her now, ten years later, her wisdom and intellectual curiosity amazed him. She never seemed to tire of asking questions of any kind and she always analyzed the answers, mulling them over with her spiritual sixth sense. Her sharp little black eyes twinkled with intelligence. Her slight, prepubescent body quivered with excitement and anticipation as Ishnoki carefully instructed and nurtured her in the mysteries of religion.

"You see, Lo-tah," he said, "*Me-daw-min,* the Sky, is our father and *Aki,* the earth, our mother. The father warms his woman, fertilizes her, provides nourishment for her, and loves her. In return, *Aki* gives birth to his many children, the oldest of whom are our people, the Anishnabeg. The many spirits which move among us and work both for us and against us were provided by *Gitchi-Manitou,* the greatest of all spirits and creator of souls."

The child absorbed all of this, then characteristically had

questions. Her dulcet voice was music to Ishnoki's ears. "What do the spirits do?" she asked.

"*Ka-be-bon-ni-ca,* the North wind, brings the snow. *We-eng* brings restful sleep, and his ugly brother, *Pau-guk,* brings death. *O-jeeg* is the spirit of fish and *Mich-i-bou,* the hare. But the greatest of all the spirit children is *Michi-mak-i-nac,* the Great Turtle, who is the special protector of the Anishnabeg. Only he is visible to us always, floating in the straits of the Great Water, *Michi-Gaumee,* and constantly on guard for his people."

Immediately another question came from the child: "How do you know all these things?" she said. "Do the Spirits talk to you?"

"Yes, child," the old *shaman* answered. "To some, special gifts are given. The West Wind, *Ka-be-yun* made love to a mortal woman and from her womb came a god-man who was born on the back of *Michi-mak-i-nac* and was named *Man-a-boz-ho.* He is the teacher of those who especially seek to know the Spirits and gives to them powers to heal and hear. These favored few are the *Midewiwin,* and I am one of them. You child, have the special gifts. Listen closely, and the spirits will speak to you too."

"Then I will one day be *Midewiwin* too?"

"No, child."

"Why?"

"No female has ever been a *Midewiwin.*"

"Why?"

"Lo-tah!" a harsh voice cried loudly, making her jump and believe that the Spirits were too quick to contact her, when she realized that the irritated voice belonged to her father.

"I must go," she whispered, rising rapidly.

"Remember, child," the amused Ishnoki said, "the voices of Spirits come from within. Listen with your heart."

She shook her head affirmatively and ran in the direction of her father's voice.

🐢 🐢 🐢

IN THE OHIO RIVER VALLEY, between the Monongahela and Youghiogheny Rivers, a young Virginian colonial officer, acting under orders from Robert Dinwiddie, the British Royal Governor of the colony, established a small, dilapidated stockade which he christened 'Fort Necessity.'

The fort was in the Great Meadows between Chestnut Ridge and Laurel Ridge, part of the foothills of the Allegheny Mountains. It was built fifty miles south of the French fort called Duquesne (after a governor of Quebec), and was established to defy French colonial claims to the area and to send a message to Quebec that the *Anglais* had no intention of allowing Louis XV to challenge what they considered possessions in *British* North America.

The young officer's name was George Washington, and he had been busy recruiting allies from among the Indians, especially a Delaware *Sachem* from Beaver Creek called Half-King. Half-King was a disaffected former French ally whose father had been killed by the French and who had been insulted by Sieur de Marin, the commandant at Duquesne, by accusing his departed parent of treason. He was more than willing to inform young Washington of French strength and military movements, to recruit other Indian allies, and to personally take up arms against them.

De Marin was convinced that the longer Washington stayed in the area, the stronger the British claim would become as Half-King convinced one *Sachem* after another to join the English cause. This development was made known to the royal governor in Quebec by de Marin.

All of this information was then directed to Commandant Beaujeu at Michilimackinac and finally referred to Charles Langlade to address to his Indian allies. Within two weeks, Langlade had gathered a force of three hundred and started south.

Minavavana, his son Wenniway, Tcianung, and most of the other warriors of their camp had gone with *Akewaugeketanso*, providing a wonderful climate of freedom for Lo-tah who now had many opportunities to visit with Ishnoki and learn from him.

From *L'Arbre Croche*, La Fourche, Okinochumaki and Jean-Paul were among fifty warriors who also went. Matchekewis brought his band from Che-boy-gan and Mshike led his Potawatomi. The French garrison provided twenty-five soldiers as well as volunteers led by Langlade which included Ignace Bou-rassa, Jean Cuchoise, Jean-Baptiste Cadotte and François Cardin.

Constante had become almost hysterical when her husband had agreed to go. She told him she hated the English for forcing such a confrontation, she hated Charles Langlade for asking her husband to go, and she hated him for agreeing to do so. She sobbed and paced and generally carried on to such a degree that he finally told her he would withdraw. Much to his surprise, she said no. She collected herself, declared that she was acting like a fool, and begged him to forgive her. He kissed her gently on the forehead, wiped away her tears, and promised to return. He knew it would be terribly difficult for her to be left alone, but it was partially to break her almost neurotic dependence on him for emotional support that he had agreed to go. Charlotte, now pregnant, agreed to stay with her, and of course the loving priest promised to watch over her and Joseph Louis.

Even so, his absence was a terrible cross for Constante to bear. She suffered as an alcoholic suffers in abstinence. Her ad-diction was, and always had been, François. Moments without him were like days and those days reminded her of earlier times when she was chained to Joseph Ainsse, or worse memories of a ragged, dirty, woman on the floor of a wigwam, chewing on ran-cid meat, the reward for. . . .

She spent much time in prayer and many hours in the com-pany of her sweet priest who helped her to stay in communica-tion with the God who loved her so much. The continual reitera-tion of his redemptive message gave her wonderful comfort. She asked Jesus for peace and received it. She asked Him for courage and it was likewise given to her. She came to be dependent on Du Jaunay to such an extent, that it became necessary for him to force another separation similar to the one she was attempting to deal with.

He talked to her one morning about it when she awakened him before dawn to help her in the recitation of her prayers and to listen to her fears about François. He had, with Domitilde Langlade, been with the Amiots most of the night, helping Marie to care for her eight children and tend to Jean-Baptiste who had suffered a terrible burn at his forge and was unable to function.

He had had little sleep, and his nerves were raw. "Constante," he told her, holding her by the arms and staring into her frightened eyes, "you have come to lean on me as you lean on your husband. I am not your husband, and François is not you. You must learn to stand up on your own and be strong."

Tears began to run down her face. She felt betrayed, disoriented and confused. She had believed that Du Jaunay would never desert her in her time of need and she was crushed by his mild upbraiding. "You . . . you had promised to always be there," she whimpered. "I believed what you said."

"I was wrong. I cannot always be there for you Constante, and neither can François or anyone else. I could die today. François could never return." At this she began sobbing hysterically, and though he held her close to him, he continued with the harsh truth. "No human being can help you, Constante. You have felt the comfort of Jesus Christ. You know He is there for you. You do not need *me* to have *Him*. Only He can be with you always and never disappoint or desert you, only He, child."

"He wasn't with me in the Chippewa village, or when my baby died," she lamented.

"Yes child, He was," the Jesuit whispered. "It's just that *you* were not with *Him*."

She stopped crying then and looked at him with eyes that were frightened, yet hopeful.

"Now you have Him," Du Jaunay said. "The only way you can ever lose Him is if *you* walk away."

"If François does not return . . ." she moaned.

"He will get you through that too. He has conquered death. He opened up the grave. You have nothing to fear—ever again."

A faint smile appeared on her delicate, pale lips. "I'm sorry to have been such a burden, Father."

"You have not been a burden, Constante," he corrected, "only an occasional annoyance."

She looked at him with such a seriously hurt expression that he began to laugh heartily and uncontrollably. Before long, she was guffawing too, and as Marie Amiot came to the door of the rectory to tell the priest that her husband was improving, she heard the hilarity inside and wondered what was so funny.

🐾 🐾 🐾

CHARLOTTE AND CONSTANTE were very close companions for the weeks after their husbands' departure. They shared their mutual burdens and worried about the future together. But as the weeks passed, Constante seemed to grow steadily stronger emotionally until it surprised Père Du Jaunay one day to overhear a conversation in which Constante was acting the comforter to Marie Bourassa and Domitilde Langlade and assuring them that in their faith, they had nothing to fear and their sons would return. The supplicant has become the missionary, he mused, and winked at Constante as he passed by.

As it turned out, their prayers were answered when Charles, François and Ignace all came back safely, having accomplished what they had set out to do. The young officer, Washington, though valiant in defense, had been forced to surrender his 'Fort Necessity' to Sieur de Marin and Charles Langlade and retreat with the remainder of his force back to Virginia.

There were very few casualties on either side and the victorious French and Indian forces were ecstatic over having driven out the British and strengthening their claim to the Ohio River Valley and the territory the English called 'Penn's Woods.' What the French did not know was that while Jean-Paul and Charles elaborated on their conquest to their wives, the British government had ordered General Edward Braddock, Commander-in-Chief of all British forces in North America, to launch a large-scale invasion of the area with its ultimate aim, the capture of Fort Duquesne.

The British authorities believed that it had been colonial incompetency and cowardice that had caused the failure of their first expedition and had therefore put this military operation in the hands of the regular British army. Washington was sent along as an adjutant, but had been stripped of his command.

Langlade had not been home more than a few months, just long enough to see the birth of his daughter, Charlotte Catherine, when he received a message from Sieur de Marin that a regular British army was to move on Duquesne from somewhere in

Virginia when spring weather made it possible to travel. Could the Sieur de Langlade enlist his Indian allies and come to their aid?

Charles immediately sent runners, and by late May had marshalled forces consisting of one hundred Canadians (French volunteers), and five hundred Indians. They arrived at Fort Duquesne in late June and de Marin was grateful for their presence.

François Cardin had opted to stay with Constante, but Ignace, Cuchoise, Cadotte, and many other Canadians were part of the force as well as the Ottawa, Potawatomi, Chippewa, Sioux, Winnebago, Huron, Miami and Minominee. The Great Council had been called to its commitment. La Fourche and Jean-Paul were particularly eager for this engagement. Having experienced the spilling of real English blood in the battle for Fort Necessity, they wanted to continue in what Wawatam had convinced them was a holy cause. Once again, Minavavana, Wenniway, Tcianung, and Matchekewis represented a portion of the Chippewa contingent.

De Marin huddled with Langlade and the various chiefs as soon as they arrived, informing them that scouts had reported that Braddock had come up the Potomac from Virginia and had left Fort Cumberland on Wills Creek with over two thousand men. He was hacking a road through the Allegheny foothills toward Duquesne. Later information indicated that he had left his baggage train under heavy guard about twenty-five miles from Duquesne and estimates were that he would reach the French fort at his present rate of progress at about mid-July.

De Marin's strategy was to keep inside the fort, wait for the British arrival, and slug it out from a superior defensive position. The French commandant believed that they could hold off any siege indefinitely and to stay inside the stockade walls gave them a decided advantage. Charles was not in agreement with this plan and told the commandant so. He explained that allowing the British to lay siege would also give the *Anglais* time to gather their Delaware and Fox allies who were presently scattered and not a threat. Furthermore, he explained, the French had a predominantly Indian army, and the long boredom of a siege, not suited to Indian tastes, would result in many desertions.

Charles presented an alternative, in which he suggested that the Indians and Canadians should conceal themselves in the woods near the fork of the Youghiogheny River and Turtle Creek, about ten miles from the fort. It was a naturally defensible position and the perfect place for an ambush. Braddock would have to pass by it to reach the fort and the Indians and Canadians understood this type of warfare much better. At the very least, their forces would weaken and cripple the advancing British army, leaving them in poor shape to attack Duquesne which would be well provisioned and garrisoned with regular French troops. At best, the French soldiers would not have to fight at all.

De Marin was hesitant at first, but the strategy made sense, and Langlade was heavily supported in his plan by the Indians and Canadians. Minavavana in particular thought that the name of the ambush site was a good omen, pointing to the tattoo of the turtle on his belly.

Finally, de Marin relented and Charles moved his forces out, deploying them as suggested and awaited Braddock's arrival. At sunrise on July 13, 1755, as the French and Indians watched from dense thickets and foliage, the British forces appeared on the opposite side of Turtle Creek. Braddock, leading the column, was prepared to cross immediately. His aide, the man Langlade recognized as Washington, seemed to be discussing the wisdom of such a move as he pointed to the opposite shoreline, apparently indicating its value as an ambuscade.

Braddock, redcoat and white wig shining brilliantly in the sun, waived aside the colonial's objections and, taking a last look at the opposite shore, ordered the column to advance. The creek was shallow but wide, and Braddock seemed pleased that nothing had happened. Several hundred British soldiers were in the middle of the stream.

At this point, Charles fired his Charleville, signaling the attack as six hundred warriors and Canadians leapt from hiding, assaulting the column, tearing it to pieces in front and moving rapidly across the creek to confront those who had not yet arrived.

Braddock, his horse shot from beneath him by Langlade's initial burst, grabbed another mount and signaled retreat, but it was too late. The British soldiers rushing up from the rear interfered with those attempting to withdraw and confusion reigned. The Canadians and Indians found easy targets in the scarlet uniforms of the British, blending themselves into the forest background and picking them off unmercifully. The water of the creek soon matched the color of the *Anglais* uniforms, and the grand British column fell into ignominious flight.

Jean-Paul, spotting the *Anglais* commander, took careful aim and drilled a ball into the officer's side. Puncturing one lung, the bullet bounced off a rib and lodged next to Braddock's heart. The mortally wounded man was lifted from the wet sand where he had fallen and tossed rudely onto a cart as Washington formed a small contingent of colonials and tried to cover the British retreat. Langlade was very impressed once again with the young Virginian and believed that greatnesss was in store for him.

Charles and his Indian allies did not pursue, but scalped the bodies of those left behind, then returned to de Marin at Duquesne and informed him that the enemy had been routed. The commandant grinned broadly when told by the excited Jean-Paul that he had an unusual scalp, holding up the wig that Braddock had lost when shot from his horse.

The victory celebration at Duquesne lasted long into the night. After a day's rest, Langlade, Minavavana and La Fourche led their people back to Michilimackinac and the other Indian bands returned to their homes. Pon-ti-ac was taken back to *D'étroit* by his followers, sporting a gaping stomach wound, but he was one of the few casualties on the French side and his injury would heal.

Braddock died on the trip back to Virginia. The British left behind four hundred dead and took back almost as many wounded. Thus began the fourth and greatest of the colonial wars between France and England, appropriately called the French and Indian War, which would last for the next seven years and settle once and for all the question of empire in North America.

LANGLADE RETURNED to Michilimackinac and hurried to the arms of his two Charlottes, who were delighted to see him, the older one covering his face with kisses, the younger layering his coat with drool and dampening his left hand which held her tiny *derrière.*

The day following his warm reception, he noticed that a new cabin was under construction next to his parents on the *Rue du Diable,* placing the Langlades in the center between the Cardins and this new occupant. He inquired of his wife who the new-comers were and she informed him that a fur trapper named Laurent Du Charme had moved his family into the fort during Charles' absence.

Langlade was awed when he met the man. He was huge, tip-ping the scales at over three hundred pounds, with a very swarthy complexion and the blackest, thickest beard Charles had ever seen. He had been born in Montreal, but the city had be-come too crowded for him and he had brought his wife, Mar-guerite Amable Metivier Du Charme, with him to settle in the wilderness. He had stopped at Michilimackinac to simply provi-sion his canoe, but had liked the area so much that he had de-cided to remain.

By the time Charles returned from Duquesne, the cabin was almost completed. All of this independent domesticity surround-ing her made Charlotte desirous of having her own home. They had been living, since their marriage, with Augustin and Domi-tilde and though his parents had been very good company and entirely gracious about sharing their home, the addition of a child, the lack of privacy and an increased wish for indepen-dence forced Charlotte to badger Charles for their own living quarters.

So it was, that Charles began construction of his own cabin, west of Cardin's, a site chosen by Charlotte to be close to Con-stante, on the *Rue du Diable.* His father, his brother-in-law, François Cardin and Laurent Du Charme all assisted him. Du Charme was a most likeable fellow, gregarious and happy, whose strength was indispensible when trying to lift the heavy logs for the walls into place. He was always joking and laughing, and generally exhibited a *joie de vivre* which those who knew him frequently envied.

Strangely, Charles did not like him. Being meticulously serious himself, and often subject to moodiness when inactive, he distrusted anyone who seemed happy all the time. But perhaps the real source of his displeasure was that Du Charme seemed to have no loyalties, except personal ones. He had told Charles that to risk one's life for a friend or relative was a noble undertaking, but to sacrifice life for such a philosophical thing as a country was foolishness. He said frankly that he did not care who won the war, and that his only real concern in life was Marguerite and comfort.

When Charles suggested that such an attitude, if everyone possessed it, would bring ruin upon the world, Laurent retorted by expressing that if peace were the result, which it surely must be, then the world could do with a little 'ruination.' Seeing the disapproving scowl on Charles' face, he said he hoped that he had not offended the Sieur de Langlade, and invited Charles and his family to dine with his, in compensation for any offense he may have given. Charles haughtily declined. But the next morning, Du Charme was hard at work on their new cabin and Charlotte was so impressed with the man's devotion to the construction of their little home, that she begged Charles to try and get along. Besides, Marguerite was extremely popular with the other women of the community. She was always happy it seemed, like her husband, and perfectly willing to help anyone in any crisis. She loved to talk with people instead of about them which added to her acceptance. She was devoted to her husband and shared his philosophy, although she was less vocal about it.

Constante, Charlotte, Domitilde, and Marie Bourassa all made the Du Charmes feel more than welcome, compensating for Charles' sour attitude. The Du Charmes were, as yet, childless, though they seemed to take great pleasure in spoiling Joseph Louis who spent much of his time in their company and exceeded the women in their welcome. He often went also to the deserted cabin which his 'father' had built and where he had been born. Though he had been inside it many times, his curiosity about the place was only natural and he wished to see what it would look like when occupied and tried to imagine his *père* sitting by his hearth after a long day of work in the carpenter shop next door.

It was always easy for the eleven-year-old boy to dream. He spent hours in the old carpenter shop, handling Joseph's old tools and imagining what it would be like to construct a chair or a wagon or a church. But the thought of such labor bored him and he was often stricken with guilt, fearful that the ghost of his father could read his thoughts and be disappointed that his son had so little feeling for the trade which had been his art and livelihood.

Joseph Louis had discovered, when listening to the visiting Jean-Paul or La Fourche, that his real interest lay in languages and he eagerly sought out anyone who could assist him. He had found that he loved and appreciated the spoken word and what could be communicated from one human to another in melodious sound. He was, by nature, an intellectual and not a craftsman. Domitilde, whom he referred to as 'aunt,' was the first to teach him the foreign sounds of the Algonkin language. Later, he began to converse with Okinochumaki and Jean-Paul. Marie Amiot instructed him in the Sac tongue, and when the Pani woman became the slave of the Langlades, he badgered her until she gave him lessons in her language. He even picked up some English from Père Du Jaunay, though it did not particularly please Uncle Augustin or Charles to hear him say 'hello' instead of ça va.

Though the Ottawa and Chippewa both spoke Algonkin, he was very curious about their differences culturally and the various intonations in their dialects. He had such a wonderful ear for sound that the slightest inflections or accent aroused his inquisitive senses and he would proceed to study until he had mastered the exact sound.

The Ottawa were familiar to him, since they were so often in and out of the fort, but the Chippewa seldom visited and thus robbed his acquisitive mind of an opportunity to store, in packrat fashion, more information. Thus one August day, when most of the men of the fort had recently returned from the expedition against Braddock, he determined to visit the Chippewa village and talk to them.

He lied to his mother (he was not sure why, but somehow he believed it necessary), and said he was going to visit the Ottawa at *L'Arbre Croche*. She was hesitant at first, but he knew the way and it was not far from the fort. With a promise to return before dark, he left and instead of turning west, headed in the opposite direction toward what he knew to be Chippewa territory.

He returned two hours later, running through the water gate into his cabin and his mother's arms, in tears. François saw that his face was badly bruised and his nose bloodied. After Constante had comforted the sensitive boy and he had calmed sufficiently to be lucid, François demanded an explanation.

Joseph Louis related that he had begun to cross the open meadow leading to the Chippewa camp. Constante interrupted him harshly and scolded him wrathfully for his dishonesty and deceitfulness. He was not allowed to continue until she drew a promise from him that he would never attempt to go there again without permission. After making this pledge, and explaining, at length, the reason for his desire to visit the Chippewa, he continued. "I . . . I crossed the meadow, *ma mère*. Do you know it?"

Constante looked at her husband. "*Oui,*" she said. "I remember it."

"Wuh . . . well," he stuttered, "I saw three of the Anishnabeg there."

"In the meadow?" François asked.

"*Oui,* papa."

"Well?"

"Two of them were older, like Jean-Paul Langlade maybe. They shouted and ran toward me, whooping and yelling. I got scared . . . ." He began to cry again and several minutes elapsed before he could continue. "They jumped around me like crazy people and said they would make soup of me. I am ashamed, papa, but I was so frightened. I begged them not to hurt me."

"It's all right, Joseph," François said. He was trying to remain calm, but his face was reddening with anger. "What did they look like?"

"The one had painted braids and wore a funny cap with an animal head on it. The other had a crazy look in his eyes. When I was knocked down, I saw he was missing a toe on his foot."

"Wenniway and Matchekewis," Constante moaned.

François nodded. "Why did they hit you?"

"They didn't," the boy answered, as if they were not quite intelligent enough to understand.

"Who did?" François asked impatiently.

"The third one."

"Who?"

"The boy," he repeated, "the boy who was with them. They said I was a coward and a fool. They told him to hit me. I fought back, papa, but he was too strong." Joseph Louis sobbed again as Constante washed his face and kissed him.

"Why was the boy with them?" François asked.

"I don't know," Joseph replied.

"You don't know who he was?"

Joseph Louis thought for a moment, his natural memory for words sifting until it found what it needed.

"They called him Sans-Père," he said.

Chapter
10

Lo-tah's Vision

At THE AGE OF THIRTEEN, Lo-tah, in spite of her special spiritual gifts, began her menstrual cycle like any ordinary girl passing into puberty. She had been irritable for several days, her stomach felt cramped, the sun hurt her eyes and she generally felt out of sorts. When the blood appeared, Natomah showed her how to use cattail cotton to absorb it and went to Ishnoki to inform him, as was proper to do.

Among the Anishnabeg, male teen-agers were sent into the forest without food or water to seek a vision and a post-pubescent name. Girls, on the other hand, were expected to go to the 'sweating lodge' and seek their vision, usually prophetic and profound. The Anishnabeg regarded the beginning of the menstrual cycle as passage into womanhood and believed that a woman would never in her life be closer to the *manitous* and spiritual revelation.

Ishnoki had been waiting anxiously for this moment because he knew that Lo-tah's experience would somehow be especially revealing. He had made certain that the shelter was prepared according to proper spiritual tradition and he saw personally to every detail.

Several squaws were in attendance to maintain a constant, misty vapor in the interior of the 'sweating lodge.' Ishnoki had been sure that Lo-tah would have, as was characteristic of her inquisitive mind, a thousand questions for him as they had ascended the steep hillside. But she had been strangely silent, apparently lost in her own thoughts. She had stood stoically at attention during the hours it had taken to ready the site for purification, and moved only when told to do so. She seemed detached and far away, in direct contradiction to her pragmatic and social nature.

Ishnoki was concerned for her. He knew that she was gifted by the *manitous* with exceptional insight and awareness. Most young women who were brought to this place had to be silenced from their nervous giggling, but Lo-tah was serene, almost absent. Ishnoki wished to be gone from this women's place as soon as possible and return to the normal daily activity of the village below. Here, he felt insecure and secondary, as if the gods regarded him with disfavor.

After taking one final survey of the hut to assure himself that all was in order, he gave the final ceremonial instructions to the two attending squaws and began his descent. Looking back into the blank eyes of Lo-tah, he shook his head and herded the remainder of the loquacious women down the hill. Once their footsteps had faded away, the two remaining squaws approached Lo-tah fearfully and removed her clothing with such hesitation to touch her, that one would have believed they were handling fire. When they pulled the loose smock over her head, they were amazed at the child's physical development. Her breasts were almost completely formed and her hips showed the curves of a woman. Though the squaws discussed her body's attributes freely in front of her, she paid no attention and remained silent.

She slipped out of her moccasins as the squaws, avoiding her eyes, removed her bone necklace and beaded headband. Thus unclad, she was ushered into the lodge and the hide flap was fastened behind her. The steam rising from heated stones in the center of the hut was suffocating and gave a ghostly mien to the dark interior. Lo-tah knelt in the dust, stretching her arms in the direction of the concealed sky and throwing her head back until her raven hair barely swept the earth, began to sway in time to a mysterious rhythm, heard only by herself. She closed her eyes and a soft moaning escaped the trembling lips as beads of sweat poured from her cinnamon skin in tiny rivulets and her ebony hair clung to her dewy back.

Self-blinded, she fought in her stupefaction to see the vision that she knew was within her. Hour upon endless hour, she undulated. Her sweating body danced, quivered and wriggled, oblivious to pain, hunger, thirst and heat. Her reverie could not be hindered even by the intrusion of the old squaws who entered at various intervals with more heated rocks and water.

As her physical condition weakened, her mind became more distant. She no longer saw the bark walls of the lodge, nor did her body feel the earth beneath it. She became a spectre, uplifted from and transcending the world. Her movements eventually began to slacken until finally she stopped, staring blankly into space.

The vision came slowly, slower than most perhaps, because her spirit demanded true visions, not hallucinations or imagined dreams concocted by the mind to allow the body respite from its torture.

As her reverie totally imprisoned her, the roof of the wigwam parted and she saw above her a black sky, roiling with human bodies, both red and white. They were covered with sores and wailing in agony as they bobbed up and down in a black liquid resembling oil. Most of them were desperately trying to climb onto the back of a huge turtle which floated in the inky brine, but they were so covered in the putrid slime that as they crawled upon the shell of the great reptile, they would slide back down into the oily mess. They were afflicted with such suffering that Lo-tah winced and tears fell from her eyes.

Far away, in the center of that misery and clearing in the mist of her mind, was a small light that grew brighter and gained in intensity as it drew nearer. The light took form as it approached. Suspended above her, clearly discernible through the overpowering brightness, stood a man in white robes. He was dark, like the Anishnabeg, and yet he was not one, for his long, wavy hair fell in light brown strands to his shoulders and he wore a beard, a physical impossibility for Lo-tah's people.

He did not speak, but hovered above the wriggling mass of human anguish around him and looked upon them, and her, with such kindly benevolence that she felt complete inner peace. The light radiating from his smile surrounded her with an aura of well-being and security. She no longer saw the hellish, squirming mass of suffering men. It was as if the beneficent being gazing upon her with such perfect tenderness, had willed it away. She felt loved—not because of beauty or usefulness, but simply because she existed. She smiled unconsciously, wanting to touch this 'Spirit of Peace,' with His arms outstretched as if to comfort the whole world. Love reached her from the silent and namelessly beautiful spirit, and her heart was full and grateful.

Knowing her fulfillment, the light lost its shape and faded into the bark ceiling of the hut. Lo-tah gradually became conscious of the choking steam and darkness. She rose, left the wigwam, and passing the curious squaws, who sat clucking around the fire in the sunshine, went to cool herself in a nearby stream. She was oblivious of the lascivious eyes which followed her, staring at her nakedness from behind a hawthorn bush. The eyes, centered between two brightly-colored braids, ogled her lustfully below the otter cap covering the foolish head that contained them.

🐚 🐚 🐚

WHEN HER 'TIME OF BLEEDING' PASSED and she was allowed to speak to men again, Lo-tah went directly to Ishnoki as she knew instinctively that he would be anxious to hear of her experience. She found the old man sitting by the shore, staring at the island of *Michi-mak-i-nac* which was becoming obscure because of the low-lying rain clouds which were racing across the dark sky toward him.

He was apparently lost in thought, for when she touched him on the shoulder, he jumped nervously. His hearing was going bad and he had not noticed her approach.

As she sat next to him, he said nothing, but kept looking out across the water as if searching for something on the ever-darkening horizon. She noticed that he was becoming increasingly emaciated. He lived pretty much on berries and rice since the last of his teeth had fallen out several years ago, and meat was no longer a part of his diet. His legs were thin and his bare chest cadaverous. He seemed lately to be always tired and care-worn, yet whenever he saw Lo-tah, he had always smiled and appeared content. Today, the smile was not there.

"You are a woman now," he said, finally breaking the silence.

"Yes," she agreed.

"What have the spirits told you?" he asked.

"I'm not sure. I saw many people dying. They were sick and covered with sores."

Ishnoki flinched. "Is that all?"

"No. I also saw a man, a white man, with a beard. He floated above all the dying people who were trying to climb on the back of a turtle."

"Did he speak?"

"Only with his eyes."

Ishnoki furrowed his brow, but kept his sight riveted on the approaching storm clouds. "What did his eyes say?"

"He loved me," she said matter-of-factly. "He seemed to love all of us, even the sick ones who raised their hands to Him in honor. His eyes told me I was His child. He said He had created all and could destroy all."

Ishnoki suddenly rose and confronted her, an expression of terrible, wrathful, awe on his face. "Lo-tah, this cannot be! You speak of the *Kitchi-Man-i-tou,* the Great Spirit. He would not come to a woman. You are mistaken . . . or you lie!"

"I do *not* lie," she retorted. Her face showed the hurt she suffered. "I have never lied to anyone, especially you."

"But child . . ."

Ishnoki pondered the quandary presented to him. It was more than his intellect could bear or his experience accept. Yet he knew she was a special woman. Omens did not lie either. "Why would the *Kitchi-Man-i-tou* appear as a white man?" He seemed to be asking himself. "Yet you speak of the Creator of all things. It must be. I am confused. Tell me again."

She related her vision to the old man a second time. He frequently interrupted her, attempting to glean every detail, but he came to the same mystifying conclusion and was more puzzled than ever.

Finally, the rain began, driving them both to the shelter of the forest. As they returned to the village, Ishnoki made her promise not to say anything about the vision and allow him to warn everyone.

"What will you warn against?" she asked.

"A great pestilence is coming Lo-tah. You have foreseen it in your vision. If it happens, we will know your revelation was true. Such prophecy is never half-correct. If the *Kitchi-Man-i-tou* spoke to you, he will let us know soon in the form of this plague. Then the earth will be turned truly upside down."

She left him feeling discomfited and nervous, but certain of what she had seen. When she entered her lodge, her father sat grinning, surrounded by many presents, and obviously swollen with pride. She waited for an explanation that was not long in coming.

"Welcome, woman-daughter," Tcianung beamed. Natomah sat by the lodge fire and looked as if she was trying to smile.

Lo-tah's curiosity was aroused. "What is it?" she said.

"Your cousin, my brother's son, Wenniway, wants you for his *noko*. He is a great warrior and brings many gifts. You must be honored. I have given my permission."

"No!" she cried. She looked from her astonished father to her mother, with pleading eyes. Natomah shrugged her shoulders and put her head down. "I will not have *him* for a husband!"

Tcianung rose from among his presents then, and slapped her violently across the face. "You will do as you are told," he screamed in rage. "You will obey your father *and* your new husband."

She ran outside the wigwam, but her father caught her by the arm before she had advanced more than a few yards. "You show no respect or obedience. You shame me in front of my neighbors. Now stop it and act like a woman!" He shook her violently until her long, straight hair snapped like a whip.

Ishnoki was attracted by the commotion, as were most of the rest of the people of the village, and he hurried as quickly as his old legs would carry him. Minavavana and his son were also lured by the perturbation.

Tcianung, seeing the approaching crowd, slapped his daughter roughly into the dust and ordered her into the wigwam. Natomah stood by the entrance, teary-eyed and fearful, but silent.

Ishnoki could not stand to see the girl treated so roughly, and he decided to put complete faith in her vision in order to rescue her. He knew he was putting his own credibility on the line, but he could not help himself. "Be cautious," he said, addressing himself to the furious Tcianung. "You are striking the mouthpiece of the *Kitchi-Man-i-tou.*"

The words of Ishnoki made the irate father hold back his hand. He looked curiously at the old *shaman*. People did not ignore the words of a *Midewiwin*. "What do you mean?" he asked.

"Lo-tah is gifted by the *manitous*. She has received a vision of death from the Creator of all things. She is special. You will be among the dead ones she has prophesied if you do not leave her alone. You know the omens of her birth. You must not treat her so."

"But she is my daughter and has defied my marriage agreement with Wenniway. Do I allow a woman to rule my lodge?"

"You are an old fool," Wenniway interrupted, addressing himself to Ishnoki. This statement raised a shocked whisper among the gathering audience. "The *Kitchi-Man-i-tou* speaks not to women. She has deceived you old man. You are blind to her treachery. I will change her." He smirked greedily at her from under his otter cap.

Ishnoki ignored him and spoke directly to Tcianung. "She must choose her own husband, if she will ever marry at all. You unbalance the *manitous* and set things wrong if you deny her."

Tcianung looked very confused and disoriented. He put great faith in the *Midewiwin* and though he knew his daughter to be strong-willed, he had never known her to lie. "But what of the contract?" he asked. "I have accepted the bride-price."

Lo-tah looked up from the dirt. She could see hope in Natomah's face and she took heart.

"You must give them back," Ishnoki answered simply. "The *manitous* will reward you far beyond any small dowry. Be strong, Tcianung! Tradition can be broken by God!"

"I will not accept their return," Wenniway shouted. "You will keep them and I see no change in our agreement."

Minavavana stared fiercely at his brother, but Tcianung relented. "The gifts are yours. I reject them," he said to his nephew. "Ishnoki is a *Midewiwin* and knows the gods. My brother is a great chief and I wish not to offend him, but my daughter speaks for *Kitchi-Man-i-tou*. That is big medicine. I cannot defy the *manitous.*"

Lo-tah got up from the ground and went to her mother, touching her father affectionately on the shoulder as she passed. Minavavana was about to speak, but as he opened his mouth, a large, white, viscous mass of bird dung splattered at the feet of Wenniway. Minavavana looked up and saw nothing, but the cry of a loon carried across the clearing. He glanced about, as if expecting to see a ghost, rubbed his tattooed belly, and turning about suddenly, returned to his lodge.

Wenniway, deserted by his father, scowled angrily at Ishnoki, then Tcianung. "You will live to regret your decision, uncle," he said. "As for you, little witch," he sneered, glaring at Lo-tah, "You are mine!" He spit in the dirt and turned to leave, as the haunting cry of the loon again drifted through the forest.

Chapter

11

Vision Confirmed

AT FIRST, the war went well for the French and much of that
success had to be attributed to Charles Langlade and Louis le
Gardeur de Repentigny.

The latter was a member of one of the oldest Canadian families in New France. He had entered the French army in 1739. In
1748, he had conducted a raid into New York from Montreal
with about a hundred Indians which had produced eleven British
prisoners and twenty-five scalps.

For his service to the Crown, the king granted a seigneury to
Repentigny at *Bawating,* as the Ojibway called it, or *le Sault de
Sainte Marie* (the Rapids of Saint Mary), about twenty leagues
north of Fort Michilimackinac across the straits. He enclosed his
estate in a stockade, and put up several buildings. For awhile,
Jean-Baptiste Cadotte and his Chippewa wife had lived on the
estate as tenants and caretakers, but found it too restrictive and
moved back to the freedom of the straits.

Repentigny had tremendous influence over the Chippewa
and, in 1756, he and Langlade led several war parties from Michilimackinac and the Sault, ravaging the western settlements of
Pennsylvania, Virginia and Maryland. In 1757, Repentigny (who
was no relation to the former commandant at Michilimackinac)
continued his raids into British settlements in the south while
Langlade grappled with colonial troops in New France under the
command of the British major, Robert Rogers.

Rogers and his Rangers fought Indian-style. They shed the

traditional red uniforms of the British army and dressed in green to better camouflage themselves. They used natural cover and gave up antiquated European techniques of linear march. In short, they became very worthy opponents, and Langlade was often occupied with them.

The corruption and administrative bungling of Governor Vaudreuil and Intendant Bigot was compensated for by the brilliant military leadership of the Marquis de Montcalm who managed to repulse an attack on Fort Niagara led by the colonial governor, William Shirley of Massachusetts, and another at Crown Point, commanded by Sir William Johnson. Almost a year later, he captured the British forts, Oswego and William Henry.

While Montcalm ably defended strategic French forts protecting the Great Lakes, Repentigny and Langlade made life difficult for the English settlements and kept the contested areas between the two countries in constant turmoil.

Thus the years 1755 and 1756 were full of military successes for the French and their Indian allies. The Indians of the straits did not fight in every battle, nor did their French counterparts garrisoned at Michilimackinac, but they contributed as mood or strategy dictated. Since their immediate area was never seriously threatened by the *Anglais,* they had the luxury of choosing when to be active and when to relax. Perhaps the only person to be continually fighting and thus absent from the fort most of the time was Charles Langlade—and that is why he escaped the pox.

No one would ever know how the dread Slaughterer slinked into the land of the Great Turtle, but He came, manifesting Himself slowly, pretending to be a small, harmless cold or an especially noxious flu, disguising Himself perhaps just for the morbid fun of it.

La Fourche was the first to make His acquaintance. The Ottawa chief came staggering into the fort one July morning, seeking his sister's advice and attention. He wobbled across the parade grounds, after sneezing rudely, but unintentionally, in the sentry's face. The young soldier had offered his assistance to the obviously distressed chief, but pride made him refuse with a shake of his scarred head. He had to get to Domitilde; she understood his weakness and she cared little that he was a leader of his people. She simply loved him.

He got as far as her cabin door, seeing with blurred and double vision the turtle hinges which held it in place, before he vomited riotously all over it and collasped.

It was Augustin who opened the door to find his brother-in-law slumped on the wooden planks of the small porch in a wet pool of his own creation. "Domitilde," he shouted, and stooped to assist his afflicted friend.

She had been cooking the morning meal for her husband and rushed to his aid as she saw her brother being dragged into their cabin. Domitilde was shocked at his condition. He was perspiring excessively and yet his strong body was quivering with chills, indicating a fever out of control. When they attempted to lift his heavy frame onto their bed, he moaned unconsciously and mumbled about soreness in his head and back.

"What is it?" Domitilde, obviously anxious and distraught, pleaded.

"I don't know."

"What should we do?" she asked. "He's very sick. Perhaps the priest?"

"I'll get him," Augustin said and headed for the door. It suddently opened inward and Wawatam and Jean-Paul stepped in. The former, visibly worried, was the first to speak. "My father has been sick. He wandered away this morning and we followed his tracks here." He looked over at the stricken man.

"How long has he been this way?" Augustin asked.

"La Fourche has been sick for almost ten days," Jean-Paul said. "He had refused all treatment. My cousin tried the big medicine of the *cicigwe,* but uncle would not hear of it. Last night, he would take no water or food. He whispered your name, Mother, all the time. He is very sick. He would not be comforted, even by Nodinens, his niece, whom he loves."

Domitilde's eyes filled with tears as she listened to her son. "Hurry and get the priest," she whispered to Augustin, who still stood by the open door.

Père Du Jaunay was at La Fourche's side within minutes. He looked at the mutilated face of the Ottawa carefully. He touched the forehead and withdrew his hand quickly as if he had encountered fire. He studied the rugged landscape of his face and drew away rapidly, his eyes widening to a dawning horror. Little, red spots, some of which showed brightly on his white scars, were scattered over La Fourche's face and were beginning to form little blisters. His bare arms and legs bore the same diminuitive circles and a very few were starting to materialize on his stomach. "It's smallpox," the priest announced to the anxious little group huddled around him.

Augustin looked shocked, but his Indian friends had never had experience with the virus. They merely looked curious.

"What is it?" Domitilde asked.

"I've seen it before," Augustin replied. "It can kill."

Domitilde seemed very frightened and knelt by her brother, laying her cheek on his burning forehead.

"Woman!" Augustin barked sharply. "Get away from him. It's very contagious. Get away!" He pulled at her arm, but she refused to move and wrenched it free again.

"My husband," she said, "I have never disobeyed you, but he is my brother and he has always cared for me. I *will* take care of him. I will not allow *Pau-guk* to have him." She looked apologetically at the priest. "It is a figure of speech, Father, a remnant of my heathen days. Forgive me." She turned back to her husband and bowed her head. "Death will not take him! I will pray to Jesus and stay by him. He *will* live!"

"Of course he will," Du Jaunay assured her. "I will stay too, if it is all right, Monsieur Langlade?"

Augustin nodded his head in confused assent.

The priest immediately ordered Jean-Paul and Wawatam to leave and not risk contamination. Having seen the condition of their relative, they were not loathe to do so.

Before they left the fort however, the two stopped at the cabin of Charlotte Bourassa Langlade to visit Jean-Paul's sister-in-law, again pregnant, and his small, blonde niece, whom he doted on. They made yet another visit before returning to their own lodges and families, to the Chippewa village, Wawatam thinking it necessary to inform old Ishnoki of the pestilence, since the wizened little *shaman* had told him of Lo-tah's vision, and this seemed to bear some relation to it. The two men thus acted unwittingly as bearers of the Slaughterer by carrying His tiny agents from one place to the next.

🦋 🦋 🦋

DOMITILDE SAT CONSTANTLY and heroically by her brother's sick bed as he rolled about deliriously, babbling about bears and turtles and other things she did not understand.

He vomited incessantly and she was kept busy cleaning him and the bedclothes for he was too demented to be directed to the wooden bucket on the floor. She put cold compresses on his fevered brow despite the fact that the red spots had become ugly skin eruptions which seemed to swell larger each day with a milky pus.

The pox had spread to his torso and his fever soared. Domitilde never left his side during those terrible days. Augustin offered to watch the patient as did others in the fort who had heard of the tragedy, but she refused all assistance. She slept on the floor next to their bed, ready at any moment to change a compress or clean up a mess.

Augustin helped her as much as possible, and Père Du Jaunay came every day to pray over the tortured pagan. The priest was amazed at Domitilde's devotion to her brother as was Wawatam who came often to check on his ailing adopted father.

It was her constant devotion to him that probably saved his life. Within two weeks after his arrival, the fever finally broke. The blisters dried up and scabs formed which eventually began to drop off leaving brown spots and little craters in the skin which would be an interesting addition to La Fourche's already disfigured countenance. But he did sit up one morning, looking confused at his surroundings, and announced to his weary sister that he was hungry.

Many rejoiced over his recovery, but Domitilde was not one of them. Her devotion to her brother had been rewarded by contracting the disease herself and within hours after his return to consciousness, she collapsed and replaced him in the down bed.

One by one, other occupants of the fort began to fall to the dreaded pestilence. Among these were Jean-Baptiste Amiot,

René Bourassa, Joseph Louis Ainsse, Marguerite Du Charme, and François Cardin, as well as several soldiers of the garrison.

In the Chippewa village, old Ishnoki contracted the pox that Lo-tah's vision had so accurately predicted and though he was terribly ill, he was able to smile when Lo-tah, who was constantly by his side, told him that Wenniway, the scoffer, had also become a victim of the virus. He had given it to Sans-père who passed it on to his adopted parents, Wawiekuimig and Au-saw-way. Tcianung also contracted the pox as well as Maingaus and many others. Miraculously, Minavavana completely escaped, but the pox made him a widower.

In the Ottawa village, though Jean-Paul and Wawatam had been two of the primary carriers, they did not become victims of the pox, though both their wives, Nodinens and Tibikki did, as well as Okinochumaki and many others.

Constante Cardin put in a horrible month, tending both her husband and son. Twice in that time, she collapsed from exhaustion and predictably, Père Du Jaunay was there to help her back to her feet. Her courage was remarkable and the priest was awed by her emotional and spiritual strength. She did not become hysterical, or fret about the injustice of her position. Rather, she spent her time in prayer and tending to the afflicted, her only relapses being physical, since she drove herself unmercifully.

Augustin Langlade tended to Domitilde as best he could. La Fourche stayed with him, and in spite of the toll the disease had taken on him, he was remarkably helpful.

Laurent Du Charme spent every moment with Marguerite except for those brief hours of respite when he slept, relieved by the indefatigable priest, who seemed to be everywhere. The devout and simple trapper whose philosophy was to live and let live, did not know how to cope with the Slaughterer, and lost fully eighty pounds of his bulk in the struggle. For the first time in his life, he found it difficult to eat.

In time, the pestilence left, leaving behind physical scars on many of the survivors and emotional scars on all of them.

Domitilde Langlade died quietly in her sleep, not disturbing her husband and brother who dozed at her side. When Augustin awoke to find her fevered brow turned cold, he wept bitterly. He looked at her emaciated frame for a long time, remembering their first night on the bed which held her dead body. He kissed her withered hand gently and recalled how she had fallen at his feet and grasped his legs on their wedding night, so fearful of displeasing him and becoming again a burden on her brother, who now stood stoically by, fighting back his own tears.

She was given a beautiful, Christian funeral by Père du Jaunay, and buried in the little Catholic cemetery outside Ste. Anne's. La Fourche, who was to live to great old age, thanks to his gentle sister, came four times each year to her grave, without fail and in accord with the seasons, to honor her memory. Augustin put fresh wildflowers there every day in spring and summer. He missed her so much that he would never remarry. Domitilde lived vividly in his mind and the hearts of their sons.

François Cardin recuperated in time to attend the funeral of the son who had never borne his name. Constante mourned him deeply, but she thanked God for His Saving Grace and the return to health of her husband. They let the secret of the boy's parentage be buried with him. No one ever knew him by any other name than Joseph Louis Ainsse. He was buried next to the carpenter who was his namesake, but had never been his parent.

Charlotte Bourassa and Ignace were forced to grieve for their father, René, who was one of the last victims of the smallpox at Michilimackinac. Augustin was a great comfort to Charlotte during these times and to Marie Bourassa who was often taken by fits of despair.

Jean-Baptiste Amiot left Marie Anne a widow to care for the six remaining children, as two of them preceded their father to the grave.

Marguerite Du Charme recovered, by the grace of God, as did several others, mostly soldiers. In all, the Slaughterer took eleven souls from Fort Michilimackinac, before he went away laughing upon the wind and howling his mocking good-bye through the pine forests.

At *L'Arbre Croche,* Tibikki and Nodinens tried valiantly to defy the Murderer, but He got them finally, and their offspring, leaving Wawatam and Jean-Paul to comfort each other in their terrible loneliness.

Okinochumaki, unlike his sister, was more successful in his struggle, but the pox still claimed twenty-six of the Ottawa, his adopted people.

Among the Chippewa, Tcianung was the first to die. At his funeral, when his corpse was placed upon stilts to keep it from the wolves, Natomah, his widow, and Lo-tah, his daughter, both cut off their little fingers, a custom which was beneficial to the mourner, since physical pain superseded, and thus helped to ease, the emotional trauma. Minavavana now had his brother to mourn, as well as his wife, but Wenniway, fully recovered, smirked viciously as Lo-tah and her mother grieved.

Sans-Père recovered and was again, as his name seemed to promise, without a father. The smallpox had taken Wawie-kuimig, though his mother, Au-saw-way, survived, but only long enough to perish in the following winter from pneumonia. Without paternal guidance, he spent more and more time in the company of Wenniway and Matchekewis, emulating them. The latter, living several leagues away from the straits at Che-boy-gan, avoided the disease altogether.

Two days after her father's death, Lo-tah was tending old Ishnoki who looked as though he would survive. He had fought off the fever and the terrible pox blisters had scabbed over. He had become lucid again, and smiled gently at the teen-aged seeress who had voluntarily become his nurse.

She had watched over him almost constantly and as his senses returned, the bloody wrap around the stump of her finger indicated that although she had been spared the pestilence, she too had suffered.

"Who?" he said weakly from the mat on which he lay, pointing at the absent appendage.

"Tcianung, my father," she answered.

"Your vision was true, Lo-tah," he said, making no further reference to her loss. "You *are* the favored one of the *Kitchi-Man-i-tou*. I did not always believe it was possible. Forgive me." He reached out his hand to her and she grasped it with her uninjured one.

"I am what I was born to be," she said. "There is little else I can do. I would know nothing without you, old friend. You believe I know everything, yet I am only a girl."

"A woman," he corrected. "You said so yourself."

"I can be wrong," she sighed.

"No," he rejoined. "Only when you say you can." He smiled in that wise way of his, but the twinkle in his eyes suddenly changed to fear as he grasped his right hand to his pock-marked chest. Horrible, searing pain stabbed his heart and he turned very pale. He winced, his face a mask of suffering, before dropping back onto the mat. Lo-tah covered her mouth and shouted: "No, no! What is it?"

In a weak voice, clouded with agony, he moaned: "Tell my Okinochumaki and Tibikki I will see them." He knew that his granddaughter was dead, but he had become delirious from lack of oxygen.

"I will, I will," Lo-tah promised. Great tears formed in her eyes as the *shaman* closed his for the last time.

"Climb on the back of the Great Turtle old friend," she sobbed.

12

Quebec

THE YEAR 1758 BEGAN WELL for the French when they beat the English decisively at Fort Ticonderoga. But their success was not long-lived. Superior numbers, more money, a larger colonial population, established colonies and better roads, providing superior lines of communication and provisioning, finally began to take their toll. However, it was the appointment of a new and more capable Prime Minister by King George, which ultimately turned the tide in England's favor in North America.

That new executive was William Pitt (the Elder), who developed new strategies, directed British strength at key areas instead of trying to attack the whole French frontier at once, dismissed incompetent officers and replaced them with competent ones. He did a better job of organizing and enlisting colonial aid, and forced the French to fight European style, only engaging in major battles when that advantage could be used.

The result was one British victory after another, beginning with the fall of Fort Duquesne, which Braddock had so miserably failed to accomplish. The *Anglais* attacked in such large and concentrated numbers that the French were forced to withdraw when their Indian allies, bored with waiting, had deserted only days earlier. The French commandant had retreated out of strategic necessity, never firing a shot and leaving the stockade burning behind him. The British quickly rebuilt a stronger, more defensible structure, which they proudly dubbed Fort Pitt.

On July 26, 1758, Jeffrey Amherst, one of Pitt's best choices for command, conquered the fortress at Louisbourg, opening the Saint Lawrence to invasion. In the following summer, Sir William Johnson, the man the Iroquois called *Warraghiyagey* (He-who-does-much), lived up to his nickname by storming Fort Niagara and raising the Union Jack over the southern approach to New France.

Thus unprotected, there was no question that the next target of British interest would be Quebec, the capital and oldest city of French America. The harried French commander, the Marquis de Montcalm de Saint-Veran, rushed the major portion of his French troops to its defense, and called upon all Frenchmen and their Indian allies to congregate there and assist in repulsing British aggression.

The relentless Langlade was quick to respond to the Marquis' appeal and led a large contingent of French *coureurs de bois,* Chippewa, Ottawa, Potowatomi, Huron and Winnebago to Georgian Bay, up Lake Nipissing and the Mattawa River to the Ottawa River and by portage to the Saint Lawrence. The journey took them over a month and a half, and by the time they arrived and reported to Montcalm, the huge British army, commanded by General James Wolfe, had descended the Saint Lawrence and was approaching Quebec rapidly by forced march.

Montcalm, without advice from Langlade, decided to deploy his troops outside the city rather than await a siege and moved them into position on the wide, flat area below the heights of the city known as the 'Plains of Abraham.'

Charles and his five hundred French irregulars and Indians were ordered to the center of the French line and by dawn, the red coats of the British were in formation across from them, a few hundred yards away.

Jean-Paul, the widower and orphan, was at his half-brother's side, as were La Fourche and Okinochumaki, both scarred by the pox. Minavavana, Wenniway, Matchekewis and the young Sans-père represented the Chippewa, as well as Jean Cuchoise and Jean-Baptiste Cadotte. Ignace Bourassa, François Cardin, and Commandant Beaujeu leading forty French regulars, came from Michilimackinac and Pon-ti-ac was there, now fully recovered from the deep stomach wound he had suffered years earlier against Braddock. Mshike still led his Potowatomi.

As the British made their approach, the French cannon tore devastating holes in their lines, but each time, the enemy would regroup and continue their advance. By mid-afternoon, both sides had counted terrible artillery losses and as yet, there had been very little hand-to-hand combat.

By evening, the British had won several yards of territory and firmly entrenched themselves, obviously not intending to give up one inch of the hard-won ground.

The French troops spent the night building earthworks, embedding sharpened logs into the mounds of dirt in front of them and pointing the lethal ends toward the English camp. Montcalm believed that if these would not stop the English advance, it would at least inhibit their forward movement.

At night, their work completed for the day, Charles, Jean-Paul, Okinochumaki, and La Fourche sat around a fire, awaiting the next assault, which they knew would probably occur at dawn.

Jean-Paul and Charles spoke gently about their mother. Charles, who normally showed little emotion, was visibly shaken as he expressed his regret at her passing. "She was a good woman," he said, staring into the fire, "full of love and devoted to her family." He glanced over at his uncle who glared fiercely into the flames, his jaws clenched. "I regret," Charles continued, "that I was not there to help her, or at least to say good-bye."

"Our father finds it difficult without her," Jean-Paul said. "He sits alone at night and will not allow us to speak of her when we visit. He drinks too much of the English milk that robs a man's mind. He has suffered much at her loss. He cries when he thinks no one sees."

"Her spirit is with us," La Fourche said.

The other men looked over at him and decided silently among themselves to speak no further of Domitilde Langlade.

"Jean-Paul," Charles said, "you have also lost your wife and child. The pox is a hateful thing. It leaves people solitary and alone. I haven't been home enough to talk to you about it, but Charlotte and myself, we would be honored if you would share our roof. Your nieces would be happy to have their uncle close by."

Jean-Paul smiled sadly and shook his shaved head, moving one moccasin back and forth nervously in the dirt. *"Akewau-geketanso,"* he began, "you are a great man and a good brother. You have always been my friend. But you and I are different. I am full Ottawa and have never been comfortable in a cabin or wearing the tight clothes which seem so natural to you. I must live among my people as you must live with yours."

"Your people are mine too, brother," Charles responded.

"Yes, you have always stood by us. But your father is French, your wife is French, and your ways are French. You are Charles Michel Monet de Moras, Sieur de Langlade. I am, and always will be, simply Au-san-aw-go."

"You will always be my brother. We both came from the womb of the same woman."

Charles' voice broke slightly at his reference to Domitilde. Jean-Paul put his dark hand on his half-brother's shoulder and squeezed hard. "La Fourche knows that the Great Turtle has given you a special task and his close protection. I am only another warrior, but I love you, Charles." He got up and moved away from the fire. Charles watched the departing silhouette of his sad brother and then at the grotesque face of his uncle, whose good eye scrutinized him closely. "He is right," La Fourche grunted.

"I know, uncle," Charles said, "but it hurts me to see him so sad and alone. He has lost mother, wife and child. It is hard."

"He is a man and an Ottawa. He will be strong. He will follow his own path now, and you must follow yours." La Fourche laid his head back and closed his good eye. "Sleep," he ordered, "the battle will come early."

But Charles could not sleep. He sat watching his uncle and Okinochumaki as they dozed. The younger man, still mourning his sister Tibikki and his grandfather, Ishnoki, slept fitfully. Charles liked the youthful warrior, perhaps because he was so much like him, quiet and given to brooding. Okinochumaki had become a close friend to Jean-Paul and the two were rarely separated. When Jean-Paul returned to the fire, he lay down next to his friend and fell asleep instantly after wishing his brother *bon soir* and encouraging him to get some rest.

Charles looked out at the dark horizon, dotted with the light of English campfires. He wondered what tomorrow would bring. The British had an immense army which would meet them on an open plain. He had never fought that way before and his heart thumped loudly against his chest. He decided that it was best not to know the future.

His gaze rested on his uncle who began to snore loudly until Charles threw a pebble at his broad chest, causing him to open his eye, smile broadly, and return to more silent rest.

Charles never could quite get over the terrible scars the aging warrior bore. He did not have the coin in its socket and his one eyelid sank deeply into his face. The bearclaw marks were white and jagged, and brown cavities left by the pox dotted the remainder of his features. His tattoos, plus the war paint carefully applied for the coming engagement, gave him a wonderfully ugly appearance. Yet Charles knew that La Fourche had cared for his own mother long beyond the normal time, before deserting her to the elements, and then only at her insistence. He had raised and supported Charles' mother, adopted Wawatam and now, he knew, would look closely after Okinochumaki and Jean-Paul. He had never married, though many squaws would have loved to be his, in spite of, or perhaps even because of, his appearance. Charles knew he had never started a family of his own in order to care for others, a responsibility he felt as a leader of his people. In Charles' mind no one, not even his own father, would ever be held in his own heart with more respect or regard.

"Good night, 'Pitchfork'," he said to the slumbering figure. "Sleep well."

At dawn, the British marched. As they descended the hill onto the Plains of Abraham, the French and Indians, behind their earthen defenses, stood aghast at their numbers as line after line of the redcoated enemy came toward them, bagpipes blaring and feet shaking the earth beneath them.

Once again, the artillery took its toll, but the lines regrouped and marched patiently forward. From Charles' vantage point, the red lines did not seem to be composed of human beings, falling and filling in mechanically, until they suddenly ran forward yelling at the top of their lungs.

Hundreds of them rushed close enough to be under the range of French cannon and they plunged into hand-to-hand combat. Since Charles' group was at the front/center of the French forces, they were the first to feel the brunt of the English onslaught.

Bullets and arrows filled the air, whizzing and buzzing like locusts as the redcoats ascended the earthworks, stepping on the dead bodies of their comrades, shielding them from the sharpened logs. As the first of the enemy topped the mounds of dirt, Charles plunged into the fray, killing one Englishman instantly with his Charleville and stabbing the next with his knife. Suddenly, he felt a searing pain in his thigh and looked down momentarily to see a rivulet of blood running from a small, tidy hole in his leg. As he looked up again, a big *Anglais* swung the butt of his musket at him, driving him to the ground.

Jean-Paul, seeing his brother's distress, raced forward with his tomahawk and split the skull of the English giant who was about to administer the *coup de grâce* to Charles. Other Ottawa quickly followed, but Jean-Paul had been surrounded as he stood in front of his fallen brother. As he raised his arm to strike again, Jean-Paul was pierced through the neck with a British bayonet, his severed jugglar spouting blood in a bright, red, stream. Okinochumaki quickly dispatched his friend's killer with an arrow in the chest as La Fourche pulled the stunned Charles away from the center of the conflict. Matchekewis and Minavavana with their four hundred Chippewa, moved forward to cover their retreat as the Marquis de Montcalm positioned French marines in the center to prevent their line of defense from crumbling.

Matchekewis, wild-eyed and reveling in the gore around him, caught a bullet in the arm while a British bayonet opened a gaping, red wound along Minavavana's cheek. Wenniway's otter cap had a hole shot through it and Sans-père was shot in the groin. French marines fought valiantly and many died, but still wave after wave of redcoats washed over the earthworks and the French line, now shattered, broke into pell-mell retreat.

Charles Langlade, his arm slung about his uncle's shoulder, was vaguely aware of the conflagration around him. He remembered seeing the Marquis fall from his horse and the panicked cries of blue-uniformed French regulars as they fled the red tide. He did not know, as he was pulled away from death by La Fourche and the wounded Okinochumaki, that a few hundred yards away, Au-san-aw-go, the Squirrel, lay in the dirt, surrounded by dead and dying *Anglais,* staring at the grey sky with vacant and unseeing eyes.

Book Two

Alexander Henry

"Welcome!" said he, "Hiawatha,
To the kingdom of the West Wind!
Long have I been waiting for you!"

— LONGFELLOW

Chapter

1

———

Montreal

MONTREAL DID NOT HAVE the appearance of a city under occupation. The misty night air of August carried its usual sounds and scents. The acrid smells of burning lamp oil, and horses and leather, drifted above the hearty voices of the French peasants who, escaping the twisted, narrow, labyrinthine streets, rested after a day's labor, as on any other day, in their rude cottages. Candlelight twinkled gaily from the unshuttered windows and open doorways, spilling onto the cobblestone streets and creating a checkerboard pattern of light and shadow.

Lamplighters moved through the streets now, as before the war, like bees, moving from flower to flower, lighting the way for those who found it necessary to move about in the inky fog.

Almost one year ago, the regular French army had pulled down the *fleur de lis* of the Bourbon kings and returned to the homeland that most of the *habitants* of Montreal had never seen. The Union Jack now dominated the elevation of Mont Royale in the center of the city. Though the bustling frontier colony had received its name from this hill, there was nothing really very regal about it except that the king's representatives (of both nations) had maintained their headquarters and residences on its summit.

Perfumed mademoiselles, their hair curled in the latest, most exquisite French fashion, rustled their pastel gowns, billowing beneath the constricting boned stomachers as they daintily placed themselves on the velvet, buttoned cushions of elaborate *voitures,* or carriages, which would take them to some debutante's ball or young virtuoso's recital. Wigged *seigneurs,* officials of the former French governor, were busily negotiating with the new British commander, just as they had with the feudal nobility of France—to obtain some position of prominence or authority which would permit them to maintain their luxurious *maisons* and continue to pamper their wives and daughters.

Montreal was an island in the Saint Lawrence, the great river that winds its way from the Atlantic, through the citadel of Quebec, to this city and, through various tributaries and portages to the Great Lakes of the northwest. From the apex of the hill that bore the little chapel established in 1642 by Paul de Chomeday, Sieur de Maisonneuve, the city's founder, one could see the twinkling lights below, even through the Saint Lawrence fog that masked all but the royal hill, which had become a center of civilization in the wilderness of Canada and had served as a catalyst for further French expansion.

From the height of the city, one could regard the bustling traffic along the Saint Lawrence where half-wild *voyageurs* and *coureurs de bois* returned from the wilderness with their furs. Landing their fragile craft at the great market along the *Rivière des Prairies,* they would disembark with hard-won plunder and, trading it for one-tenth its value to crafty and more literate men, return to their families with their meagre profits, in the outposts and Indian villages of the great forests.

Such a man was Laurent Du Charme who had arrived in Montreal after sunset, sold his furs for what he considered a fair profit and proceeded along the narrow, cobblestone paths of the waterfront to his usual haunt, a tavern that provided food, ale and bed for the night at a reasonable rate. He had come several hundred miles in the past few days. His canoe had traversed many waterways since his departure from Michilimackinac, to bring his furs, obtained from trapping and trade with the Chippewa and Ottawa, to this bustling center of commerce.

The man he had dealt his merchandise to had not, as expected, requested his license, knowing full well that he had none. Interestingly, Du Charme was to discover that the British required none, except from their own people, a policy which gave the conquered French a considerable advantage.

He was hungry, having consumed the remainder of his provisions, only a little dried fish and black tea, at dawn. He had foolishly eaten without planning, a fault which had caused him discontent on more than one occasion at the end of a journey. His dark skin was a mass of welts at every exposure from the virulent bites of ravenous black flies and mosquitoes who had heroically drilled for food through the stinking *l'huile d'ours* (bear fat), applied and suffered as a deterrent to their parasitic thirst.

His attention was momentarily diverted from his growling stomach by the raucous vociferation of a half-naked courtesan whose ample bosom spilled over the ballustrade of a bordello balcony just above Du Charme. She bawled obscenities at a customer in the street below who had apparently dishonored her with a visit to one of her competitors across the way.

Her rough beauty put him in mind of another appetite, but Du Charme, for all his braggadocio and vaunted boasts of conquests made in youth, was a devoted husband. His *petite fleur*, as he was fond of calling his wife, Marguerite, was a very capacious, heavy woman, which made her *nom de guerre* somewhat of a contradiction in terms. Yet she was not fat like Du Charme himself who, had he ever had the opportunity to measure it, would have been surprised to learn that he carried around the better part of three hundred pounds. His energy and rugged profession were conducive to the maintenance of a slim figure, so that the sustenance of his bulk required a great deal of attention —and he was not inattentive, particularly to the present rumbling in his stomach.

Yet his size did nothing to hamper his lifestyle in the wilderness. He could launch a canoe (a very difficult task for many smaller men), effortlessly and without creating a ripple in the water (though he found himself portaging more often than others when traveling the more shallow streams). He tramped many hundreds of miles in the course of a year without interrupting the flow of his normally heavy breathing. (He always breathed rapidly, even while sleeping.)

His magnitude did not seem to ever inhibit Marguerite who loved him devotedly and spent much of her time in the kitchen to aid him in preserving his dimensions. Her strong, broad hips moved quickly between hearth and table, her sympathetic voice always offering more. To her, Du Charme's body was a growing testament to her love and proof positive of her devotion to him. His mere presence proclaimed loudly to others that his wife was a good cook and cared for him well. She was proud of him and of herself.

Du Charme had approached her in their downy bed, framed by rough pine boards, every night of their married life except when Marguerite had the pox and when his trips to Montreal forced their separation. She had always accepted him enthusiastically. Unlike many of the more sophisticated of her sex who had been raised to regard their bodies as instruments to be used for achieving power, money or prestige or worse, to fear them as vessels of sin, Marguerite reveled in the pure pleasure of the act. She had no inhibitions or rules beyond the simple morality of privacy and monogamy. She had borne Laurent two fine, strong sons (the twins, Louis and Pierre Augustin), three years ago. It was Du Charme's firm and characteristically unscientific belief that the twins had been conceived as a result of making love to Marguerite twice in one night. This novel idea led to many repetitions, satisfying Du Charme and making Marguerite feel even more needed, desirable and fulfilled (though no more twins ever came of it.)

Theirs was an idyllic life, and Du Charme was one of those rarities of the human race who was capable of recognizing his own happiness. So, it was not unexpected that he should stroll quickly past the bordello, scratching his black beard in amusement.

Within moments, he was standing in front of the weathered tavern which had become so familiar to him over the years. The old sign, with its grotesque gargoyle peering down with strange pride, as if crouching on the ramparts of the *Notre Dame de Paris,* creaked on its rusty hinges in the river breeze and proclaimed the *Auberge du Diable* in faded letters.

Du Charme had been attracted by that sign seven years earlier. His cabin in Fort Michilimackinac was situated on the *Rue du Diable,* and the word, hellish as it might sound, reminded him of home. He had ventured into the place, discovered it adequate and, finding security and comfort in familiarity, had failed to ever look for better.

Now he passed under the sign into the light of the open passageway and the dry warmth of the fire he had been anticipating, his booted moccasins moving like ballet slippers across the plank floor.

The room was untidy. Dried mud covered the floor by the entrance, testimony to recent rains. Rough wooden chairs and tables were littered about the place in no particular order, standing wherever other customers had placed them for their own convenience, though at twilight, the room was yet awaiting the night's crowd.

One other customer occupied the place. He was slumped in a chair by the fire, table in front of him, staring vacantly at the wall opposite. Du Charme's eyes moved instinctively to the wall to see if there was anything there worth staring at, and found nothing. Indeed, it was the only wall in the tavern without some sort of ornamentation. (Du Charme particularly liked the wall behind the bar which was covered with small paintings of various types of wild berries and vines surrounding, like a frame, the portrait of a regal-looking woman whose scarlet dress was cut so low that the pinkish hue of her nipples showed just above the white, lacy trim of the dress.)

Beaver pelts, dried and stretched, adorned another wall, placed there with little regard for geometric order. Scattered among them was the largest collection of animal traps that Du Charme had ever seen. He had heard, more than once, fascinating lectures from the *aubergiste*, Émile, who seemed to enjoy nothing more than to expound upon the value of these iron contraptions which hung from wooden pegs, safely above the reach of acquisitive customers.

Yet the wall at which the young man stared, held nothing. His view, if indeed he saw anything at all, beheld only the log and mortar wall which was common to every dwelling on the waterfront.

Du Charme halted in the center of the room momentarily and looked at the solitary youth studiously, an action that would have captured the attention of anyone else not so deeply involved in the apparent study of a blank wall.

Du Charme noted, as he resumed his stride toward the bar and the welcoming grin of Émile that the young man was obviously English. A British musket, popularly known as a 'Brown Bess' leaned against the table. His powder and ball pouch bore the 'G.R.' (George Rex) of British military issue. Yet the standard lobster uniform did not adorn his slim frame. Waistcoat and jerkin, and the white stocks winding around his neck, belied his genteel pretensions if not his gentle birth. His sad, blue eyes, gazing blankly, looked old and tired, contradicting the rest of the face which was youthful. Light, brown stubble bordered the square jaw and tightened lips, matching the hair which fell in a long, pony tail upon his slumped shoulders.

Du Charme greeted Émile happily. He had come to know him well over the years. Émile rejoined with a hearty *"Bon soir,"* but noted that Du Charme's attention seemed riveted on the desolate young Englishman.

"He looks very unhappy, does he not?" asked Émile, poking Du Charme in his shoulder as the trader dropped his Charleville musket and bed roll.

"Mais oui. I have not seen too many young men whom God has gifted with such a face, look so sad. Have you talked with him? What is the matter?" Du Charme pointed a thumb in the direction of the Englishman.

"Non, mon ami. He came in here two hours before you and has sat there with his one tankard of rum ever since. He seems not to want to speak with anyone. Perhaps he *needs* to speak, Du Charme. What do you think, heh?"

Du Charme nodded gravely. Émile had tried valiantly to rescue the unhappy man from his painful reverie, but his attempts at conversation were met with bored expressions and monosyllabic responses which indicated to Émile that his customer was only recognizing him at all purely for the sake of propriety that was customary in one of his training. Émile had shrugged and given up.

Du Charme, however, found the man to be of great interest since his own happiness often depended on the contentment of those around him and this sad soul seemed such a challenge to his own innate desire to see the world at the same peace with itself as he found in his own life, that he could not resist the urge to interfere.

Winking at Émile, he grabbed the two mugs of hot, buttered rum he had ordered in his meaty hands and, proposing to sit directly across from the young man and block his hypnotic attachment to the wall, he glided heavily across the room. Yet, upon reaching his destination something in the youth's eyes made him sit at the end of the table, leaving his companion to continue his melancholia, as if disturbing the line of vision of those unblinking, blue eyes would somehow damage his delicate psyche.

He decided that perhaps the best approach would be to emulate the behavior of the Briton, as sometimes aping the actions of an angry person can turn that anger into laughter and reflect back upon the transgressor the foolishness of his actions. With this half-thought, half-feeling lurking somewhere in his subconscious, Laurent Du Charme seated his massive frame upon a wooden bench, which groaned under his weight.

He loudly slammed the mug of rum in front of the still-transfixed figure next to him, studying carefully the stoic face as the left cheek twitched almost imperceptibly. He then placed the other mug in front of himself and, pressing his hands against his cheeks, cradled his head, placed his elbows on the edge of the table, and brought his face to within a few inches of the right ear of the young man who was struggling to ignore him.

Du Charme's face was so close that his breathing caused the hair on the Englishman's head to wave softly, as a field of wheat might ripple under the influence of a gentle, summer breeze.

The face that had appeared so afflicted and sombre moments before, now betrayed a curious uneasiness. Du Charme could see that his tactic was at least drawing the fellow's thoughts away from his depression though not his eyes away from the wall.

The young man wanted desperately to turn his face and look upon the source of the breathing that disturbed him and caused his hair, annoyingly, to tickle his ear. Yet the wall was safety and security, providing the oblivion that allows an unconventional escape from reality. Still, this monolith had broken that catatonic comfort and now sat staring at him—or so it seemed—since he would not move his head to find out.

Suddenly, the whole thing seemed infinitely absurd to the young man and curiosity tore his eyes away from the wall to behold his persecutor. Head turning, he saw a sight most ludicrous. The trapper's hands, resting snugly against the sides of his face, caused his great jowls to be drawn together in an absurd pucker. This prunish *façade* was such an assault on the young man's depression that his natural proclivity to good-naturedness gradually found expression in a reluctant, tight-lipped smile.

The moment of levity was brief as the grieving man regained his grip on his self-mortification and his expression shifted quickly to anger. "What do you want, sir?" he demanded.

Du Charme removed his huge hands from his face and scowled just as angrily, the lines in his face indicating that this was not natural to him. This unexpected aggression caused the Englishman to shiver slightly as fear began to replace his own irritability.

"I have brought you a mug of Émile's delicious rum. Since I offer it to you freely, I expect you to drink it graciously." The Frenchman grabbed his own mug and, lifting it in the air shouted, "*à votre santé.*"

It was obvious to the Briton that he expected his pale table mate to do the same. The rum did look inviting. He reached for the mug and drew it slowly to his lips. The greasy, hot smell of it caused a wave of nausea to envelop him for a moment, but the rich, warm liquid pouring down him seemed to soothe the feeling and the nausea disappeared. He did not replace the mug on the table until the last bit of alcohol had jumped down his throat.

Du Charme smiled approvingly and slapped the man violently on his back, temporarily recalling the nausea to its domination of his stomach.

"*Bien,*" the Frenchman cried and, laughing heartily, looped his leg over the stool and rose to his feet. He crossed the room once again to Émile, guzzling his own rum as he walked and leaving much of it behind him in a sort of spattered pattern across the floor.

He had returned before the Englishman could recapture his

hypnotic attachment to the wall, and proferred another steaming mug of rum. His expression was that of one undeniably pleased with his efforts.

"*Mon ami,* you seem to have come back to us." He smiled meatily, and repeated his previous salutation, "*à votre santé.*"

The Englishman drank heavily, but could not quite finish the second mug in one draught. He mumbled a feeble "*Merci,*" as he set the mug down hard on the table, spilling part of the contents.

"Ah, *très bien,*" the trapper snickered between gulps of rum. "I'm happy to see you feeling better. Drink up! It will not be long before you feel good again." He winked mischievously.

The younger man was fascinated with the overwhelming charm of this dark behemoth. He was grossly overweight, smelled badly, looked unwashed and his blackening teeth gave a fair indication of his lack of concern with his own body, but his personality was irrisistibly engaging.

"I beg your pardon for my rudeness, Monsieur. I have had a difficult time of it lately. Your company is welcome."

Du Charme grinned broadly and extended his hand. "I am Laurent Du Charme. How are you called?"

"My name is Alexander Henry," the young man answered, wincing from the Frenchman's iron grip.

"How do you come to be in Montreal, *mon ami?*"

The Englishman looked rather sheepish and took another drink before answering. "I came with Amherst's army, though I am not a soldier," he was quick to add.

"It's all right, Monsieur Henry. I am a man of few loyalties and even fewer politics. People are people. *We* are getting along well, *n'est-ce pas?*" He roared with laughter and clapped his companion solidly on the back a second time. When his belly quit shaking he said; "If you are not a soldier, then why are you here?"

"I'm a merchant. I came here with the army for . . . for pro-tection."

"Ah, I see." Du Charme rubbed his chins thoughtfully. "How long have you been here?"

"A few months."

"And who is the young lady who is responsible for reducing

you to companionship with a wall?"

Alexander Henry looked at the big man with an expression of complete surprise, then his cheeks reddened. "Is it that obvious?"

"*Mais oui.* A man of your age mourns the loss of his mother, his money, his faith, or his woman. You are too young to have made and lost a fortune, and if you were struggling with your faith you would be in church, not the Devil's Tavern." He paused and smiled slyly. "I trust your mother is well?"

"Yes, thank you," he lied. (His mother had died years ago, but the point was well taken.) "You have a keen eye and keener wit, Monsieur Du Charme."

"She was very beautiful?"

"Very."

Du Charme sat expectantly, awaiting a fuller explanation. Henry realized that he would have to elaborate, so he continued. "I fell in love, she didn't. She wouldn't stand with me against her father who disapproved of me."

"Why?"

"I told you, she didn't love me."

"*Non, non.* Why did her father not like you?"

"Because he did not believe me worthy of her. I did not have enough status or enough money."

Du Charme frowned. "Won't she wait for you to make money?"

"She is already betrothed to another."

"Then," Du Charme stated confidently, "you are better off without her."

The young Englishman nodded, but did not seem convinced. He sat for a long while, staring at the mug in front of him, obviously remembering what he had lost. Finally, he asked: "You are from Montreal?"

"At one time," the big man responded, "but not now."

"Where now?" Henry asked. He was suddenly consumed with curiosity about his companion.

"Michilimackinac."

"Misshi—what?"

"Michilimackinac. It is a month's journey from here," Du Charme explained, "south and west."

"That's a long way. There must be very few people there."

"*Oui*. Ottawa and Ojibway mostly."

"And you live among them?"

"*Mais non*. I live with my *femme* at the French post." He thought briefly. "I mean the British post."

"Then there are British troops there?"

"*Non, mon ami*. Our French soldiers have left, however. We are awaiting British occupation."

Alexander Henry detected a slight note of regret in his voice in spite of Du Charme's declared lack of political loyalty.

"Who then is in charge of the post?"

"A civilian, the Sieur de Langlade."

"There are no English there now?"

"None."

"Tell me more about this place."

"I cannot say another word, my mouth is too dry." Du Charme smiled and winked again.

This time Alexander Henry got up from the table. Staggering slightly, he went to the bar and asked Émile for two more mugs. Other customers began to enter the tavern. When he returned to the table, the big Canadian, his thirst satiated, began a long and enthusiastic discourse describing the straits area he loved so much. He spoke of the beauty of the forests and the clear water, the sunsets and plentiful game. He told of harsh winters and the warm *comraderie* of his neighbors. He said much about his wife and twin sons whom he seemed to miss greatly. He talked about the Indians and their culture, and the tremendous wealth to be had in furs. Indeed, he made it seem like paradise itself, which of course, it was—to him.

To the young man sitting next to him, enthralled with his descriptions, and becoming increasingly intoxicated, Michilimackinac represented opportunity. It was a chance to escape his sorrow, to escape convention, to be alone, to become wealthy—all of which he desired immensely.

In the early hours toward dawn, Du Charme helped the young man to his room and went to his own. They promised to meet again in the morning, but the Frenchman doubted if he would ever see Henry again. He would be sleeping off the rum long after Du Charme was on his way again. Still, it had been an interesting evening and it kept his thoughts away from his *petite fleur,* so that he did not miss her too much.

Two hours after he had fallen asleep, Du Charme was awakened by an anxious rapping at his door. With difficulty, he struggled out of his bed and opened the door, surprised to see his companion from the previous evening standing bleary-eyed in front of him. He spoke with the haste of one who was excited and not thinking clearly.

"Monsieur, I beg your pardon, but I had to talk to you."

"I would think you had had enough rum to make you sleep a long time, *mon ami,*" Du Charme answered amiably.

"I rid myself of it moments ago, outside."

Du Charme chuckled. The poor man did look rather pale, he thought, in spite of his outward enthusiasm.

"Enter, *s'il vous plaît,* Monsieur Henry."

The young man was excited and did not sit down, but paced back and forth in front of the small hearth which warmed the room. "I have come to ask you to help me."

"But of course, *mon ami.* What can I do?"

Henry paused for a moment, somewhat unsure of himself, then he said: "I want you to take me with you back to Michilimackinac. I want you to act as my guide. I will pay you, of course."

Du Charme had not really expected such a request, and he was somewhat taken aback. "Monsieur Henry," he said, "it would be very dangerous. There are no British soldiers there to protect you. The French population may not accept you."

"You have."

"*Oui,* but not all are like me. Most hate the *Anglais.* You would not be welcome." Du Charme looked genuinely concerned now and regretted his glowing description of the straits. He would feel responsible if anything happened to the young man. "The Indians, too, hate your people and there is no controlling *them.* They do as they please. I could not protect you."

"What about the commandant? What is his name? Langlade?"

"He could, but would not."

"Why?"

"He has fought the *Anglais* for many years. He was at Quebec. His brother died there."

Henry was quiet for a moment, running his fingers across the small table in the center of the room as if inspecting for dust. "I thought you said he was a civilian?"

"Only because he never enlisted. It is a formality. He has many Ottawa relatives and Chippewa friends. They follow him and regard him as a great warrior. He has much influence, and would use it against you, not to protect."

"When will the English soldiers come?"

"Soon, I am told."

"Perhaps they will be there when we return."

"You would be taking an enormous risk." Du Charme went to the wash basin by the bed. Émile always had cold wellwater in it. He splashed it into his face. "For what?"

"I want to trade with the Indians for their furs. There is a great profit to be made there, you said so yourself," Henry told him. "I could also run a small store for the French inside the post. The women especially would appreciate the availability of cloth and other goods. Please take me with you."

"And if I say no?"

"I will go alone."

Du Charme could see that he was in earnest. The *Anglais* would die quickly he thought, without a guide. Either way, he feared, the young man's life had suddenly become his responsibility.

"You will need a license," Du Charme said hopefully.

"I can get it today from Sir William Johnson's office. He knows my uncle well. Perhaps you have heard of my uncle? Matthew Henry? He has published commentaries on the Bible."

"*Non.*" Du Charme was a loyal, and not too literate, Catholic. "You will need two canoes and merchandise to trade, as well as *voyageurs* to do the portaging and paddling."

"I will get them."

Du Charme could see that no obstacle would be placed in his way. "Very well," he sighed, "we will leave tomorrow. But now I must rest and you have much work to do."

He guided the Briton toward the door. Henry turned to him

and grabbed his huge hand. "You are a good friend," he said.

"Wait for a month or two to judge that," Du Charme rejoined. "See if you are still alive then."

Henry laughed and went whistling down the hall to his own room.

"He is charmed and feels much better now about the world," Du Charme muttered to himself. "He is also a fool, *Mon Dieu!*" Within minutes, the big man was snoring loudly.

Chapter

2

Arrival

TOWARD SUNSET on September 8, 1761, three canoes made their way slowly past the Isle of the Great Turtle toward Michilimackinac.

Du Charme had convinced Alexander Henry to wear the clothing of a French peasant and their little company had passed through Indian country without molestation. The journey, in fact, had been rather uneventful except for the young Englishman standing in the canoe to catch a better glimpse of a magnificent bull moose, and dumping most of his wares into the river. Fortunately, they were not yet arrived at Georgian Bay, or all of his goods would have been lost in its depths.

The novice became equally enthused when he spotted the stockade wall of Michilimakinac as they paddled around the point. The three *voyageurs* in his hire joked again about the man they called *geurs de lard,* or literally, 'pork eater,' a term synonymous with neophyte. They did not realize that he spoke fluent French and understood all of their sarcasm. Fortunately, he did not mind, since he was too taken with the beauty of his surroundings. But when they pulled their canoes ashore, he told them in perfect French that they should not assume everyone to be as ignorant as themselves and after they unloaded the canoes, he would pay them. They did, grumbling among themselves, and blaming each other for not being more careful with their insults.

Marguerite Du Charme, a twin in each arm, came running through the water gate to smother her Laurent in kisses and attend to his baggage while he squeezed his small sons and tickled them until they were squealing with pleasure. The Englishman would have recognized them anywhere.

Having dismissed his frowning and embarrassed employees, who embarked immediately with two of the canoes for Montreal, Henry stood among the goods which represented his entire fortune, and happily witnessed the domestic scene. After a few moments of this innocent ribaldry, Du Charme, signaled by his *petite fleur,* introduced his companion.

"Monsieur Henry," he announced grandly, "This is my sweet *femme."* He put one arm around her and compressed her to his side.

It's fortunate, Henry thought, that his wife was not so petite as her nickname indicated or she may have been crushed to death by her gigantic spouse. He noted that she had a kind face that was not unattractive except for the pock marks along her forehead and cheeks. He could see that there was little intellectual depth in her eyes, but a pleasantness and mildness resided there that was so charming that Henry did not believe it possible that she had ever had an enemy.

"It is my pleasure, Madame Du Charme," Henry said, bowing deeply. "Please, call me Alexander."

"And I, Marguerite," she answered, blushing mildly and giggling.

Other residents of the fort were slowly approaching the trio, coming to greet Laurent Du Charme and find out the latest news. Most were quite friendly to the Englishman they unexpectedly encountered, though they believed him to be Canadian at first because of his apparel. The only one he found to be intentionally cold, in fact, was the acting commandant, Charles Langlade.

Henry noted that when he spoke to the man in English, his smile vanished immediately and the hand he had extended was withdrawn. He bowed then, ever so slightly, but only after his wife, who seemed very cultured and amiable, frowned at her husband in disapproval.

Langlade looked savage even though he was meticulously dressed in the clothes of a cultured man. His hair was jet-black, straight, and fell to his shoulders, Indian style. His complexion was dark and his eyes almost black. Henry noticed that he walked with an obvious limp and the scowl seemed to be almost natural with him.

"I must tell you, Monsieur Langlade," the Englishman said, "that I have the highest respect for the French people. I came here to earn my living and not as a representative of the British government. I am sorry for your recent loss, of which Monsieur Du Charme has informed me; your brother, I believe?"

"Half-brother . . . and friend," Langlade muttered in broken English. "And I must tell you, in all candor, that I have little regard for your people and I *am* an official representative of my government. You have a right to stay here, established by force of arms, but I do not have the obligation to receive you with a respect I do not feel nor am I bound to show you any diplomatic courtesy."

His intentions thus stated, he turned and left abruptly. Père Du Jaunay, who had come upon the scene just in time to hear Langlade's rude speech, moved toward the stranger and, in the name of Christ and the *true* church, he formally, but stiffly, welcomed the young man. It was difficult for the priest to do, since the visitor was a heretical protestant. Du Jaunay too, had his prejudices.

Du Charme attempted to apologize for both of them after they departed, as did François Cardin, although his wife, Constante, seemed to share the feelings of the Jesuit and was distant. Ignace Bourassa and his widowed mother, Marie, in-laws of Langlade, were surprisingly cordial.

By the time darkness had fallen, Du Charme, Cardin and Ignace Bourassa had helped the young man to bring his goods up from the beach and store them in the deserted barracks, which Du Charme arranged to have locked. After a hardy meal prepared by the affectionate Marguerite, in which his host enjoyed six servings, Alexander Henry bedded down on the floor of the Du Charme cabin, and listened to the giggles of Marguerite and the groaning of their bed as Du Charme, regardless of his guest, continued his nocturnal habits. Pleasant thoughts of a new life and a rich future floated through Henry's mind as he eventually drifted off to an untroubled sleep.

🦋 🦋 🦋

THE NEXT DAY, again with Du Charme's assistance, Henry was able to move into a cabin of his own. It was an old one that had been left deserted by a French trapper, Jacques LeFevre, fifteen years earlier, and it was located immediately next to the residence of Charles Langlade. It was in such poor condition that Langlade had often considered burning it down after he had built his own home close to it. But procrastination and the danger that fire represented to a wooden stockade had made him hold back. Now, according to frontier etiquette, he was forced to relinquish ownership of it to whoever wished to claim it, and Henry, with Du Charme's encouragement, made that claim.

By evening, with Du Charme's help and the assistance of a couple of the Amiot boys, Henry was able to make the place habitable. The chimney had to be relined with clay, so the first night was rather chilly without a fire, but Henry was content. He had a place from which to begin his trade, and he would soon be a thriving merchant, he was certain. In the evening, François Cardin brought him two freshly killed and dressed rabbits for which Henry was extremely grateful. He roasted them over an open fire outside his little cottage and with the remains of some hard bread, which he had left over from the provisions for his voyage, it made a passable meal.

He worked until long after Du Charme and the Amiots went to bed, repairing shutters, building a new door, putting up shelves. He left the fort only to relieve himself occasionally and then returned assiduously to his labor.

By the end of the second day, he had built a counter to display his goods and to separate him from his clientele. He had invested everything he owned in this stock of wares and spent many hours hauling them from the deserted soldiers' barracks to his little trading post and arranging them in proper order. He had luxurious wool blankets in many colors, kegs of rum, skinning knives, traps, flintlocks, pots, pans, kettles, tin oil lamps, small looking-glasses, hatchets, axes, skeins of cotton calico, rope, and a myriad variety of trinkets which he knew would appeal to the Indian population and bring him many furs.

He had made an agreement with a reliable banker in Montreal to reprovision his stock every four months and to receive the furs as payment at the same time. The profit would be placed into a special account and drawn upon for remuneration to the banker for his services, the balance, his profit, to be put into an account until he wished to draw upon it. He had been assured by Sir William Johnson, when he obtained his license, that a postal messenger would run between the fort and Montreal every three months to keep in close contact with the garrison which was to arrive at any day to take official control of the post in the name of King George.

By the third day after his landing, though he had no living space, he was prepared to conduct business, relying on gossip and curiosity to bring him his desired patrons.

Marguerite Du Charme was his first customer. She wandered into the little store, holding the hands of her chubby, three-year-old boys and admiring the calico cloth which was so popular among French trappers. Henry, seeing her fascination with it, gave her enough of it to make shirts for the twins and included a bright, red and white wool blanket, thanking her for her generous hospitality. She was so elated that she kissed him loudly and went running off to tell Laurent, the twins waddling behind her like large goslings.

He sat down on the stool behind the counter, lit his clay pipe, and was mocking himself on the shrewdness with which he had just cut into his profits, when he looked up to see an Indian standing in the doorway.

Henry had seen many Indians before, but never up close and never to try to converse with. The man who stood before him was close to six feet in height and wore breechclout, leggings, and moccasins. His bare chest was muscular, but small, and he was, altogether, quite thin. The only ornamentation on his body was a tattoo on his left hand and the bone of a small animal which was thrust through his nose. He wore his hair in the Mohawk style that Henry had seen frequently in his travels through the colony of New York. The main point of interest to the Englishman however, was a wicked-looking hatchet which was lashed to the upper leg in a kind of buckskin sheath. Henry guessed him to be only slightly older than himself.

The Englishman's first thought was how to communicate with the savage. He tried French, and much to his surprise, discovered that he understood it and spoke it fluently.

"Bon jour," Henry said. "Welcome."

"I am Okinochumaki of the Ottawa," was the reply. "I was told an *Anglais* had come to our land, alone and unarmed. I did not believe anyone would be so foolish, so I came to see for myself. I was wrong, there are such fools." He waited calmly to see what the reaction would be to his insult, never once changing the bored expression on his face.

Henry could feel the anger rising in his throat as it constricted and his hand gripped his clay pipe tightly. But he knew that success in this country would depend to a large extent on how well he could get along with these people. So he choked back his anger and searched for an appropriate answer. "Fools go among enemies," he retorted. "Brave men go among the Ottawa and wise men seek them as friends. So I count myself both brave and wise, not foolish." Henry thought he detected the bare beginning of a smile at the corner of the warrior's mouth. He felt slightly encouraged.

"I have killed many *Anglais,*" Okinochumaki said.

"It does not surprise me, for one of such great courage."

"How do you know I have courage?"

"Because you are Ottawa. My people have spoken of it. They respect your warriors for their bravery in battle, but the battles are over."

"For whom?"

"For all."

"Perhaps," the Indian said, "perhaps not." Taking a final look around him, he turned and left as abruptly as he had come, not waiting for Henry to reply.

🦋 🦋 🦋

B‍Y THE END OF THE FIRST WEEK, Alexander Henry was able to look upon his efforts with some satisfaction. During the day, his little shop had been frequented by many of the Canadians of the fort who had purchased almost one quarter of his wares and he had been able to accumulate many furs which he stored in the small attic above his store. Laurent Du Charme had made certain that the young entrepreneur had met everyone and he was beginning to feel more comfortable and socially accepted.

In particular, besides the Du Charmes, he got along very well with François Cardin and Ignace Bourassa. But he also frequently conversed with Jacques Parent, a resident of the fort now for less than a year.

Charles Langlade remained a mystery to him. Charlotte, his wife, was always polite and his two diminutive daughters were petite little ladies who rejoiced over tiny sticks of peppermint which the English merchant gave them and which their father made them return. They were so cute in their doll-like ruffled dresses as, with extended and pouting lower lips, they did as their 'papa' had ordered. But Henry cheered them up considerably when he promised them even larger sticks when he and their father became friends. Though they were enthused, Henry believed that that possibility was remote. The brooding half-breed would not speak to him at all unless directly addressed, and then his answers were curt and to the point.

He saw Langlade frequently, due to the proximity of their living quarters, separated only by a short fence consisting of sticks pounded into the ground at close intervals to keep rabbits out of the Langlade garden. But all he ever received was a hard glare from those black eyes.

When Charlotte entered the Englishman's post to satisfy her own curiosity, she had been very pleasant and explained to Henry, but for her husband's hatred of the *Anglais,* they could have been friends.

The evening of that same day, he heard Charles shouting at his wife, flinging epithets with abandon, obviously infuriated with her for showing any kindness to a man he considered his enemy. Alexander felt remorse at having been the cause of that fine lady's difficulty.

He understood the age-old rivalry between his own country and France, and he knew that wars created hatred, but the other occupants of the fort seemed to accept him. Though the priest and Cardin's wife were cool, they were warming, and Constante had even made a purchase from him. But Charles Langlade was not to be won over. The more pleasant Henry tried to be to him, the more distance seemed to develop between them.

Outside of his attempts at friendship with Langlade, by the end of the first week he was established and accepted, and his business was thriving. He was in the process of building an addition onto the old LeFevre cabin which would soon become his living quarters, and he had managed to make it comfortable. What remained, however, was the most difficult obstacle, and the one that had to be overcome in order for his enterprise to be truly successful —developing a clientele among the Indians.

The only one he had seen since entering the land of Michilimackinac was the gaunt-looking Ottawa who had come to his shop and whose name he could not remember. That man had been less than friendly, but he had hoped that his diplomatic words had made at least a partially favorable impression. He had learned from Du Charme that Ottawa and Chippewa bands lived within minutes of the fort and were frequent visitors, but as far as he could determine, they didn't exist. He knew that after the novelty of his shop diminished, so would his business with the small French community, and he would have to depend upon trade with the Indians and the British garrison, neither of which seemed too anxious to make an appearance.

Exactly one week after his arrival, when the September sun had lit the evening sky in blazing colors of orange and red, he happened to be sitting outside the fort on the water's edge, throwing stones at the gentle waves, when he noticed a black, solitary vessel floating in the strait, silhouetted against the gloaming. The canoe was as yet about a league away, but it was rapidly approaching the fort from across the water.

At first, he believed that the craft must contain Indians, but on further consideration he reasoned that this was improbable, since the Indians who lived in this region would be hugging the shore on which he stood and not coming directly across the strait.

As the canoe approached him, Alexander Henry was overjoyed to see that it was a white man, dressed in English clothing. When he beached his craft, Henry was there to greet him and help him disembark. "Hello," he shouted joyfully.

"Good evening," the other man said. He was a handsome fellow, perhaps in his late twenties, with a black beard and a prominent nose. He spoke with the trace of an accent which Henry could not quite place.

"It's good to see another Englishman here," Henry said.

"You are the first?"

"Yes."

Henry introduced himself and invited the newcomer to spend the night at his cabin. He readily accepted and they talked beside Alexander's hearth well into the night.

The new arrival was Prussian-born, his family moving to England when he was a child. He said that they had left Berlin because they were Jewish and the authorities were beginning another local, political persecution, which his family was determined not to endure. His name was Ezekial Solomon and though thoroughly Anglicized, the appellation and his obvious religious practices had caused him a degree of difficulty in England too. At the age of twenty-five, he had come to North America, and made a rather successful living as a cloth merchant in New York. But the Dutch traders in the area, anti-Semites all, had forced him out of business when he became too prosperous and cut into their profits. When his wife died, he had decided to move as far away from civilization as possible, and when the British victory gave this area to King George, Solomon had made up his mind to attempt a new life in the northwest wilderness. He had come from New York about a month ago, but the guides he had hired were ruffians who had stolen his other two canoes while he slept, leaving him destitute and alone. He had decided to continue to Michilimackinac anyway and report the crime to the post commandant in hopes of recovering some of his wares. He was surprised to learn that the British garrison had not yet arrived.

After they had bedded down for the night, Solomon, sleeping on the floor by the hearth as his host had done his first night at the Du Charme cabin, Henry lay awake for quite some time, excited at the prospect of a new friendship and a comraderie with someone his own age and nationality. He discovered, as he lay thinking about the day's events, that he had not given a thought to the girl who had jilted him in Montreal since he had met Du Charme in the Devil's Tavern. He was enjoying himself as never before.

Ezekial Solomon, who was warm and comfortable for the first time in many days, fell asleep thinking how refreshing it was and how lucky to have met a person with so few prejudices as Alexander Henry.

🐝 🐝 🐝

In THE ENSUING WEEK, Solomon and Henry became fast friends. Alexander helped Ezekial to build his own *poteaux en terre* cabin, although the latter had insisted that the structure be established outside the walls of the stockade. When Henry warned him that the Indians were not altogether friendly and tried to represent to him the foolhardiness of his intentions, Solomon replied that it was better to start outside than to be driven outside and, he believed, the Indians would probably have fewer reasons to hate him than his own countrymen. The Jewish merchant was really quite astonished by his friend's *naïveté*.

Henry provided his new companion with a 'Brown Bess' musket, a hunting knife, and several traps on credit, with Ezekial's insistence that the loan be repaid from his first profit on furs—with interest.

The little cabin was completed in just a few days with Alexander's assistance and help came once again from the personable Du Charme. Solomon was completely taken with the Du Charmes. He had never met a family so genuinely happy and constantly cheerful. As Laurent showed him how and where to lay his traps (though the training would be of little use until winter), the initiate was astonished to discover that his teacher seemed unconcerned that he was training a competitor. When Solomon alluded to this fact, Du Charme responded by saying that people were more important than money, and there was wealth enough for all.

By the end of Ezekial Solomon's first week, two more Englishmen arrived. They were, like Solomon, interested in trapping and trading with the Indians for furs, so Henry was able to keep his post store as a little monopoly. Their names were Stanley Goddard and Henry Bostwick. They came to Michilimackinac in four canoes, manned by hired *voyageurs,* in much the same manner as Alexander had done.

When Henry and Solomon greeted them enthusiastically, and Henry introduced Ezekial, they were polite, but formal, and refused any offers of assistance. They resisted any attempts to meet the French *habitants* and remained aloof. They were granted permission to construct a 'row-house' by Commandant Langlade along the northwest wall of the stockade, fairly isolated from the rest of the community and they went about their business, secluded from their fellows as much as possible.

That is why, two days after their arrival, Solomon and Henry, who were sharing a meal of whitefish in the latter's cabin, were surprised when the two men came to the door.

As Henry allowed them entrance and welcomed them, he noticed that they were agitated and visibly shaken. After serving each of his visitors a mug of good English rum, he inquired into the nature of their call.

Bostwick, somewhat of a dandy who came from an aristocratic Virginia family and spoke as though he were holding his nose, was the first to speak. "I must thank you for your excellent rum, Mr. Henry," he began. "My associate, Mr. Goddard, and I did not come here to exchange pleasantries, however. To come right to the point, we were visited this afternoon by several savages who identified themselves as Ottawa. One young, rather thin fellow spoke enough English to act as interpreter."

At this point, Mr. Goddard, unable to contain himself any longer, interjected. "They threatened us, if you can imagine it!"

Mr. Bostwick frowned at his companion who looked rather sheepish and muttered, "I beg your pardon. Please continue."

"They came upon us while we were unloading our goods," Bostwick said. "Their leader, a rather ugly fellow with a deformed face, informed us that if we did not absent ourselves from the post and this entire area by morning, that we should be obligated to defend our lives."

"Why?" Solomon asked.

"He didn't say, but I know he meant it. When I explained to Monsieur Langlade what had happened, he told us very frankly that the French had signed a cease-fire with our people, but the Ottawa had not. He further stipulated that the Indian population was not under his jurisdiction and that we should address our problem to the Superintendent of Indian Affairs for our government."

"Which is?" Henry queried.

"He told us that Sir William Johnson currently held that post," Bostwick replied.

"He's at Montreal," Goddard wailed, "and when we told him so, he just smiled and turned his back on us. I think he *wants* the Indians to kill us. You can't trust a Frenchman."

"It was clear from our conversation that the commandant intends to leave us to our own resources," Bostwick added.

"What are we to do?" Goddard whined. He was beginning to get on Solomon's nerves.

"Did the Ottawa say anything in reference to us?" Ezekial asked.

"The scarred one told us that his threat extended to all Englishmen in the fort," Bostwick replied.

Henry looked at Solomon and the two young men recognized from the worried tones of the other two, that they were all in great peril. He was not sure what to do. Without a British garrison, they were defenseless and the gates to the fort would not be closed against their enemies. It was already late afternoon, and by the time they could load their belongings and leave, the sun would have left the sky. Henry did not want to travel at night through hostile territory. Besides, to leave now would be to admit failure and attempt another start elsewhere. The thought sickened him. "I intend to stay here," he said, breaking the silence.

"Myself too," Solomon concurred, winking at his friend. "I have been moved out of too many places. I don't intend to move again until *I* decide to."

"Gentlemen?" Henry looked to his visitors for their opinion.

"Yes, perhaps it would be best," Bostwick said. "I have a good musket and a sufficient amount of powder and shot to hold off an army. There's no guarantee that they won't try to kill us if we left the fort tonight anyway. We're probably safer here."

Henry and Solomon were looking at Goddard, whose lower lip was trembling, but seemed to have committed himself to whatever Bostwick decided.

"If you wish, you may all spend the night here at my store," Henry suggested. "We can fortify it as much as possible, and force the savages to attack us in small groups by coming through the doorway. I don't believe they will use fire; that would endanger their French friends."

"A good suggestion, old fellow," Bostwick said cheerily. "We'll get our things and return shortly."

"I don't know what will happen to whatever you can't carry over here," Solomon said.

"We'll have to deal with that later," Bostwick rejoined.

As the two older men left, Solomon glanced at Henry and smiled weakly. "You're about to find out what it's like to be a Jew," he said.

Henry laughed. "I don't think I want to know."

🦅 🦅 🦅

THE NIGHT PASSED VERY SLOWLY for the four isolated Englishmen. Henry had decided to say nothing to Du Charme or any of the other Canadians, fearful that any involvement on their behalf would cause retaliation against them later or at least put them in a position where they would have divided loyalties. If they were able to somehow get out of this situation unscathed, it would be important to keep the friends they had and solve the problem with the Ottawa diplomatically if at all possible. Any Ottawa deaths would mean that their opportunities for trade would be ruined and they would be forced to leave anyway.

It was curious that their only visitor that evening should be the priest, who had come to apologize for his previous rudeness. He was surprised to find all of the Englishmen huddled behind the counter and the door barricaded as he had passed by the window. When Henry finally realized who he was, he and Solomon hastily removed the crates which blocked the doorway and sheepishly signaled the priest to enter.

Père Du Jaunay looked about him as if he had just landed on the moon and awaited an explanation. Henry was quick to provide it. "I must apologize, uh, Father," (the priest could see that the Protestant was uncomfortable with the term), "but we are only trying to protect ourselves."

"I see," the Jesuit said, looking suspiciously around the room. "And who threatens you? The French army is gone." He looked at all of the muskets and ammunition. "Although I think they would have had a difficult time breaking in here to steal your rum."

Henry chuckled and Solomon smiled broadly. Bostwick did not see the humor.

"The Ottawa have been to see Mr. Bostwick and Mr. Goddard and told them that all Englishmen must leave the fort by morning or die. We do not intend to do either." Henry again looked at Solomon for support.

"The Ottawa? From *L'Arbre Croche?*" Du Jaunay seemed surprised. "Who was it exactly who threatened you?"

Bostwick spoke up. "Some ugly ogre with a badly scarred face."

Du Jaunay smiled. "That would be La Fourche."

"The Pitchfork?" Henry's French was not flawless, but he knew enough to translate this. "You know this man?"

"Yes, I do," the priest replied. "He's a good man and would not normally threaten anyone unless antagonized. But he lost his nephew to the *Anglais* at Quebec, and a few of his scars can be attributed to your people."

"Then you believe his threat to be in earnest?" Solomon asked.

"*Oui.*"

"We have spoken to Monsieur Langlade, but he offers no assistance," Bostwick interjected.

Du Jaunay laughed. "I'm not surprised."

"Why?"

"La Fourche is Langlade's uncle."

The four Englishmen looked around at each other. "No wonder," Solomon stated succinctly.

After a moment of silence in which the priest inspected Henry's stocked shelves, he said: "How do you hope to protect yourselves? You will die."

Henry scrutinized the Jesuit carefully. "Then you suggest that we try to leave?"

"Non," Du Jaunay said calmly. "I would not do that. The Ottawa are camped in the forest just to the west of the stockade. They have no intention of allowing you to leave peacefully."

"Then what are we to do?" Solomon said.

"You will have to stay where you are. La Fourche will talk before he attacks. I would suggest that you offer him many gifts and hope you can buy your way out of your situation."

"Do you really believe that will appease them?" Goddard asked hopefully. "Can they be dissuaded with presents?"

"From what I know of La Fourche, I doubt it," the priest told him.

"Then why do you bother with such unstable advice?" Solomon snapped. He was visibly irritated at this man of the cloth who seemed so flippant about their uncomfortable situation.

"I came here because I feared that my first meeting with Monsieur Henry was not very pleasant. My conscience bothered me, and I prayed. I am afraid that the answer I received was somewhat of a reprimand. I allowed my personal feelings to interfere with my sacred duty, and I should like to correct that error." It was obvious that the cleric was waging some sort of internal war with himself. "I would like to spend the night here," he suddenly announced, "and do what I can to prevent any shedding of blood. Our Lord did not want us to kill each other senselessly." He looked at Solomon. "You are not a Christian?"

"No."

"Neither is La Fourche. Perhaps the two of you can find some common ground. In the meantime, I will pray for you both."

Du Jaunay made it obvious that he was through conversing. He walked to an empty corner of the room, knelt, took out his rosary, and began his prayers.

Ezekial and Alexander talked long into the night. Only the priest, after several hours of prayerful solitude, was able to sleep. Goddard and Bostwick sat silently, the former staring nervously at the door.

As the first grey light of dawn broke the ashen, September sky, Goddard, standing at the lone window, announced that a party of about two dozen Ottawa had just entered the fort. The Langlade house, next door, was silent as was the rest of the stockade.

The Englishmen quickly awakened the dozing priest and wordlessly the cleric moved to the door, removed the board which barricaded it, and stepped outside. Solomon and Henry joined him on the plank porch as the other two slammed and fortified the door behind them. Solomon turned to protest, but realized that time would not allow them to reenter, so he faced the Indians and awaited whatever fate had in store.

The Ottawa were colorfully painted and feathered, led by La Fourche, with the Indian who had visited Henry acting again as interpreter.

"You have not left," La Fourche said through Okinochumaki. "You are dead men. Did not your brothers tell you of our ultimatum?"

Henry opened his mouth to reply, but stopped when the scarred one drew his tomahawk from his belt. Solomon lifted his musket.

"Wait!," the Jesuit said. All eyes shifted to the priest. "The *Anglais* have many gifts for your people."

La Fourche eyed Du Jaunay suspiciously. "The 'Black Robe' has always been a friend to my people. He has always spoken the truth. Why does he now stand with our enemies?" He nodded his head in the direction of the Britons and spat in the dust. "We do not want their gifts. They have tried to murder our people and have fought with our father, the French king. We do not accept gifts from our enemies." Others of the Ottawa nodded in concurrence and began to draw their own weapons.

Solomon said: "Your idea doesn't seem to be working, priest." He fingered his musket trigger nervously.

Du Jaunay ignored the remark and tried again. "La Fourche is a great warrior. He has little cause to butcher defenseless traders. Besides, when the *Anglais* redcoats come, they will punish you and your people. You will bring much sadness on the Ottawa if you act unwisely."

"We will kill them too."

"And they will send more. You know they will."

La Fourche remembered the hordes of redcoats descending the Plains of Abraham at Quebec. "They have brought much grief to my lodge. Au-san-aw-go's spirit cries out for vengeance. We do not fear retailiation. Stand aside, 'Black Robe'!"

As the Indians took several menacing steps forward, and Alexander and Ezekial aimed their muskets at the chests of the nearest savages, the shrill and distant cry of bagpipes drifted through the open water gate. Clearly, the sound was coming from across the lake. At that moment, an Ottawa brave came running across the parade ground shouting, *"Anglais, Anglais."*

It was then that the two young men, backed against the log wall of Henry's store, realized that the British garrison had finally arrived.

🦋 🦋 🦋

THE ENGLISH GARRISON had marched into Fort Michilimackinac shortly after sunrise on the twenty-third of September. La Fourche and his Ottawa had withdrawn without a word, leaving the British merchants sighing deeply with relief, but not without some apprehension as to their prospects of financial success. The confrontation with the savages had left them alive, but their enmity gave the entrepreneurs little hope for any kind of lucrative dealings with these people. On the positive side, the experience had given both Solomon and Henry a new friend. Du Jaunay had stood bravely with them, and Alexander had been very impressed with the Jesuit's courage and innate sensitivity to their suffering. The priest was a good man who cared for people and was able to overcome his own intellectual certainty that as a Protestant and Jew they were both destined for hell, with his natural loving heart. Though he made little of his role in their rescue, and immediately departed when the crisis had passed, they knew that the few moments he had delayed their enemies, had meant the difference between life and death for at least two of them, and perhaps all.

Bostwick and Goddard had run past the two younger Englishmen as soon as they saw that the Ottawa had left. Neither of them paused to thank Alexander for the shelter he had provided, nor had they shown any remorse for abandoning their brethren to their fate. They went to the British commander as soon as the redcoats arrived to report the incident, but by that time, the Ottawa were safely back at *L'Arbre Croche*. Bostwick did come back later to thank Henry for his assistance, but no apology was ever made to Henry for barring him from his own cabin during the confrontation and Alexander was too relieved at his own rescue to make much of it.

Henry was not surprised to see Langlade, as the official representative of the French government, come out of his cabin next door to receive the conquerors. It was obvious that he had been watching the entire proceedings and when Henry said as much to Solomon, the latter expressed his view that the Frenchman would have enjoyed their demise immensely and was probably very disappointed when it did not occur.

The commanding officer of the British was Captain Henry Balfour of His Royal Majesty's 60th Foot Regiment. He had brought with him only twenty-eight soldiers, but this was merely an advance detachment, and more were expected shortly.

Langlade had been ordered by representatives of the former French government in Montreal to take command of the post until the British arrival and then execute its formal surrender, which he did. Captain Balfour accepted the ceremonial sword provided for the occasion from the half-breed, then ordered that the French civilian population turn out to the parade ground.

The Du Charmes, Cardins, Parents, Bourassas, Amiots, etc. all gathered on the *Rue Dauphine,* faced the parade ground, and listened intently as Balfour explained the occupation policy.

All current residents of the fort were allowed to keep their property and their professions. Citizens of the British Crown would be given first consideration for new settlement. Anticipating the Quebec Act, which would come two years later, Balfour announced that the practice of the Roman Catholic faith would be tolerated and self-government would be permitted wherever practicable. Du Jaunay, listening from the steps of Ste. Anne's, heaved a sigh of relief, as did many others in the audience.

Balfour further informed the civilians that his own presence among them was temporary and that he would be departing within the week for another assignment. Until the permanent commander arrived, he would be leaving Lieutenant William Leslie in charge, whom he then introduced to the assemblage.

Leslie was a soft-spoken man in his mid-twenties with a high, intelligent forehead, receding into a meticulously curled white wig, tied in back with black ribbon. His bright, scarlet uniform was immaculately clean and perfectly tailored to fit his slim figure. His beautiful white teeth shone from his almost feminine mouth as he smiled and bowed gracefully when he was presented to the civilians.

When all the announcements had been completed and social amenities attended to, a detachment of redcoats, to the accompaniment of one bagpipe and a drum, marched to the flagpole in the center of the parade ground, and lowered the *fleur-de-lis*. As the symbol of French greatness descended, tears filled the eyes of several of the French citizenry.

Charles Langlade took the flag from the British sergeant and reverently folded it, holding it under his arm. As the bright stripes of the Union Jack were raised above them, he thought of Au-san-aw-go and Domitilde. For the first time, he was glad they were not alive.

Chapter
3

Wawatam's Dream and The Maple Grove

O<small>N OCTOBER THIRD</small>, when the forests of Michilimackinac were ablaze with the rich colors of autumn, Captain Balfour, as promised, departed with a two-man escort for his next assignment, leaving Lieutenant Leslie in command. The latter's prominence did not last long. After only five days, the permanent garrison arrived with the new commander and Leslie was demoted to adjutant.

The new authority was a twenty-year veteran colonel named George Etherington. He promptly called a meeting of all British subjects at the post headquarters which had housed, most recently, the last French commandant, Beaujeu.

Henry, Solomon, Bostwick and Goddard all obeyed the summons. In attendance also was Charles Langlade, Lieutenant Leslie, and the only other commissioned officer, Lieutenant John Jamet.

Jamet's family possessed a French heritage. His ancestors had been part of the French army which had assisted Charles II in the restoring of the Stuart monarchy to the throne of England following the disastrous Commonwealth of Oliver Cromwell. After the Restoration, instead of returning to France, Jamet's family had remained in England and become citizens of that country. Though that was several generations earlier, the lieutenant had been raised to speak his ancestral tongue and to appreciate French culture and customs. Thus he was a logical choice to be assigned to Michilimackinac.

246

Charles Langlade seemed very pleased with the presence of Jamet and the two conversed pleasantly in French. Langlade was especially pleased when the lieutenant praised the half-breed's courage and spoke of his reputation as a soldier in British military circles.

Etherington, on the contrary, Langlade instinctively disliked, and this point of view was shared by Henry and Solomon, in spite of their loyalty to the British crown and mutual aversion to Langlade.

The new commander was an effete snob who treated his subordinates with disdain. Although he viewed Langlade as an equal, he treated Leslie and Jamet as if they were the contents of a chamber pot, and this elitist attitude irritated the Frenchman.

Henry and Solomon disliked him for the same reasons. Etherington seemed to have more in common with Bostwick, and they talked amicably while the new commandant ignored the younger men. What really angered Henry was the man's obvious snubbing of Solomon.

When they had first entered the man's quarters, their host had told Ezekial that he had asked to see only the *British* residents. Solomon told him that he did not know whether that was a reference to his slight Prussian accent or to his Judaism, but neither mattered because he was a British citizen. Etherington had then smiled sarcastically and remarked to Bostwick that citizenship apparently no longer depended upon birth, but rather money, which led Solomon to understand that it was not his accent which bothered the new commandant. Such an attitude disgusted Henry, and because his feelings were quite apparent, Etherington ignored him as well. The only time he spoke to either of his younger guests directly for the rest of the evening was to praise Ezekial for his common sense in constructing his home outside the stockade. Solomon ignored the comment, but winked knowingly at Henry, as if to say, 'I told you so.'

Although the meeting was uncomfortable for Henry and his Jewish friend, they were pleased to note that Langlade had little use for Etherington either, giving Henry some hope for a common bond with his nearest neighbor.

Bostwick and the colonel got along famously, perhaps because they shared somewhat the same 'petty bourgeois' attitude toward their fellows. But Henry recognized it as a dangerous philosophy to possess in the wilderness. In the streets of London, it was possible to suffer such pretensions, but Henry and Solomon had both seen enough in the last few days to convince them that people had to depend on each other here, and snobbery was a dangerous luxury that Etherington would be ill-able to afford.

The colonel informed them that they were free to move about and pursue their livelihoods as they wished, but, he said, turning to Langlade, the French would be required to take a public oath of allegiance to the British crown, or be treated as prisoners of war and deported to Fort Niagara for trial.

Henry and Solomon glanced at Langlade whose face was furrowed into a terrible, dark scowl. His black eyes blazed with fury.

Lieutenant Jamet, attempting to avoid further offending the man he regarded with great respect, suggested to his superior that perhaps Monsieur Langlade could simply give the colonel his word in private that he would attempt no rebellion or sedition. Surely, he said, Monsieur Langlade's stature and rank would insure his honesty and integrity in such a matter as this.

Jamet's diplomatic ploy was well-conceived, since it appealed to Etherington's hierarchical senses. After roundly abusing the young lieutenant for volunteering advice without being asked for it, he conceded that Jamet's suggestion might be best for all concerned.

(As it turned out, Jamet wrote a very inoffensive loyalty pledge for Langlade to sign, and this made the transition as easy as it could be, under the circumstances. Langlade signed it, not overlooking the service to his pride that Jamet had provided.)

Langlade excused himself, bowing only slightly as he departed, wishing that he could have slapped the foolish Etherington senseless and then handed him over to the Ottawa squaws to see how grand he would have acted under their skilled hands. La Damoiselle's ghost would have had a good laugh.

Solomon and Henry also made their excuses and left, while Bostwick and Goddard remained to share the colonel's brandy and laugh at his tasteless jokes, well into the evening.

The following day, all of the male population of the French community, with the exception of the Sieur de Langlade, gathered at the parade ground and repeated individually the oath of allegiance to King George III. The haughty Etherington smirked as Du Charme was the first to repeat it, followed by the worn, tired, and hung-over Augustin Langlade.

There was some defiance. Ignace Bourassa refused at first to assent to the oath and a detachment of British troops had placed him in the guardhouse to await shipment to Niagara. After much pleading and begging by his desperate mother, and being reminded by his sister that he was the widow's sole support, he finally relented, but not without considerable regret.

The two older Amiot boys spat in the dust after repeating the oath together. Père Du Jaunay had added an addendum, voicing his belief in the pope as the 'Supreme Head of the Church,' in France, England and throughout the world.

This did not seem to disturb Etherington, who continued to grin happily, surveying his little realm with the look and stance of a petty king.

By noon, all the residents of Fort Michilimackinac were officially British subjects.

🦋 🦋 🦋

LIEUTENANT JAMET was able to convince Colonel Etherington that he should allow the Indians to move freely into and out of the fort as long as they came individually or in small groups.

The colonel had doubled the guard and announced that no savages would be allowed inside the post. Langlade and Henry found themselves in a strange alliance in protest over this policy. The Frenchman did not want his relatives and friends to be deprived of their visitation rights, and the British merchant wanted their trade. Neither could be accomplished without Indian access to the post, so they had both protested to Jamet, and the lieutenant, diplomatic as always, had managed to change the commandant's mind.

Etherington's prejudices extended to the Indians, whom he

regarded as ignorant barbarians, incapable of thought or any noble emotions, and it never surprised him that the vast majority of them had sided with the French in the great war now past, attributing that phenomena to their ignorance and not his own attitude.

Fortunately for Henry, Etherington kept his thoughts to himself (except for occasional conversations with Bostwick and Goddard who had become his frequent companions), and allowed Leslie and Jamet to handle relations with the savages, not wishing to dirty his delicate hands with such distasteful and mundane affairs.

One sunny, mid-October day, Henry was laying planks for a porch/entrance to his shop, when he spotted the ugly Ottawa chief coming through the water gate. He was with another, younger Indian, and after being delayed momentarily by the red-coated sentries, he and his companion headed directly toward the Langlade cabin next door.

Seeing his opportunity, Alexander rushed inside and selected a clay jug filled with rum, a splendid steel knife, a small looking-glass and a hatchet. By the time he returned, the two Ottawa were fifteen feet from him. La Fourche stopped and glared hatefully at him, but the other Indian looked at him with antipathetic nonchalance.

Henry continued to approach them in spite of the chief's malicious countenance. La Fourche's hand grabbed the hilt of the huge knife at his hip and he signaled Alexander to come no closer. The merchant stopped for a moment, then took another step forward.

"I would not move any closer," a familiar voice said. Henry looked away from the menacing figure in front of him long enough to see Langlade standing in his own doorway. "I have never known my uncle to threaten idly, *Anglais.*"

Henry stopped. "I want to speak with him," he said, nodding at La Fourche.

"Go right ahead," Langlade replied.

As Henry looked at him, he believed he saw the Frenchman smile for the first time in their short acquaintance.

"I don't speak Ottawa."

"Neither does he," Langlade scoffed. "There is no such language. He speaks Algonkin, and has very little patience. Perhaps you had better communicate with him, or step out of his way."

"Would . . . would you interpret for me?" Alexander stuttered.

"Me? Why should I do that?" Langlade was obviously enjoying the merchant's discomfort.

"For the sake of our mutual dislike of your replacement," Henry managed to stammer.

Langlade's cruel grin softened somewhat. "All right," he said matter-of-factly. "What do you want me to tell him?"

Henry released a breath, never taking his eye off La Fourche's though the reflective glare of the sun on the copper eye made it difficult. "Tell him I want to be his friend. Tell him I have gifts for him."

Langlade spoke rapidly in Algonkin. When he was finished, La Fourche's expression did not change, but his companion, who had stood by silently disinterested, now scowled fiercely also.

Henry looked up at Langlade who was grinning from ear to ear. "What did you tell him?"

"I told him you wanted to be his friend," Langlade joked, "and that you had brought him a glass so that he could admire his own beauty."

Henry looked up at his antagonist helplessly. "Now he believes I am mocking him."

"I think so, *oui*."

At that moment, the younger Ottawa muttered something to Langlade which he quickly translated to Henry. "My cousin thinks that perhaps you should experience what is necessary to obtain such beauty."

Alexander was becoming more frightened by the moment. Sweat broke out on the back of his neck and he looked appealingly again to Langlade. He knew the Frenchman was his only link to these savages and he would not cooperate.

The younger Ottawa turned to Langlade and again said something. Henry, in spite of his fear, was impressed with the Indian's noble bearing. Despite his split earlobes and the ring in his nose, he could not help believe that this man would have made a capable barrister, or impressed an audience from a pulpit.

Langlade answered him very quickly and as he did so, the smirk vanished. The Frenchman then turned to Henry. "Wawatam asked me if I was interpreting correctly. I will not lie to a friend. I told him no. He has asked me to be accurate and since I respect him highly, I will, for his sake. What do you want me to tell him?"

Henry was quick to respond. "Please tell him that I want to be his friend. I had nothing to do with the deaths of his tribesmen and want only good for them. I have gifts to offer as evidence of my words and I would be honored if they would accept them." He proferred the presents as Langlade translated for him.

Wawatam solemnly stepped forward, took the hatchet and the rum, and then moved toward Langlade's cabin. La Fourche drew his knife from its sheath, but Henry stood his ground as the old warrior approached him.

He grabbed the knife from Henry, compared it to his own, then ran the new one gently across his own arm, putting no pressure on the blade. A red, paper-thin cut followed the blade.

He grunted in approval and handed his own knife to the merchant who accepted it. Then the battered chief took the looking-glass and held it in front of his mutilated countenance. He grinned broadly, exposing blackened teeth, said something in Algonkin, and turned to follow Wawatam.

Henry heaved a sigh of relief and triumph as the two disappeared inside the cabin. Before Langlade could shut the door behind him, Henry asked: "What did he say?"

"My uncle said that you were right. A glass is a good thing to have, because such beauty as he possesses should be admired." He paused for a moment by the door, then a slight smile appeared. "You were lucky, *Anglais.*"

"I intend to learn Algonkin, Monsieur," Henry retorted.

"That would be wise," Langlade said. "It is not good to depend too heavily on one's enemies."

He shut the door and left the merchant to his own thoughts.

🦋 🦋 🦋

Du CHARME had not seen much of his young friend since helping to get him established. In fact, he was unaware of the confrontation which had taken place with the Ottawa just prior to British occupation.

He had been away laying his traps (for food, not furs) and had returned to find the British garrison settled in. He had taken the oath of loyalty with little consternation and now sat in Henry's store visiting and pulling on his pipe.

As Du Charme cheerfully related the recent history of his whereabouts, Henry organized his wares and watched over the chicken 'stovie' which was bubbling in the kettle on the hearth. Both men were enjoying a touch of rum as the leaves of this late October afternoon rustled across the parade ground and playfully skittled through the open cabin door.

When the huge man had finished his narrative, Henry informed him of his difficult conversation with La Fourche and Wawatam and his desire to learn the Algonkin tongue.

"Well why didn't you say so, *mon ami?*" he bellowed. "I can teach you."

Henry looked up from his work. "You know it?"

"*Mais oui.* It is a good thing to learn since it is the language of the Chippewa as well."

Henry was delighted and could not disguise his excitement. "When can we start?" he cried.

"Whenever you wish."

"Now?"

Du Charme shrugged. "I suppose so, why not?"

They began with simple vocabulary and another glass of rum.

Du Charme grabbed a blanket off the counter. "This is *wabowayan,*" he said.

Henry repeated it as well as he could. Du Charme picked up a spool of thread, "*Asubab.*" He pointed at the broth bubbling in the black kettle. "*Nabob.*"

With each word, Henry tried to commit it to memory. After two hours, and no flagging of enthusiasm on the Englishman's part, Du Charme began to regret his promise. Henry's thirst for knowledge seemed to be insatiable and the tutor was becoming quite bored and anxious to get home to silence the grumbling in his stomach. Henry's broth and Du Charme's interest had grown cold together, yet Alexander had given no thought to his own, or his guest's sustenance.

"Tomorrow is another day," Du Charme sighed at last, looking out the door at the setting sun filtering through the cracks in the stockade wall.

Henry seemed to be aware of his friend for the first time since his lessons had begun. "I'm sorry, Laurent. I've kept you from your family."

"And my dinner," Du Charme added.

"Of course. Forgive me. I'm just very anxious to learn."

"I know." Du Charme began to move toward the door and at first he thought the sun had vanished. It took his eyes a moment to adjust and another few seconds for his brain to register that the light was gone because someone, quite large and broad-shouldered, was standing in the doorway, blocking the fading rays of sunshine.

As the figure stepped inside, Henry recognized him as the Indian with the split ear lobes—Wawatam. After making his entrance, he stood staring at the merchant for a few moments as if he were trying to decipher some secret, knowing his familiarity with his language from previous visits. As he related the purpose of his visit, Henry was pleased to discover that he could identify a word here and there. One such word was *inabandumowin*, or dream. This intrigued him and he waited impatiently for the translation from Du Charme, as the dialogue stretched into five minutes.

Finally, Du Charme began to speak in English and the young merchant listened with rapt attention, not even bothering to greet his friend Ezekial who had come to visit after his day's work was completed, as was his habit. Solomon was not offended, but listened to Du Charme's loose interpretation as he seated himself comfortably on a rum barrel in the corner and lit his pipe.

"Wawatam explained to me that he lost his parents as a child and La Fourche adopted him," Du Charme began. "That makes Langlade and Langlade's deceased brother, Au-san-aw-go, his cousins. He told me that the death of Au-san-aw-go has left an empty space . . . you would say, eh, void . . . in many people's lives, especially his own. Wawatam belongs to the *cicigwe* (rattlesnake) degree of the *Midewiwin,* or Grand Medicine Society. He learned the practice from Ishnoki, the great *shaman* of the Ojibway who lived close by, but has since died.

"He has had a vision, which he says is big medicine. To make a long story short, he says that the spirits have told him that his cousin is dead, and to rest his spirit, a replacement must be found to fill the space. The replacement must come from among the people who killed him, the *Anglais*. He says the spirits have led you here and you must be his new cousin!"

Henry was flabbergasted. "Tell my friend, er cousin, I am deeply honored."

When Du Charme translated, Wawatam's eyes became moist. He strode across the room and gave Henry a big bear hug, almost lifting him off the floor in the process. Henry returned the embrace and was genuinely touched by the Ottawa's emotional outburst. Wawatam, for his part, was obviously very pleased. Henry noted that he smelled heavily of the rum he had accepted earlier.

When Wawatam finally released his new relative, he spoke for several minutes, and without waiting for Du Charme to interpret, walked out the door and headed for the water gate leading out of the fort.

"*Sacré bleu,*" Du Charme exclaimed.

"What did he say?" Henry asked anxiously.

"He says that you and he are now one. You are family. You are like the *atcab* and *asawan,* the arrow and the bowstring. One is of no use without the other. Therefore your life is under his protection and his is under yours. You both have a solemn responsibility to protect each other. Your lives are of no value without this bond."

"All this from a dream?" Henry asked.

"The *Midewiwin* take their dreams very seriously." Du Charme paused for a moment, then laughed.

"What?"

"Your cousin has a sense of humor."

"What do you mean?"

The Frenchman snickered again as he headed for the door

and his *petite fleur.* "He says that you must protect one another."

"Yes?"

"He says his job will probably be more difficult than yours."

🍁 🍁 🍁

Henry's lessons continued almost on a daily basis, and Ezekial Solomon began to find some time to listen to Du Charme's instruction as well.

The Frenchman spent a good deal of his time at the merchant's little store, and when Marguerite protested his absence, she found herself preparing additional food so that Henry could dine with them. In the next month, Henry was able to speak with the priest several times, and papist or not, Alexander was convinced that he had never met a more sincere cleric, or one who was less hypocritical. The 'Black Robe,' he knew, was concerned for his soul, but he was not judgmental, nor did he condemn. Their conversations occurred more frequently, and friendship began to develop.

Madame and Monsieur Cardin were also quite amicable and visited the little shop often. It seemed that Madame Cardin's increasing warmth was directly related to the priest's, but Henry dismissed the idea as improbable.

Langlade continued to isolate himself from the English, although Henry had a sneaking suspicion that the brooding halfbreed probably liked him better than any other *Anglais* at Michilimackinac, if it was possible for him to tolerate any of them.

As November approached, Henry met the Indian woman Marie Amiot for the first time. Her sons had always been very personable and had been a great help to him in his first week at the post. He had rewarded each of them with a little gift, as well as material for their widowed mother to make dresses for her daughters who had grown into dark, attractive teen-agers. She had come to thank him personally, and had drawn from him a promise to visit her little cabin.

Augustin Langlade was almost as mysterious as his son. He came to the shop on occasion to purchase rum and tobacco, but never spoke a word. Henry suspected that he knew no English. Unlike his son, the elder Langlade seemed sad and lost. He was not intentionally rude or malicious, but seemed to care little for life and was oblivious of those around him. He had become somewhat of a recluse and appeared to prefer it that way. His face was old and care-worn, and his beard was speckled with gray, matching his hoary head.

Ignace Bourassa was a frequent visitor as well. Henry was often puzzled by this man who had been willing to be imprisoned rather than take the oath of loyalty, but was so individually friendly to the British. He seemed to be able to separate politics from his personal relationships, something his brother-in-law, Charles Langlade, was incapable of doing.

Colonel Etherington was rarely seen. Bostwick and Goddard were his frequent companions, but they went to his quarters, not he theirs. The commandant did not socialize at all with the new British subjects of Fort Michilimackinac, nor did he fraternize with his men. Lieutenant Leslie and Lieutenant Jamet ran the day-to-day affairs of his command. It was they who drilled the troops, they who issued the orders, they who attended to each detail.

The French community was extremely friendly to the officers (with the exception of Charles Langlade). The common soldiers were, by and large, pleasant and polite, although their drinking and dice games would sometimes disturb the civilian population, at which time Jamet's natural bent for diplomacy would come to the fore and make short work of the difficulty.

Wawatam visited his new 'cousin' several times in the ensuing weeks, delighting Henry and giving him an opportunity to put to practical use, his language lessons. In time, he became proficient enough for the Ottawa to assume Du Charme's role as tutor—a situation which was a great relief to Marguerite and her twins, who now were able to see more of their husband and father.

Wawatam, Henry discovered, was a very patient teacher, and as his proficiency in the language grew, he learned a great deal about his friend personally, and Ottawa culture and customs in general. He also heard much about La Fourche, and through

Wawatam's descriptions, came to admire the old chief, though he did not see him again that year.

One day in early November, while he and Wawatam sat talking by the fire in Henry's shop, three Indians came through the door.

They were all young yet, two of them probably in their mid-twenties and the third, younger still. Wawatam told Henry they were 'Anishnabeg' (Chippewa), the first the merchant had seen since his arrival in the straits area, two months ago.

The one who seemed to be the authority weighed over two hundred pounds and had a wild look about him. Henry overheard one of his companions refer to him as 'whirlwind.' The other older one, obviously subordinate to the first, wore a strange turban made of otter skin with a small hole in the middle of it. Strange-looking braids bordered each side of his face.

The third member of this trio was barely twenty years old, but much fairer than the other two and without the high cheekbones and black, silky hair characteristic of the Chippewa. He was obviously of mixed blood.

Wawatam seemed to know the intruders and called them by name in a friendly manner, but the one addressed as Matche-kewis (whirlwind) merely grunted in acknowledgement as he began to handle Henry's merchandise. The other two, Wenniway and Sans-père, followed suit.

Alexander saw an opportunity to establish rapport with these men and their people, so as each admired a particular object, he told them, as well as he could in Algonkin, that they should consider it a present from him. They seemed not to understand him, so Wawatam volunteered a translation.

They paid no attention to the Ottawa's words either, but following Matchekewis' lead, began to scoop up merchandise in their arms, loading up as much as they could carry of whatever took their fancy. They were making a shambles of Henry's neatly organized shelves and counter. Sans-père, in fact, leapt over the counter and proceeded to hand his companions whatever items they requested.

The Englishman, believing that they had simply misunderstood him, attempted to explain what he had meant, but the words failed him. He looked helplessly to Wawatam. His 'cousin,' seeing his distress, stepped forward and blocked the door as the transgressors prepared to depart with their booty.

🦊 🦊 🦊

Out of the way, Wawatam," Matchekewis growled.

"You have taken what does not belong to you," Wawatam said calmly.

"Gift-giving is customary for friendship," Wenniway said, smiling slyly.

"He has fulfilled that custom and you well know it, Minavavana's son. Take what he offered you in friendship and leave the rest." Though Matchekewis' free hand slipped to the knife at his side, Wawatam did not budge.

Henry was picking up enough of the dialogue to know that trouble was brewing. He felt drops of perspiration running down his spine under his blouse, despite the coolness of the air.

"He is *Anglais*," Matchekewis muttered disdainfully. "We will take what we want and leave him his life. It is enough!"

"He is my brother and friend. You will not take what belongs to him."

Matchekewis, his insane eyes burning, drew his knife. Still Wawatam remained immobile. He looked over at Wenniway. "Your father would not be happy if you killed La Fourche's son. It would cause lasting enmity between your people and mine."

Wawatam's words appeared to have some impact on Wenniway, but Matchekewis kept his knife at ready. Wawatam's obligation to protect Henry was indeed going to be a trial.

The young merchant had learned enough of Indian pride to know that bloodshed was imminent. Finally, stumbling pathetically in his half-learned Algonkin, Henry suggested that his 'cousin' allow his Anishnabeg friends to depart, with the understanding that they could pay him later. This compromise would save face for both sides, probably save Wawatam's life and perhaps his own, and leave some hope for a decent relationship with the Chippewa, although Alexander expected that he would never be paid.

Wawatam, seeing that his new relative was serious in his proposal, and catching an assenting nod from Wenniway over Matchekewis' shoulder, stepped aside and the Chippewa departed.

When they had gone, as Henry began to put the mess aright, he asked Wawatam if all the Chippewa were like those three. The Medicine Man told him that Matchekewis, the whirlwind, was more spirit than human, a phrase that Alexander was to learn in the figurative expressions of the Ottawa, meant insane. Wenniway, he further related, was spoiled and weak. Sans-père, he said, was stupid, and simply followed.

But, he added, they were not representative of the Anishnabeg, a noble and courageous race. Minavavana, the primary chief of the Chippewa band, he believed, would someday come to friendship with Henry as he was now a friend to himself and La Fourche.

But he would doubtless not have to worry about the Chippewa for awhile since they were leaving any day to winter in the south and would not return until the maple-sugar-making-moon, *ickigamisigegizis,* or April.

Wawatam laughed, slapping his 'cousin' on the back and explaining that the Ottawa of *L'Arbre Croche,* unlike their Chippewa brethren, wintered where they were, near the fort, and his language lessons, which Wawatam reminded him he needed badly, would continue without interruption.

🍁 🍁 🍁

WAWATAM WAS AS GOOD as his word. He came to Henry's shop several times each week during the freezing, snowy months of winter and instructed his willing pupil diligently. A true son of Demosthenes, Henry gave his all to his lessons, and by the time the snow began to melt away, he had become quite proficient in Algonkin.

The greatest benefit of Wawatam's visits was not his teaching, however, but the solid friendship that developed between them. Henry was convinced that he would have gone out of his mind with boredom had he not had the companionship of his Indian friend.

The winter months were the busiest of the year for the trappers of Michilimackinac since the furs they sought were at their thickest in cold weather, and therefore more valuable. They also spent much time hunting game, and when they returned to the fort from a wet and frigid day in the forest, they tended to stay close to the warmth of their fires and families. Thus Henry did not see much of them.

The only other consistent visitor to his little post was Ezekial Solomon who, like Henry and Wawatam, had no family. The three of them discussed their varied religious beliefs, tried different recipes, drank a good deal of rum and tea, and passed the violent winter in relative comfort.

Occasionally Henry saw Du Jaunay. The priest was always invited to one house or another for a meal. It was obvious that he was regarded with sacred awe by many of the Canadians and that was not without merit. The priest was, in Henry's opinion, a good candidate for canonization. His life was a constant service to those around him. He conducted Mass and heard confessions which one would expect from a cleric, but he also was the first to be present in any emergency. He tended the sick, ministered to the troubled, gave what he had to the hungry, protected the threatened (as in Henry's case), helped construct sheds and dwellings, chopped wood, sheltered orphans and widows, and still found time to perform the sacraments and proselytize the fallen. He was, in short, a marvel, and Henry never ceased to be impressed by his integrity, industry, humility and courage.

He and the good Father had several interesting discussions during which Du Jaunay tried to convince the Anglican of his error, but to no avail. Yet the conversations helped to pass the time while the straits were buried in ice and snow, and gave Henry still another companion.

When the temperature began to rise, and dark clouds were replaced with fairly constant sunshine, Alexander Henry decided to make a visit to the Chippewa encampment when he heard from Du Charme that they had returned recently from their southern wintering grounds to tap the maples and process the sugar, which they consumed year-round.

He was not only curious about how this was done, but he also wanted to meet the Chippewa leaders, and establish some rapport with them so that he might encourage their trade.

With this in mind, and without telling anyone, he headed east from the fort one April morning, in the direction of the maple grove where Du Charme had said the Chippewa were encamped.

He knew he was taking somewhat of a risk, having experienced the hostility of Wenniway, Matchekewis and Sans-père, but he believed that the leaders of this band, particularly the one called Minavavana, would be less biased and more receptive.

He could have taken Wawatam along with him for protection, or a Canadian, like Du Charme, but he believed the Chippewa would interpret their presence as a lack of trust on his part and leave a bad impression.

So he left the fort, alone and unarmed, anxious to test his knowledge of Algonkin. He carried with him only some small trinkets, two fine skinning knives, a jug of rum, and his own naïveté.

As he labored along the beach, he kept looking inland as Du Charme had told him. The Chippewa, he said, never camped far from the big water and he would be able to see the smoke from the many fires necessary to boil the syrup.

He had walked perhaps two miles or more and seen nothing. He came upon a rock which had been so weathered by wind and water that it made a smooth sitting place and he could not resist the temptation to rest.

He dropped his pack and plunked down in nature's chair. His breathing, visible in the cool, crisp air, began to slow. Partly from relief at deliverance from his burden, and partly to see his frosty breath, he heaved a sigh and looked about him.

The sand, dotted with clumps of heavy, dry grass, like topknots, stretched to the very edge of the pines and cedars, towering behind him at a distance of perhaps fifty feet. His attention was captured by a scuffling noise among the dead leaves at the edge of the forest floor. There, scurrying among the fallen trees and branches, were two chipmunks, fighting anxiously over an acorn. They were not alarmed by the presence of the human intruder. Years of experience had taught their kind that man rarely sought them out for food or fur.

Henry, amused, thought it time that they learned to cow before their two-legged master. He grabbed a round stone from the sand and pitched it in their direction. They took no heed of it, but as it ricocheted among the trees, it disturbed a partridge which rose swiftly into the blue sky, beating its wings furiously.

Henry smiled and turned his head to absently search the shoreline on either side. As he looked to the east, he could see nothing but budding branches from the deciduous maples and elms and birches that survived in small camps among the legions of evergreens. His eyes followed the shoreline until it disappeared, then drifted across the bright expanse of blue water until they discerned a dark shape against the horizon. The great island floated along the surface of the lake, seeming to possess a life of its own. The Algonkin word for it, he knew, was *Michi-mak-i-nac,* Isle of the Great Turtle, and as Henry observed it from this distance, it did seem that the tree-darkened hills of the island could be mistaken for a gargantuan shell. 'It's very beautiful in any case,' Henry mused.

It had an eerie quality about it that forced a separation of the blue sky with the blue-green of the lake, and mysteriously established an interesting perspective between the earth and the heavens. The Indians, Henry had learned, thought it to be the home of their primary god, 'Gitchi' —something? Anyway, it was the arbiter in some eternal misunderstanding between the world and the sky above it, though he thought all of it to be superstitious mythology.

His eyes, reluctantly, broke away from the island and looked to his left. There he observed the straits of Mackinac, connecting the lake to the west called *Michi-Gaumee* (Great Water), by the Chippewa, with the lake called Huron to the east.

Across the strait, on the northern shore, was the mission of St. Ignace, founded by the French Jesuits, who had named the place for Loyola, their founder, and who had died to bring their faith to the Indians. The now-abandoned mission stood as a monument to their failure.

The sun floated briefly behind a cloud and he was suddenly aware of the cold air blowing in across the open water. As the breeze shifted, and the sun returned, Alexander became cognizant of a very definite and pleasing aroma, coming somewhere from the woods behind him. The odor was so inviting with its candy sweetness, that he decided to investigate. He rose cautiously, moved into the enveloping foliage, and disappeared.

He walked deliberately among the ferns and liverwort underfoot as the sounds of human activity and the smoke of many fires blended with the sweet scent that he now recognized as maple sugar.

His ears gradually picked up the additional sounds of laughter and human voices brattling in Algonkin. His heart beat with celerity. He halted on the forest floor, peering ahead through the filtered woodland light at a small rise which appeared to be the last obstacle to a clearing beyond. Smoke floated lazily through the towering maples and gave to the scene a haunting quality which, for a moment, mesmerized Henry and held him in his frozen stance.

Curiosity began to overcome his disquietude, however, as he realized that there was no enmity or hostility in any of the sounds proceeding from what had to be the Chippewa camp. He saw no evidence of any previous passage through the area in which he stood. The scattered patches of snow, still clinging to tenuous existence in the early spring, were without any human tracks, leading him to assume that if he approached the camp from this direction, it would be unlikely that he would be surprised by some returning warrior.

Once he had reached the little knoll, he lay on his stomach in the cold, damp leaves, and looked down at the clearing below. Wigwams of the Chippewa dotted the perimeter. Smoke rose from the center of the clearing where women poured the maple syrup from large, moosehide bags into boiling kettles. Children and the younger women carried birchbark vessels from the trees to the pots where the sap was melted down into a sweet, sticky syrup. The syrup was then poured into the moosehide bags until it cooled, then ladled back into the kettles to convert it, by vaporization, into hard, maple sugar.

Some women stoked and fed the red-hot fires and others constantly stirred the bubbling mixtures with maple branches to move the moisture to the top of the boiling kettles where it would evaporate.

The peaceful scene, with its absence of bellicose young men, created an idyllic setting and a feeling of comfort spread through Henry's chilly limbs. The odor of maple was intoxicating. The smell of it sweetened the air like perfume. Children roamed about freely, playing what appeared to be some savage form of 'king's tag,' which produced ribald laughter and created distracting movement which, in a European setting, would have provoked indignant reprimands from furious adults who lived by the maxim, 'children should be seen and not heard.'

But here, in Eden-like innocence, upbraiding the children would be paramount to sacrilege, their behavior seemed so naturally to fit the setting.

From his vantage point, Henry could see virtually the entire camp, and he wondered where the men were. Except for a few old ones, who did not contribute any labor to the project but sat in small groups puffing pipes, eating the hard-won sugar, and talking quietly, the village was free of any adult males.

Henry wondered if they might all be hunting (which seemed unlikely) or if they might be away at war (with whom?). Their absence puzzled him and made him uneasy. He had the eerie sensation that he was being observed, and kept glancing back over his shoulder to make sure the male population was not standing behind him, poised to murder him for his intrusion. Yet each time he looked back, he saw nothing but the forest, silent and undisturbed.

He wanted very much to walk from his hiding place and speak with some of the old men below, but he was afraid that they might misinterpret his actions, with the warriors away from the camp, and sound an alarm which would bring them running. Henry believed that under the circumstances any returning warriors, seeing an intruder in the midst of their women and children, might fire first and ask questions later. So, he contented himself with observation.

Among the erratic chasing of the naked, joy-filled youth,

Henry's eye was distracted by a young Chippewa woman who passed within twenty feet of his hiding place at the top of the knoll.

Her beauty was such that it momentarily interrupted his breathing and he was not conscious of this impromptu, biological reaction until he became dizzy and his body, scolding him for his inattention, began to rebel and forced him to inhale and exhale vigorously.

She was, perhaps, twenty years old, or even younger. Her hair, blue-black, glossy and resplendent, flowed down her back to her hips. Her arms were slender and alluring, ending in fragile, diminuitive hands, that looked, somehow, strong. Her legs, bare from the knee down, were lithesome and supple, softly muscled in attractive curves.

She stopped for a moment, seeming to sense something, and looked in Henry's direction. His face was hidden by a small fern, and he was certain that she was not able to see him, yet she looked right through him.

Her forehead was high and delicately feminine, sloping down toward a piquant nose surrounded by roseate cheeks. Her mouth was tantalizing, with a full lower lip and thinner upper one, which gave her a naturally pouting expression when her mouth was closed. It had all the charm of a spoiled six-year-old, who has been told that she must go without supper.

Yet the most distinguishing feature of her lovely face was her eyes. They were large, with ebony pupils that glistened even in the shadows where she stood. They were voluptuous eyes, brazen and vulpine, yet also strangely tranquilizing. They were mysterious, like strange, dark pools in an oasis. The sojourner longed to drink from them, but danger could lurk there.

Some children shouted at her, calling her name, and she suddenly turned and waved at them. The femininity and attractiveness of the name seemed to fit her. Lo-tah began to stroll toward the group of little girls who came rushing toward her. There was something very sensual about the way she walked and Henry imagined what her hips would look like under the loose-fitting doeskin dress. She walked on her toes rather than her heels, the long, silken-black hair caressing her hips.

She was loved, it was obvious to Henry, especially by the younger children who now circled about her in some sort of ritual game. She smiled, erasing the pout, then pretended to suffer horribly as the delighted children threw imaginary missiles at her. With a shout, she suddenly dropped the empty birch vessels she had been carrying, and chased the children away, laughing in great merriment at their frantic escape. One little girl, in her excitement, turned away from the trees and up the center of the camp where the kettles bubbled and boiled and where the shouts of the squaws reminded her, she was forbidden to play.

She stopped quickly, realizing her error, and backed away from the squaws, two of whom were approaching her with their maple branches poised to strike. Apparently, Henry thought as he observed this, that all was not as idyllic as he had supposed.

As the child retreated before the wrath of the advancing squaws, she caught her foot on the exposed root of a gnarled and ancient maple, lost her balance, and amid shouts of fear and warning, toppled backward, directly into a kettle of boiling syrup.

A sharp *"s-s-s-s-s-s"* split the air. It could be heard even above the child's agonized screams as the hot maple lava enveloped her waist. Her feet, arms and head thrashed wildly as she howled like an animal in her distress. She could not escape the sticky torture of the bubbling sugar as it clung to her like death itself.

"Great God!" Henry muttered under his breath. Without regard to his own position, he burst from his hiding place and scrambled down the hill. By the time he reached the wretched child, she was alternately laughing and screaming hysterically as the burning liquid consumed her flesh. She thrashed and writhed in agony, unable to help herself as the young beauty Henry had been admiring was trying desparately to liberate the child from her private holocaust.

Henry pushed the young woman aside as the rest of the inhabitants of the camp stood with mouths agape, astonished as much by his sudden appearance, seemingly from nowhere, as with the tragedy at hand. He found himself unable to grip the thrashing limbs of the hysterical child until, mercifully, she swooned. In her relaxed state, however, her arms and legs dropped limply against the sides of the red-hot kettle, and again the hissing sound of burning flesh slithered through the air like some great and evil reptile.

Henry, in one Herculean effort, snatched an arm and a leg and pulled the tortured child from the inferno. He laid her limp frame on the cold ground, barely conscious of the searing pain on his stomach and thighs where the fiery syrup had dripped on him as if in vengeance for his theft of the child. He was breathing rapidly as he ran into the trees, returning in an instant with hands full of snow, which he sprinkled onto the steaming waist of the child. He made a second trip, and soon the squaws, understanding that he meant no harm and, recovering from the initial shock of his sudden appearance, began to imitate his movements. They followed his example silently and efficiently except for one wretched woman, apparently the child's mother, who held the limp head in her lap and wailed unceasingly.

Henry did not know what else to do, once the little girl's midsection had been blanketed with snow. He listened at her still undeveloped breast, and could detect a faint, but steady heartbeat. The problem now lay in removing the hardening maple syrup around her waist, which hid the grotesque disfigurement of her torso underneath. As he reached to remove the snow, he felt a restraining hand on his shoulder.

He swallowed hard and turned to see who had stopped him. Much to his relief, he recognized the placid countenance of his 'cousin,' Wawatam. The Ottawa had come to see Henry at his store, and finding him absent, had followed his trail to the Chippewa camp. He had, in fact, been watching his friend while he lay on his belly observing the village below, probably accounting for Henry's feeling of being watched. When he had heard the screams of the child and saw Henry disappear over the knoll, he had followed. Henry was too busy ministering to the child to notice (though he had walked right by Wawatam when gathering snow to cool the burning syrup).

Wawatam was a recognized *shaman* who had been taught by old Ishnoki and many of those observing knew him and trusted his skill as a healer. No one was happier than Henry to see him. He surrendered his patient gratefully and wordlessly, because he hadn't the slightest notion of what to do next and he wanted to be absolved of responsibility for her.

Wawatam removed his *penegusan*[1] from his belt and also produced his magic rattle, or *shishiquoi,* while the mother of the child, less hysterical now that her baby was in competent hands, moved a short distance away to pray to the Great Turtle. Henry noticed that she was being comforted by the young woman named Lo-tah whom he had admired and recently thrust aside so roughly. He raised the courage to look at her, and she returned his stare with her consuming black eyes. He had feared that Lo-tah would be angry with him for the unintentional roughness he had meted out to her, but those alluring orbs rested affectionately on him as she held the bereaved squaw. He thought briefly of leaving, but her eyes held him prisoner and he remained immobile, perplexed by the way she studied him. She almost seemed to be flirting with him, but she was so savagely beautiful that he found it unlikely that she could be attracted to a mere mortal like himself.

He was absolutely captivated by the pouting half-smile, and when she moved her tongue across her upper lip, he thought he would faint. His heart beat wildly. There was something in the way she looked at him, the tilt of the head, the smile, the movement of the brazen, black eyes, that communicated a very real message to his heart, that was seductive and sensuous, but full of love and fidelity. It was not the look of a whore, but that of a beautiful bride, taking her husband to bed on her wedding night.

Wawatam nudged him slightly as the medicine man positioned himself to work on the unconscious child, and only this physical jolt could bring Henry back to reality. He looked away then, but glanced back at Lo-tah every few minutes to find her eyes riveted to him while her delicate hands stroked the head of the grief-stricken mother, the same, strange, mollifying smile on her provocative lips.

Wawatam, after careful consideration, which had been accompanied by several tugs on the gold ring in his ear, began to remove the snow from the silent victim. Further scrutiny re-

---

[1]Medicine bag made of otter skin.

vealed a hard crust of syrup which clung stubbornly to the tortured skin. Without any apparent emotion that could be discerned from his placid expression, the medicine man began to peel the offending substance from the inert body. The child squirmed involuntarily, in spite of her unconscious state, as several layers of bloody tissue came with the hardened syrup.

Henry looked quickly at the beautiful Indian maiden across from him and was surprised to see no fear or revulsion for this grisly scene, but sympathy dominated her sweet visage and a slight wrinkling of her forehead indicated an inner pain which she shared with the child.

Once the crust was removed (it seemed to Henry as if days had passed), Wawatam ordered the few attending squaws (most had returned to their work), to gather some sort of black and rotting vegetation with which he covered the torn and bloodied torso. This seemed to have some affect, whether good or bad, Henry could not immediately discover, but the child began to mumble and moved her arms slowly, as if mesmerized.

Just as relative calm began to be restored to the village, as is often the case, the patient suddenly regained consciousness and screamed in such piercing agony that Henry, his senses rebelling against the hellish sounds, leapt backward. Wawatam made no effort to pacify the writhing child, but stood over her, brandishing his rattle and hopping slowly from one foot to the other, chanting in monotonous rhythmn. The savage grunting of the pathetic figure at his feet had little visible affect on him.

While still attempting to recover from the alarming moans of the miserable sufferer, Henry's attention was captured by other sounds that foretold, perhaps, some hardship for him. He realized that a strategic withdrawal from the camp was now impossible as the noise of armed warriors moving quickly toward the encampment echoed through the woods. They had come from the permanent camp almost a league away. Henry had not realized that the village in which he stood was a temporary one, used only for processing the maple sugar, common labor in which warriors took no part. They had come in reaction to the screaming child as they suddenly plunged from the darkness of the forest into the soft and smoky light of the clearing, with weapons at ready and angry scowls upon their savage faces.

Henry shuddered as he surmised their number to be at least fifty, the early returnees from the wintering grounds in the south. They stood perfectly still once they were aware that there was no danger to the camp, and they stared at the lone white man in their midst as he, in turn, gawked at them.

Wawatam, unperturbed, continued to perform his little dance around the whimpering child as though nothing had happened. His eyes were closed and he seemed to be caught up in some sort of somnambulistic trance from which nothing could distract him.

The Chippewa moved slowly toward Henry out of the smoke and mist as demons would approach a damned soul, their eyes on the stricken child. They were fierce-looking men, their heads shaved except for the tribal scalplock. Several had bones through their noses and rings in their ears. Some had feathers attached to their hair and one fellow wore an unusual neclace made of fish vertebrae. They wore buckskin jackets, some of them festooned with beaded designs, and all wore the *mitases* leggings, partially exposing their buttocks. Their loins were covered in brightly-colored breechclouts.

The Englishman tried to present as calm an appearance as possible. He had been told by Laurent Du Charme that Indians in general, and the Chippewa in particular, could actually smell fear on a man, much like animals, and they reacted violently against it as if it were some sort of pestilence to be exterminated.

Many of the warriors wore fur capes against the cold, as well as fur hats made of beaver, otter, raccoon and other furs. Those valuable commodities did not escape the capitalistic eyes of Alexander Henry, whose existence in this wilderness would depend upon the trade he could initiate with these frightening people—if they would allow him to survive long enough to establish it.

As the Chippewa approached him, their ranks suddenly parted to allow two impressive-looking warriors to the front.

One of them looked to be in his thirties (though Henry found he was rarely correct in guessing the ages of Indians), a particularly bellicose man-at-arms who looked as if he had planned to go hunting, but now had no need to, since the game had wandered into camp. He babbled something to the older man who stood next to him and was apparently in charge. He was a noble-looking savage who had the appearance and bearing of the intellectual. Without the rings, feathers and hairstyle, and dressed in different clothing, he could have passed for an Italian university professor, though he was without the academic pall and his biceps bulged against the bracelets on his arms. The professor broke the silence. "Why are you here?" he asked flatly.

The question was simple enough and Henry was surprised to find that he understood this first Algonkin sentence perfectly. It was fortunate that he did, because Wawatam continued to ignore him and the Chippewa men and concentrated entirely on his patient.

"I came into this camp to help the child," he said in almost flawless Algonkin, pointing to the suffering girl. He was relieved to see that they had already discounted any culpability on his part in regard to the little girl's condition. At the same time, he was becoming increasingly exacerbated at the racket that Wawatam was creating with his rattle.

"Why are you here?" the Indian repeated. At first Henry feared that the chief had not understood him, but then realized he wanted a fuller explanation.

"I was down by the shore and I smelled the maple," he said cautiously, signifying one of the boiling pots. "I was curious, so I followed the scent" (he couldn't help pointing to his nose), "and then, when I saw the child, I came into your camp to help her. I intend no harm." He almost laughed at himself for having made such a ludicrous statement. In his present predicament he was in no position to do harm to anyone but himself.

"Umm," the Indian grunted. He never took his eyes from Henry, but spread his arms as if to indicate the vastness of the wilderness around him, then repeated the question: "Why are you *here*?"

Slowly the trader began to understand that the professor did not want an explanation of his presence in the village, but rather he wanted to know why Henry was in this part of the world at all!

"I have come to trade with you." He pointed at the beaver

pelt dangling from a warrior's waist. The way the man looked at him made Henry feel uncomfortable. It was a greedy look, like a starving man regarding a venison roast. "I have a license from Sir William Johnson, Superintendent of Indian Affairs in the Northern Department . . ." He reached into a pocket in his pantaloons, then realized how ridiculous this kind of explanation was.

"I have come from the English king to help you. I have things that you are in need of and you have things that the English king wants. My name is Alexander Henry. I come in peace, as a friend."

"I am Minavavana, the Grand Saulteur," the professor rejoined. "Lo-tah foresaw that the French king would fall asleep." Henry glanced quickly at the young woman who still regarded him with her magnetic eyes. It was obvious that it was she to whom the chief was referring. "But he will awaken and the children of the Great Turtle will be punished if they offer their hospitality to the *Anglais*. I, myself, have killed many *Anglais,* but they have too many to kill them all. The French have lived among us, shared our lodges and our women. The *Anglais* only kill. Our Ottawa brothers to the south and west tell us that all English seek to destroy us. If these speak the truth, then *your* words are twisted."

Henry realized that his next few words would have to be chosen carefully if he were to live. Wawatam still ignored him. "The French king will not awake. He and his people were defeated forever by the English king. You have no reason to fear the wrath of a sleeping man."

"*You* have reason to fear, *Anglais*. The Anishnabeg are awake!" These words came from Niskigwun[2], Minavavana's companion, who was known for his bad temper.

"I have brought gifts for you," Henry said, remembering at once that he had left them at the top of the knoll in his haste to help the child.

"The Anishnabeg do not take presents from their enemies," Minavavana said.

"Your son did," was Henry's abrupt reply. For the first time,

---

[2]Ruffled feathers.

the chief lost his composure, the professorial air turning to a vicious scowl.

"The *Anglais* lies," he shouted, bringing his hand across his torso in a swift, chopping motion.

"He does not lie, Minavavana." The voice came from behind Henry and he turned to see Wawatam standing there, facing his antagonists. The child rested peacefully at his feet, still covered with the black mosses. "Wenniway and Sans-père from your village accepted presents from this man and also took other things for which they have agreed to pay. Whirlwind was with them too. He speaks the truth. I bear witness."

Niskigwun looked hatefully at the Ottowa. He could sense the animal escaping the trap, and he did not like it.

"Where is my son?" Minavavana asked of no one in particular.

"He and Sans-père are at the village of Matchekewis, the Whirlwind, to the south," Niskigwun answered.

The chief paused and resumed his academic poise. "My good friend Wawatam has never lied. If my son has accepted you, I accept you also." He then stood silently, like a bellboy in a hotel, awaiting a tip.

Wawatam nudged the beaming Henry and motioned toward the hill from which he had descended. The Englishman immediately caught the hint and in moments, had returned with his presents.

He gave one skinning knife to Niskigwun who took it reluctantly, and the other to Minavavana along with the small cask of rum. The two men immediately turned and left, disappearing into the forest with their following as quickly as they had come. Once again, harmony was restored to the village. Henry, visibly relieved, began to relax. He felt a terrible need to urinate.

"We must go now," Wawatam whispered. "They are still watching." He nodded his head in the direction of the trees.

Henry looked at the child, who was moaning deliriously as several squaws lifted her onto a sort of cot constructed of saplings and pine boughs, and took her to a nearby wigwam, accompanied by her attentive mother.

Lo-tah, obviously concerned, watched their departure, then

turned her gaze once again upon the Englishman. Her expression told him that she shared none of her people's prejudices toward his race.

Summoning his courage, he stepped toward her and gently placed one of his trinkets, a beaded necklace, over her head. Her eyes never left his. His hands lingered ever so slightly on her delicate neck. "For your beauty," he said.

He tore himself away then and followed Wawatam up the little knoll down which he had stumbled, it seemed, hundreds of years before.

Chapter
4

The Horse and the Star

HENRY SAT AT THE SMALL TABLE in his shop, shortly before dawn, looking out the little window at the rays of sunshine which promised another beautiful June day.

His thoughts for the last few months had been dominated by the Ojibway woman, Lo-tah. Wawatam had explained that she was some sort of seeress who had the gift of prophecy, and certainly her bewitching eyes indicated a power not possessed by most other people, but he did not bother his heart or his intellect with the supernatural. 'Spirits are for wine cellars,' he had once joked to his uncle, a deeply religious man. Yet for some reason, that particular pun now seemed rather sophomoric to him. He wondered why, then ridiculed himself for giving the subject any consideration at all.

He had not seen Lo-tah since their meeting at the maple sugar camp, but her face drifted into and out of his mind almost constantly, both during his waking hours and while he slept.

His dreams of her ranged from gentle conversations to tempestuous lovemaking. Several times in the last week, he had awakened to find himself sweating and panting vigorously. He occasionally imagined that she had died or left the area forever, and those thoughts always left him deeply depressed and morose. His life had changed permanently since meeting her, but he was not certain why. His habits and daily routine had changed very little. He tried desperately to put her from his mind, with little success.

His business was thriving. The risks he had taken to develop a clientele among the Indians were paying off. The Ottawa frequented his shop more and more. Even La Fourche became a steady customer, having developed a taste for rum and peppermint sticks. With the addition of some Chippewa customers, Henry's stockpile of furs was growing rapidly, as was his bank account in Montreal. He had had to double his orders to the banker and sold his wares faster than he could replace them.

Of the three Ojibway who had visited his store, only Wenniway, Minavavana's son, had ever returned. He had wanted to purchase some rum, but when Alexander reminded him that he had not yet paid his previous debt, the young warrior exited angrily, promising Henry in a frighteningly sarcastic tone that he would pay him back in the course of time, indicating that the Englishman might be better off to carry the debt.

He had awakened with a start early this morning, as remnants of a dream about Lo-tah began to weave together with his returning consciousness. She and Wenniway had been part of the dream together, and somehow she had been hurt by the chief's son. Henry's heart pounded with hatred and jealous rage as he remembered the nightmare. He shook his head, as if such an action would erase the ugly vision.

He finished the last of the strong tea he had prepared for himself that morning, drew on a pair of pantaloons, tucked his nightshirt into them, and stepped onto his porch, squinting at the soft, summer sun.

His attention was captured by acrimonious commands issued from outside the southern stockade wall where the land gate stood open to the blue spruce and white pine bordering the edge of the wilderness beyond. The silence within the fort and a drum roll from without, brought him to the realization that the entire regiment was outside the walls, blocked from his view.

His curiosity got the better of him. He returned to his cabin, hastily finished dressing, and progressed toward the land gate. Since the garrison was outside, and his stock was basically depleted, he had little concern about leaving his shop unattended.

As he passed through the portal, he was startled to find the entire garrison (with the exception of Colonel Etherington), in full dress uniform, standing at rigid attention in neat, red, rows, and staring with blank faces at a pathetic soldier who was apparently being disciplined, a muffled groaning emitting from the unfortunate man.

He was seated on the 'wooden horse,' a device commonly used in the British army for petty offenses, particularly in the colonies. It was, as the name indicated, a horse made of wood, but the 'riding' surface consisted of two boards which came together at a peak, like a roof, thus causing the 'rider' to split his legs apart at an excruciating angle, and sit on his crotch, rather than his buttocks. Heavy stones dangled in mid-air, attached by ropes to the victim's ankles, producing maximum discomfort. His hands were tied behind his back so that he could not use them to relieve the pressure to his groin by pushing his body upward. As if to further humiliate him, a rocking horse head had been attached to the device and that, coupled with the fact that he was totally naked, presented a rather ludicrous and tragi-comic picture.

Henry noted that Lieutenant Jamet stood rigidly in front of the assembled troops and it was obvious from his frowning countenance that he was not relishing the barbaric task that apparently had fallen to him.

"It's not a pretty sight, is it?" Henry recognized the voice of Ezekial Solomon behind him. His friend was standing in front of his tiny cottage, just outside the southern gate at a distance of twenty-five feet. Alexander walked over to join him.

"No, it isn't." Henry was pleased that Solomon did not regard him as less than masculine for his squeamishness. "What did he do to deserve it?"

"The lieutenant said a few minutes ago that he violated the colonel's order not to leave the post. I understand he went to see an Indian woman." Henry thought immediately of Lo-tah. "I hope he had a damn good time. That horse will put him out of it for awhile. If he still has the courage to visit her a second time, he'll be planting splinters in her." Solomon chuckled innocently, but could see from the expression on his friend's face that he was concerned for the sufferer, so he changed his own to one of proper sobriety. "This isn't the first time it's happened and it won't be the last," Ezekial sighed philosophically. "It won't kill him."

"How can this be tolerated?" Alexander fumed. "Is it a crime to want a woman?" Henry was speaking as much for himself as for the rider.

"Soldiers have to obey," Solomon replied. "I don't know if he raped the woman, was in love with her, or paid her. It's all the same. British troops messing with Indian women could cause bad feelings."

"You know the colonel to be a bigot," Henry said. "Why do you defend him?"

Ezekial became irritated. "This isn't England, Alexander. Parliament doesn't stand by waving the Bill of Rights every time someone is accused. Out here, the law is brutal—and not only to the transgressor. Breaking the law could mean destruction, not just for the victim, but for all of his fellows too. So they make sure you don't transgress."

"What if the authority transgresses?"

"Then we all suffer." His face softened somewhat. "Don't be so concerned friend, he'll be up and around in a few days."

Henry studied his companion. He showed no appreciation for the cruelty he witnessed, yet Alexander saw no remorse in the tiny, black eyes, staring intently at the victim from either side of his prominent nose.

"It doesn't annoy you?"

"Of course it does."

"Then why do you stand here and watch it?"

Solomon looked rather irritated at this uncharitable remark. He had sensed a note of accusation in Henry's voice.

"I really don't have much choice," he snapped. "I live *outside* the fort, remember?"

Henry felt awkward and embarrassed. In the course of his righteous wrath, he had forgotten that Solomon was himself a frequent victim of the authorities, causing him great suffering and scornful treatment. "I'm sorry, Ezekial. Forgive me. It was a thoughtless and crude remark."

"Don't let it bother you," Solomon responded. "Looks like the troops have seen enough."

Lieutenant Jamet was mustering the regiment back inside the walls. The lone malefactor remained on the horse, his face revealing his bitter agony. Henry abhorred the ignominy of his plight. The wooden horse seemed to mock civilization and the denuded man to repudiate culture. Worse still, was the hypocrisy of the cursory Christian powers who forced his friend to live without the protection of laws or king. His good humor had vanished and been replaced by a distressing, vexatious mood.

Ezekial Solomon seemed to read his mind. "Don't get too deeply involved in Everyman's condition, Alexander. You'll see a lot of suffering yourself. You can't afford to suffer for everyone else."

Henry nodded his head in acknowledgement, but not in agreement.

"Besides," Ezekial continued, "you're a civilian. You can hump every squaw from here to Montreal, and never have to take a ride." He laughed heartily at his own joke, and drew a smile from Henry.

The rider, naked and still in his torment, mistook Ezekial's laughter for derisive enjoyment of his plight. His moaning was interrupted by a bitter, whispered, curse. "Dirty Jew."

🦋 🦋 🦋

As SUMMER PASSED INTO JULY, Henry became increasingly restless and bored. He began to sleep less and drink more. With his stock depleted and still waiting to be replenished from Montreal (the canoes were now weeks overdue), it was necessary to close his shop to all, except for the few soldiers who might need a plug of tobacco, or a cask of rum. This idleness gave him too much time to think and his thoughts inevitably strayed to Lo-tah.

He had not slept well again the night before, tossing in his sleep and dreaming of savage faces which leered at him from behind bushes, while Lo-tah wept for him, shedding tears of blood. His restive mood was not at all ameliorated by the fact that he had not seen her again, though he kept hoping she would appear one day in his store.

He breakfasted on a bowl of *sagamity*, washed it down with a little goat's milk (fresh from the nanny that Laurent Du Charme kept behind the common stables outside the fort), and sat down, not relishing the thought of another whole day in solitude. He lit his pipe, deliberated for some time, then slowly rose from his chair, paced about the room and, without purpose or plan, wandered outside, taking his 'brown bess' with him.

Within half an hour, he found himself on the beach, walking leisurely eastward. He strolled along the sand for an hour, stopping to skip stones across the water, or to observe a raccoon slip hurriedly into the dense pines, a limp field mouse in her maw. Once he saw a bull moose, majestically antlered, gulping greedily from the water of the lake as if to empty it. Another time, a blue heron with a shiny minnow in its long bill, glided gracefully into the sky, its wings beating smoothly, dragging its burden of long, inert, legs.

Henry was unconscious of any purposeful direction. The sun had become extremely hot as morning passed away, and he decided to leave the beach and seek the cool shade of the forest. The difference in temperature was dramatic as he moved further into the woods. He was certain that sunlight had never touched the ground over which he strolled and he wondered how such huge numbers and variety of vegetation could subsist without it.

Meandering aimlessly, he and a small, lost fawn startled each other, the infant running as best it could on wobbly legs, in search of its mother. Birds of every color flitted through the trees above him and filled the forest with their songs.

His musket was slung carelessly over his shoulder and in spite of the many creatures he had seen, the thought of using it had never entered his mind. For some reason, which he could not grasp, he felt at home here. Though he had been born in a city, hundreds of miles away, this was where he was at peace. He felt he had been conceived here, then cruelly taken away to live in some foreign place. Nature, God, or instinct had brought him back. Even the fort, which sat in the midst of it, was too enclosed to tolerate. He began to understand why Wawatam always felt caged when he visited the stockade, and was eternally anxious to leave.

As he lifted his eyes to look ahead, the color of the forest changed from dark, mossy green to lime, and Henry realized slowly that the metamorphosis was effected by the addition of more light. Continuing on his course, he discovered a small clearing, abundant with wildflowers, which dazzled him with their color and perfume. He did not know it then (nor would he ever), that he had stumbled upon the meadow where François Cardin and Constante Chevalier had met so many times. His eyes gradually became accustomed to the bright sunlight, and as they did, they detected movement in the center of the clearing.

His heart beat violently as he recognized the girl he had seen in the maple grove, whose haunting eyes had tortured his mind so many times since then. It was at that point that he felt as if he was suddenly awakening for the first time since he had left his bed that morning. He felt as if he had actually been drugged and led to this spot, though he could remember every detail of the hours passed.

She was alone, standing in the radiant sunshine of the meadow, facing him, but apparently unaware of his presence. She walked slowly, a dark Eve in Eden, her slender calves and ankles parting the black-eyed susan, buttercup, and Queen Anne's lace as she moved. She held her coal-black hair, kept shiny with oil made of eagle's fat, away from her face with delicate, long fingers as she stooped to gather a bouquet.

Henry marveled that a creature so savage and close to the earth could yet be so unearthly, feminine, and softly beautiful. She walked with better grace and demeanor than the noble ladies of European courtiers, and her spirit seemed to him more virtuous than Ruth or Esther. She was innocent, because she did not know the word, nor understand its meaning. She was the carnal voice of nature and, like the flowers she held, naturally seductive.

Henry watched her lustfully, knowing that the intoxicating eroticism he felt was the weakness of his own nature and not attributable to her, any more than it was the fault of the flowers that they aroused in people, a desire to pick them (as Lo-tah was doing), and thus disrupt their virginal existence.

Her face was a study in Romanesque perfection as the wide, black and sparkling eyes gazed hypnotically across the painted meadow. Her nose was thin and delicate, being well-set in her face and complimenting the wide, engulfing eyes. Her delicate and sensuous mouth accented her high cheekbones, flushed with the natural glow of robust health which the ladies of Europe had to simulate with their rouge.

She sat down among the flowers and, removing a small beaded band from a pocket in her deerhide smock, she tied it around her forehead, apparently to hold the dark, silky strands of hair away from her face. Henry noticed that she still wore the little beaded necklace he had given her. Quite by accident, she saw him standing at the meadow's edge, gaping in dumb admiration.

She smiled at first, politely, as one who would greet a stranger. But the smile melted slowly into an expression of earnest desire. She gazed long and hard at his ruggedly youthful face. His blue eyes said everything, and she read them with anticipation.

She rose slowly and moved toward him. She did not take her eyes from his. She stood in front of him, studying him, fondling the necklace and staring deeply into his soul. Gentleness and kindness were there, yet not disguising the tremendous passion and desire behind them. The look he gave her was almost frightening in its intensity and devotion.

From that moment, the world ceased to exist for them. They had found a better, immaterial, incorporeal sphere. It was a place divinely inspired and created. They had fled the world and found each other—found home.

Life from this point on, would never be the same. Though they would live among others, they would be whole only with each other, as they were this moment. It was like stepping off the face of the earth, never to return, but only observed from a distance. For him, there could never again be any happiness without her. Flippancy about love and devotion would vanish. She had become the center of his life and being. His every longing would be her. Every beautiful thing would be compared to her beauty. No decision would ever be made again without consideration for her. In a sense, he had become a prisoner, who had found perfect freedom in chains.

He could not look away from her and stood dumbfounded, only barely grasping the significance of this moment for his existence. She had become the grand obsession of his life, his *raison d'être*. He loved her, but the word sounded too weak and tawdry to describe his feelings. Adoration? Worship? These too, were insufficient. She *was* him. He would no longer be able to survive happily without her.

This she realized and shared. The intensity of her emotions and the knowledge of the power they would have over each other terrified her. They were linked by some spectral umbilical that could be severed, leaving them without nourishment or sustenance. They had gone from liberated adults to dependent children in the space of a moment. The horrifying thing was that they were helpless to do anything about it. It was not anything they had planned, anymore than they had decided to be born.

The only way to end their slavery would be to end their lives, but the terrible sweetness of it would not even allow that option. Therefore, they would live to fight off the terrible eventuality of separation. Life from this moment, would be a struggle to maintain their addiction to one another. They were now hopelessly one. Like some narcotic habit, they would fight to keep it, or suffer all the pains of hell at its loss.

All of this was felt, but unspoken between them, as they stood in the meadow, gazing into each other's eyes.

Her head moved forward, reaching for his face, and she kissed him softly on his cheek. "You know," she whispered in his ear, then turned and walked quietly away, never looking back. She moved gracefully across the clearing, her lissome figure swaying rythmically in perfect harmony with her long hair. In moments, she had disappeared into the forest.

Henry ached to follow her. He wanted with all his being to hold her. He had to have her. He *knew* she was his. Why didn't he follow her? Why had he stood like some drooling cretin instead of returning her kiss? For some reason he had been unable to move and, he had sensed intuitively, that she controlled him and had not intended more to happen or it would have. His hands were shaking uncontrollably, and as he watched her outline blend with the shadows of the forest, he fell to his knees and began to weep.

It was too late to follow her now. What if she was waiting for him just beyond that stand of trees? No. He knew she would not be there. Her eyes had told him that she loved him. He could see it when she ceased the pleasant stranger *façade* and looked at him in that bewitching way. She would not give herself to him then. She was giving him time to come to the knowledge of what she already knew. She had known for quite awhile.

🍁 🍁 🍁

From the time of their second meeting, Henry's mind could conceive of nothing or no one but the Ojibway girl. He had told Solomon of their meeting in the meadow, but when he revealed to Ezekial that he loved her, the more skeptical of the two had laughed out loud, offending his infatuated friend. Henry had refused his company for days afterward and their friendship was sorely tried. Only an abject apology from Ezekial restored their amicable relationship and Solomon suspected that it would never be quite the same. It seemed that Alexander no longer needed friends or company. There was no question that he had changed radically and become distant. Ezekial's visits, once a daily occurrence, soon dwindled to every other day, and eventually to once a week. Finally, he quit coming at all, hoping that his friend would recover from his lunacy soon, but undesiring of his company until he did.

Wawatam still came around, and when he did, Henry bombarded him with questions about Lo-tah and her people. The *shaman* told him that her name meant 'Lost Fawn,' after an Indian maiden of legend who had committed suicide by throwing herself from an arched rock which stood hundreds of feet above the rocky shoreline of the isle of the Great Turtle. She had done so, Wawatam related, because her father had forced her to marry a warrior of her tribe, when she really loved a Sky Spirit who had seduced her. When she died, her ghost crept from the shattered body, broken on the rocks, into the sky where it joined the Sky Spirit and floated away, happy in achieving in death what she could not have in life.

Her namesake was deeply revered by her people for her prophetic powers, and though her father was dead of smallpox, she was provided for collectively by the tribe, a very unusual circumstance.

Minavavana was her uncle, the Ottawa explained. Many signs and omens had heralded her birth. She had been counseled and trained in spiritualism by the great Ishnoki, now deceased, who had also trained Wawatam and had been grandfather to Okinochumaki and Wawatam's dead wife, Ti-bikki. Alexander was surprised to learn that his Indian friend had been a husband and a father. He was very sympathetic when he learned of their deaths from the pox, but Wawatam took no notice.

As when he learned Algonkin, Henry was an indefatigable student, particularly concerning the present subject. He learned that Lo-tah lived with her mother, Natomah; that Minavavana wanted her to marry his son, Wenniway (a cause for further enmity with Alexander); that she was eighteen years old; and because of her special standing in the village, one should be cautious in their treatment of her.

Henry raged about the girl being expected to marry her cousin, about the inferiority and bad temper of Wenniway, about the corruption of his character, and the great beauty of hers. He mumbled something about Vulcan and Venus, which Wawatam did not comprehend and, bored with his companion's tirade, and feeling confined, the *shaman* left Henry to his ranting.

When the new shipment of goods arrived from Montreal and the Chippewa came *en masse,* she was among them. Had he been able to escape any contact with her, he might have been more comfortable. But she confounded him with her smile. She never spoke, only looked directly, almost brazenly, into his eyes. To him, it seemed an open invitation. Whether it was or not, something held him back, and she maintained her silence. When she left his shop, he wanted to scream that she should not go! But he could only look after her longingly, while some barrel-shaped squaw diverted his attention to a pot that she wanted to purchase. When he looked up again in anxious anticipation, Lo-tah was gone, and a terrible emptiness swallowed him. Even the activity of the day could not bring him back to reality. Mundane existence was too frigid and void. That day, he cut twice the necessary wood for the evening fire, then forgot to light it. He also forgot to eat, and when the next melancholy morning came, he was still awake, cold and hungry.

Dawn had not yet broken the wilderness sky when Henry lay in bed, staring at the planked ceiling and thinking of Lo-tah. She remained in his head as he built a fire, boiled water for his tea, and cut a slice of dried, smoked trout, chewing the salty flesh slowly and sipping his tea absently. His mind puzzled over the uncomfortable feeling that he would never touch that lovely girl again, or worse—that someone else would.

He thought of his dream to mix in London society and to visit the great, royal palaces of Europe, entertaining princes with his tales of the wild, American northwest, and impressing the perfumed and white-bosomed ladies with his wealth.

But those thoughts paled next to the vision of lying next to the warm body of Lo-tah on soft furs of rabbit and doe by a fire in the 'Moon of the Crusted Snow,' reveling in the warmth of her while wind and time raged outside.

He stared at the uneaten fish and dropped it on the table. The sun was just beginning to peek over the window sill, opening the curtain of mist onto an empty and meaningless day. He could not face it. He got up, turned off the oil-burning lamp, pulled on his boots, and went through the door, locking it behind him.

It was like a grave in the compound. The only sound came from the two sentries, walking along the catwalk of the stockade wall, and they paid him no attention until he yelled at one of them to open the land gate. Henry recognized the soldier as the one who had been forced to ride the wooden horse. He had startled the scowling and sloppily-attired guard so severely that the man replied with an angry expletive, before doing as he was bid.

Once through the gate, his destination only half-formed in his mind, he passed Ezekial Solomon's cottage, where a light flickered delicately in the window and smoke curled from the clay and stick chimney. He hurried his pace. He did not want to see or talk to anyone, especially the loquacious and sarcastic Solomon. He wanted to be totally alone with his thoughts and his fantasies. It was the only way to get through the day.

He marched purposefully into the forest, but the branches and undergrowth gradually inhibited his progress and a half a league distant from Fort Michilimackinac found him stumbling along the banks of a stream in silence, his clothes damp from the morning dew. He paused, winded from his struggle with the thick, wet, vegetation. The rippling action of the stream seemed to have a soothing affect on his nerves. He took a pine needle from a green branch at eye level and bit into it. The acrid taste satisfied him. It matched his mood. He felt hopelessly and pathetically alone and no companion could make him feel any differently—save one.

He cursed his ill-feeling and shook his head as if such an action could rid him of his melancholy. He had been walking away from the meadow where he had seen Lo-tah, though that had been his original destination. He seemed to be drawn, magnetically, to this place that he had never seen before. He sat on the edge of the stream, observing the swirling eddies created by a small inlet which escaped into the exposed roots of a gnarled tree along the eroded shoreline.

Whether it was the little stream, or his depression, he did not know, but he began to think of his childhood and home. He saw himself as a young boy again, dressed in knickers and greatcoat, struggling over the snowy, cobblestone streets past the cooper's shop and the little tavern where men congregated at dusk to drink and bellow drunken tunes at the top of their lungs. He always hurried past that place, and Mr. Gronder's house, whose cranky inhabitant derived great pleasure from hurling abuse (and often stones) at frightened young schoolboys.

Always, when he returned to the thatched-roof cottage by the lane, he could smell fresh pudding, and sweetcakes bubbling in the iron woodburner and enjoy the whistling sound of sizzling mutton, bestowing its juices on a greedy fire in the hearth, as it turned on the spit.

His mother would always greet him with a smile (as if his presence brightened her life), and would comfort, and reassure him that the world was all right. His father was always away on military expeditions, and if he ever saw him, Henry could not remember him. The dreamy young man had felt (however irrationally) that it had been rather selfish of his adventurous father to die on one of these enterprises. His mother lavished her love on the boy in the absence of the father and had spent her entire widowhood in purposeful devotion to fulfilling his every need. Yet this dotage had lasted but a short time. Anne Henry had followed her husband to the grave a brief ten years later, leaving Alexander an ill-prepared orphan to face the world alone. He was sixteen then, and had toughened considerably since, but when he felt low, as now, his thoughts would turn to the only real love and security he had ever known.

He was awakened from his reverie by the sounds of splashing in the stream. The noise came from beyond a copse of cedar trees which thrust out over the brook, leaning intentionally, it seemed, to obstruct his view.

His heart quickened at the speculation that a bear could have lumbered down to the stream to quench its thirst, and he admonished himself silently for allowing his emotions to dictate his actions. He had forgotten his flintlock! He was armed with only a small, skinning knife which the bear would undoubtedly use to pick its teeth with after its meal of raw Englishman.

Henry began to slip cautiously away from the thrashing sound. His heart, beating in fear, now almost stopped during the course of his withdrawal as he realized that the splashing was accompanied by the soft humming of a youthful, dulcet, and decidedly feminine, voice. Another voice told him to continue his escape, but the siren's call was far too appealing. Like Ulysses unbound, he moved beyond the thickets along the bank, until he obtained a lucid view of a tiny clearing which touched the pebbled beach leading to the water line.

There, in the stream, nude, and cheerfully bathing, was Lotah. Her back, glistening with dewy moisture in the bright sun, was facing him as she wrung her dark hair dry in the sparkling stream. She continued her song, unaware of Henry's presence fifteen feet away.

He was awe-struck. Her body, until now concealed under her tunic, was as spectacular as he had thought it might be. Her shoulders, held high while she dried her hair, came together perfectly at the nape of her lovely neck.

Henry's eyes caressed her back, moving downward between her shoulder blades, past her small waist and rested on her sweetly round buttocks. Such beauty, he was convinced, could not be copied nor simulated by any material creature. She would have been majestic in a silk gown, perfumed and demure in the marble halls of some great castle in Europe. But it was here that her beauty was greatest. It was here she belonged, the essence of nature, her wild loveliness enhanced by her surroundings. She *was* nature, as much a part of it as the trees and streams, the animals and flowers.

Engrossed in his usurpation of this tranquility, he failed to notice that Lo-tah had discontinued her canticle and that silence reigned over the wilderness except for the rippling water and bird songs. As she turned, she betrayed no surprise at his presence.

She rose from the stream slowly, revealing her dark outline against the sparkling water. Her pulchritude forced a gasp from Henry and his breathing became quick and labored. The voice of modesty insisted that he look away, but erotic fascination held him rapt. Her eyes, dark and mesmerizing, regarded him with temerity, not in anger, but with the same ingenuousness and honesty he had experienced in their previous encounters.

She walked deliberately up the grassy slope toward him, moving past her shunned garments that lay drying in the dancing patches of sunlight filtering through the birches. She smiled boldly with pride, as Henry gazed appreciably at her firm, full, breasts, swaying above the flat and sensuous belly.

The expression on her face was neither vixen nor modest, but kind and strangely purposeful. She was ethereal, and yet earthy, bold and yet shy, questioning, yet certain. She stood before him as a part of nature with all the delicate beauty and savage lust of the world in her paradoxical face. The glowing sun sparkled in her dewy, radiant hair as, wordlessly, her arms encircled his waist and she pulled herself close to him, her eyes never deviating from his. Alexander's limbs hung inanimately at his sides. He was like some great animal trapped in a snare, too weak from hunger to struggle. His cheeks flushed, and his body shook involuntarily.

He felt that in that moment, she could read his thoughts, but he did not feel mocked, only guided, the grown man directed by the young girl, the Vestal-maid giving lessons in love to the seasoned legionnaire.

She finally lowered her bewitching eyes, and laid her head against his chest where his shirt parted, kissing him lightly on the base of his neck as she did so. His spine tingled with the tenderness and delicious warmth of her mouth.

He could feel her bare breasts rising and falling rapidly in her own growing excitement. He even imagined that she had spoken. Then he heard her distinctly. "Hen-ree," she said in soft, sweet tones spoken so lovingly that he was consumed by an overwhelming desire to give her all he had, his money, goods, or life, if only what she felt matched the adoring tone in her lovely voice.

"Lo-tah," he whispered. "Beautiful Lo-tah." His arms came to life and, with the care of a father, handling his first child, pushed the wet strands of hair from her face and, holding her small head in his hands, he kissed her tenderly, barely touching her lips. Her mouth responded eagerly. Like a hungry baby bird, she poked at his mouth teasingly with her parted lips, until he grabbed her roughly, holding his lips to hers until all breath escaped him.

She calmly brought his hands around to cradle her breasts as she felt him swelling against her stomach. She pulled him roughly to the ground on top of her. He stood up to remove his own clothing with trembling hands, as she lay back in the grass, writhing in anticipation, her dark eyes flashing fiercely.

She made love with a combination of savage, biting, lust and tender, careful affection, treating Henry's body as if it were something sacred—a temple housing a god. She reveled in the sanctity of that temple, and its desecration. As he entered her, she threw back her head in an ecstasy of pain and pleasure. As her body adapted to his invasion, she thrust her hips at him with complete abandon, dismissing concern and apprehension as if they were unworthy servants to be excused when one wished to experience nobler emotions. Henry had never felt such sensation, such overwhelming lusty pleasure, clothed in genuine inno-

cence. Sexual enjoyment seemed to be as much a part of her nature as eating and sleeping. She had been a virgin before their
encounter and he had worried, once the act was accomplished,
that she would react with tears and guilt, shame and regret. She
did not. She lay back in the grass, stretching luxuriously, her
smile revealing her happiness and calm contentment.

Once his own trembling paroxysm had ceased and his panting slowed to normal breathing, a delicious peace settled over
him. He laid down next to her and she snuggled into his arms,
embracing and kissing him again and again. He held her tightly
in the crook of his arm and sighed pleasurably, gazing into the
blue sky through the fluttering birches. A robin glided onto the
branch of one of them, outlined against the cumulus clouds.

Noticing the bird, Lo-tah pointed. "Au-pet-chi," she whispered in her child's voice.

Henry followed her eyes to the warbler above them.

"Yes. Robin."

"Yissibbin," she mimicked.

"Good," he praised in perfect Algonkin.

They laughed in the common language of love. He turned on
his side, leaning on one elbow in the grass, and began to kiss her
neck, her shoulders, her breasts. She threw her head back, smiling in pleasure and enjoying the tantalizing sensations. She
curled one supple leg around his hip, and in moments they were
lost to the world and were exploring each other again, in the
throes of a passion that transcended all other cares.

🦋 🦋 🦋

IN THE LATER AFTERNOON of that summer day, Lo-tah and Henry
sat talking quietly beneath the birches by the little stream.
Henry's knowledge of Algonkin served him well, since the
woman he adored spoke no English at all.

"You will live with me now?" he asked, assuming that she
would be happy with his proposal.

Instead, she frowned, and the natural pout of her lower lip
became more pronounced. "No," she said.

"What? Why?" Henry was mystified. "I love you, Lo-tah. I believe you love me. I have plenty of room. I can provide for you. We can be very happy."

When she deepened her frown, he began to panic. "You don't love me?"

Her eyes went wild at the horrid question. "No, no, that is not the reason, my sweet Hen-ree. You *know* that. Do not insult me." She put her hand on his cheek and smiled gently. "There are things to be done and much needs to be spoken."

"What? Speak now." He was angry, not with her, but with his own desperate impatience and insecurity. The thought of being without her for a single moment in the rest of his life made him nauseous.

"It is understood by my uncle that I will marry Wenniway." Henry started to speak, but she covered his mouth with her hand. "It will take time to convince Minavavana that this cannot be, and more time to bring him to accept an Englishman into his family."

He pulled her hand away. "Can you convince him?"

"Yes, in time."

"What else needs to be arranged?"

"Your chief hates my people," she said. "He would not accept Anishnabeg squaws in his stick village."

"He has no control over me," Alexander scoffed. "Marie Amiot is an Indian woman. *She* lives in the stockade."

"Is she Anishnabeg?"

"No, but I don't see what dif . . ." Lo-tah silenced him again.

"There is also the bride price," she said.

"The what?" He had not been instructed in the finer points of Chippewa etiquette by Wawatam. "You mean a dowry?"

"I do not know this 'doo-ree,'" she said. "All warriors must make a large gift to the woman's father. My father is dead, therefore you must give the gift to Natomah, my mother, and seek her permission."

"When may I see her? Could I come tomorrow?"

"No. I must speak with my uncle first, and you must speak to the English chief. Then we will arrange to see Natomah. She will have no objections. She hates Wenniway."

"When will I see you again?" Henry said.

"The time will come soon. Speak to your chief."

As twilight settled over the wilderness, they parted. Alexander had extracted a promise that he could see her the next day, after discussing his plans with Colonel Etherington. They kissed again, deeply, before she turned and walked gracefully up a beaten path on the opposite side of the stream.

He felt a pang of nagging regret, as he stumbled through the darkening forest in the other direction. His heart ached for her, and they had not yet been separated for more than a few minutes. He was confounded by a sudden awareness that he had always felt himself to be content. Yet he had never been happy, never been *really* content, until this day.

Inside an hour, he spotted the shadowy, needled walls of the stockade, black against the magnificent orange and violet sky, as he emerged from the wood. A light still shone from the Jew's cabin, but smoke had ceased to drift from the chimney. It was strange that Ezekial would not have a fire in the tiny hearth on a night that promised to be very cool.

As he approached the cabin, he observed that the light poured from the open door, rather than the window. Something wasn't right. He could feel it, like a man who is chopping wood and knows that if he doesn't move his hand, resting in the path of the axe, that it will cease to be his. Yet he doesn't move it until the axe motivates it.

Henry hurried his pace until the light from the cabin made his eyes squint at the open doorway. As he became accustomed to the glow, he saw that Ezekial Solomon lay face-down on the packed-earth floor of the cottage. Henry rushed to the prostrate figure and turned him over. "God in heaven," he whispered.

His friend's chest was a mass of blood, soaking the shirt which had obviously been ripped open in haste, then folded roughly over the torn flesh in an apparent effort to cover the foul deed. Henry pulled the sticky shirt aside to evaluate the severity of the wound, and found it to be superficial. It was not a murder attempt, but a deliberate act of torture.

Henry could not believe what he saw. On the Jew's chest, barely discernible through the caking blood, someone had carved the symbol of Jewish national pride, the 'Star of David.'

He wanted to vomit. He was simultaneously sick and out-raged. The victim emitted a slight moan, directing Henry's atten-tion to the face which was bloodied and bruised. Ezekial had been badly beaten and his beard, once full and black, was now grey stubble. It was apparent that the perpetrators had set it on fire.

Henry looked around the ransacked cabin. Chairs were over-turned, table legs were broken. Blankets, used for trade with the Indians, had been slashed into ribbons. On the floor, near the open entrance to the little dwelling, was a wooden bucket, filled with water. He rose, grabbed a ladle from the floor and, prop-ping the battered head of his friend, he poured the cool liquid between the parched lips.

Ezekial gulped greedily, as a child sucks at its mother's breast, more by instinct than any cognitive process, since he was only semi-conscious.

Grasping shredded bits of blanket, Henry stuffed them hastily under the wounded head as a cushion against the hard floor and, fetching the bucket and strips of fairly sanitary linen, he pro-ceeded to clean the offensive and humiliating lacerations. It sick-ened Henry, as he worked, to think that one human being could do such a thing to another.

Ezekial Solomon winced as the cold water bit into the cuts. "Bastards," Henry swore furiously as he cleansed the ugly wounds. "The bloody, stinking, bastards!"

The patient's head shifted slightly in Henry's arms as he drifted into complete unconsciousness. Henry rubbed the victim's face with the cool water, then lifted him onto a straw mattress which had somehow survived the general carnage.

He made sure that his friend was resting comfortably before storming out into the darkness, each martial step directed toward the command quarters of Colonel George Etherington.

The commandant's office was dark, but a light shone in the adjacent living quarters. Henry pounded on the door impatiently, his mind buzzing from the activity of an exciting and thoroughly exhausting day, up until a few moments ago, the best of his life. The colonel swung the door open with a jolt, catching Henry's arm in a position that would have injured him had the younger man been less alert. Etherington wore a fierce scowl and was about to cause some grief to the impertinent soldier who had dared disturb him when he recognized Alexander Henry, though his face was twisted into a horrible grimace that almost eluded acknowledgement. Etherington's own irascibility quickly converted to hospitable warmth.

"Why, Mr. Henry! This is a pleasant surprise. I had almost given up on seeing you again. Won't you come in and join me in a nightcap?"

"I'm sorry, Colonel, I'm not in the mood for social amenities. I want to know who in hell would torture a man and leave him to die."

Etherington looked genuinely mystified at this abrupt statement and Henry's savage expression began to wane slightly. He felt foolish as he realized that Etherington knew nothing about the incident. "Forgive me, Colonel, I have had a rather unusual day and I'm very angry and confused right now."

Etherington took him by the arm in a brotherly manner and closed the door. "I quite understand, old chap, don't let it concern you in the slightest." Henry could see that the man had been drinking quite heavily as he leaned against him for support. "My curiosity has been aroused. Just what has happened that has upset you so? Would you care for some brandy? It really might be beneficial." He let go of Henry's arm and swayed to a table crowded with bottles and fancy glassware.

"Yes, I guess I would, thank you. It might calm me." Henry was surprised at the luxurious furnishings in the sitting room which contrasted so much with the decor in the commandant's office. They would have been the pride of many fine houses in Europe, and looked incongruous here, within log walls.

"Commander, someone has severely beaten Mr. Solomon and I'm quite concerned for his health. The rogues also upset his household and I would imagine they have stolen his most valuable merchandise, although I don't know for certain. He was too weak to tell me."

Etherington still appeared ignorant of the affair, but not unduly concerned, as he continued to pour the brandy. "The young Jewish gentleman? Why would anyone want to do that?" Henry thought he detected a sarcastic tone as the colonel handed him his drink, seated himself heavily in a comfortable chair by the fire, and signaled Henry to do the same.

"I really can't tell you," the merchant replied, following instructions and sitting down on the edge of a chair opposite the officer. "But I know it had something to do with his being a Jew. The 'Star of David' had been carved into his chest with a knife."

"Oh, I say, that's bloody revolting! Do you have any conception who the villain might have been?" Etherington awaited Henry's reply with an expression of profound interest.

"No, not specifically. Though I have to conclude that it was someone under your command. That's why I'm here, I guess."

"I see." The colonel was not ecstatic about this observation. A tense moment of silence followed, during which time Etherington unbuttoned the stiff-collared red jacket with its gold epaulets and sipped his brandy. "Of course it would have to be someone inside the compound, but it does not follow that this person or persons would necessarily be under my direct command. That is, my dear fellow, it could possibly have been one of the civilian inhabitants of the fort."

Henry was quick to reply. "I don't think so. The Du Charmes, Bourassas, and Parents are incapable of such cruelty and certainly you would not suspect the priest." Etherington raised his eyebrows as if he would. "The Amiot boys have been gone for several days to visit their Sac relatives. Bostwick and Goddard seemed friendly enough to Ezekial and the Cardins have had him as a guest in their home. *I* didn't do it and I'm sure Mr. Solomon would not attempt suicide by carving stars on his chest. Indians would not understand the symbolic bigotry of the deed. That leaves British military personnel."

"Not quite," Etherington retorted. It was obvious that Henry had forgotten someone, judging from the triumphant smile on the colonel's face. "You have included or excluded everyone except Monsieur Langlade."

Henry had never given him a thought. "The former commandant? Oh I hardly think . . ."

"I concur," Etherington cut him short. "I don't believe you do. Let me tell you something Mr. Henry. That bloody sneak is half-

Indian, and all Indians are vicious, dull and barbaric. He probably hadn't seen any human blood for awhile and was getting thirsty."

Henry was becoming flushed and resentful of the colonel's attitude. Not that he felt any need to protect the dour and anti-social Langlade, but the Indians had not appeared to him to fit the commander's injudicious description. He thought of the dignified Wawatam and Lo-tah . . . Lo-tah.

"Mr. Henry?"

"Um? Oh, yes, I'm sorry," he muttered. "I'm very tired." His mind began to clear. "I can't say that I agree with you regarding Monsieur Langlade, or with your opinion of the Chippewa and Ottawa who live here. At any rate, the French are a very liberal race who do not hate people for who they are, but rather for what they do. Further, I have learned from the priest that Langlade has no religious prejudices."

"You would take the word of a papist? Mr. Henry, you are young and have a great deal of life to experience yet."

"My youth aside, I have seen quite a bit of people, and I am often disappointed by those who are my own. I maintain that this act was a deliberate attack by one of your men and not the Sieur de Langlade. I don't think he would jeopardize his position here for the sake of petty bigotry."

Etherington was not a man who accepted contrariness gracefully. He scratched his neck around his loosened collar and poured himself another brandy. "I am sorry to disagree, sir," he replied through tightening lips, "but despite the fact that he was once commanding here, does not qualify him to join the bloody human race."

"I believe we can agree on that point, sir," Henry rejoined. "That reasoning could also be applied to others who have held, or *now* hold, that position." The sarcastic tone could not be mistaken. Henry was angry. He had taken Etherington's remarks to heart.

"What in hell is that supposed to mean?" The colonel gulped his brandy.

"It means that this probably would never have happened if some humanity had been shown Mr. Solomon and he had been allowed to reside within the stockade. Someone would have heard him. Someone would have come to his aid."

"Mr. Henry," the colonel began, taking a patronizing tone. "Mr. Solomon is a Jew. It is *his* people who have brought world opinion against themselves. I'm not overly religious, but I am not going to mix socially with a Christ-killer. I don't believe in slicing up people for the sport of it, but social ostracism of the Jews is standard practice throughout the civilized world and there are many historic precedents to justify it. The great Ferdinand of Spain removed them from his country along with the heathen Moors. Old Fritz of Prussia couldn't tolerate them either. Our own Edward I excluded them from England. I think Mr. Solomon is beginning to learn that he cannot escape the folly of his people by running away to this part of the world, because it's the same here."

Henry could not comprehend such stilted pedantry. It defied credulity and was impossible to debate, since it was founded in ingenuous dogma. The conversation had become *infra dignitatem.* He moved to the heart of the issue. "Are you going to investigate or not, colonel?"

Etherington considered his position carefully. "Yes," he said. "I will question my men. That's all I can promise."

"May I get a doctor for Mr. Solomon?"

"I'll send the post surgeon over in the morning to have a look."

"Thank you," Henry said coldly.

"You're welcome," the colonel replied haughtily. "Good evening."

"Good-bye." Henry started for the door, then thought of the question he had promised Lo-tah he would ask. But his pride and outrage overcame him and he slammed the door, leaving behind an aura of distrust that was to mar any future relationship with the British commander.

🐝 🐝 🐝

As HENRY AND LO-TAH had made love to each other in the sweet grass of that brilliant summer day, Natomah, Lo-tah's mother and

Tcianung's widow, had gone to the lakeshore to dig for clams with which she hoped to surprise her beautiful and unusual daughter at their evening meal together. That moment of familiarity with her offspring was always the best part of Natomah's day. Since the death of Tcianung, she had expected to marry again, or starve. When neither alternative became reality, and when she saw how they would be taken care of, she offered a prayer to the Great Turtle for giving her a daughter of such rare ability and perception. Though they were well-supplied by the warriors of the village, Natomah had developed a habit of searching for food to supplement these meals. It helped to fill her lonely, often boring hours, and gave them some culinary variety. The berries, herbs, wild rice and squash she gathered were a welcome addition to the monotonous venison which had become their staple food. Clams would be an even rarer treat and they were Lo-tah's favorite.

As she stooped in the muddy water and scooped out the last of the clams with her stick, she thought she detected movement, and a low growling sound in the bushes which grew out from the shore and lay half in and half out of the water.

She decided that it was probably a smaller animal, like a raccoon or skunk because it made so little noise with its passage. But since she believed that she had more than enough clams, and the day was moving rapidly to late afternoon, she thought she had better hurry back to the Chippewa camp if she were to beat Lo-tah, who was always very prompt for dinner.

She put the last of the clams into her birchbark bag which was slung over her shoulder. It took some effort to liberate her feet from the muck, making sucking sounds as she headed for shore and creating dirty clouds in the water.

When she reached the sand, she heard another sound, presumably from the same animal, but the noise was more that of a creature in pain or distress than one which represented a threat.

Her curiosity overcame her, and she parted the bushes, stepping in the direction of the sounds. In moments, she discovered its source. A yellow-gray cur, one she recognized as belonging to the village and one she was sure she had thrown scraps of meat to on one occasion or another, had its tail toward her and was digging furiously at the base of a tree. The dog was apparently after a squirrel or chipmunk and was whining, almost unnaturally, in its frustration. As it labored, it became more and more furious, stopping only to howl in despair, then continuing its mission with frantic urgency.

Natomah laughed outloud at the comical scene, until the animal turned in reaction to the sound and she saw that his muzzle was frothing with foam and the wild eyes had a confused, hateful, look.

She did not hesitate, but backed away slowly for about ten feet, then turned and ran as fast as she could. She had seen a rabid skunk once and had also watched a teen-aged boy die from the affliction that had resulted from its bite. The Anishnabeg called it the 'mind torture.' The thought of losing her sanity and being tied to a stake while she raved and foamed at the mouth, horrified her, and spurred her feet to greater speed.

She did not realize that the dog was close until his yellow teeth sank into one of her flying legs, ripping the flesh from her calf and sending her sprawling into the dirt. As she turned onto her back and sat up to face her attacker, the mad beast sunk his infected canines into the soft flesh of her upper leg.

She muffled a scream, and beat her tormentor over the head with her fists, trying to loosen his grip. Her struggles seemed to have little effect on him, other than to make him grip tighter. His dull, idiot eyes rolled wildly in their sockets as she struck his skull with her day's catch, the hard clam shells stunning him and forcing him to release his grip.

She fought to get on her feet, but her leg had been so badly lacerated from chewing that she suspected it might be permanently damaged. She moaned as she saw her bright blood mixing with the slime from the dog's mouth. 'I am a dead woman,' she thought as the beast shook its head from side to side, slowly recovering from the effects of the stunning blow to his ravaged brain.

Natomah searched the ground for a weapon of any kind. Her hand found a sharp stick. She wanted death now. If this creature did not kill her, she would probably kill herself. She had no intention of losing her mind and becoming the object of terrible pity. Yet, she had a duty to perform before she expired. She could not let this thing live either, out of sympathy to it, and fear that it might harm someone else. As the infuriated animal attacked again, she managed to stab the loathesome creature twice in its ribs. His yellow teeth closed on her neck this time, and with the fury of insanity, ripped her throat open.

🐚 🐚 🐚

Lo-TAH DISCOVERED her mother's body at about the same time that Alexander Henry was ministering to Ezekial Solomon's wounds.

She had returned to their lodge after parting with Henry, late for the first time since her father's death. When she found the fire smoldering and unattended with no sweet aroma of food, she immediately sensed that something was wrong.

It took but a few minutes to discover from a neighbor that Natomah had been headed for the lake. Night had fallen by the time she reached the shore, and by bright moonlight, she followed her mother's trail until she discovered her mutilated body, lying quite still among some ferns, clamshells scattered about. Her murderer, himself a victim, was on top of her chest, a wet, red stick protruding from his side. It was obvious that the crows and turkey vultures had been busy with both corpses.

Lo-tah sat next to her dearest friend and wept in the moonlight long into the night. At dawn, she took the carcass of the dog, buried it, then returned to the camp to inform her uncle, Minavavana, of his sister-in-law's demise.

The great chief was obviously saddened, but typically stoic, and ordered the body of Natomah brought back to the village for a proper funeral. Her remains were placed on a platform supported by stilts near the site of her death, so that her spirit could observe the comings and goings of her people.

Lo-tah, as an unmarried maiden, now came under the guardianship of her uncle, who publicly committed himself to continue to provide for her until her marriage, which he fully expected would be imminent, since his son, Lo-tah's cousin Wenniway, had expressed his desire to be her husband.

Lo-tah was so shattered by grief that she gave no thought to her own future. She secluded herself in her empty wigwam and mourned quietly, not appearing again until twenty-four hours had passed.

At the end of that time, she left the village and headed toward the fort, needing to see the only person who could fill the void her mother had left behind.

🦋 🦋 🦋

ALEXANDER HENRY slept very little after his conversation with Colonel Etherington. He returned to Ezekial's cabin and in fact, spent the night there, watching over his friend who also slept fitfully, suffering both from his wounds and the nightmare of his degradation.

Henry kept the fire going and tried to make some order of the ransacked home. By dawn, as Lo-tah knelt weeping by Natomah's corpse, he had pretty well reestablished some order, and Solomon was deep in more pleasant dreams.

As the sun awakened on the horizon, Henry left the small cabin, reentered the stockade, and went directly to the Du Charme house. He was greeted by Marguerite and the twins, as Laurent tumbled out of bed and smiled his beefy grin. Within moments, the delicious aroma of spiced tea and biscuits filled the room.

Henry was served royally by his adopted family as he related the events of last evening. For the first time since he had met him, Alexander saw Du Charme truly angry. The big Canadian raged back and forth across the room, swearing vengeance on the 'beast' who had committed such a perverted and twisted deed. Madame Du Charme hurried her pudgy offspring through their breakfast, then rapidly dressed and rushed off to see after Ezekial.

By the time Du Charme and Henry arrived, Ezekial was sitting up in bed, smiling at the ministrations of Marguerite who clucked about him like a worried hen. Henry could see by the fresh bandages and improved appearance of his friend that the post surgeon, as promised, had already been to see him. His physical condition and emotional state appeared to be greatly improved.

"Ezekial, my friend," Henry bellowed. "You look so much better. I'm happy to see you awake and alert. What does the doctor say?"

Solomon smiled at his friend, the rift between them apparently forgotten. "He says I am fortunate that someone looked after me until he arrived. I think so too." He grabbed Alexander's hand and squeezed it hard.

"Someone has to keep an eye on you when Marguerite is not in attendance."

Madame Du Charme's cheeks turned rosy and she looked at Alexander with her 'don't be a silly boy' expression. Laurent laughed heartily at his wife's embarrassment.

"She is a wonderful lady, and certainly a much prettier nurse than you," Ezekial responded.

"Point well taken," Alexander agreed. Laurent guffawed again.

Alexander sat on the bed, his expression suddenly serious. "How did it happen?"

Solomon looked up at the ceiling of his small cabin and sighed deeply, as if he had been expecting such a question. It was obvious that he had dreaded the moment when he would have to recount the humiliating story. He set his teeth together in determination and slowly revealed what had transpired.

He had been sitting outside his cabin at twilight, enjoying the pleasant evening breeze and the solitude while his dinner warmed over the fire. Two men, both British soldiers as Henry had assumed, had come through the land gate. It was apparent that they had been drinking. Sensing trouble, Ezekial had gotten up to go inside when one of them had spoken to the other, in a loud voice meant to be overheard, that Jews were vermin and he preferred the company of rats and lice.

Solomon knew he should have ignored the remark, but the temptation was too great. Looking from one to the other, he had said that they needn't explain to him what kind of companionship they preferred, it was obvious.

They had rushed at him so suddenly that he was unable to

defend himself. He was driven inside the cabin and struck so hard with the first blow that the rest of it was only remembered in pieces. He had recalled laying face up on the cabin floor while the bigger man stood above him, a boot on each arm, while the smaller one used his chest for a canvas and a knife for a brush. He had lost consciousness then, and had awakened only for a moment to see his assailants wrecking his belongings. He had not come to again until Henry arrived moments after the villains had departed.

Silence governed the room after Ezekial finished his story, except for the squealing of the Du Charme twins who were immediately silenced by their father. Each adult hung his head as if he were somehow culpable.

"Can you identify the people who did this?" Alexander asked anxiously. "I knew they were soldiers. I told Etherington."

"The smaller one was Sidney Wickwall," Ezekial said.

"How do you know that?" Du Charme interjected.

"I heard the other man call him by name," Solomon said weakly. "You know him too, Alexander."

Henry looked appalled. "How could I possibly know him? I've never heard that name."

Solomon, worn out from the effort of recalling his degradation, was drifting off to sleep. "He was the man on the horse," he mumbled, before closing his eyes.

Henry searched his brain. 'The man on the horse?' He had seen hundreds of people on horses. What significance could that statement possibly . . . then it struck him. The wooden horse! The man he had felt such sympathy for!

He turned quickly and headed for the door. Du Charme followed.

They went directly to the barracks where military personnel were quartered. He knew that he should go to Etherington, but their previous conversation convinced him that the pompous colonel would do nothing about it. Anger controlled him now. He was furious.

He pushed past several soldiers who were standing in the doorway, Du Charme right on his heels. Inside, the barracks were dark and smelled heavily of pine and tobacco. Lieutenants

Jamet and Leslie, who were sitting at a table at the far end, rose when the two civilians entered. They had their own quarters at one end while the enlisted men slept in primitive bunks at the other. Henry recognized Wickwall, who was sitting on a log which served as a chair for the crate-table in front of him. Two other soldiers sat on either side of him on the same kind of makeshift stools. Playing cards and a pistol lay on the surface of the crate along with two pairs of dice.

Henry stomped angrily in their direction. Wickwall smiled knowingly as the two men approached.

"You . . . you *son of a bitch,*" Henry shouted at him.

The nasty smile disappeared. "Are you talkin' to me mate?" Wickwall sneered.

"You're damn right I am," Henry fumed.

"You're upset, lad," Wickwall said, the vicious grin reappearing. "But you want to be careful what you say now."

"I'm going to see to it that you pay for what you've done, Wickwall."

"And what have I done, friend?"

Du Charme saw his right hand come up from between his legs and rest inches from the pistol.

"You know damn well what you've done, you swine!"

Jamet and Leslie had come as far as the entrance to the barracks and were now approaching the scene rapidly, anticipating trouble.

"Maybe I should write it on your chest for you," Henry shouted. In his anger, he was ignoring Wickwall's hand which crept like a pale spider toward the butt of the weapon.

Henry began to step forward, not knowing yet what he intended to do. The white spider scurried now. Suddenly it stopped, just short of the pistol, a hunting knife protruding from its knuckled back, and its scarlet blood pouring onto the surface of the crate, as Wickwall screamed in pain and terror. The hilt of the knife rested securely in the meaty hand of Laurent Du Charme.

As Wickwall's hand was pierced, his huge companion, a stupid-looking fellow named Chimton and presumably his accomplice, swung heavily at Du Charme, striking him a glancing blow on his jaw.

As he did so, Henry struck the man as hard as he could, directly on the end of his nose, flattening it. Henry felt the flexible cartilege give beneath his fist and blood sprayed in torrents over it, dripping slowly down his arm and onto the floor. Chimton staggered under the blow and fell against Wickwall, pushing him backwards and forcing his imprisoned hand to rip open in a jagged pattern as Du Charme's knife, even without the pressure of the Frenchman's hand, held firm. Wickwall screamed again as Leslie and Jamet, accompanied by five soldiers, separated the men and restored order. All of this took place in less than a minute.

"What is the meaning of this?" Jamet shouted as Leslie helped the struggling, moaning Wickwall to remove Du Charme's knife from his hand. Henry saw, with some satisfaction, that it left a deep, jagged, lightning-bolt cut. Wickwall fell back onto a bunk several feet away, blubbering like a baby.

"That animal and his friend," he nodded in the direction of Wickwall and then pointed at Chimton who was sprawled on the floor, "tortured and injured a friend of ours."

"The Jew?" Jamet asked.

"Yes. They cut the 'Star of David' into his chest. He almost died from the blood loss."

Jamet wrinkled his nose, as if he had smelled something rotten. "Why didn't you take the matter to Colonel Etherington?"

"The colonel has already explained to me the 'reasoning' behind the persecution of Jews."

Jamet looked at Leslie, who was helping Du Charme to his feet.

Wickwall glared at Henry. "I'll see you both hang!" he threatened.

Jamet turned toward him and Wickwall was silenced. "Private, you have committed an atrocious act against a subject of his Majesty, King George. Do you deny it?"

"He ain't no Britisher sir," Wickwall whined. "He's a stinkin' Jew."

"Then you do not deny it," Jamet concluded.

"No. But Chimton helped me sir. He said it was a good idea."

"You could both be shot for such an offense." Jamet continued: "Lieutenant Leslie, I believe Private Wickwall and Private Chimton have injured themselves in an unfortunate accident. Do you concur in my conclusion?"

Leslie smiled knowingly. "I do."

"Private Wickwall, do I speak the truth, or would you prefer to press charges against someone? If so, I must tell you that Mr. Solomon will also be bound to press charges against his assailants, whoever they might be."

Wickwall, in spite of his limited intellect, was catching on. "Yes, sir," he said finally. "That's what happened." He glared hatefully at Du Charme.

"Monsieur Du Charme, you seem to have misplaced your knife." Leslie handed him the bloody instrument.

"Gentlemen," Jamet continued, looking at Henry and Du Charme, "are you content with my evaluation of this situation?"

"I believe we are," Henry answered, smiling, knowing that as long as Etherington was in charge, there would be no formal inquest. "Good day to you sir."

As he and Du Charme returned to Ezekial's cabin, the late afternoon sun was casting long shadows across the compound.

"Ezekial will carry that scar the rest of his life," Henry mused.

"So will our friend Wickwall," Du Charme laughed. "That's why I'll keep looking over my shoulder."

🐎 🐎 🐎

By THE TIME Henry and Du Charme had related the tale of their encounter with Wickwall and Chimton to Ezekial Solomon, who seemed very pleased and satisfied with their efforts on his behalf, darkness had swallowed the wilderness outside.

Alexander agreed to spend the night again with Ezekial as the Du Charmes went home to tuck the twins into bed. Henry was not unaware that he had promised to meet Lo-tah that day with permission from Colonel Etherington for her to live with him inside the stockade. He had done nothing but make an enemy of the colonel, and in his anxiety and anger over the condition of his friend, he had neglected to meet her.

He pictured her waiting in the meadow early that morning, having dutifully gained Natomah's blessing and Minavavana's permission, beside herself with anticipation, lingering there while she watched anxiously for his appearance.

When he failed to manifest himself, she would become worried about his safety, then fret about his sincerity. As evening approached, she would turn sadly back toward the Chippewa camp, vexed and troubled, knowing in her heart that her lover had been just that, and nothing more. She had given herself to a convincing but unfaithful charlatan and she would go away broken-hearted and hating him for his treachery.

The thought stung him deeply. The vision of her pain struck him to the core. His disquietude tormented him so, that he could neither sleep nor sit, but he spent most of the night pacing back and forth across the clay floor as Solomon dozed fitfully, seeming to share his vexatious spirit.

'Lo-tah, believe in me,' he said to himself. 'Don't run away without knowing. You have to trust. If you don't trust me, how can you love? There is more strength in *us* than that. I belong to you now, don't look for explanations. *Know* that I would have been there if I could. Wait, oh darling, sweet, life-woman, wait! Dear and precious child, Lost Fawn, wait and trust!'

He slumped into a chair and tears began to roll down his cheeks. How terrible is the sense of duty, he thought. How completely enslaving is the god, *responsibility*.

He looked over at Solomon. "Get well my friend," he said. "Because at first light I will leave you—and duty— behind and work on my own survival. If I don't find her, they can carve *me* up and use me for pig feed and I won't care. She is my savior, Ezekial. Someone else will have to be yours."

At three o'clock, he fell asleep, still sitting in the chair. When he woke up, someone was knocking lightly at the door. As he opened his bleary eyes, he noticed immediately that the light outside had blossomed into early morning. He sprang from the chair, alternately cursing himself and praying that the visitor outside would be Lo-tah. As he swung the rough, wooden door open, he recognized the benevolent countenance of Père Du Jaunay.

"Father," he gasped in total surprise. "What can I help you with?"

The priest smiled. "I was hoping that perhaps I could be of some assistance to you. Madame Du Charme informs me that your friend has been, uh, injured. I have some salve that might soothe . . ."

"Father, you are truly a blessing," Alexander mumbled as he pulled the Jesuit inside. Du Jaunay looked over the young man's shoulder to see that Ezekial Solomon was sleeping peacefully.

Henry was throwing on his boots and shirt as he invited the cleric to sit down. "Father, I have to ask you for a special favor. I have to meet someone and I'm already late. Could you stay with Ezekial until I return? I'll try not to be too long. I don't want to leave him alone yet, but I must keep this appointment."

Solomon was waking up now and looked around as if he didn't recognize his surroundings. "Alexander?" he said.

"It's all right Ezekial." Henry looked pleadingly at the priest.

"Go ahead," Du Jaunay told him. "I really did plan to spend some time talking to your friend. This will not inconvenience me at all."

Henry looked so ecstatic that for a moment, Père Du Jaunay feared that he might kiss him. The merchant banged his thigh into a table as he headed for the door. "I won't forget this, Father." He stopped then for a moment and looked deeply into the priest's kind face. "I really will not forget this."

As Henry turned and hustled away, he did not listen to the priest, who perhaps did not intend for his words to be heard. "Forget this, my son. Remember God. May you see Him through me."

Chapter

5

Confrontations

Henry headed directly into the forest, expecting to search for Lo-tah at the spot of their last rendezvous by the stream. It took him less than forty-five minutes to reach it, but he ran almost the entire distance through rather heavy undergrowth.

He sat by the little brook, under the birches, winded, waiting for her to appear, hoping that somehow she would simply keep returning until he came to her, though he had no right to expect such loyalty. Three hours passed, and as the time plodded by, his anticipation went with it. Each moment he became more apprehensive. He smoked his pipe, put it out, lit it again. He threw pebbles into the stream, carved her name on a tree, walked a few paces, sat down on a fallen pine, got up, walked back to the stream. He could not rest. He could not sleep. He could only wait impatiently.

As late morning became early afternoon and there was still no sign of Lo-tah, he decided to go to the meadow where he had seen her picking flowers in hope that she could have decided to look for him there. Again, he was bitterly disappointed.

This time he waited for less than an hour before deciding that he would not find her unless he had the courage to venture into the Chippewa camp again. He had a rough idea of where the permanent village might be, due east from the maple sugar camp he thought. In order to get his bearings, he headed for the beach and retraced his steps from his earlier visit. By four o'clock in the afternoon, he found himself in the maple camp, which was now completely deserted and reverting back to wilderness.

It was very dark under the towering trees, even though he knew that there were several minutes of daylight remaining. He headed east, in the direction the warriors had come when they had discovered him tending to the badly burned child only a few months earlier. He detected a path that was rapidly disappearing under the advancing vegetation. It was obvious that no one had used this passage for weeks, but he believed there was enough left of it to guide him to his destination.

Within fifteen minutes, the aromatic scent of burning birch logs wafted through the dense and humid air, and Alexander knew he could not be more than a few hundred yards from the Chippewa camp, though the thick foliage and increasing darkness prevented any visual confirmation.

His eyes did detect a shadow that looked different from the bony limbs and leaf masses to which he had become accustomed. But for the furry, square top, the shadow began to take human form as he advanced, and the shadow was planted squarely in the path, which had become more pronounced and discernible, the closer he came to human habitation.

A voice, speaking in Algonkin, made him stand stock-still. "Have you come to collect your money, *Anglais?*" Henry recognized the speaker as Wenniway, and his heartbeat continued its rapid acceleration. "I hope so, *Anglais,* because we have payment for you. We have seen you coming for a long while, and smelled you before then. We have been looking forward to paying our debt, *Anglais,* but we are surprised that you have come to us to receive it."

Henry suddenly realized that the crazy Matchekewis and the youth, Sans-père, were on either side of him now, making up the rest of the 'we' that Wenniway made reference to. Beyond the shadow, only a hundred feet or so, was the Chippewa camp. He could see the fires through the trees and knew that Lo-tah was near. Wenniway's vicious face replaced the shadow. He was close enough to Henry that he could smell his rancid breath which reeked with a mixture of stale alcohol and fish. The otter cap, with the bullet hole acquired at Quebec, sat firmly on his head, accounting for the square-headed illusion which Henry had noticed a few minutes earlier.

Hoping that a display of bravado might somehow impress his antagonists, he said: "Yes, I have come for payment, Wenniway. I believe you mean to cheat me so I have come to make certain that you don't."

The grin on Wenniway's dirty, painted face disappeared. Henry believed that for a short moment, he saw uncertainty in the Chippewa's black eyes. The eyes shifted from Henry's face to Matchekewis and the uncertainty disappeared as 'Whirlwind' took over the conversation. "You are not brave, *Anglais,* you are merely stupid. Your payment is this!"

Henry caught a flash of steel with his peripheral vision as the fading light reflected off the blade, speeding in a descending arc toward his right shoulder. Without thinking, he impulsively thrust his elbow backward as hard as he could, catching his would-be murderer in the solar plexus, forcing the arm of Matchekewis to veer off course only slightly. Yet the diversion, however miniscule, turned out to be the difference between a torn shirt, and a deep, probably fatal, wound.

The merchant did not wait to assess the damage, but turned and ran back along the trail as fast as he could. He did not need to look back to know that the three were following close behind, Matchekewis grunting from the effort to refill his lungs, murderous epithets issuing from his mouth.

Alexander sincerely believed that his days on this earth had come to an end. Lo-tah would find his remains the next morning, or the next, scattered about by wolves or other scavengers who had been lucky enough to find a fresh, deserted kill. She would cry, and wonder again at his failure to meet her, growing old in the mystery of it, forced to marry the animal now pursuing him, defeated by her own misplaced confidence.

He knew then that he had to live. He had to survive to explain and prevent what he knew to be her destiny without him. Anger began to replace fear. He stopped suddenly and whirled around, taking his nearest pursuer by complete surprise as he slammed his fist into the astonished countenance of Sans-père. The force of the blow, and the unexpectedness of it, drove the young warrior to the ground, stunning him momentarily.

Alexander turned to run again, but he was tackled by Matchekewis who reciprocated by knocking the wind from the unhappy Englishman. Henry moaned as Wenniway arrived to help the 'Whirlwind' turn their victim onto his back. "Now I will pay the debt," Matchekewis laughed, raising his tomahawk above the head of his prone and defenseless enemy. "Kill him! Kill him!" Wenniway hissed.

The weapon came down with deadly force and intensity. Alexander closed his eyes in a last attempt to avoid his fate. The tomahawk sunk into the soft ground only half an inch from Henry's left ear. When he opened his eyes, he realized that Matchekewis was toying with him, building fear, block by block, until terror had been fully established. The Chippewa wanted to see him cringe and beg for mercy before dispatching him.

Matchekewis' eyes rolled crazily and drool ran from his mouth, sprinkling Henry's face. The Indian laughed hysterically as he pulled the hatchet easily from the ground and brought it down on the other side of Henry's head, again missing by a hair's breadth.

His eyes gleamed insanely as Henry squirmed to free himself. But Matchekewis sat on his chest, his knees pinning Henry's arms to the ground. When the merchant tried to kick, he realized that Wenniway was holding his legs.

Matchekewis pushed his sweat-soaked hand into the dirt and drew an 'X' on Henry's forehead. Laughing wildly, he raised the weapon to bring it down into its rough target. Alexander knew intuitively that there would be no more teasing. 'Lo-tah, I love you,' he thought silently to himself, and closed his eyes.

"*Arrêtez,*" he heard an unfamiliar voice cry. It came from a few yards behind his head. "Stop it now, Matchekewis." It was a voice of authority and carried a French *patois,* even though the last phrase was spoken in Algonkin.

Henry opened his eyes. His attacker still held the tomahawk poised, but hesitant. Hope, once burrowed safely into his subconscious, began to reappear. He was aware that he could move his legs and assumed that Wenniway had obeyed the voice immediately and released him. Sans-père lay close by on his back, blood trickling from his open mouth. Matchekewis still did not move. He stared blankly ahead as if under some hypnotic spell.

"Get off him and move away," the voice commanded.

Incredibly, the pressure on his chest began to ease as Henry realized that Matchekewis was doing as he was told. The Chippewa's blank expression was changing to a belligerent glare as he looked in the direction of the voice.

"You don't want to kill him now friend," the voice said. "Matchekewis is too great a warrior to slaughter an unarmed man."

Matchekewis mumbled barely coherent words. "He is not a man. He is a bitch-pup."

"There is always truth in what 'Whirlwind' says," the voice agreed. "Would you take pride in drowning a helpless pup?"

Matchekewis thought this over for a moment. "You are right, Cuchoise," he said, looking down at Henry. "I will take his life some other time, when it has more meaning." He looked triumphantly at the downcast Henry, making sure that he heard the threat. "If you want to live *Anglais,* keep to your stick-house and away from the Anishnabeg."

He spun around and marched away, down the path toward the Chippewa camp. Wenniway, frustrated and irritable, helped the dizzy Sans-père to his unsteady feet and the two of them followed Matchekewis, the latter staggering for a few yards before he regained his balance.

Henry sighed deeply and got up, turning to greet his deliverer, hand extended. He was surprised when the man, who was obviously Canadian, but dressed in Chippewa clothing, did not take it. The man had long, black hair and a beard which completely covered his mouth, even when he opened it to talk. Henry was not sure of its location.

"I could have just as easily watched you die, *Anglais.* You don't mean nothing to me. Those men," he pointed after the retreating trio, "They're *my* people. I only stopped 'em because it would bring greater trouble on them than you're worth."

"Well," Henry said, "I guess I'm not that fond of you either. But I am very grateful to you for saving my neck."

Cuchoise smiled under his beard in spite of himself. "Rub that mark off your forehead. You look too much like Cain." He began to walk slowly away in the direction of his 'people.'

"You live with them?" Henry called after him.

But Cuchoise did not answer and continued on his course until he was lost in moonlit shadow.

🦋　🦋　🦋

IT TOOK HENRY the better part of three hours to find his way back to Ezekial Solomon's cabin. He had remained close to the Chippewa camp for almost an hour, hoping that he could somehow find a way to enter the village and see Lo-tah or that she would miraculously come to him. But he knew that both of these options were only wishful thinking. He finally determined to retreat and live to fight another day (promising himself that that day would be tomorrow), and wandered back in the direction that he had come.

He was sore from his struggle with Matchekewis and his cohorts. Little blood-sucking, nocturnal mosquitoes flew around him, dining luxuriously on his flesh and leaving payment in the form of little white lumps that itched miserably. He heard sounds in the black forest surrounding him which disturbed him and caused him to change direction, never knowing for certain whether the noises were made by man or beast. It was the former he feared.

After several such adjustments and over an hour of arduous and painful stumbling in utter darkness (the moon had disappeared under a cover of black clouds), he realized he was lost. Another half an hour found him, by pure luck, on the shores of the strait, and from there he managed to find his way back to the fort and relative security.

He did not enter the stockade, but skirted it in order to reach Ezekial's home near the southern gate.

He was weary from the evening's ordeal and his primary hope was that he had not inconvenienced the personable priest to the point of an unpleasant confrontation that would lengthen his misery and the period of time before he could retire to the oblivion of his bed.

He opened the door, grateful for the light and warmth that

blanketed him as he stepped inside. Ezekial slept peacefully in his humble bed. The priest, dozing in a chair by the fire, the 'Vulgate' of Jerome cradled in his lap, snapped to alertness at the sound of Alexander's entrance.

Henry sensed instantly that something was out of place. There was a certain unfamiliarity about the room that he did not immediately recognize, but within a few seconds, was able to place. There was an object on the floor in front of the unattended and expiring fire which was covered by one of the red wool blankets that he sold in his store.

The priest, contrary to being irritable, seemed to be perfectly content, even unnaturally amiable, as the young merchant's curiosity drew him closer. Henry did not trust this unexpected good humor. Du Jaunay smiled as if he was privileged to know a joke to which the tardy Englishman was not a party. He had had that feeling before and it usually ended in some sort of embarrassment for him. The priest continued to smile at him with that 'your private parts are showing' grin. Henry experienced increasing discomfort as he drew near.

Suddenly, the bundle on the floor moved. The blanket slipped away to reveal, unbelievably, the object of his day's exhausting adventure, sleeping peacefully and innocently in the shadows cast from the hearth. He laughed from the irony of it. "How . . . where . . . ?"

Du Jaunay was quick to explain. "She came here early this afternoon looking for you. She is a delightful child and very communicative. We have been conversing most of the day."

"You mean she's been *here* all this time?" Henry thought of how close he came to death while Lo-tah was sitting in Solomon's cabin chatting amicably with the priest. She looked so beautiful, so sweet, lying there.

"*Mais oui.* She has told us much about you. She seems to have become very attached to you and it's quite obvious from your expression that the feeling is reciprocal."

"It is."

"Was she your, uh, 'appointment'?"

Henry's cheeks reddened and his eyes fell to the floor, absently perusing his muddy boots. "Yes."

"Then it's easier to understand your urgent haste this morning."

"Father, I hope I have not inconvenienced you too much. I know I have been gone all day and . . ."

Du Jaunay raised a hand. "I have enjoyed myself immensely! Mr. Solomon and I have been exchanging our philosophies. This day has given me an opportunity to do a little proselytizing. The girl . . ."

"Lo-tah," Henry interjected.

"Lo-tah," the priest corrected, "seemed very interested in my crucifix. When I asked her why, she said she had seen 'the little man' before. She wanted to know who He was. God works in mysterious ways my son."

"I guess He does, Father." Henry looked with adoring eyes once again at Lo-tah, then back to the priest. "She said she had seen the Christ before? How?"

"In a dream."

Henry nodded his head. "She is noted as somewhat of a visionary among her own people."

"Well her curiosity afforded me the opportunity to speak of the Lord to her. She was very interested and attentive. She has a quick mind. The lesson was not lost on Mr. Solomon either." He nodded toward Ezekial who had just begun to snore. "In all, it has been a rewarding day, so do not apologize."

Henry moved to a chair and seated his weary frame. He pulled off his boots, leaned back, and sighed heavily. "I'm surprised she stayed here and didn't leave to look for me elsewhere."

"That's probably because of what Mr. Solomon told her," Du Jaunay said.

"What did he tell her?"

"He said that he believed that you were probably going to the Chippewa camp, although he failed to mention for what purpose."

"I still don't understand why . . ."

"Monsieur Henry, it seems that the young lady is afraid to go back. She has, I believe, run away. She spoke very rapidly and I don't practice my Algonkin very often, but from what I could comprehend, her mother was killed and she is now in the care of her uncle."

"Minavavana," Henry mumbled.

"*Pardonnez-moi?*"

"Nothing, Father, go on."

"Well, apparently she fears her uncle will force her to do something that she is very anxious about, but she would not elaborate. It was at that point that she asked about the crucifix, and our conversation never returned to the original subject. But it was obvious that she didn't want to go back and risk a confrontation with her new guardian, so Mr. Solomon invited her to stay and await your return. She fell asleep about an hour ago. I was nodding myself when you came in. Did you see her uncle?"

"No. I couldn't get to the village at all. But I believe I understand the reason for her timidity."

"Look." Du Jaunay pointed at Lo-tah who was sitting up, apparently awakened by the sound of their voices. When she saw Alexander, her face changed from sleepy dawn to bright daylight as she rushed across the room, jumped onto his lap, and embraced her lover eagerly. Due to the presence of the cleric, Henry's response was less flamboyant, but just as genuine. He held her tightly for a moment, whispered something the priest could not hear, then stood up and held her at arm's length.

"What happened to your mama? I am sorry."

Lo-tah's smile changed to a frown and her naturally pouting lower lip became very pronounced. "She has gone to the spirit world." Tears formed gently in her dark eyes. "It was she who guided me here. I cannot go back. Minavavana would have me be his son's bride. He is blind to the spirits and to his own child's evil. I will obey my spirit-mother and my heart." She put her arms around his waist and rested her head gently on his chest as tears fell down her face.

Alexander stroked her long hair unconsciously, attempting to soothe her. "You were right to come to me," he said. "I could not come to you until today. My friend . . ." he pointed to Solomon who had quit snoring and was moving restlessly, "was hurt. I had to help him. I was afraid you would think that I had no feeling for you. Forgive me, dear Lo-tah."

She looked at him, an expression of complete surprise slowly replaced by a returning smile. "I did not know you did not come. I failed also, Hen-ree. I was mourning Natomah."

"You mean you weren't there, by the stream, either?"

"No."

"Well, today is filled with ironies." He smiled down at her youthful, pretty face. "What are we to do?"

"I will be your squaw, here," she answered firmly.

He thought of his 'discussion' with Etherington. "I'm afraid I have made somewhat of a mess of things." The way she looked at him, questioningly, yet full of trust, stabbed him with guilt. "The chief will not allow me an Anishnabeg wife inside the stick-wall."

"Why?" she asked. Her innocence drove the guilt-dagger deeper.

"He does not trust the Anishnabeg. He has already punished one soldier for 'having' an Indian woman."

"He is not a good chief," Lo-tah said bluntly.

"Probably true," Henry agreed.

"Why then do you obey him?" Henry found it terribly difficult to think in the face of such simplicity coming from a face of such beauty.

"I don't know. I just have to do it," he said finally. He knew the answer was stupid, but his tongue could produce nothing better.

"Obedience is superior to wisdom?"

"Yes," he admitted. "I guess it is."

She turned away from him, apparently deep in thought and sat on the floor below the small window. "If this were true among the Anishnabeg, I should have to marry Wenniway."

"I'm glad it isn't." Henry sat down again.

Du Jaunay had gone to the door without Henry noticing. *"Bon soir,* my son."

Having recovered from the initial shock of her presence, Henry now realized how rude he had been to ignore the man who had spent his entire day and evening assisting him. "Forgive my neglect of you, Père Du Jaunay. I seem to have become a to-tal boor. It's just that my mind is completely preoccupied with my own problems and concerns. Please pardon my idiocy."

"I cannot clear your mind my young friend, but I take no offense and, perhaps, I can offer you some suggestions, if you wish?"

"I do wish. Please."

"The girl, if Mr. Solomon agrees, could remain here. She needs a place to stay and he requires a nurse. It might be mutually beneficial, *n'est-ce pas?*"

"A capital idea, but . . ."

"This would, of course, be only a temporary arrangement until we can change Colonel Etherington's mind."

"You believe that possible?"

"With some help, *oui.*"

"What help?"

"I want you to talk to some friends of mine. I believe they could assist you."

"Of course, anything."

"I will arrange a meeting." The priest paused, then spoke in English, knowing that Lo-tah would fail to understand. Henry was surprised to discover that their entire conversation had been in Algonkin.

"You will marry the girl?"

"Yes, of course Father. I love her."

"You know I cannot perform the sacrament of marriage unless you are both members of Holy Mother Church?"

"I know."

The priest turned to leave.

"Father?"

"Yes, my son."

"You are a good man."

"*Non,* my son. The words are contradictory. I am only a man of God. *Bon soir.*" He winked at Alexander and closed the door behind him.

"*Bon soir,* good priest," Henry said to the closed door and strode across the room to join Lo-tah who awaited him with open arms.

🏵 🏵 🏵

THE JESUIT called for Henry the next afternoon. The young Englishman, the Jew, and the Chippewa girl had spent the morning in pleasant conversation. Henry had acted as interpreter between his friend and Lo-tah, who was so diligent in her attendance to every need of the injured man that he felt genuine remorse at having ever mocked Alexander's relationship with her and soon developed an appreciation for his friend's obsession.

She was, he told Henry, the very epitome of beauty, the perfect representation of sensitivity, a complete model of intelligence and compassion. He received no argument from his infatuated associate.

When Père Du Jaunay rapped on the door, interrupting their noon meal and their pleasant companionship, Solomon was almost resentful until he discovered that the intruder was the Jesuit whose company he had so enjoyed on the previous day.

"Monsieur Henry, can you come with me now?" The priest asked after informal greetings had been exchanged.

Alexander looked at Solomon. "Go ahead," Ezekial said, "and while you're gone I'll try to repay you for all your kindness by stealing your girlfriend."

"That isn't possible," Henry retorted. "She loves only me."

"Ah, but she hasn't seen the fancy design on my chest yet. I understand Indian women love tattoos."

"But not on such an emaciated frame as yours," Henry joked.

"We'll see," Ezekial challenged.

Henry was happy to see his friend in such improved spirits. He had been so miserably depressed at first that Alexander had feared for his sanity. He was recovering and becoming more himself. He could not help but believe that the vengeance exacted on Wickwall and Chimton by Du Charme and himself had contributed to that healing.

With a kiss, he parted from Lo-tah, explaining that he would return shortly. He exited with the Jesuit.

They went inside the fort. Du Jaunay led him directly to the Cardin cabin which, of course, Henry recognized.

"How can the Cardins help?" he questioned, as Père Du Jaunay rapped at the door.

"They have suffered much to be together. *They* know what

you are learning. They also know Jamet quite well. Some influence will be needed to change Etherington's mind. He won't listen to me."

Constante opened the door, smiling warmly at Du Jaunay. Henry believed from that expression that much had been confided between them. He thought she was quite an attractive woman for her age, but her face belied a difficult life and her pursed lips indicated a rigid personality that found little room for nonsense. Her husband, amiable as always, stood directly behind her, his sturdy, muscular frame contrasting with her middle-aged plumpness.

"*Bon jour,* Monsieur Henry," he said. "*Entrez, s'il vous plaît.*"

Alexander followed the priest inside and smiled at Constante whose expression was polite, but not warm.

The sitting room of their rather expansive log home was nicely furnished with comfortable chairs and quaint little tables covered with lace doilies. The tea service, set neatly in the center of the room, indicated that the Cardins had been expecting their visitors. Du Jaunay helped himself to the tea and small cakes as if he were sitting in his own parlor.

"It is good to see you, Monsieur," Cardin began. "I trust that your business prospers?"

Alexander had always liked his host. He was straightforward and honest and his comment was not simply idle curiosity. Henry believed that the man was really interested in his success.

"It does, Monsieur Cardin, *merci.*" He looked at Constante who was watching Du Jaunay devour his cake and tea as a vigilant mother might oversee her undernourished child. The Jesuit paused from the pleasure of his Epicurean labor when he realized he had become the center of attention. All three were looking to him to continue the conversation. He set aside the cake and took a hasty swallow of the hot, spiced tea. "Monsieur Henry is in love," he stated flatly. Red roses bloomed in Alexander's cheeks. "He has met an Indian woman named Lo-tah, and he wishes to marry her."

"How fortunate for you, Monsieur," Cardin said, honest felicity apparent in his features.

"Lo-tah?" Constante suddenly became quite animated.

"Tcianung's daughter?"

"Her mother's name was Natomah," Henry answered. "I don't know her father's name."

"Was?" Constante asked.

"Her mother died two days ago. Her father, I believe, died in the smallpox epidemic."

Both Constante and François looked so sobered by his remark that Henry was dumbfounded by their reaction.

"Joseph Louis, their son, perished of the same affliction," the priest explained.

"I'm so sorry to have been the cause of unhappy memories," Henry said.

François rapidly composed himself. "You had no way of knowing Monsieur. I hope our temporary grief was not the cause of too much discomfort for you."

Henry simply shook his head. Silence reigned for a few moments, before Alexander's curiosity forced his tongue to action. "Do you know Lo-tah?"

It was Constante's turn to cultivate facial flowers. "I cared for her when she was a little girl."

"They brought her here?"

"*Non*, I lived among the Chippewa." Tears formed in Constante's eyes, watering the roses which were gradually fading in her cheeks. François reached across and held her hand. She grasped it until her knuckles turned white.

Alexander could see that the question upset her, so he did not pursue the subject. Again, the little group fell into silence. Du Jaunay rescued them. "I have brought you together," he said to Henry, "Because François and Constante are two people very much like you and your Chippewa woman. They love each other very much and, like you, circumstances worked against them. They know what it's like to be separated. They had no help, and a lack of sound advice and open entreaty to those who love *them*, almost destroyed their lives. I think it would benefit them greatly if they could assist you in resolving your unhappy situation."

He turned to François and Constante. "Monsieur Henry has been told by Colonel Etherington that he may not bring Lo-tah inside the walls of this post, I believe primarily because of the commandant's own prejudices. It is impossible for them to live among the Chippewa because the girl has disobeyed her uncle, Minavavana, who is her guardian. He wishes her to marry Wenniway, his son and her cousin."

Constante interrupted in a shaky voice. "Wenniway, that pig!" She almost spit the words. "It's unwise to marry someone you do not love."

"Exactly," the priest argued. "That's why she has run away and come here. She is with Solomon, the Jew, outside the fort. But you see why they *must* live inside the stockade?"

"How can we help?" Cardin asked.

"Jamet is a good friend of yours, *n'est-ce pas?*"

"Oui."

"Can you get him to influence the commandant to change his mind? He will not listen to a papist priest and he and Monsieur Henry are not on the best of terms. I don't believe he would listen to *any* Frenchman, but Jamet is technically English."

Cardin looked over at Henry who sat tensely on the edge of his chair, elbows resting on his knees, and face expectant.

"Oui, I will try."

Henry believed if anyone could change the commandant's mind, it would be the diplomatic Jamet, who spent the vast majority of his free time in the company of the Cardins. "Thank you, Monsieur," Henry said, rising and grabbing the Frenchman's hand. "I will be in your debt."

As he and Du Jaunay prepared to take their leave, Constante put her hand on Henry's arm to stop him. "You really love her?" she said.

"Yes."

Constante looked into his face for a long time, then she reached up and kissed him maternally on the cheek. "God bless and preserve you both," she whispered.

🌺 🌺 🌺

CARDIN DID TALK to Jamet. The lieutenant shared with François the story of Etherington's terrible addiction to alcohol which was getting worse each day. Jamet recommended that Henry make a gift of rum to the colonel, and he would try to broach the subject to him at that time. There was little doubt, he said, that within hours after receiving his gift he would be extremely inebriated and, under those conditions, he might be persuaded to relent and allow Henry to bring his prospective bride into the stockade.

Henry suspected that he might have been able to accomplish the same thing without having to use François Cardin as an intermediary, based upon his previous association with Jamet in the incident with Wickwall and Chimton. Nevertheless, he was glad that Du Jaunay had brought them together. He had learned something about the Cardins that he would have remained ignorant about without the priest's intervention. He felt a sort of comraderie with them (he wasn't sure why), which broadened his friendship and enriched his existence. He believed that he could count on them now to help him at anytime, and he was certain that that had been Du Jaunay's intention in bringing them together.

As it turned out, Jamet's ploy worked to perfection. Henry gave Etherington the rum, he drank himself into a stupor, and Jamet got him to sign a paper agreeing to Lo-tah's residence with Alexander Henry.

There was a minor crisis the following day when Etherington spotted her outside Henry's cabin, but when Jamet produced the written order, signed by the commandant (he, not surprisingly, did not recall signing it), he gave in and Lo-tah moved in with Alexander. Etherington, realizing he had been duped, was never cordial to Henry again and Lieutenant Leslie now had to countersign anything suggested by 'that mongrel,' Jamet.

Lo-tah continued to nurse Ezekial, and within a few days, he was up and around. His health restored, and his dignity reinforced, Solomon never went anywhere without his muzzle-loader, and Wickwall avoided him like the plague. Ezekial had promised (and made it well-known), that he would shoot Wickwall on sight if he ever made the smallest threatening gesture toward him again.

As autumn approached, Henry and Lo-tah spent a great deal of time in the company of the Cardins and gradually, as trust was established between them, heard the story of their difficulties. Henry was amazed at the strength of their commitment to each other and marveled at their courage.

Lo-tah spent most of each day with Constante and with Père Du Jaunay, who was a constant visitor. Both of the latter took the opportunity to proselytize, and Lo-tah rapidly became an able catechist. She wanted to know everything about the 'little man on the cross,' and her curiosity often drove her patient teachers to exhaustion. When Constante told her of the crucifixion and the reason for it, tears formed in her eyes and she mourned for the 'gentle man.' When she listened to the Easter story, her face positively glowed and she commented that she knew that *He* could not be dead. Père Du Jaunay gave her a crucifix of her own, which she wore proudly and she bent Henry's ear each evening, repeating the stories of Noah's Ark or Joseph's robe of many colors.

The vision of the 'Jesus Spirit' haunted her dreams and she would often wake in the middle of the night in response to some foreign sound, look at her sleeping lover, and wonder if the Holy Ghost had come with 'tongues of fire' to possess her as He had done to the Apostles at Pentecost. When she asked the priest about her dreams, he told her that it was indeed the *Spiritus Sancti* working faith in her and she would soon be a Christian and be baptized into the 'True Church' and partake of the Mass.

She wanted very much to be a part of the religious community. When the French, Catholics all, attended Vespers, or went to morning Mass, she felt guilty and strangely deprived by not going, but Alexander would not attend, and though he gave her the freedom to do as she wished, she would not go without him.

He tried to explain to her the difference between the English church and what he called 'the papists,' but she could not comprehend it. To her, their mutual belief in Jesus, the Christ, would surely be sufficient to overcome any other considerations, but alas, this was not the case. Henry loved the priest, and religion was not an integral part of his life, but he was a firm Protestant, and could not be budged.

In spite of this, Lo-tah and Henry were extremely happy.

Henry's business prospered and Lo-tah was making many friends. They were married in a quiet civil ceremony conducted by Lieutenant Jamet (one of the stipulations that Du Jaunay had placed on assisting them was that the priest would allow no philandering, even though the marriage would not be recognized by the church.)

Henry and Lo-tah spent their evenings together in the cabin by the fire, or walking along the beach in front of the stockade wall and watching the glorious sunsets. They made love often and with such intensity that Henry felt somehow that they were both driven by an urgency that foretold of disaster. Yet he pushed such horrid thoughts from his mind, and reveled in the wonderful beauty of their time together. Lo-tah was the perfect wife. She was a perfect lover, a tremendous helpmeet, an interesting conversationalist, slow to anger and quick to forgive, displaying every virtue of her sex and few of the faults.

Such an idyl was too good to last, and one bleak and rainy morning brought affirmation. Minavavana and his son, Wenniway, along with the ever-present orphan, Sans-père, were granted permission to enter the stockade by Etherington for the purpose of 'trading' with Mr. Henry. They had brought gifts for the commandant and he had not failed to be impressed with these bribes. He announced to Lieutenant Leslie in rather slurred speech, that the Chippewa chief was a 'fine chap'—for a savage.

Thus it was that the angry chief and his jilted son came storming into Henry's shop and found, as they had suspected, their wayward relative, Lo-tah.

They also found François and Constante in attendance along with Ezekial Solomon. Lo-tah sat with Constante and François around a small table by the fire. Alexander, as usual, stood behind the counter, attending to his store and chatting amiably with Solomon who had planned to run his traps for rabbit or squirrel for the first time since his return to health on this morning, but had been waylaid by the weather and out of boredom, had come to visit.

When the Indians slammed the door behind them and stood dripping by the entrance, Solomon picked up the 'Brown Bess' which never left his side. Lo-tah did not move. She was caught in the belligerent glare of her cousin and uncle. Henry, half expecting some such confrontation, remained quite calm.

Minavavana spoke first. *"Anglais,"* he shouted, "you have brought my niece away from her people without my permission. I am her guardian and parent. You have violated my wishes and I will not tolerate this treachery. Do you wish to die? Why do you act so foolishly?"

"The 'Grand Saulteur' has been misinformed," Henry replied. "I did not bring Lo-tah here, but she came of her own volition. She chose to be with me and has become my *noko,* my woman. I love her. No deceit was intended, nor any insult."

When Minavavana heard the word *noko,* his nostrils flared and the turtle design on his chest swam with his angry breathing. "I am her parent. Am I to have no say? She has been promised to Wenniway and I will take her with me!"

"She will stay here," François said quietly as he stood up and drew his knife. Solomon squared his rifle, aiming at the neck of the turtle which was right over the chief's heart.

Constante Cardin had remained frozen in her chair since the Indians had entered. She stared hard at Sans-père, whose light complexion and soft features reflected back to her, mirror-like, her own image. Though he was now full-grown, she remembered him instantly as her own, and trembled for what he had become. She looked at Wenniway who had, as a teenager, raped her. These memories flooded back on her and her stomach revolted against their recall.

Resolve hardening on her face, she stood up. "Minavavana," she said, "your son is an *oqui,* a devil. He hates everyone and disgraces you with his conduct. Lo-tah cannot be a companion to such a one as this. God smiles too much on her." Though she trembled and tears formed in her eyes, she did not waver.

Wenniway glowered at her with diabolical eyes, malevolence apparent in every line of his twisted, painted, face.

"Would you rather have her the companion of a whore?" Minavavana said. His glare burned right through Constante and she collapsed in her chair, covering her face with her hands and moaning softly.

François stepped forward, his knife extended. Minavavana

looked at him with utter disdain as the other two Chippewa lifted their tomahawks in defense.

Lo-tah quickly stood up, placing her hands on Constante's shoulders and comforting the tortured woman as she spoke. "Minavavana!" she said. "You are my uncle, my father's brother, and I love you. But I will not marry Wenniway. You remember a time when Tcianung, my father, did not accept his bride price." She pointed at Wenniway without looking at him. "Tcianung's wishes have not changed with his death. I have had visions which Wenniway has laughed at, and yet many of our people bear the pock marks on their flesh of the truth of that vision. Your own *noko,* my revered aunt, has an even higher insight, for she is in the spirit world. Part of that vision was of the *Kitchi-Manitou* whom I now recognize as Jesus, the Christ. Constante is right about Wenniway. He is an agent of the great *oqui,* Satan. I will die before I would be his. My husband," she looked coyly at Alexander, "will provide a just bride-price, but I will not leave him. My heart and Jesus tell me differently. I will remain!"

Minavavana's anger began to dissolve slowly into a realization of the truth of the situation. His son, in spite of the chief's devotion, was a miserable excuse for a man. He was basically a coward, cruel and stupid. Minavavana's extreme love for his only offspring had often covered those faults. But he knew the verity of these people's accusations.

He knew too, that any forcing of the issue would probably end in his own death or, a more terrible consequence, the death of his beloved son.

Yet his greatest fear was to unintentionally defy the spirit of his brother and offend the *Kitchi-Manitou* who would withdraw the protection of the Great Turtle from him and make the tattoo on his chest, which he wore with such great pride, meaningless. There was little doubt of the authenticity of Lo-tah's visions, which had been confirmed time and time again.

He thought back to the day of her birth and he remembered the many omens. The problem now presenting itself, was how to withdraw without leaving behind the impression with everyone that it was out of fear for his own physical safety. He knew that he could never allow that to happen and still live with himself.

He had to show the assemblage that it was not fear of them which was driving him away.

He stepped toward the counter and stood directly opposite Henry, staring fiercely at him, but not moving to strike him. Ezekial Solomon, determined to protect his friend, kept his musket pointed at Minavavana, only a few feet away. Tense moments passed before the chief turned and walked toward Solomon, who kept the turtle in the sights of his 'Brown Bess.' The stoic Chippewa, expressionless and calm, continued forward until the cold barrel of the musket touched his chest. Ezekial could not pull the trigger. He sensed, somehow, that Minavavana intended no harm, but was establishing his courage with bravado. The chief pushed against the deadly pipe with his chest, hands resting at his sides and actually forced his armed opponent to step back. When Ezekial took no action, he turned away contemptuously and sauntered over to his niece.

He looked at her long and hard, and Lo-tah believed she saw love somewhere behind the fierce, belligerent, *façade*.

As he strode toward the door, the 'Grand Saulteur' intentionally bumped Cardin, who still held the knife in his hand, then purposefully turned his back on the Frenchman, daring him to use the weapon. François lifted the blade as if to strike, and held it there. The few seconds that it took for him to wisely lower his arm seemed like an eternity to the small gathering.

Minavavana did not move again until he was sure that Cardin had lowered the knife. Then he passed deftly between Wenniway and Sans-père and out the door, having proved his point with a melodramatic flair.

Wenniway and Sans-père, obviously confused by their chief's desertion, had not the stomach to continue the confrontation. But Wenniway could not resist a parting volley. "I still owe you, *Anglais*," he threatened in Algonkin, "but now the debt extends to your squaw as well. I *will* pay you both!"

He made a defiant gesture with his fist and stalked out of the building. Sans-père said nothing, but glared at the tiny group with wild eyes, puffy and swollen from his broken nose. Words were not necessary. His unbridled hatred for them was felt by every occupant in the merchant's shop and none felt it more keenly than Constante Cardin, who sobbed with miserable penitence as her son passed through the door into the grey and stormy world she had fled.

Chapter

6

The Beaver Hunt

IT RAINED ALMOST EVERY DAY in that month of August, turning the parade ground into a field of mud and keeping the occupants of Fort Michilimackinac busy patching their roofs and digging trenches to keep the water from collecting in grey and stagnant pools around their cabins.

Inside Henry's cabin, however, life was sunny and pleasant. The wet weather produced a constant stream of visitors during the day who sat by the warm, dry fire and sipped tea with Henry and his wife.

François and Constante were frequent visitors along with the Du Charmes, Père Du Jaunay, Jamet, and the ever-cheerful Solomon who, for the first time in his short life, enjoyed the company of a group of Gentile friends whose loyalties went unquestioned and carried no conditions. They all fell in love with Lo-tah whose extemporaneous actions, acquiescent demeanor, and dulcet voice, coupled with her intelligent innocence and consuming beauty, captivated everyone she met.

Henry, too, was popular. He was generous (and could afford to be), helpful, polite, intelligent, and, importantly, a good listener.

These shared qualities, coupled with the eventual inactivity produced by the prolonged bad weather, inevitably brought others to the Henry cabin, including Ignace Bourassa and Marie Amiot. This circle of friends created a small oasis in the desert of Anglo-French hatred, that was refreshing to those who shared it, and created black envy in those who did not.

Wawatam, Henry's 'brother,' had not forgotten their friendship either and was a frequent visitor after Alexander's marriage. He highly approved of Lo-tah and was fascinated by her visions which he wanted a complete account of and he, in turn, explained his dreams. Both of them, he said, had been led to Alexander through visions and they were, therefore, spiritual cousins. The bulk of any discourse between them unfailingly had to do with the supernatural. Wawatam was accepted into the little club as a full member and his stories, appearance, and personality made him a popular attraction.

Even after the rains finally stopped, the little group would often meet at Henry's shop, when time allowed, and converse well into the evening.

September saw the promise of a spectacular autumn as the trees began to turn early. October exploded with orange and red and yellow. The sun, hidden so long in August, made up for its absence by shining daily in October and using its refractive rays to intensify the stunning colors. The lake, often calm in these beautiful days, assisted the sun by acting as a gigantic looking glass, reflecting the color back to the sky and giving the inhabitants of the straits a double picture of nature's artistry.

Ironically, in the midst of all this pulchritude, the Anishnabeg of Michilimackinac began the long journey south to their wintering grounds. Minavavana had made no further attempt to see Lo-tah before his departure, and had accepted Henry's bride price consisting of three fine hatchets, four wool blankets, three kegs of 'English milk,' a musket with powder and shot, beads, trinkets, dice, a spinning top, and six clay pipes with tobacco. No one in the memory of any of Minavavana's people had ever received such a large dowry. Henry sent the gifts with Wawatam when the Ottawa went to visit the 'Grand Saulteur' and he reported that the Chippewa chief had accepted the presents without comment or emotion, indicating his assent to their union. Wawatam also related that Minavavana was entertaining a group of Ottawa visitors from *D'étroit* whose leader, he told Alexander, was a great warrior named Pon-ti-ac, whom Wawatam had met before as a young man.

It seemed that Minavavana and Pon-ti-ac were closeted together in many secret meetings, and when Wawatam inquired about the Ottawa's presence in the Anishnabeg camp, the 'Grand Saulteur' said they had come to talk and would not elaborate any further.

The Chippewa left for their winter camp shortly after Pon-ti-ac's departure, intending to stop only at the Chippewa settlement at *Che-boy-gan* to visit briefly with Matchekewis before sojourning to *le grand Sault* (the Grand Rapids).

With the Chippewa gone, Lo-tah and Henry spent many beautiful fall days walking through the forests of Michilimackinac, hand in hand, watching the animals prepare for the hard winter to come, listening to the geese honking overhead as they followed the Chippewa south, and strolling through the ever-thickening layer of dry leaves. The air was cool and fresh and clean and, Henry believed, he had never felt more wonderful or at home.

In the dark evenings, when visitors had gone and the wind whistled off the lake through the now bare trees, Alexander and Lo-tah would lie together in the bed that he had made and he would try to teach her the rudiments of English. But the closeness of her body and its wonderful, shapely nakedness would drive him to distraction and they would make love to each other, while ominous clouds crept over the land of the Great Turtle.

Winter struck in full force before the first week of November was gone. Henry and Lo-tah awoke one morning to find that it was still dark in their cabin. Alexander was convinced that it was at least an hour since sunrise and even on a grey and cloudy day, enough light could be found inside to see by.

Upon further investigation, he discovered that the snow, which had begun at midnight, had fallen and blown with such fury that the windows were drifted over with it. It took him the better part of the morning to dig his way out and clear a path to his shop which would allow other occupants of the fort to reach his little store to purchase things they now depended upon (especially old Augustin Langlade who was continually drunk and depended upon Alexander for his supply of rum).

Autumn never returned. The straits were buffeted by continual blizzards and no one, not even old Langlade, could remember a more brutal or punishing winter. Between Christmas Eve and the beginning of the new year, the fort was like a white tomb, blanketed in a hoary shroud from continual snowstorms and sub-zero temperatures. Footprints could not be seen on the parade ground outside and there was little evidence of any kind of life except inside the dwellings. Life became monotonous and often dull and the inhabitants of the fort, especially the British garrison, became very restless.

Du Charme, hardy and cheerful as ever, waited patiently for the weather to break, and when the sun at last shone again one icy, frigid January day, he strapped on his snowshoes, kissed Marguerite and the twins, and went out to lay his traps. The pelts would be at their thickest, and he looked forward to a rich harvest. He puffed on his clay pipe as he ventured forward, bundled in layers of clothing and his own fat which, he was convinced, would keep him adequately warm.

He headed out the water gate and as the miserably cold sentry swung the big doors inward, snow, which had been drifting against the outside, collapsed in a huge pile in the opening. The sentry sighed, knowing that he would have to shovel the snow out of the way in order to close the gate again and Colonel Etherington was very adamant about it being closed, since the snow would then find its drifting way inside and make movement within the compound difficult.

Du Charme, his snow shoes firmly attached, simply walked up the little hill. The sentry watched with disgust, knowing that later in the day, the damn Canadian would want to get back in. Other eyes too followed Du Charme's progress, hateful eyes, glaring from the barrack's window that the Frenchman had just passed.

As Du Charme disappeared on the other side of the little snow-knoll, the eyes looked down at a hand that often ached with the cold, a hand whose dominant feature was a white, jagged, and lightning-shaped scar.

🍇 🍇 🍇

LATER THE SAME AFTERNOON, the sentry had to open the gate for Wawatam who had come to visit his 'brother' and 'sister.' The sentry was very irritable because it was the second time in several hours that he had done it and the task always pulled him away from the little brazier which kept him from freezing.

Wawatam was welcomed cheerfully by Alexander and Lo-tah who were starved for company and who had missed *him* in particular over the past few weeks. He had been absent from them for a reason however, and had struggled through the deep snow to tell them about it.

He smiled broadly and pulled at his split earlobes as he announced proudly that he had taken a new wife. Her name Henry found difficult to pronounce, and when he tried to repeat it, Wawatam laughed heartily. She was called Ozah-guscodah-wayquay, or in English, 'Woman of the Glade.' Wawatam said she was very young and pretty and could carry many loads of firewood at once. She had a full belly and broad hips, he bragged, that promised fertility. She was such a good woman, he boasted, that even though he had lived with her for a month, he had not yet had to beat her.

Lo-tah congratulated him and embraced him affectionately which he seemed, strangely, not to enjoy, but he accepted Henry's warm handshake and was very pleased that his *Anglais* brother approved of his choice.

They sat talking for over an hour before Wawatam got around to revealing the other purpose of his visit—that being his wish that Alexander would accompany him that afternoon on a beaver hunt. He stated that the animals were much easier to obtain in the winter without using traps, and he would like to teach his friend how it was done. He concluded his invitation with an admonition that it was not good to be inactive or one should grow fat and lazy. Henry could not resist such an invitation as he felt his small, but increasing, paunch.

After leaving the grumbling sentry behind, they headed for the river which wound its way south from the straits. This was a favorite habitat of the beaver because it was slow-moving and several little ponds had been formed by the creatures on its edges, surrounded by birch, aspen, and poplar, which were the preferred foods of these beasts.

While journeying toward this furry gold mine, Wawatam told Henry that the beaver in summer were very intelligent and difficult to catch, but as the cold weather set in, they became slow thinkers. Indeed, he related, the beavers were, at one time, a kind of people, who had the power of speech. But the Great Spirit took this ability away from them lest they became superior in understanding to mankind.

Wawatam stated further that the beaver were still much like the Ottawa, building their homes, fighting for their mates, reproducing, and hunting for their food, while living in relative harmony within their natural surroundings.

By the time they reached the pond, the fickle sun had disappeared behind dark storm clouds, and the temperature dropped several degrees, making both men uncomfortable even though they were heavily dressed.

Many small trees along the shore had been felled by the industrious animals they sought, and several wooden igloos jutted out of the ice in the center of the pond.

Wawatam hacked down a small but sturdy sapling with his hatchet and proceeded to strip it of its branches. He motioned for Alexander to do the same. This accomplished, he stepped out onto the ice and headed for the nearest beaver 'house.'

As soon as he reached it, he began using the pole he had fashioned to tear the building apart, casting sticks and debris every which way, as he pried them loose from their foundation. Henry worked assiduously by his side, learning by imitation and enjoying the warmth the labor created.

Once they had fashioned a large hole through the top, Henry and Wawatam looked inside and saw that the home was empty. Henry was disappointed, but his teacher showed no discouragement whatever, strolling to the next 'house' and prying at it with the sapling.

After they had opened all four of the homes and found nothing, Henry was prepared to begin the trek back to the fort empty-handed until Wawatam patiently explained that he had not intended to find the beaver there. The purpose of their labor had been to drive the animals from their lodges which, he pointed out, they had accomplished, since all of the dwellings were deserted.

Henry's patience was wearing thin as the temporary warmth provided by their physical efforts had begun to dissipate and he was shivering.

Wawatam, displaying Job-like constancy, explained to Alexander that the beaver, who invariably lived in families (except for the 'old bachelors'), would now move to washes near the banks of the pond. These were small hollows that the animals used for temporary shelter and as exits from the ice-covered water, which were never frozen over very thickly because of the continual passage back and forth, of the warm-blooded fur bearers.

It was now a simple matter of walking along the edge of the pond and tapping with the stick until the sound indicated an empty space underneath.

This took less than five minutes. When the 'clunk, clunk' of the stick on the ice changed to a 'clink, clink,' Wawatam stopped, the expression on his face similar to a child who has just entered an unattended candy shop.

He stood over the spot and brought the sapling down hard on the thin layer of ice, shattering it instantly. Underneath, Henry could see the brown backs of a beaver family, swimming furiously in confused circles in the shallow wash. Wawatam reached into the cold water and pulled the largest one out by the hump of his neck.

The rodent was huge, weighing between thirty and forty pounds, and Wawatam had everything he could do to avoid its sharp foreclaws and snapping incisors. He finally had to put the creature on the ground and it immediately made a bee-line for the wash. It was too slow and clumsy on land, however, to make good its escape as Wawatam grabbed hold of its flat, foot-long tail, hoisted it in the air again, and swung it around, smashing its head violently against a tree.

In spite of the violence of the blow, the beaver was only stunned, but Wawatam deftly dispatched the unfortunate creature by slitting its throat, being careful not to bruise the succulent flesh below the head.

He then returned to the wash, grabbed the next one and duplicated his earlier procedure. The last three were only kittens and Wawatam left those to mature, moving on to the next hollow.

When they had collected six prime animals and emptied out three washes, they decided to head back. It was snowing, and Alexander's hand was throbbing from a nasty gash inflicted by one of the beavers now slung over his companion's shoulder. He had wanted to try lifting one of the beasts from the water, but its fur was slippery and the beaver, a large male, had twisted suddenly and sunk its prominent, sharp teeth into the meaty portion of Henry's hand, just below the wrist. Wawatam had killed the assailant with his knife, but the wound bled severely and soaked Henry's deerskin mittens.

As they labored through the snowy woods toward home, Alexander experienced a great deal of satisfaction, watching the dead beaver flop gently against Wawatam's back, its pink tongue hanging limply from its open mouth.

He was thinking that he might make a necklace of the pearly weapons which had maimed him when he almost ran into Wawatam. The Ottawa had stopped suddenly and was staring at a large, dark object laying on the snow-covered ground. Around it, the snow was turning red.

🐾 🐾 🐾

LAURENT DU CHARME had laid his last trap when he looked up at the sky, roiling with dark clouds. 'Another bad storm coming,' he thought as he shouldered his Charleville and shuffled his snowshoes in the direction of the fort and Marguerite.

His stomach had been complaining for the past hour and he had hurried through the latter part of his task in order to avoid the brewing storm, but also to satisfy his gnawing hunger.

It had been four hours since he had last consumed any food, and he looked forward to the venison roast and wild rice that Marguerite had promised for that evening.

He also anticipated the time spent with his sons who were curious and bright and, crawling up on his knees, often fell asleep there, their curly heads resting securely on his large stomach.

Absorbed in his thoughts of home, Du Charme did not hear the footsteps behind him until it was too late. As he began to turn, his upper back exploded in a bright flash of pain. The world spun around crazily, his mind mixing with the wild clouds above, as another bolt of lightning pain penetrated his lower back.

He dropped to his knees, struggling to stay conscious. The swirling white ground was fading into darkness. He was falling into a dark pit, which he was sure went on forever. Blackness covered him before he hit the bottom.

Above the pit, in the real world of ice and grey-white cold, a scarred hand removed the hilt of a large, hunting knife from Laurent Du Charme's massive body and, kicking the prone figure violently in the ribs, the owner of the hand laughed in hateful triumph before strolling happily away, whistling a martial British tune.

As the sound vanished, Laurent Du Charme's blood began to put some color into the white wilderness, but Mother Nature, in rebellion against it, opened the impatient clouds, which proceeded to cover up the color and the crime.

🦋 🦋 🦋

WHEN ALEXANDER FIRST LOOKED at the snow-covered lump in the path before them, he thought it was perhaps a dead bear, because of its size. He was alternately outraged, fearful, and sad when he brushed the snow away to reveal the face of Laurent Du Charme.

His skin had turned blue from the cold and loss of blood, and icicles formed on his beard. When they removed the snow from his back, they discovered two huge, gaping wounds, one near the left shoulder, and the other on the lower right side of his back.

Incredibly, his iron heart was still beating, but very faintly. Two things had worked in the Frenchman's favor. The extreme cold had helped to congeal his blood and prevent fatal and irreversible loss. Further, the layer of fat surrounding his structure and thus his vital organs, coupled with the strata of clothing he wore as protection against the cold, had prevented the blade of the knife from plunging to an immediately lethal depth.

Still, he hovered near death. Exposure and shock were working their evil, and both Henry and Wawatam knew that he must be transported to the fort as quickly as possible.

They were still a good two miles from the stockade, the snow was now coming so thickly that their vision was severely impaired beyond a few feet. Perhaps worst of all, their three-hundred-pound friend was incapable of moving under his own power.

Wawatam seemed to know exactly what to do. Within just minutes, he had constructed a rough travois, which they rolled Du Charme onto, covering his massive frame with whatever bits of clothing they could spare.

Then, shouldering the poles which held the skeletal structure together, lashed with the sinew strings from Du Charme's mammoth snowshoes, they began to haul their precious cargo through the deep snow. They left their catch behind them.

Several times they became stuck in the drifting snow as darkness fell, and twice the makeshift transporter came apart, causing interminable delay. Henry's wounded hand throbbed violently, but Du Charme's weight required the use of both hands. The wind and snow snapped at them maliciously and Alexander began to fear that they would all die, but Wawatam plodded on like some inhuman automaton, and the Englishman refused to complain.

They finally entered the gates of Fort Michilimackinac after midnight, half-frozen and completely worn out. The Cardins and Père Du Jaunay, along with Ezekial Solomon and Lo-tah were all huddled in the little Du Charme cabin, comforting Marguerite who was frantic with worry. They came running when they heard the shouts of the sentry.

Book Three

———

Attack!

And they stood there on the meadow,
With their weapons and their war-gear,
Painted like the leaves of Autumn,
Painted like the sky of morning,
Wildly glaring at each other;
In their faces stern defiance,
In their hearts the feuds of ages,
The hereditary hatred,
The ancestral thirst of vengeance.

— LONGFELLOW

Chapter

1

Conspiracy

Laurent du Charme, much to the relief of his family and friends, did recover, although it was a terrible winter in which he had to depend on his friends to provide for his family. Henry chopped double loads of firewood, Lo-tah and Constante Cardin assisted with the chores and meals, and Ezekial Solomon ran two lines of traps, his own and Laurents', giving the lion's share of the profit to the man who had so unselfishly given him his start and aided him in his distress.

Du Charme healed very slowly in spite of the wonderful attention he received from Marguerite. The wounds had been severe, he had lost a considerable amount of blood, and the long exposure in freezing temperatures had complicated his recovery with a severe fever.

Over a month passed before he could sit up and eat. He lost over forty pounds in that thirty-day period and, at two hundred and sixty-five pounds, Henry thought he looked better, but Marguerite was concerned and flitted about him like an old hen over a new chick.

His left arm would never be the same. The blade had done extensive damage to tendons which caused his arm to hang limply at his side during the first months of his recovery. Eventually, he would use the arm, but he would never lift with it very well again, raise it above his chest, or have much sensitivity in the fingers of his left hand.

There was little doubt in Du Charme's mind, or his circle of friends, as to who had attacked him. When they asked the sentry if Private Wickwall had left the fort at anytime during that day, they were told that he didn't think so, but he had been given a break, rather decently he thought, by Private Chimton, who had offered to watch the gate while he took the opportunity to warm himself for half an hour in the barracks.

When they confronted Chimton, he stated emphatically that Wickwall had not left the stockade during his short tenure on duty. The heavy snow of that night had literally covered the would-be killer's tracks, and no hard physical evidence could be found. Though none of the British soldiers believed they had seen Wickwall at any time during that afternoon, they could not be certain that he was absent, and Chimton was sure that Wickwall had been with him, conveniently providing the alibi in exact minutes.

A protest to Colonel Etherington proved to be fruitless, since Henry was out of favor with the commander and there was, after all, no hard evidence and no substantial testimony. So although many were convinced of his guilt, Wickwall, for the moment, went unpunished.

The winter seemed to drag on interminably. As expected, it was one of the worst in the strait's history and people kept basically to themselves, with the exception of those assisting the Du Charmes.

Two events helped to break the monotony of winter's enforced inactivity. Father Du Jaunay, as proud as if he were her biological father, baptized Lo-tah into the Christian faith in the church built by Joseph Ainsse. All of the circle of friends attended, including her husband who, though a stubborn Protestant, was proud of his wife and her conversion to Christianity—even papal Christianity. Du Jaunay had tried to convince Henry that he should follow suite, but no amount of cajoling, proselytizing, patience or example, could move his recalcitrant and, in his opinion, wayward friend, to a new baptism.

In March, with not even the slightest indication that spring had to be near, Lo-tah quietly announced to Alexander in her broken English, that she was 'filled with a baby.' She was not sure how he would react, but when he danced around the room, went running to the Du Charmes, and came rushing back to smother her with kisses, and generally acted like a witless child, she assumed that his queer antics indicated approval.

He had always been a gentle lover, but he became even more so after her announcement, and she had to work at seducing him, such was his fear of hurting her or the child. It made him all the more lovable in her eyes, but she found him difficult to understand and she decided she would be happier when the child was delivered so that he could go back to treating her as he always had.

In April, water ran almost constantly as the sun set about its mammoth task of melting five feet of snow and ice. It was a Herculean effort, but the hot sun was equal to it, cleaning its hoary, Augean stables with fiery efficiency.

Temperatures rarely dropped below sixty-five degrees in April, and by the end of the month, traces of the horrible winter existed only in small patches of snow in the denser areas of the forest and the side of the stockade which was always in shadow.

The Chippewa, as usual, returned in about the middle of the month, to drain the maple trees of their sweet nectar. Though Henry saw very little of them, squaws moved in and out of the fort, bringing the sugary candy to Etherington, who apparently had more than one addiction. The commandant seemed to have changed his mind (about these Indians at least), and as time progressed, the Chippewa gained an accessibility to the fort they had never had since the French surrender. Apparently, they too recognized Etherington's susceptibility to subornation.

The warm weather also opened up the Great Lakes and brought to Fort Michilimackinac the person of Mr. William Tracy, who was Alexander Henry's liaison with Montreal. It was Mr. Tracy who took the young merchant's profit to Montreal and dealt with the banker who held his accounts.

Tracy arrived on the second of May, 1763, and spent the day with Henry and Lo-tah. He had met the latter just after her marriage in the fall and, like everyone else, he thought her delightful.

He was about fifty years old, had a white beard and hair that gave him a rather grizzled appearance. His face was weathered and wrinkled and red. He always seemed to be good-natured and loved the freedom of his life. In fact, he had never married or had any children because of that libertarian creed.

He surprised Henry when they sat down to converse by explaining that he was not as yet prepared to transport his furs back to Montreal, but was planning to make a trip to *D'étroit* first. There was a merchant at the stockade there named Dunne who wanted to develop the same business arrangements with Tracy that he and Henry now shared. The idea was perfectly acceptable to Alexander, since his books were not prepared for his banker and he could use the additional time.

Tracy wanted to talk to the fellow at *D'étroit* in person since he had only communicated with him by post, and get some measure of his reliability before concluding any agreements. He thought that asking the new British commandant there (a man named Gladwin) about Dunne might be helpful also.

So after a delicious dinner of whitefish and corn, he bid Henry and Lo-tah *adieu,* promising to return within a month when he had concluded his business in the south. He left Alexander's supplies that he had brought from Montreal with the young merchant, evidence of the trust between the two men in their two-year association.

On the same day that Tracy left, Laurent Du Charme, with Marguerite's assistance, put on his clothes (which now hung on him), and walked outside his cabin for the first time since January. The air was intoxicating to him. It seemed so fresh and clean after the confined spaces of the smoky cabin.

He and Marguerite walked out the water gate, frowning darkly as they passed the barracks where Wickwall resided, presently unseen. Like Solomon, Du Charme now carried his musket with him constantly and, in spite of his good nature, looked for the slightest excuse to 'rid the world of that vermin.'

The sunset that evening was so beautiful that they sat down, backs against the stockade wall, and lingered until well after dark. The sky blazed with orange, purple and red, reflecting off the clear water. Gulls wheeled recklessly in the cool air, devouring mayflies which swarmed in the sky above like locusts.

The two of them conversed quietly for a while and then just sat looking at the moon which appeared slowly in the sky over the lake, dividing the strait with a bridal veil beam of light which came to the shore only yards away from where they sat. Marguerite snuggled closely to her husband as he talked about the twins, now tucked safely into bed, and how they had argued about the moon's reflection on the lake. When one had stated that the light followed him, the other had vehemently argued that his brother was wrong because the light was following *him!* Laurent had explained that the light followed both of them at the same time and they had looked at their father, puzzled and confused, while Marguerite giggled. Now, she was content to simply rest happily in the knowledge that Laurent was still alive and with her.

The sentry had left the gate open, expecting the Du Charmes to return shortly. It had remained open during their hour's absence because he was determined not to double his effort.

As the contented couple rested quietly against the stockade wall, they heard the opposite gate, the land gate, creak open on its rusty hinges. Curious, they stood up and walked slowly to the end of the stockade wall and peeked around the corner. Du Charme's sharp eyes immediately spotted a solitary figure walking across the short spanse of open ground which separated the fort from the edge of the forest to the east.

The bright moonlight made it possible for him to judge that the person was a male and, from the aristocratic style of clothing, and the distinctive, almost arrogant gait, that the night walker could only be Charles, Sieur de Langlade.

Du Charme was very curious about this man who was so secretive and anti-social. He had not seen Langlade since last summer. Although Langlade's wife, Charlotte, was often at Mass with the two little girls, and always seemed to be very amiable, Langlade himself was rarely seen outside his cabin or at any social event. He appeared to go to great lengths to avoid other people and, outside of frequent visits to *L'Arbre Croche,* and occasional calls upon his father and brother-in-law, he saw no one. He was often absent from Michilimackinac on one errand or another, which seemed to suit him and gave rise to a variety of rumors concerning his whereabouts, none of which, Du Charme thought, were accurate.

As the mysterious figure strolled purposefully across the open field, unaware of his observers, Marguerite detected some movement along the edge of the forest and pointed it out to Du Charme. The cause of the motion became apparent quite rapidly as four men stepped from the cover of the woods and headed in the direction of Langlade. Although Laurent and Marguerite could only see them as dark shadows, it was apparent from the feathers and loincloths which flapped in the gentle, spring, breeze, that they were Indians.

Du Charme was convinced that one of them, due to his size, bearing, and haircut, was probably the Chippewa chief, Minavavana. Another was wearing a squared hat, which could only belong to Wenniway. It was fairly accurate to assume that the third was probably Sans-père, who was the chief's son's ever-present companion. The fourth, Du Charme did not know.

The Indians met Langlade about one hundred yards from the forest's edge, and the five of them stood talking quietly for the better part of fifteen minutes before the white man turned back toward the fort.

The Du Charmes could hear nothing of the conversation between them, the distance was too great and those being watched had no reason to believe that they were, because weeks ago Etherington had removed the sentries from the walls (apparently feeling more secure after almost a year of command and the recent gifts from his Chippewa friends) and limited his guard to one sentry at each gate.

When Marguerite and Laurent discussed the event later that evening in bed, the latter expressed curiosity at so clandestine a meeting, but his wife ridiculed his suspicions stating that Langlade had many friends among the Chippewa and that their meeting in the field was probably necessary because of the limited access of the Chippewa to the fort, and Minavavana's desire to avoid any contact with his niece, Lo-tah. Laurent did not agree, and would have had trouble sleeping because of the matter if Marguerite had not undressed and turned his thoughts to sweeter things.

❦ ❦ ❦

WAWATAM AWOKE in the middle of darkness about a week later and stared at the roof of his wigwam, observing the birchbark patterns and listening to his new wife's quiet breathing, before rising and stepping outside under the starry canopy of the spring night.

He had been very disquieted and restive since he had first tried to sleep and, once accomplished, it had been an extremely uncomfortable slumber.

His mind had been clouded with black, somber dreams which still dominated his consciousness. He had pictured the 'stick house' of the *Anglais,* devoid of human life. Grey wolves moved about the compound, devouring the mutilated bodies of the *Anglais* soldiers and civilians while turkey vultures darted in and out, attempting to get their share.

The vision made him doubly uneasy because his 'brother' was among them. He cared little for the *Anglais,* and in point of fact, disliked most of them intensely. Their deaths meant some vindication for La Fourche and his own people, and revenge for the dead Au-san-aw-go, Jean-Paul Langlade.

But he loved Alexander Henry and he liked Ezekial Solomon. Their deaths would be regretted by him and dishonor his promise to protect Henry. This could not happen. He sat by the dying village fire where several young bachelors slept, until the first light of dawn, then got in his canoe and paddled toward the fort, arriving at Henry's store in time to catch the newlyweds at breakfast.

He related his vision to Alexander who, much to the Ottawa's disappointment, did not seem very impressed or concerned. On the other hand, Lo-tah looked petrified. "When did you dream this?" she said in a voice that sounded musical, yet strained.

"In the darkness, the time of embers," the *shaman* replied.

"Time of embers?" Henry asked.

"About two of the clock, my husband," Lo-tah explained.

"Why did you want to know that?"

"Because," she said, looking gravely at Wawatam, "I had a

similar dream at about the same time."

"Was it the same?" Wawatam asked.

"Yes, brother, except for one thing." Lo-tah frowned as if trying to understand what she had experienced.

Henry looked at them both as if they were from another planet. He had his doubts about the authenticity of their dreams, though he could not explain how they could share them. *They* certainly believed what they were saying, but his intellect was in rebellion against what it viewed as unreasonable. "The one difference," Henry said, "what was it?"

"In the center of the wolves and vultures . . . and bodies," her voice was shaking with emotion, "there was a red ball."

"A what?" Henry said.

Lo-tah looked at her lover, trying to erase the image of carnage she had seen in her sleep the night before. "A wooden ball Hen-ree," she said, "like the kind they use in 'baggitiway.' "

Wawatam anticipated his question. "It is a game played with sticks and a ball," he said. "Our French brothers call it *le jeu de la crosse.*"

🐚 🐚 🐚

On the same spring day, Laurent Du Charme mentioned to Alexander, offhandedly, how he and his wife had witnessed Langlade's meeting with Minavavana. The Frenchman was very surprised when he discovered how much interest his English friend showed in such an insignificant event.

Du Charme had convinced himself that it was nothing more than a social visit, the time and place, as Marguerite suggested, made necessary by Etherington's strictures on the Chippewa within the fort itself.

But as Henry talked about the visions of Lo-tah and Wawatam, Laurent began to feel uneasy again, knowing that what he had been accepting as explanation might well be rationalization.

Henry was the first to make a concrete statement concerning what they both were thinking. "I believe they intend to assault the fort," he said after a long period of silence. "They have many reasons to hate the English and we have not really given them any cause to change their opinions. I know that Wenniway and Matchekewis, who was the fourth person you saw, I suspect, would both love to tear my throat out. Sans-père has good reason too!" he added, pointing to his nose.

Du Charme understood why Wenniway hated Henry, but he did not know why Matchekewis or Sans-père should dislike him any more than any other Englishman.

Henry proceeded to tell him then about how he had broken Sans-père's nose and how Matchekewis had tried to kill him. All three were strong influences on Minavavana who, as the 'Grand Saulteur,' wielded enormous influence both among the Anishnabeg and other Indian peoples.

"The fact that he is talking to Langlade indicates some kind of conspiracy, I'm convinced," Henry told Du Charme, "and I don't feel very secure right now. The garrison consists of only thirty-some troops, and I don't believe they would be capable of repelling an attack on the stockade, especially if the Canadians," here he paused and looked apologetically at Du Charme, "should decide to be interior allies."

Laurent shook his head sadly. "I think, *mon ami,* we had better go see the commandant."

WHEN THE TWO MEN went to talk to Etherington three days later (he made them wait for an appointment in spite of the fact that he really had no pressing business), they were not terribly surprised to find that Private Wickwall answered the door and admitted them. The villain had become the colonel's eyes and ears, and made himself very useful. That usefulness had not gone unrewarded. Du Charme had everything he could do to keep from strangling the smirking, little worm, but Alexander put a restraining hand on his shoulder and both men tried to ignore him as best they could.

When they informed the commandant of their suspicions, he laughed aloud and did not attempt to mask his contempt for their opinions. "Gentlemen," he began in his condescending manner, "it may surprise you to discover that the people whom you seem to be so frightened of, have been in and out of this post frequently in the last month and have given no indication whatever of any kind of belligerence. On the contrary, they have gone to extremes to solicit our friendship with gifts and other overtures of cordiality. I believe that you may be allowing personal prejudices to cloud your judgment. I know that you, Mr. Henry, have reason to favor the Ottawa," he glanced at Wickwall and winked, "but the Chippewa really seem much more civilized and personable. I remember *you* insinuating to *me* that I permitted bias to affect my policies. Perhaps, sir, a bit of self-examination is in order?"

Alexander's face was reddening with anger. Etherington picked up a piece of maple sugar from a crystal dish and plopped it in his mouth. He did not offer any to the others.

"Colonel," Henry said, trying to control the hostility and aversion he felt for the bewigged dandy, "isn't it possible that the Chippewa are attempting to flatter you to put you off your guard? Mightn't they be trying to lull you into a false sense of security?"

"No, Mr. Henry," Etherington retorted. "I don't see that as a possibility. In the first place, savages of any kind are not capable of sufficient thought to execute such a ruse. Secondly, *I* am not susceptible to such tawdry and boorish methods."

Henry had to force back the temptation to giggle over the frivolous and preposterous remarks. "I think, colonel, that *you* need the self-examination. Don't sell Indian intelligence short. They may not have attended Cambridge or Oxford, but they are *not* stupid. As for your last statement, we *both* know that you can be bribed, quite easily actually."

Wickwall stepped forward. Du Charme's musket was immediately leveled right at him. He quickly retreated. It was Etherington's turn to get angry as he poured himself some rum attempting, without success, to remain calm.

"Get out!" he shouted. "I might remind you Mr. Henry, and your Canadian 'friend,' that you live within the walls of this compound and therefore, civilian or not, you are both under my jurisdiction. I could have you arrested!"

Henry turned to leave knowing that he would not get anywhere with the colonel, and before Du Charme followed, he said
to Etherington in a very soft tone of voice, "All *Anglais* might be
safer in prison if you don't take your enemies seriously." When
he reached the open door through which the furious Henry had
already passed, he turned: *"Bon soir,"* he said grinning, and
closed the door behind him.

They could both hear Etherington screaming at the top of his
lungs after their departure, and less than twenty minutes later,
as they sat in front of Du Charme's cabin, smoking, they saw
Wickwall run out of the commandant's quarters and come racing
back, Lieutenant Leslie close on his heels, throwing his red officer's coat around his shoulders.

🦇 🦇 🦇

At MIDNIGHT on the night of May twenty-ninth, a bat flew over
the meadow where Constante and François had found comfort in
each other's arms years earlier and where Alexander Henry had
fallen in love with the Chippewa maiden, Lo-tah.

The creature flew over this field almost every night in its nocturnal search for small rodents and large bugs.

This night, it was startled by a bright light to which its sensitive eyes were entirely unaccustomed and it shrieked in surprise
and fear. Below was a fire, and fire meant that men were near.
Realizing instinctively its dilemma, the winged mammal rose
swiftly in the air, returning to roost in a nearby cave, upside
down, until darkness was complete and it once again felt secure
enough to venture forth.

The light came from a bonfire which was so large that, were
it not for the trees and dense foliage surrounding the meadow,
the illumination it provided could have been seen from Fort
Michilimackinac.

Four hundred Chippewa and Potawatomi Indians stood
around the fire, awaiting their turn to enter a wigwam, constructed that same afternoon for the purpose of passing the purple wampum.

Minavavana was the first to enter and leave, followed immediately by Matchekewis. The warriors were heavily painted and Charles Langlade thought, as he observed the ceremony, that they were almost beautiful in their war costumes.

Squaws kept adding wood to the huge fire as warriors drank from three kegs of rum—two of them part of the bride price that Henry had paid for Lo-tah, carefully preserved and saved through the winter. The third was a gift from Langlade.

Preparation was complete. Pon-ti-ac had already begun. 'We must move now before the wind carries the secret,' the 'Grand Saulteur' thought as he watched Wenniway and Sans-père enter the ceremonial wigwam.

Within two hours, the fire had dwindled to a large bed of ashes and the *Wabana* or firewalkers, moved forward to prepare for their ordeal, invoking the protection of *Michi-mak-i-nac,* the Great Turtle.

🦃 🦃 🦃

On THE FIRST OF JUNE, a terribly hot and humid day, Minava-vana and Matchekewis visited the quarters of Colonel George Etherington. Their presence was noticed immediately and curiosity began to spread through the compound regarding the intentions of their call. Both the Chippewa chiefs remained closeted with the commandant for over an hour before they walked down the two porch steps smiling happily and carrying a British flag, apparently a gift from the colonel.

Details of the conversations were not to be had, but the rumor circulated among the residents of the fort, both military and civilian, Canadian and English, that some sort of special event was being planned for the following day to celebrate the birthday of His Majesty, King George III on the occasion of his third year as ruler of the British Empire and twenty-fifth year of his life.

Etherington did not know that the decisions made in his meeting with the 'agreeable and witless savages' would dramatically affect many lives, including his own.

Chapter

2

———

Baggitiway

On JUNE 2, 1763, Alexander Henry slowly opened his eyes and then looked at the slumbering Lo-tah whose head lay on his chest. Her body was snuggled so close to him that he almost felt that she was a literal, physical, part of him.

Her innocent face, devoid of care or strain, was a child's face; lovely and sweet, filled with *naïveté*. Her long, dark eyelashes, so feminine, matched her silky, black hair which lay over her cheek, partially obscuring her face.

Her delicate, slim arm was curled securely around his bare chest, and one beautiful, brown leg lay parallel to his pale one, while the other was bent and rested comfortably over his groin.

He discovered that he was becoming aroused and was about to wake her, when he decided that perhaps she should rest. He reasoned that her pregnancy was undoubtedly causing her to be fatigued, since she had rarely slept after dawn before the conception, and now often slumbered well into the morning.

Reluctantly, he wriggled quietly out of her embrace, got up, and put on some clothes before stoking the ashes of the fire to heat some tea. He heard the clanging sound of hammer and anvil and knew that one of the Amiot boys, probably Antoine or Philippe, was working in the blacksmith's shop. They were good boys, Henry thought, devoted to the care and support of their widowed mother and their siblings. They were always ready to assist others, as they had done often with his neighbors.

The sun, glowing bright and yellow in the sky, promised another hot and cloudless day. The water for the tea began to bub- ble in the pot over the fire. He went to it and poured himself a cup, burning his thumb in the process and cursing his own clum- siness as a white blister began to erupt in the midst of the red, raw, skin. He sucked on it, giving himself a rather infantile ap- pearance as Lo-tah awakened and smiled dreamily at him from their bed. He removed his thumb from his mouth quickly and gave her a sheepish grin, which she pretended not to notice.

She threw back the blanket and stepped gracefully onto the rough board floor, her tawny, athletically delicate body again ex- citing her husband. He was amazed that after weeks of preg- nancy her belly was still so flat. She looked only mildly bloated, as if she had just overeaten. She raised her arms and stretched luxuriously before slipping into the shift made of doeskin and decorated with intricate, beaded designs, that Henry liked so much.

She took a jar of deer tallow from the shelf where most of the pots and pans were hung, and made him stick the injured digit into it, explaining that this method always worked for burns and had done miracles for the little girl whom Henry had rescued from the maple kettle on the day they had first seen each other. Lo-tah kissed him gently as she told him that the child, despite being terribly scarred, now led a normal existence and was, thanks to him, very much alive.

Incredibly, the salve did work, as the throbbing in his thumb subsided. Lo-tah went to work to fix breakfast while he went af- ter water from the common well, whistling cheerfully and thinking about what responsibilities lay before him that day.

He knew that Mr. Tracy would be returning from *D'étroit* at any time. In fact, he had expected his arrival days ago, and he still was not ready with his accounts. Nor had he written the let- ter to Sir William Johnson that he wanted Tracy to deliver, ex- pressing his fears regarding the enmity of the Chippewa and the clandestine behavior of Monsieur Langlade. He determined that immediately after breakfast, he would procrastinate no longer and complete the tedious paperwork so that his conscience would rest easier and he would not delay Tracy when he arrived.

At the well, he met Marguerite Du Charme. She was pleasant

and cheerful as always and she waved to Père Du Jaunay and Philippe Amiot who were conversing pleasantly outside the blacksmith's shed before greeting Henry. *"Bon jour,* Monsieur Henri," she said. She always pronounced his surname like the French first name and in spite of many attempts at correction by her husband, she just couldn't get it right.

"Bon jour, Marguerite," Alexander replied as he took her bucket and drew the water for her. "It looks like it will be hot again today, the kind of weather Laurent despises. You will have to work to keep him cheerful."

"I can do that without much effort since he is eating like a normal human being again," she replied. "I will have to prepare something delicious for *souper* and assist him in gaining back the weight he has lost. He looks so, so . . . *unhealthy* when he is thin, don't you think?"

Henry had never thought of Du Charme, who now tipped the scales at about two hundred and eighty pounds, as being thin, but he shook his head affirmatively, knowing that it would please her.

She smiled, happy with his answer, then wrinkled her broad forehead into a frown.

"What is it?" Henry asked. She scowled so seldom that it looked unnatural on her.

"I forgot. I cannot prepare a good meal early today. It will have to wait until tonight."

"Oh? Why?" Henry wondered aloud.

"He wants to watch the 'baggitiway.'"

Henry dropped the water bucket he was lifting over the lip of the well and the cool liquid splattered on his pantaloons.

"Ah Monsieur Henri," Marguerite exclaimed and rushed to his assistance, attempting to pat dry his trousers with her apron. Her excessive fussing aggravated him, but he tried to hide it since the least indication of annoyance would bring tears, and that would only frustrate him more. "It's all right, Madame," he said, helping her to her feet. He grabbed her by both of her solid arms and made her look at him. "Marguerite, what did you say about 'baggitiway'?"

"Oui," she said wiping the front of his shirt. *"Le jeu de la*

crosse."

"Where?"

"On the open field outside the stockade."

"When?"

"Today. You wish to see it too? Laurent is going to go and . . ."

"Who will the contestants be?" Henry interjected quickly before she lost track of the subject.

"The Chippewa and Potowatomi." She looked at him as if he didn't understand anything. "The commandant sent invitations to observe to all the people of Michilimackinac. You surely must have received one? You are *Anglais,* and it is to celebrate the *Anglais* king's birthday, which is today."

"May I see the invitation?" Henry asked. He was feeling increasingly uncomfortable for some vague reason that, intellectually, escaped him.

"Oui, if you wish to refill that bucket and carry it to the cabin, I can show you right now."

Henry lowered it into the well quickly, brought the water up, and followed Marguerite toward the Du Charme cabin. Once inside, he greeted Laurent who was seated by the hearth, still in his nightshirt and munching on some goat's cheese which he appeared to be relishing.

When Marguerite informed him of the reason for Henry's early morning visit, he got up, whacking Pierre on the *derrière* as he passed him and got the 'invitation' off the chest in their bedroom.

Henry was surprised that the paper was written in French in a smooth, small, almost feminine script. The solicitation was signed by Etherington, but probably written by Jamet. Du Charme interpreted for Henry. It read:

To all our Canadian friends, Greetings:

In the name of His Royal and Sovereign Majesty, King George III, ruler of England, Ireland, Scotland, and Wales. It is our privilege to invite you to an exhibition of native skill and friendly competition in a game of *le jeu de la crosse* to be held without the fort, June the second, in the year of Our Lord, Seventeen Hundred and

Sixty-Three. This attraction will begin at three of the clock and continue until completion. The event is in recognition of the birthday of His Majesty, and all Canadians now under British suzereignty are encouraged to attend.

George Etherington

George Etherington, Colonel
HMS 60th Foot Regiment
Fort Michilimackinac

When Du Charme had finished, he smiled in his charismatic way. "I want to see this very much. I am told it is as close to actual warfare as you can get and yet no one dies. Still, I have heard that often the contestants are badly maimed. Few white men ever get to see this. Will you go too?"

"I'm not sure I'm supposed to, Laurent. I did not receive an invitation and it is written in French. If it were intended for my people, wouldn't it be in English? Why is it addressed only to Canadians?"

"I talked to the soldier who delivered the paper last night and he said the entire garrison would be turned out in dress uniform to witness the game. It really is fascinating to watch I'm told. You see . . ."

"Laurent," Henry cut him off abruptly, "does this game use a kind of ball?"

"*Mais oui,*" Du Charme answered, "a wooden ball, painted red."

ON THE WAY BACK to his own cabin, Henry decided that he would not speak to Lo-tah of the matter until it was absolutely necessary. Her dreams and visions were real enough to her and this could only mean confirmation of what she had prophesied. She would be frantic with worry. As much as he loved her, he had little faith in her divinations and felt small need for alarm, but he could not shake the ominous feeling that shrouded the happiness with which he had awakened.

As he had promised himself, he got to work on his letter to Sir William Johnson as soon as he returned to his own cabin and wrote with an urgency that was disturbing. Still, he felt strangely relieved after its completion and relaxed somewhat.

At noon, Lo-tah brought him some soup made of goat's meat and wild sweet potatoes. It was delicious and he had a second helping before returning to his books. As the sun rose higher and hotter in the sky, he began to doze slightly, resting his head on his accounts books.

He woke an hour later to find that Lo-tah was gone. He got up and went out on the wooden porch, thinking that perhaps she had left to see Marguerite Du Charme or Constante Cardin. He was wrong in both cases. He saw her just as she passed through the land gate by Ezekial's cabin, laboring under a bundle of clothing which she obviously intended to wash in the stream about a quarter of a league into the forest behind the stockade. She had not disturbed his nap to inform him and he was very glad that he knew where she was, or he would have worried. But he was determined to upbraid her when she returned for carrying so heavy a bundle such a distance in her condition.

He would have chased after her to tell her then, and to assist her, and there were many times in the next few days that he wished he had, but Madame Parent had come to purchase some cloth, and he had to tend to her.

She remained for about fifteen minutes and when Alexander stepped outside again, Lo-tah was nowhere to be seen. However, while he stood there, Colonel Etherington, flanked by Lieutenants Jamet and Leslie, and followed by Private Wickwall, came out of his quarters and headed for the land gate, following in Lo-tah's footsteps. The thirty-odd soldiers of the rest of the 60th Foot Regiment poured from the barracks as did many of the Canadians from their homes. A regular parade passed down the *Rue Dauphine* on their way to the 'game,' but he did not see Goddard or Bostwick or Solomon, the only other British civilians besides himself. Outside the stockade wall, hundreds of Potowatomi and Chippewa warriors were gathering to take part in 'baggitiway.' They were whooping and hollering and pushing each other in good-natured fun while the stakes were set up at opposite ends of the field.

Inside the compound, Alexander Henry turned back to his accounts, thinking that he would perhaps finish his books and then wander out to observe the contest that had begun outside, judging from the noisy cheers.

No sooner had he sat down again than Mr. Tracy came running through the open door of his shop, breathless and looking tired and frightened. "Henry," he shouted. "What the hell are you sitting *here* for?"

Alexander was so startled by his sudden appearance and tone of voice that he did not reply at first and when he did try to answer, the old man cut him off.

"Don't you know there's a huge crowd of savages out there? Get your musket man and let's get outa here!"

Henry smiled. "No, Tracy, you don't understand. It's a game. They're playing la crosse to celebrate . . ."

"Don't be an ass, boy. You're the one who don't understand. I just come from *D'étroit.* The Ottawa, Shawnee and Chippewa are laying siege to the place. Major Gladwin was prepared for 'em, but he ain't gonna last long if he don't get some help. Hell, I barely got outa there alive. A savage name of Pon-ti-ac has the whole northwest frontier in an uproar. You really think them boys out there is playin' ball cause they love young Georgie? They're gonna kill ya. Yer sittin' ducks!"

Alexander was flabbergasted. He regretted, not for the last time, that he had not listened more acutely to his instincts. "Mr. Tracy," he pleaded, "I can't leave now. My wife, Lo-tah, isn't here. She's outside the fort somewhere."

The grizzled messenger stared hard at Alexander for a moment as if he couldn't decide whether he was crazy or stupid. "Hell, man, she's Chippewa ain't she? They won't hurt her!"

"But Du Charme and Cardin, the priest . . ."

"They's Canadians, boy. They's friends. The red men ain't gonna harm them neither. They's after Englishmen, which both you and me *is!* Now c'mon, I ain't waitin' no longer."

"Mr. Tracy," Henry stumbled over a chair as he followed him to the door. "We have to get to Ezekial Solomon."

The old man stopped at the entrance. "Who's he?"

"A good friend of mine, an Englishman."

Tracy spat tobacco juice on the porch. "Well, where is he?"

"Out there," Henry replied, pointing toward the noise.

"He's watching the game?"

Henry shook his head. "No," he said. "His cabin is there. They're probably playing right outside his door."

Tracy whistled through his remaining teeth. "Then he's a dead man. I can't wait any longer. Are you comin' with me or not?"

"I can't leave my friends or Lo-tah. I just can't."

"God be with you boy," Tracy said and started down the porch steps.

At that point, a red ball came flying over the stockade wall, rolled to the middle of the compound, and came to a stop about fifty feet from where Tracy and Alexander Henry stood gaping.

🏐 🏐 🏐

OUTSIDE THE FORT, Ezekial Solomon had looked out the front window of his little cottage as the crowd began to gather. He had no idea what was about to transpire, but experience had taught him that anything out of the ordinary usually meant trouble, so he remained inside.

Indians gathered by the hundreds along the bare field in back of the post, laughing boisterously and sporting many different colors which had been painted on their faces and torsos with great care and precision.

When he saw the English soldiers walking out of the fort, it was obvious that they were coming to observe the test of skill (or whatever it was), that the Chippewa and Potowatomi were preparing.

Ezekial watched the Indians as they drove a painted post into the ground near his isolated cabin and put another in the earth two hundred yards away at the opposite end of the field. Most of the men were carrying clubs, about four feet in length, which curved at the end into crude rackets. They were used to advance a ball toward the opponent's post, the object being to touch the post with the ball and score a point. Since about four hundred braves were involved in the game, it promised to be brutal. The Chippewa were opposing the Potawatomi and, unbeknown to Solomon, Colonel Etherington had a significant wager placed on the former.

As he looked upon this strange gathering, Solomon felt that something looked out of place, awkward, and he couldn't quite place what it was until he noticed the squaws of the combatants lounging against the stockade wall, congregating near the gate entrance. Though the weather was sultry and hot, these women had blankets thrown over their shoulders, as if they were uncomfortably cool.

Minavavana stood by the soldiers and held a red piece of cloth. Four hundred Indians gathered around the ball and watched for the 'Grand Saulteur' to drop the cloth, signaling the contest to begin. Matchekewis appeared to lead the Chippewa. Solomon also spotted Wenniway and Sans-père.

When Minavavana let the material fall from his hand, Matchekewis struck the Potowatomi nearest the ball a violent blow across the head, scooped up the wooden ball, and hurled it as far downfield as he could, two hundred screaming Chippewa following it at top speed. Contestants were struck with the rackets far more often than the ball, and players tripped, gouged and battered each other in an attempt to move the ball forward while the other side reciprocated by trying to fling it back. The British and Canadian audience cheered for their favorites. The majority of the British, following their commander's lead, seemed to be pulling for the Chippewa.

Solomon noticed that Minavavana did not participate, but seemed to be above all the hoopla and had moved only to retrieve the red cloth which he held in his fist. His face was very serious and he appeared to be rather nervous, glancing back and forth at the squaws who seemed not to notice the contest, but stood stoically by the gate as if they had been placed there for some purpose.

Gradually, Solomon began to understand the true purpose of the 'games' just as Minavavana let the red cloth fall a second time. At that exact instant, the warrior in possession of the red ball, using his racket, hurled it over the stockade wall and all four hundred warriors, in unison, raised a thunderous shout that was indistinguishable, but definitely belligerent, as they poured through the open gates of the fort in hot pursuit.

Etherington was smiling, even laughing, at the savages until the squaws discarded the unnecessary blankets to reveal hatchets, knives, tomahawks and war clubs hanging from strings tied about them, strategically placed for purposes of concealment.

They handed them to the racing warriors and Solomon saw, with horror, that they were attacking the British soldiers some of whom simply stood, dumbfounded, while others tried to flee for protection into the stockade.

It slowly dawned on Ezekial that he himself was in extreme peril. He was in a totally isolated position, surrounded by hundreds of belligerent Indians, and no avenue of escape.

He moved away from the window and barred the door just as some Chippewa warriors slammed against it and began battering it down. He reached for his musket as glass from the window sprayed inward and several savage faces appeared.

The last thought he had before the leather hinges of his door gave way was: 'Oh Lord, is there no place in this world where a man might be left alone?'

Chapter

3

___

The Massacre

TRACY DID NOT WAIT for the red ball to roll to a stop, but was running toward the water gate and his canoe before the first Indian plunged through the opposite gate. Henry went inside his shop, slammed the door, and barred it.

He moved quickly to the window and was about to close the curtain, but the scene of horror outside held him with rapt attention. He froze.

Lieutenant Jamet had run inside the fort, trying to get to weapons which had been left, stacked carelessly in the barracks. He had been knocked to the ground by one of the Chippewa with a blow to the head from a la crosse racket and he was on his hands and knees only a few feet from Henry's porch, trying to shake off the effects of the injury and clear his mind.

As Alexander watched, the Indian who had struck him down, held Jamet firmly between his knees, as if he were riding him, and deftly began to make incisions in the poor man's head as he screamed in terrible agony. The savage gripped his hair then and, pulling viciously backward, ripped the scalp from his skull, revealing a mass of bloody tissue underneath. The victor shook his trophy in the air while Jamet writhed like a worm on a hook, dangling between the legs of his conqueror. Mercifully, the Chippewa ended the unfortunate officer's hellish suffering with a blow from his tomahawk which split his head in two.

Jamet's body slumped to the ground, the grey contents of his skull, once the organ for all his thoughts, oozing onto the

365

ground.

Henry's temporary paralysis ended when the murderer looked in his direction. He ran to get his 'Brown Bess' from over the fireplace when he realized it would avail him nothing against four hundred savages, so he looked around to find a place to hide.

He had noticed, through the window, several Canadian occupants of the fort, including the Cardins and Parents, standing outside their homes watching the massacre, some horrified, others apathetic, but none were harmed by the invading horde.

This observation gave Henry the hope that he might be able to survive by concealing himself in one of their homes. He slipped out the back door of his shop and headed for the nearest Canadian house, which was that of his immediate neighbor, Charles Langlade. The Cardins and Du Charmes were too far away and too exposed to the view of the enemy. Langlade, as doubtful as it seemed, was his only hope.

He hopped the little fence surrounding the Langlade home and ran through their garden to the door in the back that he had seen the dainty Langlade girls move in and out of many times.

It was open, and without knocking, he stepped quickly inside. He became cognizant of his own fierce breathing and made a tremendous effort to calm himself. He felt more secure for the moment. He was in the kitchen and he walked rapidly through it and down a narrow hallway to the parlor where he found the entire Langlade family. Charles was observing the massacre calmly from a window, while Charlotte and the children huddled in a corner, wincing from the terrible screams they could hear outside.

"Monsieur Langlade," Henry addressed the swarthy half-breed, who scowled darkly when he saw the merchant in his home. "I am desperate and need your assistance."

Langlade looked at him with utter disdain, almost distaste. *"Que voudriez-vous que j'en ferais?"*[1]

Henry was sick to his stomach from witnessing the fate of Lieutenant Jamet and his own wild fear. "Please, Monsieur. If

---

[1]What do you expect me to do?

you could hide me . . ."

Langlade stared at him with pitiless eyes. "This is a matter between your people, the Anishnabeg, and their allies. France is no longer involved. I can do nothing."

Slowly, Henry's fear began to turn to anger. "I know, Monsieur Langlade, of your influence with these people. You could do something but you won't. You are determined to see all Englishmen dead. I know that you have probably used that influence to encourage this barbarism, but it will avail you and them nothing. More British troops will replace them and these Indians—as well as their accomplices—will be punished for their crimes!"

Langlade looked from the desperate man to the window again. The shrieking cries of the victims and triumphant shouts of their conquerors, created an appalling, hideous, din.

"I did not invite you here, Monsieur Henry. I did not welcome you when you came to Michilimackinac, nor did I ever pretend to be your friend. As far as I am concerned, you do not exist. Now leave my house, you are frightening my children."

Henry continued to stand where he was and looked at Charlotte Langlade whose expression was one of pity and sympathy. "You know," he said, looking back at Langlade who continued to stare out the window, "that you send me to my death."

"Your government has condemned you," Langlade answered calmly in his deep, resonant baritone. "That, and your own folly."

Unarmed and without shelter, Alexander decided to resign himself to whatever might await him outside. But before he turned to leave, he could not resist a parting barb. "God forgive you, Monsieur Langlade, and may your children always remember the image of their father this day."

He had hoped to raise some angry retort from Langlade, but the dark eyes continued to stare out the window, ignoring him as if he were already dead.

Henry retreated back down the hallway toward the kitchen, intending to try to sneak out the same door he had come through, unobserved, and by some miracle reach one of the open gates or, failing that, one of the other Canadian homes. He could see through the tiny kitchen window that his own home was being ransacked by the Chippewa.

As he approached the kitchen door, a hand grabbed his arm and he spun around instinctively to defend himself. But the countenance that confronted him was a pretty female face, distinctly Indian, and for a moment, he could not place who it was. For one exuberant instant, he thought her to be Lo-tah, but as his head cleared, he could see that she was not, though she was almost as attractive.

He let out a startled "What?" when she touched him and her eyes grew wide with fear. "Please, be quiet," she said in Algonkin, "the master will hear you and suspect."

At that point, keying on the word 'master,' Alexander recognized her as the Pani woman, Langlade's Indian slave.

"Suspect what?" Henry whispered.

The Pani woman produced a key from her pocket and signaled him to follow her. Having little choice and no other viable alternative, he did as he was bid. She brought him to a door in the kitchen which, when opened, led to a small garret. She instructed him to mount the stairs and conceal himself there. Before doing so, he paused. "Why are you doing this?" he said. "Why do you risk your master's wrath?"

She hesitated, uncertain as to whether she should say anything, or even proceed any further. "I hate Langlade," she said finally and resolutely, "but I hate them more." She motioned her head in the direction of the noisy *mêlée* outside. "They took me from my people. Perhaps I can rob them of one victim. Now go!" She pushed him roughly forward and closed the door.

He was instantly enveloped in darkness as he heard the key catch in the lock behind him. He felt his way up the stairs slowly, trying not to stumble and make any noises that could be heard by the family below. When he reached the top, more light was available from cracks between the logs. He saw that he was in a small attic. Several barrels were stacked in one corner and an old canoe, obviously no longer seaworthy, lay upside down on the floor nearest the far wall.

Henry, fearing detection, crawled slowly across the floor until he reached the outside wall. There, an aperture between the logs afforded him a view of the grisly scene below.

He recognized the boots and clothing of old Mr. Tracy on a body whose head was now being used as a ball. Several young bucks were joyfully belting the dreadful sphere back and forth between them with their rackets, shouting victoriously as their bloody blows extinguished the facial features of the thing that had smiled at Henry less than ten minutes ago.

A few feet away, three Chippewa had wrestled a British redcoat to the ground and, having dispatched him with a tomahawk, cut open his torso from throat to groin, scooped up his blood in their cupped hands, and quaffed it amid shouts of triumph.

His stomach churning in nauseated agony, Henry espied Père Du Jaunay, discernible in his black robe, moving from one group of savages to the next, shouting at them to desist, and even striking one of them as the Potawatomi slit the throat of a hapless soldier.

Minavavana, who stood in the center of the carnage, ordered several braves to remove the priest to his rectory which they did, while he resisted their unkind attentions.

Since the water gate was behind him, he had no idea that Laurent Du Charme was, at the moment, surrounded by five warriors who refused to let him move. Matchekewis had promised that Du Charme's wife and sons would die if he made any attempt to assist his *Anglais* friends and so he, although in less peril, watched as helplessly as Henry.

In a few moments, it was all over. Bodies were dragged into the compound and dumped in a careless pile near the center of the parade ground. Alexander noticed that several prisoners were being brought forward who, for one reason or another, were still alive. It was a great sense of relief to notice that one of them was Ezekial Solomon, but ironic that two of these fortunates were Sidney Wickwall and Colonel Etherington, whose lack of foresight and swollen ego were as much to blame for the slaughter as the Chippewa and Potowatomi butchers.

The general massacre being concluded, Minavavana now ordered a house-to-house search for those who were missing. Several Englishmen had had the same idea as Henry, that is to seek safety in a Canadian home. In point of fact, Sans-père had

caught one British soldier just as he entered the door of the
Cardin cabin and, while the mother who was unknown to him
watched in horror, he slit the man's throat and eviscerated him.
He left the corpse on their doorstep, its intestines unfolding in
wet loops. Grinning through a wicked face smeared with blood,
he returned to warn his chief that others might be attempting the
same.

Thus it was that several Chippewa, including Sans-père and
Wenniway, entered the Langlade home, searching specifically for
Alexander Henry.

The object of their search could see them, since the floor of
the garret was also the ceiling of the room below and he observed the savages through a crack in the boards. Wenniway and
Sans-père were both completely covered in the blood of their
enemies, and their actions were wild and boisterous, yet they
showed respect for Langlade. Charlotte Langlade took the children to another room, not wanting them to observe the bloody
intruders.

The two warriors were soon joined by Minavavana and
Matchekewis. Langlade welcomed them like old friends, in the
name of the French king. The 'Grand Saulteur' asked the
Frenchman if he had seen any trace of the *Anglais* merchant, and
Langlade replied frankly that Henry had come to him seeking
shelter, but that he had sent him away.

When Wenniway asked if he was sure that Henry had left the
house, Langlade replied that he did not watch him go out and
they were free to search the house to satisfy themselves on the
subject. Henry began praying that they would not become curious about the door in the kitchen, but Minavavana asked about it
when he saw it and Langlade informed him that it led to the garret. Since it was locked, Minavavana wanted to know why and
his Canadian friend, having no reasonable explanation, offered
to open it and investigate.

Some delay was occasioned in looking for the key, which
gave Henry's tortured mind sufficient time to think. He crawled
across the floor, trying not to make the slightest noise. At first he
thought it might be wisest to conceal himself beneath the over-
turned canoe, but upon further reflection, he feared it might take

too long and create too much noise, so he quickly scrambled behind the barrels in the corner as the door opened and his pur-
suers began to ascend the stairs

The corner in which he was, was completely black for want
of light, and the barrels blocked his view, but he believed himself
to be completely hidden from view. The only way he could be
discovered, he reasoned, was if the Indians should move the barrels or he should make some sound which would alert them to
his presence. In order to avoid the latter, he attempted to hold
his breath so as not to create the slightest whisper.

The Chippewa had reached the landing of the garret he could
tell, by the vibrations their feet created on the floorboards. He
prayed silently to himself and tried not to move at all.

When he opened his eyes, he could see through a gap between two barrels, a dark leg and bare foot, standing close
enough that if he moved a barrel and reached out, he could
touch it. The foot was missing a toe and could only belong to
Matchekewis.

The Indians righted the canoe to look beneath it (at which
point Henry thanked God he had decided not to use *it* for his
refuge) and, apparently satisfied by their incomplete search,
thanked Langlade for the inconvenience and descended the
stairs, this time leaving the door unlocked.

When the door closed, Henry exhaled, but did not move from
his hiding place, cramped as it was, for an hour. Within half that
time, the Indian voices outside went away and after another
thirty minutes, he worked up the courage to move to the outside
wall again and look at the compound below which was becoming
more difficult to see in the enveloping darkness.

The heat and humidity in the attic were almost unbearable
and became worse as Madame Langlade and the Pani woman
began to cook the evening meal, heating up the chimney which
passed through the garret just a few feet from where he sat. As
he looked outside, sweat dripped in his eyes and stung them,
blurring his vision.

The hole that he had looked through before, he noticed,
could be widened by removing some clay which would afford
him a better view. So he stuck his thumb in the hole and began

to work it out. The digit stung when he put pressure on it, reminding him of the burn he had sustained only that morning (which now seemed hundreds of years ago), the one his wife had treated so tenderly. "Lo-tah," he said aloud, the sound of his own voice frightening him. He began to weep, wondering where she was now.

He attempted to toughen up, and with clearer vision, washed clean of salty sweat, he worked the clay chink loose and looked outside.

The compound was littered with the dead. Mutilated corpses, most of them soldiers, were strewn everywhere. A big grey dog, one he had seen before, was busy tearing at one of them, while turkey vultures were descending from the sky in large numbers to join in the feast. The red ball lay where it had rolled to a stop, completing the portrait of Lo-tah's vision. Henry turned away in revulsion, his stomach churning. He wept again, bitterly and hard.

Below him, the Langlade family ate in silence. They had no idea that they harbored a fugitive in their attic. The smell of food drifted up through the ceiling into Henry's sanctuary/prison. The pangs of hunger chewed at him with pitiless constancy, but helped to take his mind off his mourning.

He began to realize that he had a great deal to be thankful for. He was not among the dead, now being devoured outside. He was alive enough to be hungry and frightened, which counted for something. While he still breathed, there was hope.

He forced himself to look outside again in response to shouting voices. As he surveyed the scene, it became apparent that the sounds were coming from Laurent Du Charme who stood in the midst of the slaughter swinging at the vultures with a tree branch and kicking at the dogs (there were now three of them), to drive them away from the bodies which were beginning to smell in the heat.

François Cardin, Père Du Jaunay, and the three eldest Amiot boys, were hauling the corpses to the cemetery near the church on makeshift stretchers. Ignace Bourassa was digging shallow graves there.

Henry wanted very much to call out to Du Charme, but he

knew that Langlade would hold him there at musket point until the Chippewa would arrive to take him away. The mere sight of his giant friend warmed him and gave him hope.

Slowly, a plan of escape began to form in his mind. He assumed that within two or three hours, the family whose house was his temporary shelter would be retiring to their beds. When he was certain that they were asleep, he would go down the stairs, slip quietly out the back door, and run the distance of a few yards to the Du Charmes who could, he was certain, find a way to smuggle him out of Michilimackinac *after* he had found Lo-tah and armed himself properly. Perhaps she was with them even now? He had no way of knowing, but the thought of her being only a few hundred feet away in safety gave him cause for hope.

He settled back to rest for a few moments and waited until he could no longer hear anyone stirring below. He was utterly exhausted. The emotional and physical strain of the day had worn him out. He laid his head back and rested it on the hard floorboards, promising himself that he would only close his eyes for a few minutes.

He awoke to the sound of rolling thunder, flashes of lightning, and driving rain. The lightning was brilliant and the brightness of it zig-zagged through the room in streaks.

Henry sat up and looked eagerly through the gap in the wall at the parade ground below. The bodies were gone and the stockade appeared strangely normal. He looked behind him in reaction to a dripping sound and saw that the roof was leaking, a pool of water having formed on the floor about fifteen feet away.

He was about to get up and descend the stairs, when the door below opened up and candlelight illuminated the walls of the passageway leading to the garret. Henry stumbled backwards looking for a place to hide, but by the time he turned, Charlotte Langlade had seen him.

Knowing he had been discovered, he turned and faced her as she stepped on the landing. Her eyes were wide and frightened, but she stood her ground. She held a wooden bucket in her hand. Henry conjectured that she had been awakened by the pool of water seeping through the floorboards into her bedroom below. She had come to catch the leak in the roof and wipe up the excess water which was disturbing her sleep.

They stood staring at each other for a few moments, neither of them quite knowing what to say. Finally, Henry spoke, as much to break the tension as anything else. "Don't be afraid," he whispered. "I'm not here to harm anyone. I'm only trying to stay alive."

"Charlotte!" her husband shouted from below. "Have you put the bucket in place? The bed is getting wet."

"*Un moment,*" she cried and moved to the puddle, wiping it up with a rag and placing the bucket beneath the drip.

With a quick glance at her pathetic intruder, she hurried down the stairs and closed the door behind her.

As Henry watched the light fade down the narrow stairway, he decided that he had to leave at once or lose the opportunity. He didn't know whether Charlotte Langlade would tell her husband of his presence in their house or not, but he wasn't going to wager his life on one sympathetic look. He moved slowly across the floor, trying to be as noiseless as possible, though the boards creaked loudly.

He felt his way around in the dark, being guided by occasional flashes of lightning, until he reached the top stair. As he began to descend, he heard footsteps approaching the door again and he was certain that Madame Langlade had betrayed him. But the door never opened. Instead, he heard the key fitted to the lock and heard the latch snap. Though he remained undiscovered, he was again a virtual prisoner, and his heart sank.

He did not sleep the rest of the night, but remained curled up against the slanted roof interior, resting behind the barrels in the event of further intrusion. The dripping water afforded him some refreshment, but his stomach ached with hunger. He had not eaten since Lo-tah had prepared the noon meal over twelve hours ago.

He wondered where she was. Did she come back with the bundle of laundry in the middle of the attack and was she now hiding in the forest somewhere wondering about his fate? Was she taken by the Chippewa? Tracy . . . poor Tracy, had said they wouldn't harm her, but he didn't know the terrible hatred of

Wenniway or the insanity of Matchekewis.

He tortured himself with these thoughts until dawn. The storm had abated and the sun rose on this day as it had the day before, sultry, hazy, and hot. 'Lo-tah, where are you?' His soul screamed it out, but the answer was silence.

His thoughts were interrupted by voices below as the family rose from their beds. The smell of tea and biscuits drifted upward, adding to his misery and increasing his depression. The garret was already stifling and he was perspiring profusely. He returned to the bucket many times until it dried up.

He remembered his uncle, the Bible commentator, Matthew Henry, reading him a poem by a Puritan named John Milton. One line read: "They also serve who only stand and wait." That seemed to be his only remaining option. There was really little else he could do. His only relief from the monotony of sitting quietly was to look through the gap in the logs. He watched Marguerite Du Charme fetch water from the well and recalled how he had stood there with her about twenty-four hours earlier, a free man, looking forward to returning to his wife and a warm breakfast.

If he had said something about the game of 'baggitiway' to Lo-tah when he saw the Du Charme's invitation, perhaps all of this would never have happened. Or if he had not fallen asleep at his desk, or Madame Parent had not come into his store, perhaps he would be a free man, with Lo-tah, hiding in the woods behind the fort somewhere. If, if, if—it didn't help to speculate. It only made his heart ache more fiercely.

As he observed Marguerite Du Charme returning to her cabin, he wanted to cry out to her for help. Surely Laurent would come running to his aid. But if Langlade disarmed him, the big Frenchman would be turned over to the Chippewa and treated as an Englishman. Henry's conscience would not bear the responsibility for the death of his friend, and so he continued to sit, motionless and in silence, hoping for a miracle.

Half the morning had passed when a sharp knocking at the main door below indicated visitors. At first, clinging to his natural optimism, he hoped that it might be Wawatam who had come to visit Langlade, his cousin. The voices (there were two of them), sounded vaguely familiar, muffled as they were, speaking in Algonkin.

Alexander had not realized until that moment that no Ottawa had been present at the massacre, and he knew that the Chippewa and Potowatomi were brothers, in the 'Council of the Three Fires' with the Ottawa. What had happened to them? Why were they not involved?

His hope dissolved rather rapidly, however, when he recognized that the voice's familiarity was due to his having dealt with these men before. A look through the floorboards confirmed his suspicions. Wenniway and Sans-père stood in Langlade's parlor.

Their conversation revolved around his absence. They explained to Langlade that the *Anglais* merchant was nowhere to be found among the dead or the prisoners and they were convinced from talking to Madame Parent, that he had been in the fort when the attack commenced and must still be.

They were certain, they said, that the fugitive was hiding in a Canadian home and they had already searched Du Charme's cabin, the Cardin house, and Père Du Jaunay's rectory, these people being suspect because of their well-known relationships with Henry. But the Chippewa had been unable to find a trace of him in any of those places. Sans-père said that it would go hard with any Canadian who hid an *Anglais*. Minavavana had instructed them that such a traitor would be treated as an *Anglais*, along with his wife and children. Langlade voiced his approval of this plan and was about to wish his Anishnabeg brothers *adieu*, when Charlotte, clinging fiercely to her daughters, confessed that she had seen Henry in their house during the night and was now, at that moment, concealed in their garret. She was telling them now, she said, as they were not here at the time she had discovered him, and she did not want her children to be harmed.

Charles Langlade said nothing, but the look he gave to his wife was so fierce that it might have withered a less formidable woman. It spoke of betrayal and deceit. She had not said anything to him about Henry's presence in their house, that was obvious, and might have kept her secret completely were it not for fear of her children's safety.

Above them, Alexander Henry's heart almost leapt from his

chest and panic began to overtake him. He looked about wildly for some sort of refuge, but there was none. They knew he was there and would tear the attic apart until they found him.

Knowing there was nothing else to be done, he stood up in the room, having to stoop somewhat to prevent his head from colliding with the roof, and turned toward the staircase to confront his fate, as the key turned in the lock below, the door opened, and the Chippewa ascended the stairs.

Chapter

4

Discovery

As the ridiculous hat and ugly, bitter countenance of Wenniway appeared before him on the landing, Alexander Henry made a pact with himself that he would die with decorum and honor. He was determined not to beg for his life or to show any trace of fear. He tried to force his mind to command his knees and hands to quit shaking. It took all his courage just to control his bladder and he ridiculed himself for his fear. He faced Wenniway and Sans-père, however, with admirable composure, although he was filled with an inner trepidation that bordered on panic.

"So, *Anglais,*" Wenniway sneered, "we find you hiding in this 'box'."

"I'm not hiding, Wenniway. I'm standing here where you can see me."

"It is time to pay your debt, *Anglais.* Are you ready? The debt is large." Sans-père grinned wickedly. His nose had healed crooked. 'There is something familiar in that face,' Henry thought unconsciously.

"Unlike yourself," he rejoined, turning again to Wenniway, "I pay my debts." Wenniway's smirk disappeared. He drew his knife and stepped forward. "I will end your life now, *Anglais.*"

Henry raised his hands to ward off the attack, but it never came as another Chippewa, one that Henry did not recognize, appeared on the landing of the garret and shouted at Wenniway. "Stop," he cried. "Your father, Minavavana, has said that no harm is to come to the *Anglais* until he orders it. He would be very displeased if you disobeyed him."

Wenniway stopped where he was and replaced the knife in its sheath. He was trembling with rage and frustration, and motioned the other to come forward.

Sans-père and the other Chippewa both grabbed Henry's arms and escorted him roughly down the narrow stairway into the kitchen where the bright sunlight stung his eyes, which had become so accustomed to the darkness. He held up one hand to shield them and he saw Charlotte Langlade, tears streaming down her face, looking guiltily at the floor, unable to face the man she had betrayed. Her husband stood coldly by the door leading outside, holding it open for Henry and his captors. The Pani woman was nowhere in sight.

Once outside, Henry's arms were bound tightly and he was escorted through the gate in the little fence surrounding the Langlade garden and onto the porch of his own shop where he had stood with Tracy a day earlier. He was forced inside and pushed roughly to the floor where he discovered, once he got his bearings, that the Chippewa were using his cabin for the safekeeping of other prisoners. Propped against the counter he had constructed for his business were: Colonel Etherington, Lieutenant Leslie, Sidney Wickwall, Ezekial Solomon, Henry Bostwick, Stanley Goddard, and seven soldiers of varying rank. They were bound hand and foot and looked miserable. However, Ezekial's face lit up when he saw Alexander brought in and it was obvious that Henry found some encouragement in discovering his good friend to still be among the living.

When Henry attempted to speak, Sans-père kicked him in the ribs, knocking the wind out of him while Wenniway bound his feet. Without further comment, they left the room, leaving the third savage to guard their prisoners.

As Henry tried to catch his breath, Ezekial spoke to him, trying to be as cheerful as possible. "Look on the bright side my friend," he said, "this is the most customers you've had in quite some time."

"Unfortunately I'm unable to serve them," he replied, forcing a smile and looking around the room which had been torn apart, his merchandise stolen or scattered. "It seems my inventory is somewhat depleted."

Goddard's voice, high and nearly hysterical, interrupted their attempts at levity. "Are you both mad? How can you jest at a time like this? We're going to die and you two are laughing like a pair of idiots. I hope you can manage to giggle when they slit our throats."

Solomon shrugged his shoulders. "Mr. Goddard doesn't seem to find any humor in our situation, Alexander. He's going to fret himself to death instead of waiting for the Chippewa to do it for him. Hasn't quit whining since they hauled us in here."

"I'm not whining," Goddard whined, and fell silent.

Henry, having regained his wind, managed to push himself upward so that his back rested against the table which stood in the center of the room. He was sitting directly across from the rest, who were all leaning against the counter. Etherington, minus his wig and shorn of his bright, military coat with all its adornments, looked the very picture of dejection and defeat. His head hung down on his chest and his thinning, drab-brown hair was draped over his face creating an even more pathetic portrait.

Wickwall stared straight ahead at the wall beyond Henry, but it was apparent that he, too, had lost his fighting spirit, if he ever had any. The jagged scar on his hand itched miserably but, with his arms bound tightly, there was nothing he could do to relieve it. He had no other thought but to scratch it, and ignored Henry.

Bostwick picked up the dialogue. "What are we to do?" He looked at Henry as if he had some magical solution to their dilemma, his face the epitome of woe. "They mean to murder us, I know it. We must do something!"

Solomon looked at the aristocratic face and sneered. His contempt for the elitist Bostwick was very apparent. "We will be happy to entertain any suggestions you might have, Mr. Bostwick, but personally I don't see much promise in our situation. Maybe *you* can find us a way out of this, but I doubt it. I believe, however, that panic will get us nowhere. So try to be calm and wait to see what develops."

"I haven't eaten or drunk anything since yesterday," Bostwick said, ignoring Solomon's sarcasm. "Do they intend to starve us to death?"

"I really don't think," Henry contributed, "that these people, who have butchered most of the garrison, are terribly concerned about our nutrition. When there is nothing to do, there is nothing to do. We can work on our own endurance and courage. We will need them both a great deal, I suspect. I really see no other recourse."

Bostwick was about to open his mouth again, but seeing the displeasure from his fellow captives, and realizing that he was sounding too much like Goddard, decided against it.

Henry, unhappy with the complete silence, and anxious as to the fate of his wife, asked Solomon if he had seen Lo-tah. The Jew related that he had observed her carrying a bundle past his cabin some time before the game of 'baggitiway' had begun, but had not seen her since. Henry hung his head in dejection, but quickly raised it again, determined not to let the circumstances defeat him.

As he and Solomon talked, fighting off despair, he realized that *all* of the British civilians were still alive and captive, with the exception of Tracy who had never been a permanent member of the garrison and had held no personal significance for their captors. Henry gleaned some encouragement from this observation until Lieutenant Leslie commented that perhaps the savages were purposely preserving them for some ritualistic death, which immediately dampened everyone's spirits.

Nevertheless, argued Henry, they were still all alive and essentially unharmed except for a few bruises and weakened by hunger and thirst. They should, he said, find some cause for optimism in this and hope for the best.

Fatigue eventually overtook them and conversation ceased. Most of them dozed through the humid, June afternoon. Sleeping, they discovered, as old Will Shakespeare had said; 'knitted up the raveled sleeve of care' and helped them to cast aside their worries, summoning sweet Morpheus to battle the gods of Hunger and Thirst.

By late afternoon, they were very weak and groggy, and Sleep was surrendering the field to its demanding enemies. They were roused from their torpor not only by their physical needs, but also by some sort of commotion on the porch of Henry's shop. Suddenly, the Indian sentry who had been dozing through much of the afternoon with his prisoners, came flying through the open doorway, tripped over the outstretched legs of his captives, and sprawled out on the rough floor, unconscious.

In the entryway, Henry recognized the huge bulk of Laurent Du Charme and his heart leapt for joy at the sight of him. But his happiness was short-lived. Du Charme was about to step inside, his mouth open to greet his friend, when several Potowatomi braves pulled him backward out the door and Henry saw them tumbling and wrestling in the dust. The merchant heard his ally and mentor bellow *"Par la sambleu!"*[1] as additional warriors arrived to overpower the would-be rescuer and escort him to his cabin.

Henry heard him shout in English: "Take heart, Alexander, I *will* come back!" But the prisoner doubted the truth of that statement, though he believed the sincerity with which it was spoken.

The aborted rescue attempt plunged the captives into an even deeper gloom since one option they had all silently considered, their rescue by Canadian friends, had been thwarted. Now, their primary hope for assistance shattered, they fell into silence to await their fate.

🐚 🐚 🐚

CONSTANTE CHEVALIER AINSSE CARDIN finished pouring the wine into her *matelote* (fish stew), and told François that she was going to see the priest for a few minutes. He objected at first, reasoning that the Indians outside were very excitable since Du Charme's attack on one of their sentries and were now deeply suspicious of any Canadians leaving the shelter of their homes. He also pointed out that Père Du Jaunay was one of those they were watching most closely, and anyone calling upon him would be very suspect. He reminded her that though they were Canadians, Minavavana and Wenniway would remember her defense of

---

[1]Loosely translated: "Confound it!"

Lo-tah and Henry months ago, and he would never forgive himself if anything happened to her.

Nevertheless, she was adamant. So he pulled his boots on and would only agree to her leaving the cabin if he accompanied her. She protested, stating that someone had to watch their *souper* and that he must not let it burn.

Without waiting for an answer, she stepped out and closed the door behind her. She had not gone five paces when the door opened and François came trotting after her. She scolded him, but he kissed her and said he liked his food cooked thoroughly.

They walked in silence, as they traversed the open area from their cabin to the rectory attached to Ste. Anne's. Memories flooded her. The cottage she had once shared with Joseph Ainsse stood as a firm reminder of her past and she could almost hear him, coughing violently in his little carpenter's shop next to the house. As they passed the cemetery next to the church, she saw the graves marked 'Joseph Ainsse' and 'Joseph Louis Ainsse' and her throat constricted, choking back a sob. How many times, she wondered, had she looked out of the window of that little cabin across the way at the steeple of the church as Joseph labored upon it? How many times since his death had she sat in the pews of this place that had been his handiwork, and thought of her baby, buried beneath its floor? She wondered, if their sweet little girl had lived, if it would have had her father's large ears and nose? How frivolous she thought. How silly, vain, and frivolous.

Her mind pictured René Bourassa, the gentle master. Almost her father, he had been, ironically, interred next to the man he had so wanted her to marry and whose wishes she had obeyed. She thought of Domitilde Langlade and wondered what she would think now, to find her son a party to this situation and her beloved Augustin a hopeless alcoholic? Jean-Baptiste Amiot was here in the little graveyard too, while his old squaw, Marie, struggled to raise all the children he had left her. How time does change people, she thought, and how love does leave such deep and lasting scars. She slipped her hand through her husband's and squeezed it tightly as they approached the rectory and knocked on the door.

The priest's benevolent face appeared at the door almost immediately. He looked very tired and care-worn. His grey hair was thinning rapidly and he had lost so much weight from continued fasting and simple neglect, that he looked almost emaciated. His bright, intelligent, eyes looked sad and the twinkle that always resided there had dimmed.

"My dear Constante," he greeted her, his voice as soothing as ever, "how glad I am to see you. *Entrez, s'il vous plaît.*" He motioned both of them to come in and slapped François paternally on the back.

Every time she entered this barren, little place, Constante felt like she had come home. Here, she had been pulled out of Hell. Here was safety and the portal to Heaven.

"Father," she said as he offered them rude chairs and seated himself upon an old chest. "What are we to do? Monsieur Henry and those other poor men are held captive in his shop. They are alive, but for how long?" Her eyes began to glisten with moisture and François offered her his handkerchief. "Oh, the absolute horror of these two days!" she cried. "What can we do? I can't just stand by and watch them perish. I have prayed hard to God, Father, I really have, but He seems not to hear me. I have been watching Monsieur Henry's shop ever since they took the first prisoners in there. I don't think they have been given any food or water in all that time. I believe they mean to kill them. I know you tried to stop them Father, I saw you. But we can't do it by ourselves. This afternoon, Monsieur Du Charme risked his life to assist them and he is now a prisoner in his own home. And poor Lo-tah! What has become of her? What must she be thinking! Oh Father, where is God? What can we do?"

She placed her hands over her face and wept bitterly. François put his arm around her in a gentle attempt at comfort. "She can't sleep, Father. She won't eat. She has seen too much of the horror and it won't leave her mind. I'm afraid her sanity depends upon the rescue of the survivors. She paces back and forth all day and finds no comfort. She has worn herself out with prayer. What do you advise?"

The priest looked at them both, their faces so childish and hopeful. 'What a burden God places on his priesthood,' he thought. He realized, as he looked at them, searching his weary mind and soul for an answer, that he loved them and they loved him. That's why they are here, he thought. A delicious sensation enveloped him and he knew the answer. He wasn't sure what it meant, but he knew the answer. "Love," he said simply.

"What?" François asked. He looked as if someone had just given him a very difficult riddle to solve.

"The answer is love," the priest repeated. "The answer is always love. I have tried to extinguish force with force. God does not want us to act with the devices of humanity. We cannot destroy pagan practices by practicing as pagans. Our weapons have always been—and must always be—love and faith. It is a test, you see. It is forever a test. God corrects, instructs, and tests. We have not done well. We must use *His* weapons, not ours, and believe that what happens will be as *He* ordains it. Saint Paul wrote to the Romans: 'All things work together for good to those who love God.' The key words are 'all' and 'love.' We must trust to *His* methods."

Constante listened to the Jesuit with such intensity that her face was puckered in a severe frown. But as he continued to speak, the roughness of her face began to smooth as if the sound of his voice were some miraculous antidote to the poisonous bile that had been building in her over the last forty-eight hours.

François was baffled by the priest's answer, or perhaps it would be better to say he did not see a solution. Talking about love and faith as virtue was one thing, using them as weapons was quite another, if indeed, that's what the cleric was saying. François wasn't sure.

However, Constante seemed to accept what he said as a viable course of action. She was not only no longer afraid or depressed, but smiled broadly and appeared to be very optimistic. She kissed Père Du Jaunay very tenderly on his cheek as they departed and François noticed a youthful bounce in her step that had not been there for a long while.

🐾 🐾 🐾

WHILE CONSTANTE AND FRANÇOIS had been in the rectory, Sans-père had come to Fort Michilimackinac to see the prisoners. He and Wenniway had been drinking rum taken from the King's Storehouse all afternoon. Wenniway's part in the massacre, unlike his father's, had been entirely non-political and extremely personal. He had planned to take Lo-tah back and make her his wife, after killing Henry with his own hands. Vengeance and the thrill of killing were his only motives.

His chagrin at discovering her absence can be imagined and his disappointment was doubled when Henry was nowhere to be found among the slain. When they had ascertained the merchant's whereabouts in Langlade's attic, he had been robbed again of sweet retribution when reminded that his father wanted the *Anglais* alive.

So all afternoon, he and Sans-père had been drinking rum and Wenniway had been bemoaning the loss of Lo-tah and vengeance. Sans-père had commiserated with his friend until the latter had passed out. He then determined to cheer his comrade by setting things right.

Unsteady at first, sobriety had gradually returned as Sans-père made his way toward the fort, determined to kill the *Anglais* for the benefit of Wenniway, whom he regarded, though over a decade his junior, as a brother. He knew that disobedience to Minavavana's wishes would probably end in exile for anyone else. But he also knew, even more certainly than Wenniway, that the son's power over the father's judgment was profound and Wenniway would probably be able to talk him out of such an extreme measure, especially since Sans-père was acting on behalf of Minavavana's beloved son. If not, then he would accept the consequences. Matchekewis would always take him in. He was convinced of the rightness of his task, and his determination could not be altered now by any consequences. He saw himself as acting out of familial loyalty. The 'without father man,' would avenge the frustration and humiliation of his 'adopted' brother and seal their relationship with Henry's blood.

When he arrived at Henry's store, he told the sentry at the door that he had been ordered by Minavavana to take Henry to the Chippewa village. The jailer, a Potowatomi, had no qualms about releasing the merchant and did not contest Sans-père's entrance to the shop.

Once inside, Sans-père moved deliberately to Henry whose eyes widened when he saw his enemy. He struggled to sit up straighter. "This is going to be trouble," Solomon said. Etherington did not even look up, but Goddard began to whimper until Bostwick cautioned him to be silent.

Sans-père stood directly in front of Henry, spread-eagled over his outstretched legs. His nose, the merchant noted, was crooked. It had obviously never been set properly after he had broken it. He was still covered in the dried blood of yesterday's victims and he stank, the odor of rum barely recognizable among those of dirt and sweat. Henry wrinkled his nose in disgust.

Sans-père didn't seem to notice. He had a wild, almost religious, ecstasy in his eyes. He drew his knife and Henry shut his eyes, convinced that his life was over. Instead, he felt his bonds loosen and realized that Sans-père had cut them. "Stand up, *Anglais*," he ordered in Algonkin.

Henry struggled to get to his feet, but his weakened condition and the stiffness in his legs, made it a very slow and deliberate process. When he finally was erect, his legs wobbled and his hands tingled as circulation was gradually restored.

"Remove your garments," his grinning enemy commanded.

At first Henry did not comprehend, and he stood dumbly staring at the wicked, young face before him. Sans-père's knife was instantly under his chin, pushing upward until it drew blood and Henry was standing on his tiptoes. "Take them off! Now!" he shouted. There was a measure of hysteria in Sans-père's voice which indicated that he was entirely serious and would brook no disobedience.

Henry began to undress, looking over at Solomon whose shrug of the shoulders indicated that he, too, was mystified. Sans-père forced him to continue shedding his clothes until Alexander stood before him as he had been born, naked and helpless.

Sans-père, watching his nude prisoner carefully, began to pick up the discarded clothes. He put on Henry's ruffled, white shirt which became instantly soiled. He took off the only article of clothing which he wore, his blood-covered loincloth, and threw it at Henry as he pulled on the merchant's stockings, underwear and pantaloons. Alexander's shoes did not fit him, so he tossed them aside and completed his new wardrobe by donning Henry's tri-cornered hat which had hung on a wooden peg by the door.

Satisfied with his new accouterments, Sans-père signaled Henry to move toward the door. It was obvious that he intended to take him somewhere. Alexander, knowing that he would be paraded through the compound past the eyes of women and children, forced himself to pull on Sans-père's loincloth, the only article of clothing available to protect his modesty. He struggled to keep down his rising gore, and the only thing that kept him from vomiting as he adjusted the filthy rag over his groin was the lack of anything in his stomach to expel.

As he moved toward the door, Solomon, knowing that the Chippewa spoke no English, said to Henry, as calmly as he could: "Alexander, I believe I know why he forced you to trade clothing with him. He means to kill you, and he does not want to tear your garments, which he intends to keep. Be wary, dear friend. I can't help you."

Henry feared that Solomon's statement made all too much sense as he limped on his protesting legs out the door and past the bored sentry. Sans-père was directly behind him and Henry was now convinced that the young man did indeed intend to murder him as soon as they got out of the Potowatomi's field of vision, which would be just outside the stockade gate on the water's edge, which they were now rapidly approaching.

Alexander decided there wasn't much he could do about the situation, except to make it more difficult for his captor to kill him by refusing to go any further. So he stopped abruptly in his tracks and turned to face his would-be murderer, just a few feet away from the open gate.

Sans-père was startled by this action and raised his knife. He looked almost ludicrous in the merchant's clothing, like a small child dressing in his parent's clothes and pretending to be an adult. But, unlike a child, he was anything but cute. His face was twisted in a demonic grimace. "Move!" he snarled, waving the knife in front of him menacingly.

Henry tried to keep his voice steady, though he was shivering in fear. "I won't go any further, Sans-père," he said. "I believe you intend to kill me, and if so, you'll have to do it here, where all can witness it."

Sans-père looked at him with the curiosity that a panther might display when confronted with a defiant squirrel. Then he moved, lunging at Henry, the knife flashing in the sun as it sped toward Henry's chest. Partly because of the slowing effects of the rum, and partially due to Alexander's natural quickness, the knife swished through empty air. The Englishman jumped aside, struck Sans-père on the shoulder, and raced back toward his shop with uncanny speed, his long brown hair flying almost straight out behind him.

Sans-père, knife in hand, had recovered sufficiently to be right on his heels. It was at this terrifying moment for Henry, as he raced past the rectory, that Constante and François stepped out of the door to Père Du Jaunay's living quarters.

In that instant, Henry saw her face as he ran by, and he thought he detected a smile. It was not a wicked grin or one of pleasure, but one of certainty and peace.

He heard her yell 'stop' in Algonkin and, curiosity conquering fear, he turned to see what was happening, fully expecting to be struck down as he did. Much to his surprise, Sans-père was a full fifteen feet away and Constante was standing in his path, blocking his progress. He looked confused and angry. He did not want to kill a Canadian, especially a woman. He stared at her for a moment, then started toward her. François moved beside her and she took his arm. Sans-père was completely confused. This defenseless woman stood before him, smiling. She was looking at him as if she *loved* him, but her mouth was set in determination and she had no intention, short of her own death, of letting him continue his pursuit.

Sans-père took another step forward, then paused. He cocked his head to one side, resembling for a moment a wild animal which had been charmed by soft music. He almost turned around to leave, and Henry thought for a moment that he might live after all. But the befuddled expression was gradually giving way to one of hateful obstinacy and resolution. "Get out of my way, whore!" he snarled and rushed forward. François tried to move in front of Constante, but she held his arm and kept him in place at her side.

"I am your mother, Sans-père," she stuttered. "Speak to me as a son to his mother." Her eyes clouded with tears and she gasped for air, but the sweet smile and determination remained. Sans-père stopped again. He was not certain of what she had said, more because of its unbelievability than lack of hearing. The dumb, confused expression returned.

"What?" he managed to mumble.

Constante bit her lower lip and squeezed François' arm tighter. *"Je suis ta mère,"* she repeated, first in French and again in Algonkin.

Sans-père lowered the knife, his pursuit of Henry temporarily forgotten. "My mother was Au-saw-way. She is dead. You are but a whore, one-who-lays-with-many."

Her face quivering with emotion, Constante fought to keep her composure. "Who has told you this, Sans-père?"

"It is common knowledge. Minavavana has called you such. He does not speak lies."

"No," she answered calmly, "but he does not know all the truth, and he is sometimes blind to it."

Behind her, Henry stood motionless, his mouth agape.

"What truth?" Sans-père asked. He was watching her intently, his mind clouded and unsure.

"I ran away from this place, this stickhouse and this man," she put her other hand on François' arm, "because I was afraid and felt guilty over the death of my husband. I was godless, spoiled, and childish, intent on my own pride and deserving of the guilt and misery my heart bore. I came to your village. Tcianung and Natomah gave me shelter in their lodge."

Henry cocked his head when he heard those names and stepped forward to better hear what she was saying, oblivious of his own danger.

"But Tcianung forced himself on me," she continued, choking back her anger and humiliation. "Natomah saw us together and blamed him, but he told her that I had seduced him. She believed him and they expelled me from their wigwam. I had two choices then. To return to the fort, the stickhouse, and face

François and my guilt, or to try and survive in the Anishnabeg camp. I was foolish and blind. I chose to stay." She took a deep breath and looked at François who gently tried to silence her, but she was determined to complete her confession.

"I survived as best I could that winter. I moved south with the tribe and lived off scraps of food that were thrown to me. Jean Cuchoise built a small wigwam for me, but your men had little pity. Alone and unprotected, even though I was pregnant, I was raped many times at the wintering grounds. It was by these circumstances that I began to be called a *gourgandine,* a prostitute." The tears flowed freely now and the smile had faded in the face of her agonizing memories, but she forced herself to continue. "I returned to Michilimackinac in the spring with a child. I loved the baby, though it was conceived in hate and lust. I protected it, fed it from the meager scraps that came my way. The child was my only link to happiness, my only reason for living. The child was you, Sans-père. I am your mother and Tcianung was your father. I am not a whore. I was a victim of your people and my own fear and pride."

She stopped talking and began to sob, her chest heaving in uncontrollable spasms. François held her closely, but she stiffened and resolve returned to her face, along with a loving smile.

Sans-père stood motionless, his mouth hanging open and his weapon dangling loosely from his hand. He acted like he had been slapped across the face. Then he spoke slowly and deliberately, as if he were retarded and had to concentrate on each word. "You do not speak the truth. If you did, Lo-tah would . . ." He could not complete the thought or the sentence, but continued to stare dumbly at Constante's lovely, shining countenance.

". . . be your half-sister, yes." Constante completed it for him. "You have the same father, and the man you are trying to murder is your sister's husband."

Sans-père glanced over her shoulder at the half-naked Henry, whose wide eyes and surprised expression indicated his ignorance on the subject. His eyes returned again to her smile—her loving, maternal, smile.

"Your skin is light," she continued, "like mine. Your hair is brown, not the true black of the Anishnabeg. Did you ever wonder why?"

His face became stormy and angry. "If what you say is true, why did you leave me? Why did I grow up to be Sans-père, the fatherless one? Was I so hateful to you?"

He said these words with such bitterness that Constante could see clearly that he had searched his mind often in pursuit of an answer to that question. She could see also that the answers had been found only in self-blame and abnegation.

"No, my son." She spoke these words with such conviction and compassion that his lower lip quivered. He began to perspire and feel very uncomfortable in Henry's tight clothing. "I loved you very much. But when François and Père Du Jaunay rescued me, I thought it best that you grow up among your own people and not with the shame of your mother to cripple you. Au-saw-way and Wawiekuimig wanted you and were good parents to you. I did not know they had died and you were again an orphan until you were grown. I saw no need to tell you—until now. You have a family. I am your mother and . . . and I love you!"

Tears streamed from her face and Henry could see that she wanted very much to move forward and embrace her prodigal. He was awed by the emotion which made her tremble and stagger. François held her securely, to keep her from fainting and his strength, as always, fed hers.

Henry wondered how anyone could love the dirt and blood-spattered savage who stood before them in his ridiculous costume, ready to erupt into a volcano of hate and violence at any moment. Yet the words that came from Constante were real. He realized that she had not interfered just to save his life, but because she had longed to express her feelings to a son she really loved.

Sans-père, looking about him as if the truth could be found in some physical place, avoided his mother's sweet smile and after a lifetime of doing without it, felt very uncomfortable in the presence of genuine love. "Wenniway is my brother," he said finally. "*He* is my family."

Constante recoiled at this hated name and then decided to reveal the final, painful truth. "Wenniway has always known who you are. Did your 'brother' ever tell you? Did he ever say to you how he and Matchekewis raped your mother while the little son was thrust aside? Is this your friend Sans-père? Because what I say is the truth, and whether you believe it or not, it still stands as such. Wenniway is not your brother or your friend. He is the enemy of your family!"

Sans-père rushed toward Constante, his knife raised, screaming at the top of his lungs. It was a terrible cry of anguish and betrayal. It was an exorcism of evil and it sounded like the release of Legion.

He stopped just short of her, the knife poised above her head, every muscle coiled to spring in murderous contempt, like the head of a venomous serpent.

Constante, pushing her husband aside, reached for Sans-père's trembling hand, brought it slowly to her face and, turning the blade away, gently kissed the dirty hand of her bastard son.

"Put your knife away Sans-père, my child," she whispered gently, using the weapon she had just received from her priest. She wielded God's weapon of love to do battle—and won!

🦋 🦋 🦋

Sans-père, disoriented and confused, turned and fled. Constante watched him go, then turned sadly to her husband and said: "We must get home François, the *matelote* will be burned by now."

Henry, amazed at yet another reprieve, had hoped he could conceal himself in the Cardin home or at least run for the open gate, when he became cognizant of a figure standing silently behind him. It was the Potowatomi sentry, who took him by the arm and, threatening him with his tomahawk, motioned for Alexander to return to his prison/home.

Constante and François could do nothing at that point to rescue him from his misery, but François promised they would keep trying and Alexander thanked them for saving his life, although he confessed inwardly that he did not know to what purpose.

When he was again securely bound hand and foot among his fellow prisoners, he related the strange events that had just transpired and Ezekial offered his opinion that it was nothing short of a miracle, while Lieutenant Leslie expostulated that this proved that both the French and the Indians were irrational mystics.

That evening, however, the officer changed his tune when Constante brought the prisoners bread and dried fish which the sentry allowed her to distribute. She also brought a large flask of water which François helped them to drink since the sentry would not untie their hands. After the departure of the Canadians, several Chippewa appeared, to allow the Potowatomi an opportunity to rest from his jailer duties. The prisoner's feet were untied, and with the security of additional numbers, they were allowed to stretch their legs and relieve their strained bladders outside. That evening, as the sun disappeared, taking with it the terrible heat of the day, the prisoners were much more comfortable in spite of their unfortunate circumstances. The enemies of hunger and thirst had been temporarily repelled from the ramparts of despair and Hope creeped into their makeshift prison. They talked amicably, though still bound securely on the hard floor of Henry's shop, until sleep overtook them.

As they talked of escape, and their spirits improved, Charles Langlade stepped out of his house next door into the soft moonlight. He greeted the Chippewa who were lounging casually on Henry's porch and turned in the opposite direction, intent on visiting his father.

Augustin Langlade had become an embarrassment to his only son. The old man drank to excess and was often seen staggering around the compound, the butt of jokes by British military personnel. It had given Charles tremendous satisfaction to see one of these soldiers, his father's worst tormentor, cut to pieces as Charles had watched from his parlor window while Henry begged him for shelter.

But, somehow, the triumph had not removed the shame he felt for his father's behavior. It had been a difficult two days. Charlotte had been soundly scolded by him and she had not accepted it well. She did not understand the necessary cruelties of war and he felt somehow, that their marriage would suffer for a long time. The Pani woman he had beaten within an inch of her life, and this had alienated his daughters, who were very fond of her. All of this trouble, and a drunken father to boot. Patriotism was a demanding emotion. It required one to suppress so many others.

As he approached the cabin where he had been raised, he noted that no light issued from it. He paused at the door, running his rough hand across the turtle hinges which still held the door firm, although the wood was rotting and the hinges were badly rusted. He stepped inside and called out for Augustin, but there was no reply. The moonlight illuminated the room sufficiently for him to see that it was a shambles. Dried, uneaten, and rotting food lay on the table, the surface of which appeared to be moving, until he realized from the squeaking sounds that dozens of mice were busy devouring the leftovers.

Clothes lay on the floor and tin cups were sitting here and there throughout the room. A wooden cask marked 'rum' lay on the floor near his feet, and another, resting cock-eyed on a chair, dripped the alcohol onto the floor.

Charles began to regret that he had not taken more care to surpervise the old man. He had not visited him in months. Jean-Paul would have been a better son, he thought.

Charles had never respected his father very much. Augustin had always been too content with things the way they were. He was not a fighter, a warrior. He catered too much to the whims of women and fate. He had never been a great, courageous man like La Fourche, or Minavavana. He had always been too meek and accepting.

Now, at the same age as La Fourche, Augustin, unlike his proud and fierce brother-in-law, was a hopeless drunk, an old man to be ridiculed.

'A man has to be hard,' Charles thought. 'You were never strong, *mon père,* and your weakness has brought you to this. You could never push aside what you felt, old man. I will *not* be like you.'

He called out again for Augustin, but there was still only silence to answer him. As he moved to the center of the room, leaving the door open to air out the stinking room, he noticed a dark object near the cold hearth which looked, at first, like a pile of clothes. But as his eyes became more accustomed to the dark, he recognized that this dark shape was his father.

He sighed and went to the old man. He had obviously drunk himself into oblivion again and Charles cursed his ill-luck that he would have to lift the emaciated frame into the bed and clean him up before going home. It irritated him, though he was really in no hurry to return to the four pouting females he had left moments ago.

He knelt by his father and lifted his back and head, preparing to put his other arm under the old man's legs and carry him to his bed. But there was no sour breath coming from the mouth that hung open and the eyes stared, wide open.

Charles shook him, but no moan escaped the grey lips. The son put his ear to the father's chest, but the heart that had loved him was still. *"Mon père,"* Charles whispered as he stared at the dirty, lifeless, face. *"Mon père!"*

Charles suddenly thought of a time when he was a child, when Wawatam had taken him and Jean-Paul and Okinochu-maki to hunt for *Mag-wah,* the bear. He vividly remembered the huge animal lumbering toward them, Wawatam's bow spent and useless. He recalled thinking that he was going to die when the wasted figure he now held in his arms, then young and strong and happy, stepped from the trees and coolly destroyed the raging beast, preserving the lives of his young sons.

The memory brought tears to Charles' eyes and he hugged his father close to him. *"Mon père,"* he whispered again, "I never gave you a chance. You loved me. Why didn't you demand that I love you too? I did, you know . . ." He stared at the dead eyes and gaping mouth. "No," he muttered, "you didn't know."

Charles wiped his face with the sleeve of his frilly shirt and lifted the corpse, carrying it to the bed which had not been used for weeks, the bed where Charles had been conceived while Au-san-aw-go slept in his cradle. 'So long, so long ago,' Charles thought to himself. His father's body was so wasted that he was as light as if he were made of straw instead of flesh and bones.

He laid Augustin on the bed gently and covered him with a blanket. As he turned to leave, something caught his eye in the corner of the room. It glinted in the moonlight as metal does. When he walked over to investigate, he found that the source of the light was the shiny crucifix given to Domitilde by Père Du

Jaunay, hanging from a small hook. Draped over a chair in that same corner was the dress Augustin had bought her in Montreal, her comb, her moccasins, in fact everything that had been distinctly hers. It was all there, neatly arranged in that one corner of the room as if it were a shrine.

Charles looked again at the blanket-covered lump on the bed. "You loved her that much?" he said. "When she died, all you wanted was to follow, wasn't it? Your weakness was your love, *mon père.*" He turned to leave and paused at the doorway, looking sadly at the bed and then the little shrine. "What was your strength?" He sighed in a melancholy tone, and stepped out into the night.

Chapter

5

The Isles du Castor

THE SECOND MORNING after the massacre dawned wet and cool. Though most of the prisoners were thankful for the change from the terrible heat, Henry, dressed only in Sans-père's breechclout, shivered from the cold.

His stomach was again gnawing with hunger and he prayed that their captors would allow Constante to bring them some further sustenance. His arms and legs ached miserably from lack of movement, inhibiting his circulation. His legs in fact had begun to quiver with muscle spasms and contracted so badly at times that he thought he might scream from the pain. His mouth was parched, and the gentle rain falling outside, just a few feet away, was a maddening temptation.

Since he was the only one who seemed to be awake, he had made up his mind to try and slumber a bit longer, when the noise of raucous voices outside made him struggle to see through the open doorway.

Aroused by the noise, other captives began to wake up. Solomon tried to shake the fuzziness from his brain and looked over at Henry. "What is it?" he asked.

Henry was trying to shuffle across the floor to line his vision in better perspective with the doorway. "I don't know," he whispered back, "but the voices are mostly Algonkin. I hear one Frenchman though. I can't see them through the door. I think they're off to the right at Langlade's cabin. I don't know the meaning of it, but I think it's trouble for us."

Goddard once more began to moan and kept expressing his certain belief that all of them were doomed. Colonel Etherington, irritated to distraction, told him to shut up. Those were the first words Henry had heard the commandant speak since he had been brought into his company from Langlade's garret. He did not hear him speak again.

Several Chippewa and Potowatomi appeared at the doorway. Charles Langlade was with them and, auspiciously for Alexander, so was Wenniway. Sans-père was noticeably absent and Henry couldn't help but wonder, in spite of his fear, what had happened to him.

Two of the Chippewa braves began to cut the bonds of the prisoners as Charles spoke to them in halting English. "The warrior, Wenniway, has asked me to tell you that you are to be taken out of here now and put in canoes at the beach. I don't know what your destination is. Do as you are told. You have no other choice." This abrupt statement being completed, he turned and exited.

The prisoners were so stiff and their limbs so paralyzed by lack of movement, that they found it quite impossible to stand up until circulation could be restored. Within fifteen minutes, however, all of them were standing erect, albeit on very tenuous foundations.

Their arms still bound, they were shuffled out into the drizzle, immediately raising their open mouths to the sky to take advantage of the opportunity to quench their burning thirst.

They were herded through the compound and out the open gate very quickly. The black rain clouds hung low over the lake and the rain sprinkled noisily on the grey water.

The prisoners were ushered into waiting canoes, some of them tumbling into the cold lake as they lost their balance without the use of their hands to steady them. Their captors beat them about their heads violently and verbally abused them for their clumsiness.

Henry was shoved into a canoe with Solomon, Wickwall and Goddard and four Chippewa warriors he had never seen before. He found himself silently thanking God that he was not in the same vessel with Wenniway, though he was not sure why that should give him any comfort.

He was so distressed physically that he was afraid he would die of exposure anyway. Except for the loincloth, he was naked, and when he saw Langlade standing on the shore watching the proceedings, he called out to him. "Monsieur, I beg you to give me a blanket, anything to cover me. I am freezing. I will happily pay you twice its value when I am again a free man."

The temperature had fallen from ninety degrees the day before to the low sixties on this grey dawn, and the cold, northern rain made it worse yet. Henry thought he detected a flicker of compassion across that dark face, but some inner force suppressed it.

"In your situation, Monsieur Henry, you cannot guarantee payment and you have nothing to serve as a surety. Besides, I don't believe it will make any difference in the next few hours. You will be surrounded by a *living* blanket before the day is over."

As the Canadian turned away, Solomon made an obscene gesture in his direction. Henry, in spite of his bewilderment at his enemy's last statement, and his disappointment and discomfort, smiled at the small act of defiance.

As the four canoes embarked and headed out into the lake, Langlade's ominous words hung like a pall over their heads. It was apparent that they were being taken to their deaths, but where or how they could not tell.

The Indians hugged the shoreline with their canoes, not wishing to venture into the soupy fog that was developing as the rain ceased and the clouds darkened.

As they traveled, the Chippewa in Henry's canoe talked cheerfully of their plans for the captives, not knowing that the merchant understood perfectly well what they were saying. As their conversations revealed their purposes, Alexander's stomach started to twist into knots. He began to fully comprehend what Langlade's words had meant.

From what he could glean of their discourse, the Chippewa planned to take the prisoners to the *Isles du Castor*.[1] There they

---

[1]Beaver Islands.

would be killed, butchered, and made into a soup which their captors planned to eat as part of a victory feast. ('You will be surrounded by a living blanket.')

Henry slumped in the canoe as if he had been struck in the head. Despair began to permeate his every fiber. He fell mute and seemed disinterested, a being without hope. He did not share this information with the other prisoners in his canoe. He saw no need to destroy their optimism or create a panic which would capsize their canoe and drown them, as their arms were bound and useless for swimming.

But he could not trust any further. Luck had deserted him and he knelt on the floor of the canoe, shoulders slumped, head down. The fog crept toward them across the surface of the water, screening the opposite shoreline from view. To avoid becoming lost in it, they hugged the beach nearest them. Except for the splashing of paddles, there were no sounds, the Chippewa having fallen silent to concentrate on their navigation.

Henry heard only the occasional cry of a loon, or the raucous cacophony of crows, gliding above the tall pines along the shore which were partially shrouded in mist. He had never felt such utter despondency. It began to drizzle again, increasing the wretchedness of his tormented body and dampening his spirits.

Calamity and misfortune had combined to numb his senses to such an extent that desolation replaced fear. His heart beat calmly. He began to accept. His only desire lay not in escape, but in a quick death. He thought of Lo-tah, and rapidly expelled such thoughts. He emptied his brain into nothingness and sat quietly. He ignored Solomon's voice. He even ignored Goddard's pleading with the savages for something to eat.

He did not look up when one of the Chippewa produced a piece of dirty bread and, drawing the blood-caked knife he had used in the massacre, spit on the blade, mixed the saliva with the dried blood, and wiped the red-brown mixture on the bread.

He offered it to Goddard who opened his mouth wide and stood higher on his knees to receive it. The Chippewa, enjoying this degradation, teased him with the morsel until he got bored, then plunged it into the Englishman's mouth. As Goddard chewed greedily, the Chippewa joked about how he had made the pathetic creature devour his own countrymen.

Solomon called Goddard every foul name he could think of, but the disgust and loathing the Jewish trader felt seemed to have no effect on Goddard's groveling, servile behavior. Henry took no notice and, uncharacteristically, said nothing.

This cessation of silence lasted but a few minutes before taciturnity was restored. Another ten minutes of movement through the misty waters saw them pass the poplar and aspen trees along the hilly shore, crowned by a lone, gnarled oak, which indicated their closeness to the Ottawa village of *L'Arbre Croche*. When Solomon asked Alexander what he knew concerning the absence of the Ottawa in all that had transpired in the last three days, he was met with muteness.

Solomon was not offended because he knew that Henry's silence was not a willful disregard of his question, but a symtom of quiet desparation which made him fear for his friend's sanity.

As the canoes approached *Pointe du Waugoshance,* the thin finger of land which marked the last denotation before their entrance into the great lake of *Michi-Gaumee* where the *Isles du Castor* lay, Solomon noticed a solitary figure, obviously Indian, standing on the spot where the point reached its furthest penetration into the water.

The man was shouting and signaling the Chippewa to approach the shore. Solomon saw that the lead canoe was turning in towards the promontory and he shouted at Henry to look up, but got no response. All of the canoes followed the lead vessel toward the point and Solomon thought that perhaps this might be their final destination. A feeling of dread enveloped him like the fog that consumed the lake as they drew nigh and the first canoe was beached. Solomon, now getting a clearer view of the Indian who had caused this diversion, thought he looked vaguely familiar.

As he was musing thus, the thick bushes which covered the majority of the little headland came alive with Ottawa warriors who plunged out of their concealed positions in the undergrowth and into the lake, waist-deep in the cold water. As they clutched the canoes and pulled them ashore, the Chippewa warriors, not expecting such belligerence from their brothers, were tardy in grabbing their weapons. By the time they thought to retaliate, they were completely surrounded by three hundred Ottawa warriors and they themselves were now captives.

Sometime in the midst of this confusion, Alexander Henry finally raised his head. Though he was not certain of the intent of the Ottawa, he did see some reason for the chance of a favorable conclusion to this journey and his despair began to dissipate.

He recognized the Ottawa warrior who had beckoned them to shore as Okinochumaki, the lanky savage who had been so threatening and belligerent to Henry when he first arrived at Michilimackinac. He also identified La Fourche, who stood immobile on the shore, surveying the scene through his one good eye while the copper glistened in his other socket, in spite of the dullness of the day and the absence of sunlight.

Henry searched the Ottawa party for some sign of Wawatam, but he was not in attendance. The English were pulled from the canoes by the attacking Ottawa and, Henry reasoned, based on his past experience with La Fourche, though he had met him but twice, that they were all going to die. But they seemed to be more upset with the Chippewa, whom they derided, and referred to, more than once, as traitors. The Anishnabeg were obviously confused and Wenniway, as leader of the group, approached La Fourche, and the two conferred while their respective followers and the British captives stood on the shore and awaited their decisions.

Henry judged, only by observation, since they were out of hearing, that Wenniway was extremely angry. He gesticulated with violent motions and raised his voice to such a level that what he was saying was almost intelligible to Alexander who stood and stared at the younger man, his stern, scarred face fierce, and disapproving. Wenniway lost control of his emotions to such an extent at one point in their discourse, that he raised his arm as if to strike the Ottawa chief.

Ottawa warriors moved forward, weapons drawn, but La Fourche handled the brash, young man himself. His hand struck with lightning speed, grasping Wenniway by the throat and squeezing with such strength that Wenniway's tongue protruded from his mouth and he began to lose the color in his face, the arm he had intended for a weapon now hanging limply at his side.

The Chippewa warriors, surrounded and significantly out-manned, were powerless to interfere. Henry watched this little drama with a growing sense of confidence and hope. He even managed a smile as he watched Wenniway choke.

La Fourche, having proven his point, released Wenniway and made it obvious that the 'discussion' had come to an end. On a signal from their chief, more Ottawa warriors emerged from the forest bordering the cove and carried with them a large number of canoes which were immediately launched. The British cap-tives, their arms still encompassed and apparently still in a state of bondage, were loaded into the largest of the vessels with sev-eral Ottawa warriors to guard them. The Chippewa were allowed their own canoes and were not treated as captives, but they were stripped of their weapons. They followed the Ottawa flotilla at a short distance, headed toward Michilimackinac in the opposite direction from the *Isles du Castor,* which gave Henry and Solomon an immeasurable sense of relief.

Chapter

6

Isle du Michilimackinac

THE SUN BEGAN TO BREAK THROUGH as morning lengthened to noon. Its rays dispelled the fog and warmed the chilled, traumatized frame of Alexander Henry.

As the vessel in which he was a passenger came within sight of the fort, he expected to head toward shore, but the canoes continued on course. As they glided by the palisade, Henry thought it looked haunted and unreal as if it should have disappeared with the fog. There were, of course, no British guards along the ramparts, no sign of the Canadians or Indians. It looked deserted, abandoned, even though he could hear the smithy's hammer of Philippe Amiot clanging behind the stockade wall and caught a glimpse of the Bourassa cabin through the open gate.

Only a few moments past the fort, the canoes began to glide toward shore and the passengers disembarked about at the spot where Henry had stumbled out of the forest the night he escaped Wenniway and Matchekewis through the gracious interference of the Canadian, Jean Cuchoise.

Now, he was hauled ashore and guided through the dark foliage with his fellow prisoners. His arms and legs ached and he was terribly weak from his deprivation, but it felt good to be standing in a more natural position and moving about, restoring his circulation.

By the time they drew near the Chippewa camp the Anishnabeg, who had been robbed of their prisoners, had run ahead to alert their brothers concerning what had transpired and to alert them to the intrusion of the Ottawa. La Fourche made no effort to stop them.

When the entourage entered the clearing where the Chippewa village was located, they found the 'Grand Saulteur' standing near its center, looking very perplexed and angry. The camp was armed to the teeth and ready for war, as could be seen by the number of warriors surrounding the village perimeter. It was quite apparent that they were only awaiting some signal from their bare-chested leader to attack the Ottawa and exact revenge for what they saw as a betrayal of the alliance of the Council of Three Fires.

La Fourche, seeming not the least intimidated, strode forward and faced Minavavana, whose virulent son stood by him like a child, expecting his father to set things aright.

La Fourche, his Ottawa braves grouped in a tight circle around the British captives, was the first to speak. "My brother," he began, "I come to you in friendship and peace, yet you are armed against us."

Minavavana did not reply immediately, but rubbed the tattoo on his stomach as if to coax the proper words from the guardian spirit it depicted. "Brothers," he finally answered, "do not attack those whom they call by that sacred name and steal from them what is rightfully theirs by conquest."

La Fourche did not appear to be offended by the remark, but his face was so scarred and rough that it was difficult to tell what his expression was. "Men, even brothers, must defend what is right and oppose what is wrong. You have attacked the *Anglais* stickhouse and have hidden this from us. Why did you not inform us? You have your booty. What of ours? Why were we not told?"

"There is one among you who could not be trusted to keep his silence. He is a brother to the *Anglais* who stands behind you." The chief pointed at Alexander.

"You speak of my son, Wawatam. Do you say that he would betray his people? If so, we will scatter the fire."[1] La Fourche

---

[1] I.e., break up the Council of Three Fires Alliance.

spoke in the harshest tone.

"You speak of brothers," Minavavana said. "Would you betray yours? I do not insult your son, I admire him for his loyalty. But he must betray someone. Either he keeps silence and betrays his adopted brother, or he speaks and betrays us. Therefore, in friendship to you, I refused to put your son in that position. This act of kindness has been rewarded with treachery."

La Fourche thought about his clever reply for a moment, then replied: "A true brother would keep silence as you have done Minavavana." The 'Grand Saulteur' smiled broadly at this acceptance of his point. "But, a true brother would also preserve the life of my son's brother. Where was your son taking the prisoners? Why was my son's brother bound as he is now, if you intended to preserve him?"

"My son was bringing the captives here to our village on my orders that I might better preserve them," Minavavana replied.

Henry looked at Wenniway and noticed that he was very uncomfortable and moved from foot to foot as if he needed to empty his bladder.

La Fourche remained very calm, but pursued the point. "If that is true, why were your canoes at *Waugoshance,* heading *away* from your village?"

Minavavana turned quickly and glared at his son. "Is this true?"

Wenniway appeared to be embarrassed and looked sheepish. "We were only going to display our captives to our brothers of the Three Fires. We were going to return with them immediately afterward."

Henry could not let the lie pass. "Great Minavavana, that is not the truth," he shouted. "The Anishnabeg in our canoe spoke of taking us to the *Isles du Castor* and killing us."

The Chippewa chief at first did not react. After a few moments, he turned again to Wenniway and repeated: "Is this true?"

Wenniway, shaken with anger and apprehension, simply replied, "No."

Minavavana looked back at La Fourche. "You see, no harm has been done and the *Anglais* brother is alive. My son would not disobey his father." The chief put his hand on Wenniway's shoulder and studied him carefully.

La Fourche, not as trusting, refused to accept the explanation. "If the 'Grand Saulteur' is concerned with the truth, let him call forth the warriors that the *Anglais* has spoken of and ask them if Wenniway, the son I brought gifts for at his birth, speaks falsely or not."

It was obvious that Minavavana had hoped to avoid this type of confrontation which belied his lack of confidence in his son. But he was honor-bound to submit to the test or face humiliation. He signaled the warriors who had been with Wenniway to step forward and they obediently lined up in front of him. Wenniway's eyes narrowed to cruel slits, his expression one of warning and promised retribution for any betrayal.

In spite of this, when Minavavana asked the first warrior if Wenniway had spoken the truth, the young man confidently replied in the negative, as did the next, and the next. It was a unanimous vindication of Henry's account.

During this entire proceeding, Minavavana displayed no emotion, in spite of the inner humiliation he felt. When he was through with the interrogation, he dismissed the warriors, praising them for their courage and honesty. He then turned to his son. "Leave this council, now! This is a meeting of *men!* Go!"

Wenniway whirled around and left, as much in fear of his father's wrath as in his own anger with those who had not stood by him. As he departed, he looked at Henry as if to say that the debt had reached monumental proportions, but still, would be paid.

Minavavana watched his son disappear through the gathering throng behind them, then turned back to La Fourche. "My son has dishonored me. My instructions were to bring the *Anglais* here."

La Fourche, without being too obvious, attempted to console the abashed chieftain. "I know that Minavavana has always spoken the truth. I thank him for his judgment and trust to his word."

Minavavana did not acknowledge the salute. "La Fourche has been wronged. I wish to amend our differences by dividing the prisoners between us and giving to your people a share of the spoils. Is this agreeable to the younger brother of the Three Fires?"

"It is," La Fourche answered.

Minavavana called a young warrior to his side and instructed him. Moments later, blankets, mirrors, knives, muskets, and a variety of other trophies were brought forward and placed before the Ottawa chief.

Minavavana then told La Fourche that he could choose seven of the fourteen captives and dispense with them as he chose. 'The Pitchfork' turned and went to the prisoners, singling out Etherington and Leslie, the two highest-ranking British officers (and the most desired captives), and all of the British civilians, leaving seven soldiers of ordinary rank to the Chippewa.

When La Fourche showed Minavavana who he had chosen, the Chippewa chief had only one objection. "The *Anglais* called Henry," he said, "must remain."

La Fourche looked puzzled. "Why should you want him? He is my son's brother. Though I have no personal claim on him, Wawatam will be grateful for his life and his safe return. As a relative, he should go with us."

Henry, who had been terribly relieved to be chosen by La Fourche, now listened intently to this dispute. He felt somewhat like a side of mutton being auctioned off to the highest bidder. "But he is also my relative," Minavavana said. "He is the husband of my niece."

Henry felt that this was merely an excuse to keep him in the Chippewa camp where he was much more likely to die an untimely death. He knew he was not popular with the chief, and Wenniway and Sans-père had both made it clear that they hated him with unbridled passion. He did not trust the Ottawa either, although he knew that Wawatam would protect him there and he believed that since the Ottawa had had no part in the massacre, they were unlikely to kill *any* of the prisoners and suffer the vengeance of British military authority when they now had no reason to be affiliated with the actions of the Chippewa and Potowatomi.

But Minavavana was adamant. The *Anglais* must stay with them. La Fourche knew that by the rules of Indian warfare the booty extended to them was more than generous and he no longer had a reasonable argument for taking Henry away with him. To bargain in the face of this generosity would be petty and dishonorable. "I thank the great warrior, Minavavana, for our share in this enterprise," La Fourche said. "I only ask, for the sake of my son, that the *Anglais* merchant live under your protection. I trust that he will be well when my son sees him again."

"You have my word on it brother," Minavavana replied. The two clasped each other's right arms in perfect amity, then La Fourche turned and left. The Ottawa gathered their prisoners and herded them out of the village ahead of them and back to the canoes.

"God be with you," Solomon whispered to Henry as he was pulled away.

"Somehow, I think He is," Henry answered. "Keep safe, Ezekial, until we meet on a better day."

Henry watched them go. Solomon was scolding Goddard for his whining and Etherington looked shaky and miserable perhaps as much from alcohol withdrawal as from mistreatment.

When they were gone, Henry and the six soldiers, including Wickwall, were moved into a hut which was used as a sort of jail. They were bound together, hands and feet. Henry was nearest the open entrance and as he looked out, he saw the sun break through the clouds for the first time that day.

🎖 🎖 🎖

HENRY WAS TREATED BETTER than at any other time since his captivity began. Before dusk, a squaw brought them all food, and their hands were freed so that they could eat it. They devoured it in wolf-like fashion, and their guards seemed rather amused at the scene and joked good-naturedly with their captives. They were allowed to walk a little after their meal to stretch their legs (under watchful supervision), and relieve themselves among the foliage by the edge of the camp.

Henry was also given a blanket, and when all the prisoners were back in their lodge and tied securely, a fire was built to ward off the damp chill. In spite of these comforting attentions,

Henry did not believe that they were going to survive unless something or someone should intervene. Though the Chippewa were dutiful in their ministrations, Henry felt somewhat like a sheep being attended by his shepherd until such time as the shepherd deemed the sheep's slaughter necessary. Then kindness would become cold-blooded murder. He had seen Wenniway brooding by his wigwam when they were exercising in the clearing and Matchekewis had been with him. That insane presence did not help to alleviate his fears.

Gradually the camp settled into idleness as the sun disappeared and crickets, frogs and owls began their dark chorus. Chippewa warriors, mostly young bachelors, sat around the community fire, their backs to the prison lodge, talking amicably, and playing some sort of game with pebbles. Henry, as he saw their black silohuettes against the orange fire, believed that they were gambling, because some sort of payment was being made after each round.

As he was watching thus, his mind absorbed in his prospects for survival and Lo-tah, a face suddenly appeared at the doorway, startling him so badly that his heart beat wildly at his temples. But his shock and surprise quickly evaporated and were changed to joy when he recognized the noble countenance of Wawatam!

"My friend!" Henry shouted. "My dear, good friend." Though he tried to avoid it, tears came to his eyes.

Wawatam embraced him and Henry would have cheerfully reciprocated, but his arms were still tethered. "I told you that protecting you would be a great task, my brother, but we are still the *atcab* and the *asawan,* the arrow and the bowstring."

Looking over Wawatam's shoulder, Alexander noted that a young Chippewa had entered the hut also. He appeared to be with Wawatam, but the merchant was not certain until his brother introduced him. "This is Soutache."[2] The name, Henry saw, was as much a description as an appellation. The youth had formed all of his luxuriously silky, black hair into one long, thin

---

[2]Like La Fourche and Sans-père, Soutache had a French name. It means 'narrow braid.'

braid which was pulled over his head and hung down his forehead to the tip of his nose. It was held in place by a quill headband which was pulled tightly across his forehead. Wawatam looked upon the young Ojibway with an expression of pride, as if he had given birth to him.

Soutache was very friendly and spoke in a high but strongly masculine voice as he greeted the merchant. "We are happy that you are safe," he said. "The *shaman* has told me that you are his brother and he loves you. He has been concerned for your safety." Henry guessed that the boy could not be more than thirteen or fourteen years old.

Wawatam drew his knife and deftly severed Henry's bonds. Wickwall and the others, expecting the same, moved their bodies to allow better accessibility to the ropes that held them, but Wawatam shook his head back and forth, making it clear that he had no authority over them and no interest in their fate. None of them comprehended Algonkin, so Henry was forced to tell them that he was the only one to be freed and tried to explain the circumstances. None of them were very understanding and as Henry stood up to leave with the two Indians, Wickwall called him a 'traitorous bastard,' a comment the merchant ignored. He stepped out into the cool, invigorating, night air, his blanket wrapped around him for warmth.

Several of the Chippewa braves by the fire turned and looked at them for a moment, then swung their attention again to the game they were playing.

The three walked across the darkened clearing and entered a wigwam where Soutache was greeted warmly by a Chippewa warrior and a squaw whom Henry assumed must be the lad's parents. Wawatam was accorded the respect due to a *cicigwe shaman* and invited to sit at the place of honor closest to their fire. Henry was ignored. When Wawatam introduced the merchant as his brother, however, there was much apologizing and fussing over him. They could hardly be blamed for their original reactions, since Alexander's ragged appearance hardly warranted respect. He looked very much like a slave. In addition, Henry recognized Soutache's father as one of the braves who had been on the *Isle du Castor* expedition and had been called forth to testify to Wenniway's dishonesty.

When they were all seated, Henry found, in the course of the conversation, that Wawatam and Soutache had been away, fifteen or twenty miles to the south for the last week, living together while the *shaman* taught the youth the mysteries of the *Midewiwin* society and the dogma of the *cicigwe* cult.

It seems they had traveled such a long distance to be near the pit where the 'grandfathers' (woodland rattlesnakes), kept their residence. It was regarded as a sacred training ground for apprentices of the *cicigwe*. They had fasted and prayed diligently to the spirits while the Chippewa and Potowatomi had been annihilating the garrison.

Henry's curiosity about Wawatam's absence was thus satisfied. He couldn't help but ask his friend if he had had any inkling of the conspiracy, a question that was met with displeasure and left unanswered. He also begged Wawatam to tell him anything he knew concerning the disappearance of Lo-tah. The *shaman* said he knew nothing. However, he promised to try to find out what he could in reference to her fate as soon as possible.

When the conversation with Soutache and his family ended and they began to prepare for sleep, Henry urged Wawatam to get up and guide him out of the Anishnabeg village. Wawatam seemed surprised at this suggestion and explained to Alexander that such a proposal was out of the question.

Wawatam related that upon his entrance into the Chippewa camp that day, he and Soutache had gone straight to Minavavana to inquire about the fate of the *Anglais* brother, as news of the massacre had reached their ears while they were as yet many miles distant from Fort Michilimackinac.

Minavavana had explained to Wawatam that the life of his friend had been preserved, but he was a prisoner of the Anishnabeg and must remain so until it was decided what was to be done with the captives. Until that time, because of Minavavana's respect for Wawatam, he would put Henry into his custody, trusting that the *shaman* would be able to produce him when needed. They were now, he told Henry, guests of Soutache and they would sleep there for the night. He reassured him that he had no intention of leaving Henry until he was safely out of captivity and promised that he would allow no harm to befall him. When Henry tried to protest, Wawatam asked him to be patient and trust. In the meantime, he gave Alexander some dried venison and a potent blend of tea before nodding off and leaving Henry alone with his thoughts by the dying fire, listening to the boisterous bellowing of the young men outside, and other dark noises of the night.

LA FOURCHE HEADED straight for the stockade as soon as he departed from the Chippewa village. He wanted to see his brother-in-law and nephew and obtain some advice from them on what to do with his new prisoners. He also wanted to see what the fort was like without British control, and what transpired there since he had last visited.

The Ottawa reached their destination quickly and La Fourche, Okinochumaki, and a few other warriors entered the gates while the remainder of the band stayed with the prisoners and the canoes.

The short voyage had been marred by only one incident. One of the Ottawa braves, overcome with loathing by the continual whining of Goddard, had clubbed the Englishman over the head, sending him into unconsciousness and blessed silence.

As the little party passed through the water gate, La Fourche noted a small gathering of the French in front of the church. The 'Black Robe' was standing in front of the assemblage, where a rectangular pine box, occupied a prominent place. The priest was walking around the box, waving some sort of smoking pot, attached to a small chain and chanting in a language that the Ottawa knew was neither French, Algonkin, nor English.

Charles and Charlotte Langlade and the two dainty little girls were there, along with most of the other Canadian residents of Fort Michilimackinac. They seemed to be almost worshipping the box, since their heads were all bowed in its direction and their hands were piously folded in prayer.

But as he got nearer, the chief recognized this ceremony as a funeral, and he began to wonder who had died. Many of the

Canadians turned in his direction to see who the intruder was, but observing his familiar, if fearsome visage, turned back to the ritual.

When Charles saw him, he turned aside for a moment, leaving Charlotte to stand with her brother, Ignace, and went to greet his uncle and inform him of Augustin's death. "My uncle," he said as he grasped La Fourche's hand, "your sister's husband, my father, has given up his spirit. He is at rest."

At first, La Fourche did not seem to comprehend what he was hearing, then a single tear formed at the edge of his one good eye. He was thinking of the day, so long ago, when Augustin Langlade had walked into his camp at his summons, and left with Domitilde as his wife. There was no need for the scarred chieftain to ask the manner of his friend's death. Everyone knew that Augustin had become a hopeless alcoholic.

Wordlessly, La Fourche approached the casket, removed his bear claw necklace, which he prized above all other possessions, and laid it on the rough surface of the pine box. Père Du Jaunay, ignoring the interruption, continued with the liturgy of last rites. An open hole, next to Domitilde's grave in the little post cemetery, stood waiting.

La Fourche turned to leave and embraced Charles. "I will miss him," La Fourche said.

"He was weak," Charles offered, as the only reasonable explanation for his father's passing.

La Fourche grabbed his nephew by the shoulders and shook him. Charles had never seen him look so fierce. "He was a great man!" the Ottawa shouted. "He gave life to you and was my brother." La Fourche glared at Charles. "Never dishonor his memory. You only bring shame on *yourself.*"

With this statement, he shoved his nephew aside and stomped away. The Ottawa departed as quickly and silently as they had come.

Charles was shaken by La Fourche's words. The uncle he had always admired and emulated instead of his father, obviously had thought a great deal of Augustin. He had called the pitiful drunk 'a great man.' Somehow, Charles sensed he was right.

These thoughts were suddenly disturbed by a scream and

shouts of 'get some water' and 'let him breathe.' While Charles had been occupied with private musings, he had failed to notice that the priest, in the midst of his ritual, had turned ghastly pale and, halting in mid-sentence, clutched at his chest before toppling to the ground.

The scream had come from Constante Cardin who was now on her knees in the dirt, clutching the Jesuit's limp hand and kissing it while she prayed fervently aloud for her mentor's recovery. François was trying to hold others back as the little community rushed forward in concern for their priest.

It was Laurent Du Charme who finally put his head to Père Du Jaunay's still chest and pronounced sadly; *"Il est mort."*

Constante looked to François in desperation as if he somehow had the power to bring Du Jaunay back to life. François could only kneel beside her and attempt to comfort her, but she would not allow it. She threw herself across the prostrate form of the Jesuit and wailed in such horrible anguish that many feared that she too might expire—from grief.

"Oh God, dear God," she shouted at the blue sky. "Why must you take him? He taught me to love. You demand that we love. Why does it have to hurt so much? Why do You torture me when I care?"

She put her head down and sobbed bitterly, at the same time covering the dead hand with her tears and caresses. Another hand, full of tender warmth and life, touched her shoulder and squeezed gently. In spite of her grief, she knew that everyone was looking at the figure behind her.

She turned her head and looked through red, misty eyes at the face of Sans-père.

"Mother," he said. "I have found my sister."

At that moment, Constante realized that the priest and God both knew what they were doing, and she smiled.

HENRY AWOKE to find himself alone in the lodge of Soutache. Unknown to him, La Fourche, Okinochumaki, and several Ottawa warriors had glided silently by the Chippewa camp in their canoes shortly before dawn, on their way to Montreal with Etherington, Solomon, and the other British captives.

La Fourche had spent the early hours before daybreak talking with his nephew. They had exchanged some angry words when La Fourche discovered that Charles had been fully cognizant of the conspiracy to overthrow the British and had kept it secret from his own people. Langlade's callous lack of concern for Henry's survival had also created a schism between them and the Ottawa left in a huff, determined to take his prisoners back to their own people in Montreal and exchange them for a ransom. Charles slumped in a chair and remained there the rest of the day.

Henry, waking slowly, panicked a little when he realized he was alone. He had not been outside surveillance for several days and was unused to such eerie privacy. There were noises outside which indicated frantic activity and Alexander thrust his head through the portal of the wigwam to see what was transpiring. Wawatam stood beside the lodge just a few feet away, calmly observing the hustle and bustle of squaws who were scurrying with heavy loads, headed toward the lake. It was apparent that the Chippewa were about to desert this site and move their village to some other location.

Henry left the wigwam and stood next to Wawatam, who smiled at him benignly and cheerfully as if there was nothing out of place or unusual.

"Where is everyone going?" Henry asked.

"Word has arrived in camp that the *Anglais* are sending a force to avenge the attack on the stickhouse. Minavavana has ordered that the Anishnabeg must move to the island of the Great Turtle. There," he explained, "the people will be in a more defensible position to repel an invasion and be under the direct guardianship of their protective Spirit. It is a wise decision."

"What is to be done with us?"

"We will go also," Wawatam said solemnly. "No other decision has been made concerning the prisoners."

By mid-morning, a virtual armada of canoes was assembled offshore, poised to make the passage across the strait to the Isle du Michilimackinac. The water was calm, which would make the five-mile journey considerably easier. Before leaving, Wawatam stood up in his canoe, which was floating in about ten feet of water, and held up a small dog whose feet were bound. He invoked the Great Spirit of waters, *Michi-Gaumee,* to protect them on this journey across the wide, blue, expanse, and then dropped the whining, struggling, sacrifice into the depths.

Henry watched the poor animal sink from his vantage point in a large canoe which served as transport for himself and the other prisoners. He was very uncomfortable being placed among them, since they resented his privilege of being unbound and having unrestricted freedom of movement.

Furthermore, his mobility and the appearance of Wawatam had left him with the impression that he was no longer incarcerated. Being placed in this canoe indicated that in the minds of the Chippewa at least, his status had not appreciably changed.

The journey was uneventful and as they approached the only natural harbor of the island and gazed at the cliffs rising behind it, Wawatam was congratulated by the Anishnabeg on his invoking of the Spirit of Waters for their protection.

As they beached their canoes, Wawatam informed his brother when they were reunited on shore, that this was hallowed ground and must be treated accordingly. When Alexander asked what he meant, the *shaman* replied that he must not attempt to speak to any devils or say anything insulting about turtles. They were within hearing of this beneficent and jealous spirit and must in no way offend him or his offspring.

Alexander assured his anxious friend that he could be counted on to show the proper reverence. He kidded that he was not in the habit of insulting turtles anyway, but Wawatam simply shook his head solemnly and said, "Good."

The new camp was established very quickly in the woods a short distance from the beach. Alexander was amazed at the skill and industry of the squaws who took sole responsibility for building the wigwams and hauling the household possessions from the canoes to the new residences. The men sat around talking and ignoring their diligent enterprise.

Within the space of two hours after their arrival, they had succeeded in constructing an exact replica of the village they had just left, including the prisoner's lodge where all of the British except Henry were immediately housed.

This work completed, the squaws began preparations for the evening meal as the sun lengthened in the sky by gathering huge amounts of firewood and setting out big kettles of water to boil.

In the midst of all this activity, no one noticed that beyond the woods and beach and harbor, a lone canoe struggled across the choppy, black water, as the sun blazed orange and red on the fiery horizon.

🐚 🐚 🐚

THE WOOD TURTLE had spent the better part of her day looking for the right consistency of soil in which to dig her nest and lay her eggs. She was exhausted and hungry, but would not find respite until the demands of her instincts were satisfied. After several hours of aimless wandering among the dead leaves and ferns of the forest floor, she finally found what she had been looking for.

In this spot the soil was moist, sandy and loose. Ignoring the sounds of human voices and activity close by, the turtle began to dig her nest. She worked feverishly, driven by a relentless and terrible genetic obssession.

In an hour's time, she had finished excavating. Painfully and methodically, she deposited twenty-eight white, round, leathery eggs into their shallow cradle.

Carelessly, she tossed a thin layer of sandy soil over her brood. She crawled slowly away in search of food and rest, having fulfilled the only parental task that nature required of her. She did not know or care, that she had laid her eggs only inches from a recently constructed human dwelling.

🐚 🐚 🐚

THAT EVENING, as darkness set over the Chippewa camp and the community fire popped and crackled in the center of the village, a huge man, obviously Ojibway, entered the new settlement. He was greeted with much fanfare and ceremony, so Henry believed that he had to be a person of some importance.

He was the biggest Indian Alexander had ever seen, handsome and strongly muscled. A distinctive tattoo in the shape of a snake slithered down his forehead to the tip of his nose. He strode through the camp like some sort of deity and even Minavavana seemed small and somewhat insignificant by comparison.

There was a general council of warriors called shortly after his arrival and both Wawatam and Southache's father left to attend. Soutache and his mother remained behind with Henry who was ordered by Wawatam to stay inside the wigwam and not allow himself to be seen publicly that night.

The merchant did as he was told, but watched the proceedings, peering out from behind the flap that covered the lodge entrance.

He could not hear much of what was transpiring outside, but the giant walked around inside the circle of warriors surrounding the fire, gesticulating wildly and generally working the Anishnabeg into an emotional lather.

Henry noted that Wenniway was seated opposite his father across the circle, when his usual position was at Minavavana's side. He guessed that this was probably the disgruntled parent's order since the position nearest the war chief was always the one of greatest honor and the one Wenniway had always taken for himself. At this meeting, Wawatam sat on one side of the 'Grand Saulteur,' and Matchekewis on the other.

Several kegs of rum were brought out and distributed to the council, a situation that bothered Henry. He knew that alcohol made some men sloppily emotional and others depressed. It made Indians mean, and would not be helpful to his chances of survival, Wawatam's friendship and Minavavana's pledge to La Fourche aside.

After about half an hour had transpired, there was a general whooping and hollering and amid this noise, Wawatam returned to Soutache's wigwam and sat down by the fire. When he offered no explanation as to what had happened, Henry asked him.

Wawatam's expression was strangely disquieting when he turned to look at his friend. " 'Le Grand Sable' has come into camp," he said.

"Who?"

"He is a great warrior who has heard from Pon-ti-ac, our Ottawa brother to the south. He attacked the *Anglais* stickhouse at *D'étroit.*" Wawatam hesitated for a moment, then continued. "The Ottawa and Anishnabeg were defeated there. 'Le Grand Sable' says they were betrayed by an Ottawa squaw who alerted her *Anglais* lover to the conspiracy."

"Yes?"

"He has told Minavavana that vengeance is in order and the *Anglais* captives here must be killed."

"What?" Henry's previous feeling of security rapidly dissipated. "What did you tell him? You told him this wasn't possible, didn't you?" He grabbed Wawatam's arm. "Didn't you?"

The *shaman* put his hand on Henry's shoulder. "Wenniway said that we have a prisoner here who has an Anishnabeg squaw. The squaw is missing, he said, and the *Anglais* has been set free. 'Le Grand Sable' then demanded the death of this Englishman or the spirits of those Ottawa and Ojibway who died at *D'étroit* would haunt the Anishnabeg."

"He meant me," Henry moaned.

"Yes."

Wawatam bowed his head and rubbed his chin. He seemed to be absorbed in his own thoughts. When he looked at Alexander again, he saw that all the color had left his face and he was perspiring heavily.

"Then I must die," the merchant managed to mumble.

Wawatam, continuing in his maddening habit of careful consideration of every answer, waited several moments before replying.

"Minavavana explained to 'Le Grand Sable' how he had promised La Fourche that he would protect the man named Henry. 'Le Grand Sable' threw his hatchet to the earth at the mention of the name and spit into the dust. He said the chief of the *Anglais* at *D'étroit* who defeated the Ottawa was also called Henry. Did the 'Grand Saulteur' wish to defy the ghosts of the dead? Now could he see how the spirits demanded revenge?"

"That's ridiculous," Alexander said. "Henry is my last name.

Henry is Major Gladwin's first name. It's nothing but coincidence. Surely a man can't be condemned for his name?"

Wawatam, like all his Indian brothers, did not understand the meaning of the word 'coincidence.' The word was not translatable into Algonkin and Henry had spoken it in English. "It was a bad omen," Wawatam replied.

"But it means nothing," Henry argued.

"Minavavana is determined to spare your life and keep his word, but he is not pleased about it. It will cost him too much."

Suddenly a terrible scream pierced the night causing Henry to jump like a skittish colt. Wawatam, who could not have helped but hear it, did not react at all. He almost seemed to have been expecting it.

Comprehension began to dawn in the grey sky of Alexander's mind. "My God!" he mumbled. "What cost, Wawatam? What is the price for my life?"

Wawatam looked at him with his steely, black eyes. There was no regret or indication of any compassion there. "Minavavana has traded the other *Anglais* to satisfy 'Le Grand Sable' and preserve your life."

"No!" Henry shouted and rushed for the doorway. He was stopped by Soutache's father who was entering and then held by Wawatam who had quickly grabbed him.

"It is a wise decision," Wawatam shouted at him as he wrestled with his friend. "The ghosts must be satisfied, and they will accept six lives better than one. Minavavana can keep his word and so can I. There is no other choice."

Another terrible scream penetrated the bark walls of the wigwam and Henry's conscience. "I can't live with this," he mumbled as he slumped to the ground, tears streaming down his face. "What becomes of *my* honor?"

"It is necessary," Wawatam replied putting his hand on Henry's shoulder as Soutache followed his father into their home. "You must accept it."

After a half an hour passed, the screaming finally stopped and Henry knew that it was over. For the first time in several years, he prayed for forgiveness and the souls of those who had been sacrificed.

While he was thus engaged, the ugly, leering face of Wenni-way topped by the ridiculous hat, now in tatters from constant wear, poked through the wigwam's entrance. Without comment, he extended his arm to hand Wawatam and Soutache's father pieces of birch bark with some sort of scribbled symbols upon them and then rapidly withdrew.

Wawatam looked at it briefly, then shrugged his shoulders. Across the fire, Soutache's father nodded in silent confirmation. "We must leave," he said, getting up and heading for the door-way.

Henry looked at him anxiously. "Where are you going?" He said. "What did Wenniway give you?"

"An invitation," was the reply. "We will return soon."

Without any further explanation, the two men departed and Henry was left with Soutache and the old squaw, trying to pull himself together.

Wawatam was gone for over two hours. In that time, Henry managed to gather his wits. The prayer that he had spoken had helped to pacify his troubled soul to a degree of tolerance.

The shouting, singing, whooping and hollering outside indi-cated that the captured rum was being put to use and drunke-ness was beginning to overtake a good number of the 'guests.' Henry was concerned that Wawatam might fall victim to this bacchanalian revelry. But when he returned, alone, he was very sober and very much in control of himself. He carried with him a large wooden bowl with a spoon fashioned from the same mate-rial.

He seated himself by the fire and began to sip the broth slowly as Henry questioned him regarding the fate of the other prisoners.

"All dead," was his distinct reply, "but all but two died bravely. It speaks well for Minavavana's decision."

He took another spoonful of the soup and slurped it noisily. Henry was becoming increasingly irritated at the way he ate so heartily when they were discussing the slaughter of his country-men.

Wawatam, insensitive to the aggravation he was causing, continued to eat and listen. Henry changed the subject, but was still relieved when Wawatam placed the bowl on the ground between them.

As Alexander glanced down at the dish, his eyes froze in their sockets. Floating in the broth among tiny bits of meat, was a human hand! The hideous thing had a very pronounced white, lightning-shaped scar!

Alexander's hand went to his mouth to try and stem the inevitable progress of the contents of his stomach to the outer world. He staggered outside and, falling to his knees with ungovernable loathing, sprayed the ground with vomit.

Chapter

7

Skull Cave

Wawatam pulled Alexander back inside as soon as he had finished regurgitating and reprimanded him for having left the shelter of the hut. The *shaman* tried to explain that the more he was seen, especially by the rum-soaked warriors outside, the more precarious his existence became. He also informed Alexander that 'Le Grand Sable' would kill him on sight, drunk or sober, bargain or no bargain.

The merchant was not listening. He had been so repelled by Wawatam's participation in the cannibalistic feast that he wanted nothing more to do with him, regardless of how that would affect his own fate. The 'brotherhood' between them, as far as the Englishman was concerned, could not survive such a desecration.

When Wawatam put his hand on Alexander's shoulder to comfort him, the merchant pulled away and sat silently by himself. Wawatam, looking wounded, picked up his bowl and carried it outside.

Soutache, too young to join in the ceremony, sat across from Alexander, quietly staring at him, his eyes never wavering. Finally, Alexander could stand it no longer. "What are you looking at," he snapped.

Soutache, smiled benignly. "You are wrong to push away one who loves you," the teen-ager replied.

"No one who does that is capable of loving anyone," Henry exclaimed.

"Does what?"

Henry began to believe that the whole world had gone insane. "Butchering and devouring their fellow beings. It's loathsome and devilish."

"The *shaman* does not like it either."

"Then why does he do it? No one was holding a gun to his head," Henry scoffed. "Who forced him, eh?"

"It is customary among our people," Soutache patiently explained, "to make a feast from among those captured or slain in war. The *shaman* was invited to come to this feast. To refuse would have been an insult to 'Le Grand Sable' and further endangered *your* life." A moment of thoughtful silence followed, then Soutache completed his thought. "Perhaps it is you, *Anglais,* who do not understand what love is? I know that your God instructed his followers to drink his blood and eat his flesh because he sacrificed himself for them. Are we so different?"

Henry stared at the young face for a moment and was going to try to explain the difference between symbolic sacrifice and true depravity, when the wigwam's flap was thrown back and Wawatam reentered. He looked at Henry with sad, black eyes, his distinguished forehead wrinkled in perplexity. "I returned the 'food' to 'Le Grand Sable.' He is very angry and has gone to Minavavana. Most of the warriors are drunk and their blood is hot from killing. You are in great danger. We must leave now!"

He drew his knife and went to the rear of the wigwam. Soutache's mother had fallen asleep and paid no attention to Wawatam's vandalism of her home as he cut a hole through the birchbark wall and motioned Henry to exit through it.

Alexander hesitated, then got up and headed toward Wawatam. Soutache interrupted him long enough to give him some clothes, taken from his father's wardrobe. Henry slipped these on gratefully, having possessed no garment but Sans-père's loincloth for almost two days. He still took the blanket with him.

When he reached the little hole that Wawatam had created for his escape, he put his hand on the *shaman's* shoulder. "Forgive me my friend," he said, "for things I can't understand."

Wawatam smiled. "Hurry," was his only reply.

Henry stumbled as he passed through the opening. His foot had wedged in a small hole in the sand as he left the wigwam, and when he pulled it free, it was smeared with a glistening jelly. The remains of leathery turtle egg shells clung to his moccasin. He peered ahead into the darkness and was thankful that Wawatam had preceded him and not seen his desecration of the sacred offspring of their guardian spirit. In a moment, he followed Wawatam and the two disappeared into the dense foliage behind the camp.

Down by the shore, the little canoe which had struggled across dark waters under the light of the summer moon, came to rest on the shore of the island.

Two figures disembarked and hurried away from the water's edge and into the protective cover of the forest.

🦋 🦋 🦋

WAWATAM AND HENRY struggled up the hillside. The forest was pitch black and huge pines blocked any light from the brilliant moon. Their progress was slow, since their destination, which Henry did not know, was almost straight uphill. Several times the merchant stumbled over fallen trees and had to be helped to his feet. The more they climbed, the steeper the hill seemed to get and Alexander was about to ask his guide for a moment's respite from their labor when the earth suddenly began to flatten out and they could walk with greater ease. The trees thinned somewhat and they had the added luxury of seeing where they were going.

Wawatam paused momentarily to get his bearings and Henry, gasping for air, turned to look behind him. They were standing on a kind of plateau. The tips of trees were at his feet and he could see, far below, the huge council fire of the Anishnabeg camp, made tiny by distance. He could hear the warriors, screaming and whooping in drunken revelry below, and quietly thanked God that he was not there.

Beyond the dark trees, the moon sparkled on the straits. On the opposite shore, somewhere in the blackness, was Fort Michilimackinac. Laurent Du Charme cuddled with his wife there and François and Constante held each other in comfort. His own cabin was torn apart. His own bed lay empty. Where, where, was

Lo-tah? Tears formed in his eyes. He wanted to scream at the injustice of it all.

Instead, Wawatam touched him on the shoulder and he followed again. After laboring up a rocky incline for about twenty minutes, Wawatam halted again. The lunar light was again masked by trees and it wasn't until Wawatam pulled him forward by his arm that he realized that they were standing at the mouth of a cave. Wawatam told Henry that if he spent the night inside the natural shelter, he would be safe. The *shaman* explained that he, himself, must return to the Chippewa village, but he would return for him in the morning when 'Le Grand Sable' was gone and the effects of the rum had worn off the other Anishnabeg warriors. In the meantime, Henry must stay concealed within the cave.

Wawatam opened a small pouch at his side and handed the merchant some smoked fish and corn, then bid him good-bye.

Henry grabbed his arm as he turned. "You are a good friend, Wawatam, and a man of honor. We will always be brothers. I don't approve of that 'custom' of your people, but I won't let it stand between us."

The *shaman,* grinning from ear to ear, put his strong arms around Henry and almost lifted him off the ground in a powerful bear hug. He dropped Alexander just as suddenly and sauntered away into the darkness, humming to himself.

Alexander drew the blanket around him. It had already absorbed a good deal of moisture from the heavy dew. He felt along the cave wall as he entered, and stumbled once or twice over rocks, or pieces of wood, he wasn't sure which since they tumbled quite easily and made a clacking sound on the stone floor. Yet they were round he was sure, because they rolled when he stubbed them with his foot.

He wished he had a fire, for both warmth and vision, but without ventilation the smoke would rapidly expel him from his shelter, and any light outside would be seen from below.

He lay down where he was, using one of the rock-things for a pillow and pulled the blanket over him. He tried to sleep, but his tortured mind was filled with images of floating hands and rolling heads.

To soothe himself, he thought of Lo-tah. He saw her beautiful face and innocently mischievous eyes. He could almost feel her slender, exciting body next to him and smell her silky, black hair. These happy thoughts were soon replaced with fear. He could not imagine what had happened to her (or would not). Alone and pregnant in a dark forest without food or shelter, what could become of her?

If he knew she was dead, he was convinced that he would have gone down the hill and presented himself to 'Le Grand Sable' without any compunction at all. Life without her would not matter. With these troubled thoughts, his exhausted and traumatized mind drifted briefly into welcome oblivion.

He was awakened less than an hour later by sounds outside the cave which he at first feared were the shuffling sounds of a bear whose home he might be occupying, then recognized (with greater fear) that the approaching sounds belonged to a more dangerous animal. He froze, holding his breath against the determination of his pounding heart. It was too early for Wawatam to return, and it was obvious now that there was more than one person.

He knew he shouldn't move, but he also knew if whoever it was entered the cave, there would be no avenue of escape. Crawling as slowly and noiselessly as possible on his belly, he reached the cave entrance and peered out into the darkness.

The panting, struggling sounds of at least two people were closing in. A small patch of moonlight cut through the trees in the general direction of the sounds, and he hoped whoever it was would pass through that light when they reached the top of the hill so he could catch a glimpse of them.

His wish was granted. The first figure stepped directly into the lunar spotlight and at first Henry thought he was an Englishman. He was dressed in pantaloons and stockings and a ruffled shirt similar to his own. . . . Only then did he realize the clothes *were* his own! The Ojibway haircut and bare feet could only mean one thing—it was Sans-père.

Henry searched the ground around him for any kind of weapon, and his hand closed around one of the rock-things. It would have to do. He watched in silence as Sans-père assisted the person behind him into the patch of moonlight.

Henry gasped as he said her name aloud: "Lo-tah!" Both intruders turned toward the sound of his voice. He jumped up and ran toward them, out of the darkness, his weapon held high in a striking position.

When Lo-tah recognized who the assailant was, she rushed to him and threw her arms around him. "Hen-ree, Hen-ree," she cried. Tears streamed down her lovely face. She covered him with kisses and laughed and cried alternately in the ecstasy of hope fulfilled. He returned her embraces, but kept an eye on Sans-père who had not moved.

"I love you, Hen-ree," she whispered. "I feared so much that you had been killed." She broke into tears then and Alexander lost all comprehension of the world except her. He dropped the rock-thing and held her close, kissing her forehead and whispering, "Sh-sh, it's all right. Be quiet now. Oh sweet Lo-tah! Thank God you are here!"

Her little body shivered against his and he held her closer. She raised her face to his, looked deeply into his tear-filled eyes, and kissed him with unbridled passion.

Moments later, Lo-tah turned and pulled Henry by the hand toward Sans-père who still had not moved. The Indian stood there so casually that Alexander began to relax somewhat and when Lo-tah introduced him as her brother, Henry began to understand that he was no longer an enemy.

The three of them sat outside the cave for over an hour, explaining their separate adventures and Sans-père's sudden change of heart.

Henry watched his wife adoringly as she related what had transpired since she had walked out the door of their cabin only a few days ago.

She had carried the bundle down a path through the forest in the back of the fort to a stream where she had become accustomed to washing her laundry since she had moved inside the 'stickhouse' with her husband.

When she had finished cleaning, she hung the clothes on branches to dry and had amused herself by picking strawberries and bathing in the stream. It was late afternoon before she came to the open field behind Ezekial Solomon's cabin, and she recognized immediately that something was very wrong. She saw the turkey vultures hovering in the air and the bright, red, coats of British soldiers lying on the ground in front of the land gate. The tracks of hundreds of moccasined feet in the field was all the evidence she needed to know that her nightmare had come true. Her first instinct was to rush to her home and find her husband. But a sixth sense told her that Alexander was somehow still living and that the situation there now represented extreme danger to herself and her unborn child.

She went back into the forest a mile or two and constructed a small camp for herself near the stream where she had spent the day, using the laundry to keep herself warm. She built a small wigwam of saplings and bark, and subsisted on berries and small fish and frogs that she managed to capture by the stream.

Every day she returned to the edge of the forest behind Solomon's cabin and watched to see if she could see any sign of Alexander or find any clue which would tell of his fate. She could discover nothing, but she continued to try. Several times she had an almost overwhelming urge to run to the fort and shout his name, but again, her instincts kept her away.

The afternoon of this day, she told Alexander, Sans-père had found her. At first, when he walked into her little camp, she was terrified and ran. But Sans-père caught her and as soon as he began to talk, she could tell that he had changed. He called her sister. He explained how they were related, pretty much as Henry had heard Constante explain it to him. He said he was through with Wenniway and his falsehoods and he had come to take her to find her husband, his brother-in-law.

Trusting him, she followed as he led her to the fort. She did not hesitate at the field, but put her faith in her new brother implicitly.

When they arrived at the fort, they discovered that all the *Anglais* prisoners were gone and the Canadians were gathered for the funeral of Augustin Langlade.

Henry was saddened by this news. He had always liked the old man, in spite of his drunkenness. He had been a regular purchaser of rum and Henry had always extended him considerable credit. He had always seemed so melancholy. Now he was dead.

Lo-tah further explained that she and Sans-père had entered the fort right at the moment of Père Du Jaunay's collapse. Henry interrupted her to gain a more definitive description of the fate of the priest, and when he found out that he also was dead, Henry was truly grieved. The merchant recalled how the noble cleric had stood with them against the Ottawa when Henry had first arrived at Michilimackinac and how he had stood in the middle of the parade ground during the butchery of a few days ago, valiantly trying to preserve life.

The priest had believed good works, combined with faith in Jesus Christ, could salvage one's soul. If that were true, Henry was convinced that Du Jaunay was definitely in paradise.

Lo-tah continued her narrative after Alexander's questions about the Jesuit, by relating that she and Sans-père had sat down with Constante and François, Laurent Du Charme and Marguerite, and tried to determine the whereabouts of Henry, Solomon, and the other British captives. They knew nothing, but suggested that they all go to see Monsieur Langlade who probably would.

Much to their surprise, Charles Langlade readily told them that La Fourche had informed him that Henry and some soldiers were on the island of Michilimackinac and the others had been taken by the Ottawa and, he assumed, were on their way to Montreal to be ransomed. He did not know whether those prisoners still on the island were alive, but he supposed so. He wished them a cordial *bon soir,* and shut the door on them.

At that point, Sans-père offered to take Lo-tah by canoe to the island. Du Charme and Cardin had both insisted that they be allowed to go along, but Sans-père would not hear of it, petitioning his mother to convince her husband and Du Charme that his was the wisest choice. The Anishnabeg would be in a foul mood after losing half their captives and part of their booty, and there would be no guarantee of safety, even for a Canadian. In the end, with Constante's support, Sans-père's point of view won the day and immediately after a small meal and a short rest, the two had departed in a canoe, arriving on the island after dark, less than an hour ago.

In a stroke of incredible luck, Wawatam, after leaving Henry and descending the hill, had seen the little vessel pulled ashore and had gone to investigate. It was he who had directed them to the cave where they had been reunited with Henry.

When Lo-tah had finished this discourse, Henry fired question upon question at the two of them. He wanted to know of the condition of his child and Lo-tah, beaming happily, announced that all was well. She was even beginning to show, in spite of her meagre diet.

Henry wanted to know more about Sans-père's sudden amity. He explained that he had been completely moved by his mother's explanation of his conception, and her wonderful expression of love for him. He had run away and secluded himself for awhile and came to believe that the *oquis,* or devils, had been leading him away from his real family. He had even, proudly, changed his name. From now, he said, he would be called 'Constante-fils,' which meant that he was both 'Constante's son' and a constant son. No longer would he be the 'without father man.' He had an identity. "I have a sister too," he said in shaky, emotional tones as he clasped Lo-tah's hand, "and a brother." He grabbed Henry's hand also and tears drifted down his face. Henry squeezed his hand tightly, letting him know that the new relationship was entirely acceptable to him.

"I now give you back your clothes," Constante-fils said, and began to strip off Henry's confiscated apparel.

Alexander stopped him. "No," he said. "They are yours. Keep them as a token of my devotion to my new brother-in-law."

Constante-fils broke into tears again. Henry believed he had never seen anyone quite so happy.

"What of Wenniway?" Henry asked after the young Chippewa had composed himself.

"He is no longer my friend," he replied. "I have told him this and he hates me for it, but he raped my mother and he hates my new brother and sister. He knows that all men must follow a stream of blood."[1]

---

[1] A Chippewa expression which means essentially, 'Blood runs thicker than water.'

When Henry's curiosity had been satisfied, it was his turn to explain all that had happened to him in the last few days, culminating his story with the demand of 'Le Grand Sable' for the slaughter of the captives and the cannibalistic feast that ensued. It shocked Henry that neither Lo-tah nor her new brother expressed any surprise or contempt at such unbridled savagery. He could only assume that exposure to it had innured them to civilized compassion.

When Henry had finished talking, Sans-père, *né* Constante-fils, got up and told his sister and her husband that he was going to go down the hill to the village. It was necessary, he said, to establish his new identity with his tribesmen, and he wanted to explain to Matchekewis why he had changed. He was anxious to find out how his other friend would react and if he, like Wenniway, would shun him for his new allegiance to Henry and Lo-tah. He knew he could forgive the mad chief's misuse of his mother, but he must accept her.

Promising to return at daybreak, he began his descent down the steep slope, watched by Lo-tah and Henry, unaware that a third pair of eyes followed him.

🦅 🦅 🦅

Wenniway had seen Wawatam when he came back from the cave and knew that he had taken Henry out of the village to protect him.

He had followed the *shaman* back to the beach where he witnessed the arrival of Lo-tah and Sans-père from the dense underbrush which skirted the sandy shoreline. When Wawatam had left the new arrivals, Wenniway had followed them to the cave and watched in disgust as they expressed their affection for one another. These three had destroyed him, and he was bent on their destruction.

Lo-tah had jilted him. She had refused his bride price years ago and convinced Tcianung to do the same. Then she had married the *Anglais,* guided by her silly visions and ridiculous mysticism.

The *Anglais* had stolen his woman, and to add to the insult had pointed out his lies to his father so that he had lost his place at council. Henry had escaped time after time. This time, there would be no escape.

And Sans-père, that son of a whore, had betrayed him and now conspired with his enemies, calling them 'brother' and 'sister.' The bastard would pay, like the rest.

As Sans-père began his descent down the slope toward the lights of the Anishnabeg camp, Wenniway fell in step behind him, concealed by the thick forest. As they reached the small ledge-clearing that Henry and Wawatam had passed earlier, Constante-fils paused in the moonlight and bent down to study the soft ground along the precipice which fell to the trees below.

The young man studied the tracks of Wawatam and Henry, then Lo-tah and his own. They were very clear in the moist soil. What had caused him to stop however, was the presence of a fifth set of footprints. Matchekewis had always told him that whenever you encounter something unexpected or unusual, turn around and protect your back. Constante-fils started to do so now, but too late.

Wenniway's tomahawk caught him directly in the nape of his neck, opening a red maw and exposing his spinal column. The maniacal butcher pulled it free and brought it down a second time between the victim's shoulderblades, where it lodged. With the hatchet still buried in the flesh of his former ally, Wenniway brought his left hand around and stabbed the hapless youth repeatedly in the lower back with a wicked-looking knife that had been a gift from a friend whose name was once Sans-père.

Since the victim's spinal cord had been severed immediately, the cry that started in his brain had been interrupted in transmission and lost the channel leading to his mouth. Thus, he died in relative silence and his 'brother' and 'sister' only a few hundred yards above him, knew nothing of his fate.

Wenniway struggled for several moments, trying to pull his tomahawk from the corpse. he finally had to put his foot on the body of Constante-fils and pull with both hands in a kind of jerking motion before it would rip loose. He kicked the cadaver contemptuously and it tumbled over the cliff's edge, pummeling into the trees below.

He turned back out of the moonlight then and into the forest trees, reascending the slope until he had returned to the area near the cave. When he looked toward its entrance, he saw that the other two objects of his vengenace had disappeared. He guessed that they had gone inside and his face turned to a bitter grimace as he guessed what they might be doing. He settled down to wait.

Inside, Henry lay on the stone floor of the chamber and Lo-tah snuggled next to him, her head resting securely in the crook of his arm.

They talked softly in the blackness of the cave, content for the first time in several days. Their major concern now was Henry's release from captivity. Wawatam had promised to return in the morning and would have to take Alexander back to the Anishnabeg camp, where he would resume his status as a pris-oner, the only Englishman still alive in the entire area of the straits. What would Minavavana decide then? He didn't have any idea.

How would the 'Grand Saulteur' react to Lo-tah's presence? Henry didn't want to think about it. They discussed their options through the remnant of night. Should they go to the canoe now and attempt flight to the Sault de Ste. Marie, a small settlement some sixty miles to the north? Henry didn't think so. They would almost certainly be spotted by the Anishnabeg on the open lake, and what of Sans-père and Wawatam? They could not just leave them without some explanation. They could try to get back to the fort and seek shelter among their friends. But they had an enemy there also in Langlade, and Henry feared that they would bring the Chippewa's rough justice upon their French allies if they sought their aid.

It seemed that the only viable option was for Henry to see what the Chippewa judgment would be. But he did not want to wait for Wawatam or Sans-père to return. He was very nervous about Lo-tah being discovered by Wenniway or Matchekewis if a delegation came with Wawatam in the morning.

As the first grey light of dawn began to dispel the blackness around them, Alexander determined that he would walk down to the village and, with Wawatam's assistance, plead for his freedom to Minavavana. Lo-tah agreed to wait for him there, but vowed in spite of his protestations, that if he had not come back to her by the time the sun was high in the sky, she would follow. As much as he tried, she could not be dissuaded, and so he promised himself that nothing short of death would keep him from returning.

As he got up to leave, the sun peeped over the horizon. Its bright beams shot across the water and the tops of the trees, illuminating the cave. For the first time, Henry saw clearly the interior of the place where he had spent the night and he shuddered. Littered about the floor, and piled against the back wall in careless disorder were two to three hundred human skulls! Various other bones also littered the floor, but the vast majority of the skeletal remains were heads. These were the rock-things he had kicked, used for a pillow, and had intended to use for a weapon.

Although this ghoulish collection shocked him somewhat, it did not surprise him or even repel him, and he suspected that he had seen so much horror that he, too, was becoming insensitive.

Lo-tah looked about her fearfully and quickly moved outside of the cave looking very much as if she had seen a ghost.

Henry followed her. "What is it?" he asked.

She kept staring nervously back at the cave entrance. "It is the Cave of Skulls," she said grimly.

"I know it's a bit gruesome, but . . ."

"No, no," she interrupted. "You don't understand. When a very great enemy is slain by the Anishnabeg, he is decapitated and his head is put in here, separate from his body. The dead man's headless ghost then wanders about looking for it. It is forbidden for anyone to come here. It is taboo."

Henry smiled at her innocent *naïveté*. "You are a Christian now, Lo-tah, such legends are not for you. Besides, it is Wawatam, a *shaman*, who brought me here and he was not afraid."

"You are not Anishnabeg," she said. Her lower lip jutted into the pout which had first endeared her to Henry. "Wawatam is Ottawa. No Anishnabeg has ever been inside here—until now. I did not even know that it existed for certain. It has been desecrated by me. It is a bad, bad omen."

Henry had to remind her several times of her new faith, and that adherence to such superstition was blasphemous before she would calm down. But in no way would she enter the cave again.

She seated herself on the ground several feet away from its entrance and begged her husband to return quickly. Henry leaned over her, held her delicately feminine face in his hands, and kissed her tenderly. "I'll be back shortly with Wawatam and Sans-père."

"Constante-fils," she corrected.

"I won't be long," he promised.

She put her arms around his legs as if to prevent him from leaving, hugged him tightly, and reluctantly let him go.

He started down the slope and as he glanced back, he saw that Lo-tah was still watching him. Though she was smiling, he knew that it was a mask to hide her real feelings.

Something told him to go back, to sit and wait for Wawatam's return, but he felt that the issue must be forced and he had a terrible, driving need to end the suspense concerning his fate. He had lived on the edge of death for almost a week, and he wanted it to be over. He was convinced intellectually that she would be safe and he had no reason to feel any insecurity in that regard. But, that creeping feeling would not leave him.

In the end, reason won the battle with emotion, and he moved slowly down the hill. A few yards to his left, laying on his belly, and concealed among the ferns, Wenniway watched him go. His eyes then focused on Lo-tah, leering from his blood-spattered face. She was sitting by herself, unprotected, and glancing nervously about. He looked back at the *Anglais* and for a moment frowned deeply when the merchant suddenly turned and started back up the hill. But, Henry paused again, shook his head as if to scold himself for his silly suspicions, and continued his descent to the Anishnabeg camp. It was, perhaps, that same 'something' that made Wenniway stand up after the *Anglais* had departed, and head toward the cave.

🗿 🗿 🗿

As soon as her husband had left, Lo-tah assumed the posture of the penitent that the priest had taught her, put her hand around the little crucifix at her neck, and prayed to Sainte Anne and the Lord Jesus to keep away dread spirits and bring her husband back to her safely and soon.

She was afraid, and she begged forgiveness for her sins and wished that the priest were there to give her penance and absolution. Thus absorbed in her meditation and petitions for protection from spiritual evil, she did not notice the physical devil who was rapidly approaching in sinister silence.

Henry had made his way down the steep hill to within a hundred yards of the Chippewa camp. It was no surprise to him that it was easier to negotiate the hill in the daylight than to climb it in the dark.

When he reached the bottom, he could see Soutache's wigwam about fifty feet in the distance through a stand of birches. The hole in the back had been patched already and sealed with 'wattap.'

The black flies and mosquitoes he had aroused in his scattering of vegetation during his short journey, now were plaguing him to such an extent that he stopped to exact a measure of vengeance upon them.

Realizing that he was fighting a losing battle from sheer numerical superiority, he took a deep breath and was about to continue to camp to try and find Wawatam, when his foot stubbed something soft.

His initial reaction was that he had bumped into a large mushroom of some sort. His bare feet told him that it had that consistency, cold and clammy, but did not give quite as easily. When he looked down, he saw a single, human foot. He pulled back the other dense ferns which were the natural cover to the forest floor and was appalled to find that the foot belonged to a leg that was clothed in brown, English pantaloons.

At first, he feared that it might be the remains of one of 'Le Grand Sable's victims until he recognized the clothing as his own. As he spread the vegetation apart, he knew that the corpse was Sans-père. His other leg was curled beneath him, and he was lying face-down in the damp earth. Henry's shirt, a gift that had brought tears to the young Chippewa's eyes only a few moments earlier, was in tatters and badly stained with blood. Henry felt for a pulse, but knew he would not find one. The wounds were too severe.

The attack on Henry's unfortunate brother-in-law had been swift, cowardly, and vicious. Alexander turned the body so he could see the face and touched the poor victim's cheek. "Be at peace, Constante-fils," he whispered, and closed the open, vacant, eyes.

As he stood up, he looked out at the water and blue sky beyond the village and puzzled over the violence of such a beautiful world. There was such a contrast in the sparkling sunshine radiating through the blue-green forest and the bloody, fly-covered corpse at his feet. Such incompatibility befuddled him and the simple answer, that God had created one, while man had created the other, eluded him.

When he reached the village, Wawatam was just emerging from the wigwam of his pupil. When he related the story of the murder of Sans-père to his Ottawa brother, they went immediately to find Minavavana. They discovered him sitting outside his own lodge, in some sort of consultation with Matchekewis. 'Le Grand Sable' had departed earlier in the morning at first light, completely satisfied that the spirits of those Indians slain by the English at *D'étroit* had been appeased.

The two Chippewa chiefs were discussing the events of the past few days and planning how to deal with the inevitable British retaliation when they were interrupted by Wawatam who told them of Sans-père's murder. Matchekewis glared at Henry. The last time the merchant had been this close to him, the chief of the *Che-boy-gan* Chippewa had been prepared to run a knife through his throat. Henry's hand went unconsciously to his neck.

Minavavana stood up and immediately blamed Wawatam for allowing the *Anglais* enough freedom to have committed such an atrocity.

Wawatam answered that his English brother had not committed this foul crime but he personally believed that Wenniway was responsible.

Minavavana told the shaman that his association with the

Anglais had confused his mind *and* his loyalties. Matchekewis, always a true friend to both Wenniway and Sans-père, vowed that he would disembowel Henry and throw his entrails to the dogs.

The merchant ignored these threats and asked to be confronted with the man Wawatam was accusing. When Minavavana sent for his son, the young lad who acted as messenger returned to reveal that Wenniway was nowhere to be found in the camp.

Immediately, Henry thought of Lo-tah, alone, at Skull Cave. His heart leapt to his throat. He had disobeyed his instincts again. Minavavana said that he wanted to see the body of Sans-père and Henry was happy to oblige, since it allowed him to get that much closer to where Lo-tah waited for him. His anxiety was unimaginable and he almost raced to the spot.

Close examination of the body of his friend by Matchekewis revealed an expression of surprise, followed by a violent cry. He had seen the knife wounds and they could have been made only by the unusually jagged blade of the knife that Wenniway had so often proudly displayed to him.

"It was Wenniway," he said sadly.

Henry did not wait to see Minavavana's reaction. He was running toward Skull Cave.

Chapter

8

Arch Rock

Wenniway was cautious in approaching Lo-tah. He came up from behind her with incredible stealth and his luck held. She did not turn around. He didn't know that she was so absorbed in her prayers that she probably would not have heard him if he had been shooting off a musket or shouting warning.

When he was standing directly behind her, he grabbed her beautiful, silken hair and yanked her backward, pulling her quickly into the world of reality. She did not scream, but tried to struggle to her feet to ward off her assailant. This option, she quickly discovered, was not possible, since he was dragging her across the ground toward the cave. The nerves in her head were screaming for relief from the painful pressure and her eyes bulged from their sockets. She pushed her feet and hands against the ground in a kind of an awkward reverse crawl in an attempt to alleviate the pain, but he simply pulled faster and harder.

Reaching back with her hands, she was able to grab Wenniway's arm and this, finally, gave her some measure of relief. He even released his grip and allowed her to scramble to her feet, her scalp tingling.

She tried to run, but he clutched her wrist and pulled her back. She whirled around to strike out at him, but his fist came smashing into her jaw below her left cheek, bruising the tissue and knocking two teeth from their roots.

The intensity of the blow actually turned her completely around before she collapsed on the ground, temporarily stunned and blood pouring from the corner of her mouth.

"Now I will take what has always been rightfully mine," he growled.

He pulled her to her feet and ripped the doeskin dress until he had pulled it down over her breasts. She clutched instinctively at her garments, in a pathetic attempt at propriety. He kissed her roughly on her neck, and bit her shoulder. When she struggled in her revulsion, he slapped her hard across the face with his open hand, causing the flesh to explode in searing agony.

He pushed her violently to the ground again, in the same instant releasing the knot in the cord which held his loincloth in place.

Naked, he jumped on top of her and pulled the bottom of her dress upward, forcing it over her hips. She had stopped struggling. He had knocked the wind from her when he landed on her, but worse than that, she felt something go wrong inside of her. As she struggled to regain her breath, she was sure that her baby, once growing peacefully in her womb, had been injured badly.

In a fit of anger and resentment, she flailed at Wenniway's head with her delicate hands and brought her knee up hard into his groin.

"Argh-g-g," he shouted and instinctively curled up in reaction to the cramping, shooting pain in his testicles. She rolled out from under him, stood up, and kicked him square in the face. However, her soft moccasin and petite foot inflicted little damage. She felt heavy moisture between her legs, and she knew she was bleeding badly.

She looked around for some sort of weapon and in that instant, he was up and upon her again.

He struck her repeatedly in the face with his fists, dislodging two more teeth and breaking her nose. But she continued to struggle. Her mind was stunned, confused, mortified and traumatized, but over it all, Alexander Henry dominated her fading consciousness and as long as she could see that well-loved face, she would fight.

Wenniway's pounding fists, however, finally took their toll. A final punch drove her to the ground and she lay motionless.

Since she could not protect herself anymore, her brain, reacting to violent injury, overrode her emotions and shut down, commanding her into darkness and oblivion.

Determination and character rebelled against this oblivion, however protective, and unconsciousness gave way to her martial spirit only a few moments later. Her eyes focused slowly on the ugly face of Wenniway only inches from her own. His breath stank of stale rum. She felt nothing, but she knew that she was being raped. The hideous devil had his dull eyes closed in psychopathic ecstasy and he was pushing at her like a rutting boar.

She didn't cry or slip into hysteria, but became as inert and cold as stone, waiting for the animal to get off of her. He shuddered wildly, then gradually rolled away and got to his feet. She watched him through one eye (the other was swollen shut), as he pulled on his breechclout and adjusted it.

He smiled at her triumphantly and, for an instant, even lovingly she thought, before he drew his knife. "You are a married squaw, a *noko,* and you have now betrayed your husband."

"*I* have betrayed no one, Wenniway." That he should blame her as an adulteress she thought as absurd as the little whistle added to her speech by the absence of one of her front teeth. "*You* have betrayed the Anishnabeg," she retorted. "No people would ever want to claim someone so weak and pathetic. Minavavana, my uncle, must live with great shame!"

At the mention of his father's name, Wenniway rushed at her. She tried to get to her feet, but he struck her down again with his fist. He sat on her chest and put a knee on each arm so that she was pinned to the ground. Her legs flailed in the air behind him, but accomplished nothing.

With his left hand, he grabbed a handful of her blood-soaked hair to hold her head steady. She knew what he intended. It was the common punishment for a *noko* who has cheated her husband and she tried to move her head away from the knife, but he held her too tightly.

Wenniway sat there for a moment, enjoying his triumph. He looked at the swollen, bruised face and grinned in satisfaction.

At that exact instant, he heard the sound of rolling gravel and desperate breathing, and he looked to his left. Two hundred yards below, struggling up the hill like a man possessed, was Alexander Henry, followed closely by Wawatam, Matchekewis, and about a dozen warriors.

He looked back down at the battered, bloody, face between his knees and made his decision. He brought the sharp blade to the bridge of her nose, the razor edge pressing downward toward her chin. "You have grown ugly, Lo-tah," he said, "but bruises will heal. The unfaithful *noko* must be permanently ugly so that no man will ever want to touch her again."

He pulled the blade forcefully toward him, amputating her nose. For the first time since he had attacked her, she screamed, and Wenniway, his vengeance two thirds complete, jumped from his victim and fled down an opposite slope, away from the approaching party of his tribesmen.

Lo-tah writhed on the ground in pain, blood spurting from the hole where her nose had been. She was choking in it.

Fifty feet below her and rapidly completing his ascent, Henry called out her name. His voice had a kind of desperate note to it and it shook with fear.

When she realized that he was coming and was so very near by the sound of his voice, she forced the agony of her pain aside and stood up. She clamped one dirty hand over her wounded face to arrest the flow of blood, then she turned and ran.

As she climbed the hill directly behind the cave, the remnant of her sanity forced her to think. She realized that Wenniway, though he had not stopped her heart, had killed her.

Her baby, she was certain, was dead. The scarlet stream running down her leg was sufficient evidence of that. She had been violated, and though it was no fault of her own, and Hen-ree would not condemn her, their relationship would suffer from it.

She had been horribly disfigured, and though she had done nothing to deserve it and Hen-ree would say it meant nothing to him, it would not be pleasant to kiss and caress such repulsive deformity. And when she was old, and the story of how this horrible thing happened had faded into the past, her people would look at her and whisper, "adulteress."

All of these thoughts flashed before her in an instant and she knew she could never have Alexander again. Without that, she believed, death was preferable and she wished it. Wenniway had been successful.

She knew she could not let Alexander see her this way, and so she climbed, higher and higher toward the summit of the island, refusing to listen to his desperate pleading for her to stop. She knew where she was going.

Henry would have caught up to her but for the fact that he slipped on a rock which his weight had pried loose from its moorings and he tumbled down the hill for about forty or fifty feet before he could grab a small sapling to break his fall. When he scrambled to his feet to continue his pursuit, he realized that his ankle had been badly twisted and he was hobbled.

He had seen Wenniway at the top of the ledge running and he had seen her begin to climb in the opposite direction. His mind was a mass of confused imaginings and grotesque pictures. He shouted to her again and she stopped. She seemed to be holding one hand up to her face for some reason, but she did not turn around and continued to climb.

As he forced his painful ankle to function and pursued her again, only Wawatam followed. Matchekewis and the other Chippewa ran off in pursuit of Wenniway.

Henry followed Lo-tah as quickly as he could and continued to call out her name, but she disappeared among the trees growing in thick masses on the hillside. He would have lost track of her altogether had it not been for Wawatam who followed her bloody trail and helped him to limp along it.

After twenty minutes of arduous labor, Wawatam and the frantic Englishman emerged from the trees. The *shaman* made him halt and pointed to an area several hundred feet above them.

Henry saw two massive rock formations which were joined together by a natural bridge of rock which had been formed by thousands of years of erosion. The blue sky shown below this arch and crawling along the surface of it was Lo-tah!

Henry swallowed hard and wanted to shout at her, but he was afraid he would startle her and cause her to fall. He did not want to think about how far a fall that would be or what lay underneath.

Oblivious of his throbbing, swollen ankle, he ran up the side of the cliff face struggling like a madman and murmuring; "Dear God, oh please, dear God!"

When he finally caught up to her, Lo-tah was kneeling at the top of the arch. Her back was turned to him, her hand was still at her face, and he could hear her praying.

She knew he was there, but she would not turn around. He approached her cautiously. One sudden movement either way would send her to her death since the arch over the chasm was only about three feet wide. It seemed as if a strong wind would blow her small frame from its tenuous perch.

When Henry looked below, his fear increased. Hundreds of feet down was the rocky shoreline of the back of the island which Alexander had never seen. No one could survive such a fall.

He stood at the edge of the arch and stepped forward, intending to crawl out on the bridge and retrieve the only meaning to his life and return her to safety.

But as he did so, Lo-tah, aware of his closeness, stood up. "Stay away," she warned through whistling teeth. It was not so much a command as a threat. The tone was soft, yet ominously serious, and Alexander's frightened senses told him that the voice of his love had changed. Not only was it hard and demanding, but it sounded muffled, unreal and nasal.

He halted. He did not like the sound of that voice. It was too earnest, too set in determination. His fear increased. In her present standing position, a slight breeze would push her over the precipice.

"Lo-tah, please," he begged.

"Lo-tah is dead," the strange voice said. "Go away."

"Lo-tah, our child . . . I love you so, please, *please!*" He began to cry, but she did not respond.

Wawatam, who had been standing behind Henry, had moved back into the woods to try and circle to the other side in an attempt to help. But there was no other way across the chasm except by the arch, so he returned to his friend.

Henry continued his pleas hoping that whatever had forced her to this decision could be overcome. "Lo-tah, I love you. Come down from there. By all that is holy, I swear I cannot exist without you. You *know* that. What are you doing? Think of the baby . . . ."

That eerie, unfamiliar voice broke silence again. "The child is dead and so am I. If you love me you must go away."

"But why? Why?"

As he watched her, she turned very slowly, appearing to be oblivious or apathetic about the precarious danger of her position. She looked straight at him and removed her hand from her face.

What Henry saw would never be forgotten. The sight would torture his thoughts and dreams for the rest of his life and he would always regret that he had forced her to it.

She was unrecognizable. The left side of her face was a reddish purple and so swollen out of proportion to the right side that it looked as if she had two heads. The left eye was completely closed. He could see that her front teeth were missing and where her nose had been was a grisly hole where white cartilege was barely discernible in a sea of blood.

Blood was everywhere. Her hair was matted with it. It soaked her torn, doeskin dress. It still ran down the inside of her legs and formed little pools on the rock under her feet.

When Lo-tah looked at Henry through her one misty eye, she found confirmation of her fears. On his face was such a look of revulsion and horror that she knew she had been right. But the worst emotion she found in the face she so adored, was pity, and that she could abide even less.

She turned away, and as she did she said; "I love you, Henree." As she adjusted her feet in the narrow confines of the arch's pinnacle, her left foot slipped, perhaps in her own blood, perhaps on a pebble, perhaps on purpose. Alexander would never know.

She fell silently as Henry screamed and watched her float through the air. She looked strangely as if she could fly, she seemed so composed and comfortable, until the rocky shore ended her flight. She had fallen quickly and without a sound, as a fowl shot from the sky.

Henry lay on his stomach where he had fallen, his arms outstretched over the cliff's edge, as if to save her, though he could not possibly have reached her.

He watched the waves break softly over her shattered corpse through eyes that would be eternally moist at every thought of her and every mention of her name. "Lo-tah, oh God. Oh, Lord Jesus, Lo-tah!"

He tore his eyes away from her corpse and looked out across the deep, blue waters of Michilimackinac at the amethyst sky. The cottony clouds hung low across the horizon and three of them seemed to take shape as he watched. The center one was an almost perfect outline of a long-haired, bearded man dressed in an ankle-length robe. The one to the right looked like a priest with its long gown and clerical collar. The third was an Indian woman whose outline reminded him of Lo-tah as probably everything would for the remainder of his life. As he watched through misty eyes, the clouds dispersed and blended with the others.

He stood up and tried to jump from the cliff to her billowy image, but Wawatam grabbed him and pulled him away from the edge. Henry struggled for a moment, then threw his arms around the big *shaman* and sobbed in deep, heaving gasps of grief. When he finally turned around again, all the clouds were gone.

🦋 🦋 🦋

WAWATAM STOOD WITH HENRY by the cliff's edge for quite some time while the *Anglais* gave up any thoughts of composure and cried pitifully. At last, Alexander pulled away from him and murmured a single word: "Wenniway!" Wawatam had seen death at work and he was not unacquainted with hatred, but the look in Henry's eyes scared him. It was one of possession—and obsession.

As the merchant began to limp down the hill, Wawatam followed. Henry marched on the injured ankle as if it didn't exist and struck at tree branches and bushes as he went down as if abusing them would somehow help to appease his anger and grief.

What Wawatam didn't know was that two emotions were battling for supremacy in Alexander's heart and hate was winning.

Hatred of Wenniway and lust for revenge helped to drive other heart-rending emotions away. It was so easy, so comforting to hate. It blinded even grief.

Three times Henry's ankle gave out and he tumbled down the hill, banging against rocks and trees as he went. But each time when he rolled to a stop, he got up and continued without complaint or exclamation, shrugging off any assistance from the bewildered Wawatam.

Henry did not know or care that his Ottawa friend had lost his wife and baby to smallpox, that he knew the enemy, Grief. No one had ever felt this bitter, he was certain, nor would anyone ever have such justification to kill.

As they passed skull cave, Henry stopped in front of the fast-drying blood and picked up a tuft of long, black silky hair which had belonged to Lo-tah and one of her moccasins which had fallen from her foot in the course of her struggle. He held the battered footwear to his face as if it were a beloved relic which would somehow commute his sentence of purgatorial grief.

Then, cursing the return of that expiatory limbo, he plunged back into his private hell of hate and resumed his frantic pace down the escarpment.

Years later, he would say that that short journey in which he was consumed by vengeance, had saved his life because it gave him a physical release to the injustice, hypocrisy and cruelty of the world. Wawatam knew it now, and let him go, though he continued to follow within sight of his brother.

They reached the Anishnabeg camp very quickly and Henry plunged into its center, thoughtless of his own safety. The game of prisoner and master, slavery and freedom, death and life, meant nothing to him now. Hate had afforded him two gifts; temporary surcease from sorrow, and the complete freedom of a desperate man who fears nothing.

When he saw Wenniway standing next to Matchekewis and Minavavana at the far end of the camp, he strode deliberately toward them, weaponless and still dressed in the loincloth that had once belonged to Sans-père and the breeches and buckskin jacket from Soutache. Wenniway grinned confidently, but wiped his sweating palms on his breech-clout, stained with Lo-tah's blood.

As Henry stormed toward them, Minavavana reached over and pulled Wenniway's knife from his belt and with his other arm pushed Wenniway forward.

From the expression on the son's face, Wawatam could see as he entered the camp circle that this was entirely unexpected. Wenniway had assumed that his father, as always, would protect him. But he had committed the unpardonable crime in Chippewa culture—fratricide. The 'Grand Saulteur' shoved him, defenseless, toward his enemy.

Wenniway turned to look at Matchekewis, perhaps expecting his assistance, but the mad eyes of the Chippewa chief stared through him like cold, pitiless, steel.

He whirled around to face his enemy, hoping to fend him off in an even fight. But Wenniway was afraid to die or to be hurt, and Henry didn't care about either. The Chippewa was motivated by self-preservation, the merchant, by hate. It was no contest.

Henry attacked him like a tornado assaulting a fly. In a wild series of blows, he drove Wenniway to the dirt, breaking his nose and sending him sprawling. When the Indian did not get up, Alexander kicked him viciously in the ribs and jammed his other foot into Wenniway's groin. Minavavana watched impassively.

The murderer howled in pain and scrambled through the dust. In a frantic effort to escape, he crawled to his father and grabbed his knee. Minavavana looked straight ahead, the expression on his face was the same as if he had some sort of sluggish leech attached to his leg instead of his son. It was an expression of total revulsion.

Before Wenniway could stand up, Henry kicked him again and struck him so hard on the back of his head that he spread-eagled, face down in the dirt.

In the moment that it took the killer to turn over, Henry was on him. He sat on his chest and pounded his face until it began to resemble raw meat. Wenniway pleaded for Henry to stop. Alexander was so taken aback by these cries for mercy that he actually did halt and stared at the bloody countenance below him.

Wenniway, whining and crying for mercy, lay right at Minavavana's feet. The 'Grand Saulteur' still holding his son's knife, handed it to Henry. Wenniway's eyes grew wide in horror and disbelief.

Alexander took the knife and raised it to strike. But as he looked at the stupid, whining, coward, he began to realize that hate was not going to triumph in him and that he would be saddled with terrible grief the rest of his life. He decided in that moment that he would not add guilt to it.

He stood up and handed the knife back to Minavavana who accepted it with combined feelings of gratitude and regret.

Wenniway smiled wickedly and slowly realized that he would have yet another opportunity to exact vengeance on Henry. But another hand suddenly took the knife from Minavavana's hand and, grabbing Wenniway's hair, pulled back his head and opened another bright, red, wicked smile across the murderer's throat.

It happened so quickly that no one was immediately sure who had done it. Only Wawatam, standing by quietly, had seen it clearly.

As the lifeblood ran from Wenniway's veins, the *shaman* looked at Matchekewis, who stood next to Minavavana. The crazy chief handed the bloody instrument of execution to Minavavana, then reached down and touched Wenniway's dead, battered face, and walked away. The 'Grand Saulteur' stood staring down at the knife in his hand and then at the dead son he had wanted so much to be proud of and had never been able to.

Wenniway's square, otter cap, worn and dirty, once a token of friendship that he sported with such pride, slipped off his head and fell into the dust.

🦫 🦫 🦫

A WEEK LATER, Alexander Henry emerged from the Laurent Du Charme cabin. It was approaching sunset on one of those rare and beautiful days that occur so infrequently in a lifetime of summers.

The air was sweet with the perfume of summer flowers and pine. The temperature, soothed by the breeze from the lake, was ideally comfortable. There was no wind or rain and the setting sun lit up the sky in kaleidoscopic colors.

Marguerite and Laurent followed him from the cabin along with Wawatam. After Wenniway's death, Minavavana had agreed to Wawatam's petition for Henry's freedom and the Ottawa had brought his brother from the island to Fort Michilimackinac where he had lived for the past few days with the Du Charmes. The slow healing of his broken heart and battered psyche had begun, but would never be completed. There would always be terrible, open wounds there or, at best, livid, white scars. Nothing would ever be the same.

During the course of his week's stay, many things had happened. Constante, hearing of the death of her son and Lo-tah, had borne the news with stoic integrity and saintly acceptance. It was, in fact she, who comforted Henry. She had come to the Du Charme cabin each day and prayed with the grieving widower and read to him about the resurrection and the life—something he felt sure was now Lo-tah's. He really did not grieve for her, but for himself, because he did not know how he could live his life without her. Constante, speaking from a position of experience, assured him that he could, and he must. Henry was amazed at her courage in the face of her own terrible grief, but he marveled more at her capacity for love. Her valiant life and example made him feel petty in his own sorrow, and he made a conscious effort to display some backbone and fortitude. But he also knew that displaying and being were two very different things and he would never achieve the latter.

He visited his own cabin, which had been straightened and restored to order as much as possible by Laurent and François, but it bore too many painful memories and he asked Constante to take away anything that Lo-tah had owned and burn it, which directive she obediently performed.

All other possessions he gave away to the Amiots whose large family would become larger now that the boys were men and had married Ottawa women. Two of them would be fathers soon.

He also called upon Charles Langlade, who received him with the stiff formality to which Henry had become accustomed. He offered the Frenchman a large amount of money to purchase the

Pani slave woman who had given him shelter during the attack of the fort and had saved his life. Langlade agreed, under pressure from Charlotte, and when the transaction was completed, Henry gave the happy and grateful squaw permission to leave the straits and return to her own people. As he left the Langlade home, Charlotte looked sorrowfully down at the floor. Her guilt was obvious. He turned and gently said to her: "I forgive you, Madame."

When he passed Charles on his way out the door, he paused. "May *God* forgive you, Monsieur." The Sieur de Langlade did not reply.

Lo-tah's body had been retrieved from her wet and rocky grave by Minavavana who instructed that she be taken to the fort and delivered to Henry. Wawatam, who was constantly in attendance upon his friend, had received the body and Philippe Amiot had built a pine casket for her. She was interred in Christian solemnity next to Père Du Jaunay in Sainte Anne's cemetery with François Cardin conducting the ceremony in the absence of an ordained priest. Before the week was out, another body was put to rest in the same little plot. The wooden grave marker read: 'Constante-fils Cardin, a beloved son.'

Henry, the Du Charmes, and Wawatam passed by the little graveyard at sunset and Alexander looked sadly at the wooden cross that bore the name of 'Lo-tah Henry.'

As they walked through the water gate, Laurent Du Charme tried once more to convince Henry to stay, as he had been doing for the last several days, but to no avail. In spite of his argument that the new British forces would be at the fort any day and that Pon-ti-ac's Conspiracy had failed and the British would now be safe, Henry was adamant. He explained again that he was leaving not out of fear for his physical safety (that meant little to him), but rather he feared the memories he would have to encounter each day.

Wawatam was going with him as far as Lake Nipissing and the mouth of the Fox River which would eventually take Henry to the St. Lawrence and Montreal.

They packed his meagre belongings in the waiting canoe and then Alexander turned and embraced Du Charme. "I will miss you my dear friend," he said. Du Charme's eyes moistened and he hugged the young man vigorously. Henry kissed Marguerite and she blushed. "Take care of *her* grave," he whispered.

He and Wawatam boarded the little craft and pushed out into the dark and smooth lake whose black pines bordered the brilliant orange and violet sky. A loon's haunting cry drifted across the still lake.

On the island of Michilimackinac, on Arch Rock, Minavavana stood against the blazing sky above Skull Cave. He thought of his son and his niece. He thought of the hordes of *Anglais* who would descend upon his homeland. He rubbed his tattooed belly as he watched the tiny canoe glide across the purple waters. It eventually disappeared in the descending darkness. He rode the back of the Great Turtle until the sun was resurrected.

Epilogue

ALEXANDER HENRY did return to Montreal. There he met a woman who eventually became his wife. She gave him several children. He became rich in the fur business, visited the royal courts of England and France, and died in bed at the age of eighty-five.

La Fourche became a British subject and assisted his former enemies against the colonials in the American War for Independence, helping to defeat Daniel Boone and an American force at Blue Licks, Kentucky.

François and Constante Cardin lived out their lives at Fort Michilimackinac. Major Robert Rogers, who became the commander at the Fort, employed Constante to negotiate with the Ottawa at *L'Arbre Croche* and the Chippewa at Cheboygan.

Laurent Du Charme traded furs in Milwaukee and Green Bay, later returning to Michilimackinac where he joined other merchants in establishing a General Store. Typically, he stayed away from the conflict between the British and Americans and refused to join either side.

Minavavana and Matchekewis became allies of the British, the latter fighting alongside General Burgoyne against the Americans at Saratoga. In 1794, he also fought the United States Army at the Battle of Fallen Timbers won by the Americans under the leadership of General 'Mad' Anthony Wayne. He eventually made peace and gave Bois Blanc Island in the Straits of Mackinac to the United States.

George Etherington was ransomed in Montreal by the British government and given a new command. He retired from the army after an unspectacular military career and died in England.

Ezekial Solomon married Elizabeth Du Bois. They had four sons and two daughters. He was one of the investors, with Du Charme, in the General Store, and in 1780, moved to Mackinac Island, where he helped to establish the first white community there and became wealthy in the fur trade.

Charles Langlade fought on behalf of the British in the American Revolution. He moved west and settled near what is now Green Bay. He is known today as the 'Father of Wisconsin.'

It was rumored that the medicine man, Wawatam, became blind and accidentally was burned to death in his lodge at Ottawa Point.

Fort Michilimackinac was burned by the British and the garrison was moved to what is now called Mackinac Island and the stone fortress, Fort Mackinac was constructed. In 1960, the State of Michigan began reconstruction of Fort Michilimackinac. It rests now, on its original site, at the base of the Mackinac Bridge.

Glossary of French Terms and Expressions

Adieu. Farewell.

Agréable. Worthy.

Allons. Let us go.

Ami. Friend.

Andouille. Roll of tobacco.

Anglais. English.

Arrêtez. Stop!

Auberge Du Diable. Tavern of the Devil.

Aubergiste. Tavernkeeper.

Au revoir. Good-bye.

Aussi. Also.

Avoine folle. 'Crazy oats,' a type of wild rice.

À votre santé. To your health!

Bois Blanc. Literally, White Woods, the island adjacent to Mackinac Island, covered with birch trees.

Bon Homme. Good man, jolly good fellow.

Bon jour. Good day, a greeting.

Bonne nuit. Good night.

Bon soir. Good evening, more formal.

Canot du maître. 'Canoe of the master,' a 45-foot-long canoe for carrying large amounts of provisions.

Ça va. Informal greeting, similar to 'hi' or 'how goes it?'

Ceinture flechée. Indian leggings.

Charpentier. Carpenter.

Chèr(e). Dear.

Comment-allez vous? More formal greeting, 'how are you doing?'

Coureurs de bois. Literally, 'woods runners.' Unlicensed French or half-breed fur trappers.

Derrière. Bottom, buttocks.

D'étroit. Of the strait.

Dieu. God.

Enceinte. Pregnant.

Enchanté(e). Charmed.

Enfants terribles. Loosely, juvenile delinquents.

En masse. In large numbers.

Est-ce que vous comprenez? Do you understand?

Et vous? Literally, 'and you?' Loosely, 'How about you?'

Façade. Outward appearance.

Femme. Woman.

Femme grosse. Literally, 'fat woman,' pregnant.

Fenêtre d'étalage. Store front.

Fichu. A type of triangular shawl.

Fille. Daughter.

Fils. Son.

Fleur de lis. Lily flowers on a blue background, the flag of the Bourbon dynasty.

Frère. Brother.

Gauche. Inappropriate.

Gaucherie. Poor behavior.

Gallant. Civilized gentleman.

Gallette et beurre. Butter and milkbread.

Geurs de lard. 'Pork eaters.' Loosely, rookie.

Gourgandine. Prostitute.

Grand Monarch. Great King, an allusion to Louis XIV.

Grand Saulteur. Great Chippewa, an allusion to Minavavana.

Habitants. Inhabitants, settled population.

Isles du Castor. Beaver Island.

Isle du Michili-mackinac. Present day Mackinac Island.

Jabot. A kind of blouse with ruffles and puffed sleeves.

Je. I.

Joie de vivre. Joy of living.

Je t'adore. I adore you.

Lac du Chat. Lake of the Cat, Lake Erie.

La Fourche. The Pitchfork.

Languier. Pig's tongue.

L'Arbre Croche. Literally, 'The Crooked Tree.' Name of an Ottawa village.

L'huile d'ours. Bear fat. Used as an insect repellent.

Ma *(fem.)*. My.

Madame. Mrs.

Mademoiselle. Miss.

Maintenant. Now.

Maison. House.

Mais oui. But yes, of course.

Matelote. A kind of fish stew.

Merci. Thank you.

Mère. Mother.

Mes *(plural)*. My.

Mesdames. Mrs.

Mon *(masc.)*. My.

Monsieur. Mister.

N'est-ce pas? Is it not so?

Nom de guerre. 'Name of war,' nickname.

Non. No.

Par la sambleu! Confound it!

Patois. Broken French.

Pays sauvage. Frontier, back country.

Père. Father.

Petite fleur. Dainty flower.

Poisson blanc. Whitefish.

Que voudriez-vous que j'en ferais? What do you expect me to do?

Raison d'être. Reason for being.

Rivière Grande. Grand River in the southwestern area of the lower peninsula of Michigan.

Rivière Rouge. Red River, or River Rouge, near Detroit.

Rivière Ste. Claire. Ste. Claire River connecting Lakes Erie and Huron.

Rue de Babillarde. Street of Babillarde.

Rue Dauphine. Street of the Dauphine (Daughter of the King).

Rue du Diable. Street of the Devil.

Sacré bleu. A harsh curse.

Salaire. Salary.

Seigneurs. Landed gentry.

S'il vous plaît. If you please.

Soeur. Sister.

Soirée. Party, reception.

Suis. Am.

Tante. Aunt.

Tout est perdu hors l'honneur. All is lost save honor.

Très beau. Very beautiful.

Très bien. Very well.

Va-t'en. Begone, go from this place.

Veuve. Widow.

Voiture. Carriage.

Voyageurs. Travelers. Men who guided people through the wilderness and paddled the canoes, carrying them over portages.

Voyez. Look!

Glossary of Indian Terms

Akewaugeketanso. Loosely, 'Great Warrior.'

Aki. Earth Mother.

Anishnabeg. What the Chippewa called themselves. Also referred to as Ojibway and the Saulteurs.

Asubab. Spool of thread.

Atcab. Arrow.

Asawan. Bowstring.

Au-pet-chi. Robin

Baggitiway. La Crosse.

Bawating. Algonkin word for Sault Ste. Marie, Michigan.

Che-boy-gan. Cheboygan, Michigan, not to be confused with Sheboygan, Wisconsin.

Chick-a-sau. Chickasau Indians.

Erieehronons. Iroquois, 'People of the Panther.'

Gitchi-Man-i-tou. Great Spirit.

Ickigamisigegizis. Maple sugar-making month (April).

Inabandumowin. Dream.

Jessakid. The power to summon spirits.

Ka-be-yun. The West Wind.

Kinabig Man-i-tou. Rattlesnake Spirit.

Kinickinick. Indian tobacco.

Kitchi-Gumee. Lake Superior.

Ktchimokoman. Long knives (Potawatomi expression for Englishmen).

Mag-wah. Bear.

Mas-ke-gon. Muskegon, Michigan.

Masquinoge. Muskellunge.

Me-daw-min. Ruler of the Sky, Sky Spirit.

Mez-he-say. Turkey.

Michi-bou. Great Hare.

Michi-Gaumee. Great Water (Algonkin term for Lake Michigan).

Michi-mak-i-nac. Great Turtle.

Michi-man-i-tou. Spirit of Evil.

Michi-ne-mok-in-ok-ong. Dancing Turtle Spirits.

Midewiwin. Medicine Society of Healers and Seers.

Migis. Cowrie shells.

Nabob. Kettle.

Noko. Wife.

Ododem. Totem, a mark of an Algonkin-speaking clan.

Ogema. Respected leader.

Oqui. Devil, demon.

Out-ou-ais. Ottawa.

Pani. Pawnee.

Pau-guk. Bringer of Death (Similar to the Grim Reaper of European culture).

Penegusan. Medicine bag made of otter skin.

Puk-wudj-in-i-nees. Fairies.

Red-Gee-bis. Sorcerers.

Sac. Sauk, sometimes called Fox.

Saguenaum. Land of the Sauks or Sacs (Saginaw).

Saugunash (Sagonash). English.

Shaman. Medicine Man.

Tenasie. Cherokee. Tennessee.

Tishomingo. Cherokee word for war chief.

Waboyan. Blanket.

Wahkoonun. Black lichen.

Wakama. War leader.

Wampum. Beaded belts used as a medium of exchange.

Warraghiyagey. He-who-does-much (Iroquois name for Sir William Johnson.

We-end. Bringer of Sleep.

Wen-di-goes. Cannibal giants.

List of Historic Persons
In Order of Appearance

La Fourche

Augustin Langlade

Domitilde Langlade

René Bourassa

Jean-Baptiste Amiot

Marie Anne Amiot

Joseph Ainsse

Marie Bourassa

Jean Cuchoise

Ignace Bourassa

Charles Langlade

Wawatam

François Cardin

Père Du Jaunay

Jean-Baptiste Cadotte

Minavavana

Wenniway

Matchekewis

Constante Chevalier

Pon-ti-ac

Okinochumaki

Marie Coussante Ainsse

Joseph Louis Ainsse

Charlotte Bourassa Langlade

La Damoiselle

Le Grand Sable

Pani Slave Woman

Robert Dinwiddie

George Washington

Half-King

Sieur De Marin

Edward Braddock

Laurent Du Charme

Marguerite Amable Metivier Du Charme

Louis le Gardeur de Repentigny

Robert Rogers

Governor Vaudreuil

Intendant Bigot

Marquis de Montcalm de Saint-Veran

William Shirley

Sir William Johnson

William Pitt (The Elder)

Jeffrey Amherst

Gen. James Wolfe

Louis and Pierre Augustin Du Charme

Alexander Henry

Jacques LeFevre

Jacques Parent

Ezekial Solomon

Stanley Goddard

Henry Bostwick

Capt. Henry Balfour

Antoine Amiot

William Tracy

Lt. William Leslie

Lt. Jean (John) Jamet

George Etherington

Henry Gladwin

COMMANDANTS AT FORT MICHILIMACKINAC

Louis Lienard de Beaujeu

Jean-Baptiste-René Legardeur de Repentigny

Pierre-Joseph Celoron Blainville

Louis de La Corne

Jacques Legardeur de Saint-Pierre

François Duplessis-Faber

Louis Lienard de Beaujeu

Charles Michel, Sieur de Langlade

Col. George Etherington

Bibliographical Sources

Armour, David, and Keith Widder. *At the Crossroads: Michili-mackinac During the American Revolution.* Mackinac Island, MI: Mackinac Island State Park Commission, 1978.

Bald, F. Clever. *Michigan in Four Centuries.* New York: Harper and Row, Publishers, Inc., 1954.

Catton, Bruce. *Michigan, A Bicentennial History.* New York: W. W. Norton and Company, Inc., 1976.

Clifton, James, George Cornell, and James McClurken. *People of the Three Fires: The Ottawa, Potawatomi and Ojibway of Michigan.* The Grand Rapids Inter-Tribal Council, 1986.

Densmore, Frances. *Chippewa Customs.* St. Paul, MN: Minnesota Historical Press, 1979.

Dunbar, Willis Frederick. *Michigan, A History of the Wolverine State.* Grand Rapids, MI: William B. Eerdman's Publishing Company, 1965.

Fasquelle, Ethel Rowan. *When Michigan Was Young: The Story of Its Beginnings, Early Legends, and Folklore.* Au Train, MI: Avery Color Studios, 1981.

Gérin-Lajoie, Marie, trans. *Mackinac History, An Informal Series of Illustrated Vignettes: Fort Michilimackinac in 1749, Lotbin-ière's Plan and Description.* Mackinac Island, MI: Mackinac Island State Park Commission, 1976.

Gringhuis, Dirk. *Lore of the Great Turtle: Indian Legends of Mackinac Retold*. Mackinac Island, MI: Mackinac Island State Park Commission, 1972.

―――. *Mackinac History, An Informal Series of Illustrated Vignettes; Indian Costume at Mackinac in the Seventeenth and Eighteenth Centuries*. Mackinac Island, MI: Mackinac Island State Park Commission, 1972.

―――. *Were-wolves and Will-O-the-Wisps: French Tales of Mackinac Retold*. Mackinac Island, MI: Mackinac Island State Park Commission, 1972.

Henry, Alexander. *Travels and Adventures in Canada and the Indian Territories Between the Years 1760 and 1776*. New York: Burt Franklin, 1969.

Kohl, Johann Georg. *Kitchi-Gami: Life Among the Lake Superior Ojibway*. St. Paul, MN: Minnesota Historical Press, 1985.

Lewis, Ferris. *Michigan, Yesterday and Today*. Hillsdale, MI: Hillsdale Educational Publishing, Inc., 1956.

McCoy, Raymond. *The Massacre of Old Fort Mackinac (Michilimackinac), A Tragedy of the American Frontier*. Bay City, MI: Privately printed, 1956.

Parkman, Francis. *The Conspiracy of Pontiac and the Indian War After the Conquest of Canada*. Boston: Little, Brown and Company, 1907.

―――. *Pioneers of France in the New World, France and England in North America*. Williamstown, MA: Corner House Publishers, 1970.

Petersen, Eugene T. *France at Mackinac: A Pictorial Record of French Life and Culture, 1715–1760*. Mackinac Island, MI: Mackinac Island State Park Commission, 1972.

Stone, Lyle M. *Fort Michilimackinac 1715−1781: An Archaeological Perspective on the Revolutionary Frontier*. Publications of the Museum, Michigan State University, in cooperation with the Mackinac Island State Park Commission, 1974.

MICHILIMACKINAC
A TALE OF THE STRAITS

Name _____

Address _____

City _____ State ____ Zip Code _____

Day Telephone (____) _____

Discounts	Quantity _____
	Price $14.95/book
ORDER DEDUCT	Subtotal _____
2 books $1.50	Discount _____
3 books $4.50	Shipping & Handling $2.00/book
4 books $9.00	*or* Priority Mail $3.50/book
	MI residents add 6% sales tax _____
	Total

Please make checks payable to Wilderness Adventure Books

Mail this form with payment to:

Wilderness Adventure Books
P.O. Box 856
Manchester, MI 48158
800-852-8652